LADY OF PERDITION

*A selection of recent titles by Barbara Hambly
from Severn House*

The James Asher vampire novels

BLOOD MAIDENS
THE MAGISTRATES OF HELL
THE KINDRED OF DARKNESS
DARKNESS ON HIS BONES
PALE GUARDIAN
PRISONER OF MIDNIGHT

The Benjamin January series

DEAD AND BURIED
THE SHIRT ON HIS BACK
RAN AWAY
GOOD MAN FRIDAY
CRIMSON ANGEL
DRINKING GOURD
MURDER IN JULY
COLD BAYOU
LADY OF PERDITION

LADY OF PERDITION

Barbara Hambly

This first world edition published 2019
in Great Britain and 2020 in the USA by
SEVERN HOUSE PUBLISHERS LTD of
Eardley House, 4 Uxbridge Street, London W8 7SY.
Trade paperback edition first published
in Great Britain and the USA 2020 by
SEVERN HOUSE PUBLISHERS LTD.

British Library Cataloguing in Publication Data
A CIP catalogue record for this title is available from the British Library.

ISBN-13: 978-0-7278-8909-6 (cased)
ISBN-13: 978-1-78029-646-3 (trade paper)
ISBN-13: 978-1-4483-0345-8 (e-book)

This is a work of fiction. Names, characters, places and incidents
are either the product of the author's imagination or are used fictitiously.
Except where actual historical events and characters are being described
for the storyline of this novel, all situations in this publication are
fictitious and any resemblance to actual persons, living or dead,
business establishments, events or locales is purely coincidental.

All Severn House titles are printed on acid-free paper.

Severn House Publishers support the Forest Stewardship Council™ [FSC™],
the leading international forest certification organisation.
All our titles that are printed on FSC certified paper carry the FSC logo.

Typeset by Palimpsest Book Production Ltd.,
Falkirk, Stirlingshire, Scotland.
Printed and bound in Great Britain by
TJ International, Padstow, Cornwall.

For Gene

ONE

'Right over there.' The grocer who pointed Seth Javel out to Benjamin January, in the hot and ill-lit back room on Avenue K, glanced at him once, then away. Bleak, dead eyes in the face of a man who has long ago learned to keep his mouth shut and not see anything.

January crossed the room. It didn't take him more than four of his long strides – he was a big man. There were 'groceries' in his native New Orleans – mostly in the 'back of town' behind Rue des Ramparts and around the turning basin – which everybody in town knew were actually barrooms catering to free black laborers and free colored artisans, to black sailors ashore from the ships that lined the waterfront and to slaves who 'slept out' (and a sprinkling of slaves on unpermitted leave from their duties). Other establishments, farther back in the swampy purlieux of the First Municipality, had tables set up in what were supposed to be only the back rooms and storage areas, and most nights hired musicians: piano, fiddle, guitar, cornet. Good musicians, too, reflected January, looking uneasily around him.

There was nothing like that, here.

Galveston was different.

Despite the English being spoken around him, January reminded himself that he was on foreign soil. The four-year-old Republic of Texas – or a state in rebellion from Mexico, depending on who you asked.

In New Orleans it was illegal to run a bar for men of African descent or to sell liquor to them, but nobody really expected the City Guards to come crashing through the door and arrest (or beat up) everybody in the place.

Here in the Republic of Texas, everybody looked as if they expected that they might.

No tables, few chairs. Roaches the size of a man's thumb, creeping along the boxes stacked by one wall. The smell of dirty clothes and dirty bodies, heavy in the damp spring air. The grocer sat on a bench between the door that led into the store itself in the front of the building, and the stair that ascended presumably to where his family slept. His stock of liquor remained in a packing box at his feet, ready to be closed and shoved under the stair at a moment's notice. A half-dozen tin cups weren't arranged on the barrels stacked beside him, but remained in a box of their own.

The men sitting on benches or barrel-halves, on crates labeled Havana Coffee or Finest French Mustard, didn't speak much, and nursed their cups of liquor on their knees or between their palms. A couple of sailors in the rough slops of the merchant ships glanced around them constantly, as well they should, reflected January as he made his way among the barrels and oil-jars. Even in the United States it was scarcely unknown for men ashore to simply disappear, if they were black and kidnappers thought they could get away with it.

Galveston was the hub of the slave trade between the Caribbean and the United States. What man, paying fifteen hundred dollars for a cottonhand, was going to believe his new slave's protests that he was in fact a free man, once his freedom papers had been torn up?

What captain was going to even bother calling the sheriff to help him look for a missing seaman, when the sheriff himself was more than likely being paid off by the kidnappers (if he wasn't actively one of them himself)? *He shoulda had more sense than to go ashore . . .*

'Mr Javel, sir?' January stopped before the man seated in the corner, and held out the letter, folded and sealed, that he drew from his jacket pocket. 'I got a letter here for you, from Mrs Pitot.'

At the name of the woman who'd been his landlady in New Orleans Javel relaxed, and held out his hand. He was, January guessed, in his mid-twenties, though his baby-faced good looks made him appear younger. Octoroon or musterfino: a soft Spanish-brown complexion that would have let him pass for an Italian, were it not for the African contours of nose and lips. Under the gleam of macassar oil his medium-brown locks had the tell-tale deadness of hair burned by lye.

In the heat of the spring evening – in April, hotter and stickier even than New Orleans – he retained the starched linen shirt, tight-tailored jacket, and stylish cravat of a gentleman. Gloves, too, observed January, and a pearl stick-pin in his cravat.

Javel started to open the letter, then paused, studying January: six-foot-four, massive and muscular, black as coal but dressed, not like a sailor or a cottonhand but neatly, in a short jacket and a very worn calico shirt.

No slave-badge.

'Who's your master, boy?' asked Javel, his tone suddenly friendly. 'Think he'd object to it, if I buy you a drink?'

January grinned shyly. 'Ain't got no master, sir. I'm a free man.'

Javel's smile warmed and widened, and he held out a friendly hand to shake. 'Then there's nobody can say a word against it, is there? On a hot night like this we all need one – and I think I need another.'

The night was, indeed, stifling, the more so because the windows of the little room were shuttered tight, and the door closed. Looking pleased and gratified and a trifle self-conscious, January sat on the nearest barrel and watched as Javel crossed the room to the grocer by the stair. Almost any black man who'd spent part of his life in slavery would be gratified, for it was seldom that the free people of color – the *librés* who in general despised slaves and anyone who had once been a slave – would let themselves be seen actually drinking with men who obviously had more African grandparents than they did.

But Javel had his own tin cup re-filled, and had another charged for his guest. January saw the younger man give some instruction to the grocer, and when the man disappeared up the stairs, fished in his pocket for something, his back to the room – not that anything was clearly visible through the brownish murk of cigar smoke that was illuminated only by a half-dozen tallow candles. When the grocer returned with a sleepy-looking young man Javel made another request, and from a pocket the grocer dug a notebook and a stub of pencil.

Javel tore out a page, scribbled something on it, and handed it to the grocer's . . . boarder? Son? Cousin? The youth disappeared into the front of the building. Moments later the thin board walls of the back room, against which January leaned one massive shoulder, vibrated slightly as the front door of the shop was opened and shut.

Seth Javel sat beside him again, and set the two cups on the barrel – salt pork, by the smell of it – which January had helpfully maneuvered in between them to serve as a table. 'So what are you doing in Galveston . . . Dang me if I didn't forget to ask your name!'

January grinned bashfully again and said, 'Danny, sir. Danny Squires. Long time ago, when I was first freed, friend of mine stayed at M'am Pitot's place, Cal Malsherbes. I got to know her then. When she heard I was shippin' on the *Nabby Whately* comin' down here, she asked me, would I bring you this letter? Nuthin' serious, I hope?' he added anxiously, though in fact he knew that the letter concerned the retrieval of a score of small but valuable items from a thief apprehended at the end of March. Some had been recognizable as the property of two of Javel's fellow-boarders. The letter, January was aware, asked whether Mr Javel was the owner of a blue china-silk vest embroidered with yellow roses, and a Manton dueling-pistol with tortoiseshell insets in its handle.

Javel shook his head, folded the letter and slipped it into his pocket. 'This your first voyage out? The *Nabby W*'s a good ship,' he added, reaching for his cup.

January, reaching for his own, startled, his glance flung past Javel's shoulder and a look of shock and horror convulsing his face. Javel spun to look, his hand sliding inside his coat where, January was fairly sure, a small pistol was concealed, since no black man in his senses walked around Galveston at this hour of the night without some means of protecting himself.

January had neatly switched the two tin cups before Javel turned back, puzzled – January, holding what had formerly been Javel's cup in one huge hand, looked abashed and said apologetically, 'I swear to God, I never *seen* a cockroach that big, as the one that run along the wall just now! Jesus *Christ*, I hates those things!'

Javel laughed with derision and relief. 'Texans are always bragging how everything in Texas is bigger and stronger and faster than anything in the United States or Mexico.' He shook his head. 'And in this case they're right, my friend. I've seen insects in this town that you could put a saddle on and ride! Confusion to them!' He picked up the tin cup before him, and raised it in a toast. 'May they frizzle in the fires of Hell!'

January grinned back, and lifted his cup in his turn. 'I'll drink to that, sir!'

Both men drained the liquor. January winced and made a face. 'Lord God, sir, I pity the horse that pissed that stuff! Poor thing's got to be sick unto death!'

Javel laughed again, heartily. Then his face changed. He lurched to his feet, gray-hazel eyes widening with momentary shock and fury before he collapsed unconscious across the barrel.

He was a slender man, for all his handsome muscularity. January picked him up easily, put him over his shoulder like a sack of meal, and remembered to pay the grocer two silver US dollars – the price of a box of cigars – on his way out.

The man's dead eyes met his, and January saw in them a sparkle of deep amusement.

Seth Javel didn't come to until the following evening. So deep was his stupor – January wondered what the hell had been in that drink – that when he pissed himself in his sleep, tied to a chair in a wooden shack in the swamps along Offat's Bayou west of town, he didn't even stir.

January was on the porch playing cribbage with Abishag Shaw of the New Orleans City Guards (currently on leave) when they heard Javel begin to groan inside. It had rained that day, the muggy rain off the Gulf, and they had just lit the smudges, made up with tobacco and gunpowder, as the swift twilight of the semi-tropics began to close in. Shaw gestured for January to stay where he was. January moved his chair a little, so that he sat closer to the door but also closer to the wall beside it, so there was no chance he'd be seen from within. All day, he, Shaw, and their friend the fiddler Hannibal Sefton had kept watch on the road that led back along the bayou toward town, in case Javel had friends who might look for him.

But no one had come.

January heard Javel moan, 'Oh, God . . .' like a man with the world's worst opium-headache (*No surprise there . . .*)

Shaw asked, 'Where's Selina Bellinger?'

'What? Who?' Javel's voice was thick and he was clearly struggling to gather his wits. 'I–I don't know anybody named Selina. Where the hell am I? And who the hell—?'

The slap of Shaw's open hand on Javel's face was like a leather belt striking a table. In exactly the same tone as before, the Kentuckian asked, 'Where's Selina Bellinger? An' don't tell me you don't know who that is.'

'I don't!' Javel's voice was a little clearer. 'Who the hell is she? And who the hell are you? Where am I?'

'That don't matter an' don't you lie to me.' Glancing briefly through the window, January could see his friend, like an ill-clothed scarecrow, gargoyle face framed in greasy locks the color of dead leaves, standing arms folded before their prisoner. There was an oil-lamp in the room and its grimy light showed up the wood stacked along the walls, the cobwebs that festooned the ceiling and the dead and dried wasps' nests; a sorry chronicle of how long this shed – and the land it stood on – had been deserted.

'Selina Bellinger was the little gal you seduced back in New Orleans an' got to run away with you, sayin' you'd marry her. Instead you brung her here an' sold her to one of the dealers in town, an' I ain't got the time to go snuffin' around all ten of 'em, not to speak of hangin' 'round the barrooms askin' if'n you got rid of her by a private sale.

'The girls of the school she went to give me a pretty good description of you – includin' stuff like you got long lobes to your ears rather'n short ones, an' them two pockmarks on the side of your jaw.' Shaw named two features that in fact he and January had only ascertained in the clear light of that morning, when they'd had the leisure to examine his face. Only one of the girls at the little school on Rue Esplanade – run by January and his wife – had gotten a good look at Selina's handsome lover. Though her description was a good one as to height, complexion, and hair ('He looked like he straightened it, M'sieu Janvier . . .'), all were features which could have been contested in court. 'Where'd you sell her?'

'You're crazy!' yelled Javel. '*Help!*' he then bellowed. '*Help!* Murder! Somebody—'

'We's six miles from town,' pointed out Shaw, in his light, flat-timbred voice.

'You're lying! I don't know this bitch and I only got into town yesterday! My name's Merrit, Bartholomew Merrit . . . *HELP!*'

Another ringing slap. January reflected that whatever his name actually was, he'd certainly intended for January to be the one who woke up that evening with an opium-headache, in some slave-dealer's barracoon, with the shreds of his torn-up freedom papers turning to ash in the nearest stove. 'I don't give fuck-all what your name is,' said Shaw into the ensuing silence. 'You come into town on the *Whitby* seven days ago, first of April, 1840, with a gal name of Selina Bellinger, who you got to run off with you from a boardin' school in New Orleans—'

Javel must have started to protest, because Shaw slapped him again, and continued without change of tone, '—promisin' you'd marry her. Now I want to know who you sold her to.'

'*Sold*?!? I don't know what the hell you're talking about!'

'Well,' said Shaw, 'that's too bad.' Through the window January saw the shadows jerk as the lamp was scooped off the bench it sat on, and a moment later came the splintering crash as it was thrown against the nearest stack of piled wood.

Yellow light burst a hundredfold stronger through the window.

'I swear it!' Javel screamed. 'I swear I don't know what the hell you're talking about!' The chair creaked as he bucked against the ropes, heels drumming vainly on the dirt. 'I don't know this girl—'

'Then I guess we got no more to talk about.' Shaw turned to leave the shed.

Smoke was pouring from the wood as the flame raced up and over it. The piles of cut branches, as January had seen when Hannibal Sefton had rented the shack on Sunday, were bone dry, cut probably to sell to one of the small steam-craft

that plied the shores of Offat's Bayou. He could see (he
glanced again through the window) that they were catching
like kindling.

'Stop it! Don't leave me! For God's sake—'

Shaw's hand was on the doorframe.

'Neumann! Andreas Neumann!' Javel writhed against his
bonds, as if he'd dislocate his own arms in his frenzy to pull
free. 'He's got a place on Avenue B! Oh, God—'

'When'd you sell her?'

'The second. Night after we got in town . . . Oh, dear God,
hurry—!'

How Shaw could stand there with the fire swarming up the
wooden walls and across the shed's roof January couldn't
imagine. He gathered the cards hastily from the little table on
the porch, shoved the cribbage-board into his pocket, and
retreated, knowing the brittle-dry building would collapse any
minute. Away from the smoke of the shed the night sang with
mosquitoes; the flames made a growing curtain of topaz and
gold against the low black wall of swamp oak and water holly.
The ground away from the bayou wasn't squishy, as it would
have been in New Orleans, and the whole world smelled of
the sea. Six miles along from town, not even the new commu-
nity's stink competed with the acrid smoke of the burning
shed. The stillness reminded January of the islands of the
Barataria south of New Orleans, empty and peaceful and
deadly.

He heard Javel scream something else, before a shot
cracked the night.

A few moments later Shaw's lanky form silhouetted against
the flame as he walked to where January stood.

'He told you where she was.' January felt just a little
shocked, though he knew that he shouldn't.

'Maestro –' Shaw sounded just the smallest bit apologetic
as he shoved his pistol into his belt – 'you are a godly man.
You go to church regular, an' believe God gives a crap about
humankind an' what we do on this earth.' The firelight caught
in the cold gray of his eyes. 'Now, by my calculation, if this
little gal was sold to Neumann on the second, Neumann raped
her that night, just to show her who's boss, an' I'm bettin' the

man what runs his barracoon for him did the same, soon as Neumann was outta the buildin', just 'cause he could. Third, maybe fourth she's in the barracoon –' he ticked off the dates on his long fingers – 'gettin' it from both of 'em, til she sells . . . An' if she's as pretty as you tell me, I'm bettin' she didn't stay here long. That's not even mentionin' whether Neumann's the kind what gives customers free samples to get 'em to buy. Say she's sold on the fourth; fifth, sixth, seventh . . .'

He held up his hands to show the number of days Selina Bellinger had been a slave, sixteen years old, headstrong, pretty, the daughter of a planter from Shreveport who could deny nothing to the child of his pretty Caribbean *placée*. Quietly, Shaw went on, 'You ever know a white man that bought a slave-girl an' *didn't* rape her, 'fore he left town an' every night on the road? For all we know, she coulda been sold to a whorehouse. They may still be breakin' her in. I figure I owed Javel a little somethin' for her. He's lucky I shot him, an' didn't leave him to burn.'

January nodded. 'I'd have left him to burn, myself. You think he was working with others?'

'Prob'ly was.' Shaw shrugged. 'He sure as hell sent somebody that note, sayin' as how he'd got a free black pigeon out cold on opium at the grocery last night. My guess is he works with half the dealers in Galveston. An' my guess is won't be one of 'em that'll give a hoot in hell iff'n he disappears. I'm pretty sure,' he added, 'we didn't commit a sin – given what the Bible tells us wrongdoers deserve at the hands of the righteous. An' technically, we didn't commit a crime neither. We're in the Republic of Texas now, Maestro. So far as I know, it ain't against the law for a white man to kill a black one here.'

'No,' said January quietly. He took from his pocket the tin slave-badge that proclaimed him the property of Hannibal Sefton, and hung it around his neck: ironically, the best protection he had in the western hemisphere's newest republic. 'No, it's not.'

Together, the two men started along the bayou road back to town.

TWO

Neumann's Texas Exchange stood on Avenue B, close by the bustle of the Galveston waterfront. It was built of sawn lumber, American-fashion, whitewashed, and one of the largest on its block.

January's skin crawled at the sight of it.

A line of men sat on benches along the unshaded front wall, hands on their knees, faces beaded with sweat in the compressed stickiness of the April heat. Clearly, the man who'd put the steel shackles on their ankles had ordered them in no uncertain terms not to loosen the collars of their calico shirts – starch-stiff and buttoned to their chins – nor to open the neat blue wool jackets they wore: *Who wants to buy a sloppy-lookin' nigger?*

They looked uncomfortable but January knew this wasn't the worst misery they'd had to put up with in their lives and they looked like they knew it, too. They talked quietly, squinting against the morning's cloudy sunlight, and watched the street scene before them with, for the most part, resigned interest. If any man of them remembered the family he'd been taken from – because his master needed money, or had died leaving his heirs in need of money, or because he'd stolen silverware or coffee for liquor-money or had perhaps been 'uppity' about his master bedding a wife or a child – he kept it to himself. He was now a thousand miles away from family, friends, wife, children, past, and there was for the moment nothing he could do about it.

January nodded greetings to the men as he followed Hannibal Sefton up the plank steps to the Exchange's door. Some of them nodded back, cordial. For all they knew, the thin, threadbare Hannibal, with his old-fashioned white linen neckcloth, gray-streaked mustache and threads of silver in his antiquated queue, could be bringing him in to sell. Or could be, for all his unassuming scholarly mien, a monster. January was aware of it in their glance, as they eyed the white man up and down. *This man out to buy? He decent or mean?* They studied January, too, as if trying to read whether there were whip-scars, or cigar-burns, or marks worse than those, beneath his scuffed linen jacket and faded trousers.

Rage filled January's heart, that anyone would have to look at another man that way. Would have to make those desperate calculations over a potential new life. At such times it was hard not to hate all white men.

The Exchange was dim inside, shuttered against the glare. Andreas Neumann evidently dealt in goods other than human chattels: hundred-pound sacks of coffee ranged along one wall, and on another was a counter bearing bolts of calico, and boxes of books, crates of pineapples and the inevitable, enormous cockroaches. A stairway ascended to the floor above, and to the right of it, on another bench, sat the women slaves, sweltering also in the heat. Their eyes, too, flicked to Hannibal and January as they entered.

But their glances returned, expressionless, to the four men who stood around a shackled girl in front of the bench. January guessed the hatless man – big and rosy with a jawline 'Quaker' beard and a bald patch in his fair hair – must be Neumann. The shortest of the others, whose red sunburned complexion marked him as a planter or rancher, had just opened the girl's calico bodice and pulled it down to her waist. 'Nice tits,' the man approved, and squeezed one. The girl stared stonily out over his shoulder at a corner of the ceiling. She looked about thirteen.

'You sure she'll breed?'

Neumann nodded vigorously. 'Ja, sure, she got her period regular.' His accent placed him from one of the southern German kingdoms, Bavaria or Hesse. 'Just last week, matter of fact.'

'Them tits don't mean nuthin', Jimmy,' said one of the other men, and gestured impatiently at the lascivious commentary of his companions at the remark. 'You gotta take a look at her box.'

'Oh, sure!' Neumann fished promptly in his pocket for a key. 'Sure enough thing! Help yourself. You want to take her upstairs? First door on the right as you go up.'

He unlocked the girl's shackle and stepped aside as the three men led the child up the bare board steps. January saw one of the women on the bench – a woman in her thirties, with the girl's same Fulani bone structure, the girl's same Spanish-dark eyes, turned her face aside. She didn't make a sound, but tears ran down her face.

January shoved his hands deep in his trouser pockets to hide the clench of his fists.

'Mr Neumann?' Hannibal stepped forward and held out his card, which had been printed the week before in New Orleans. The Bourbon Street address on it actually belonged to a white great-uncle of January's wife Rose. Hannibal himself was in fact a musician whose current residence was in one of the disused cribs behind Kate the Gouger's bath-house on Perdidio Street, but his respectable upbringing, and a long-ago Oxford education, stood him in good stead.

'Hannibal Sefton, of New Orleans . . . Very nice stock you have here, sir. Very nice.' He made a slight bow and tipped his hat to the women on the bench, who were linked – as were the men outside – along a single chain with ankle-fetters. 'I wondered if perhaps you might help me?'

'Of course, Mr Sefton, of course.' Neumann bowed, but his blue eyes, though genial, held the wariness of one who has dealt with every grifter and confidence-artist ever spawned.

'I understand,' said Hannibal, 'that you have – or had – a young wench named Selina on the premises recently. Octoroon, tall, slim-built; I'd put her age at sixteen or seventeen. Light eyes and a reddish-gold cast to her hair. Hair curly, rather than wooly, and unbraided reaches to her waist. She may have been claiming that she was a free woman, the daughter of a planter?'

Something shifted in the slave-dealer's eyes. But he only raised his brows, in an expression of polite inquiry.

'She is in fact the property of my wife.' Hannibal produced sale papers, dated 1836 and proving that the girl Selina had been purchased at the St Charles Exchange in New Orleans by one Ransom Hardy and deeded to his daughter Emma Sefton the following year. The papers were very convincing – during the slow summer season when no one was hiring musicians, Hannibal made ends meet by discreetly forging freedom papers for the local Underground Railroad.

'She ran away on the ninth of last month,' he continued, 'with a young man named Javel – if that was his real name. According to our cook, this Javel promised he'd take her to Kingston in Jamaica, and get her work as a free woman. We later learned that Javel is in fact in league with slave-stealers and regularly lures slaves – particularly housemaids who are not strictly kept – into escaping.'

And the fiddler shook his head, dark brows knitting at the incomprehensible unreasonableness of silly-minded wenches who want to be free.

'Someone told me that this Javel might have brought her to you,' Hannibal went on. 'I am, of course, prepared to pay you something for your trouble—'

He slipped his hand into the front of his coat.

Neumann's brow wrinkled in thought, as he waved the offer aside with a beefy hand. January's heart sank a little, though he would have been astonished had any slave-dealer divulged the name of a customer to a stranger who might well be a confidence-trickster – or in the employ of the law on the trail of a receiver of stolen goods. Slave-stealing was a hanging offense in Texas.

'The name is not familiar,' Neumann said. 'The last fancy we had in here was two months ago. Musterfino, she was, from Cuba—'

January, standing quietly in the shadows beside the women's bench, felt a quick, slight pinch of fingernails on the back of his hand. Glancing down, he met the eyes of an older woman, African-black like himself, heavy-breasted and too old, he thought, to bear children or do heavy work in the fields. 'This wife of his,' she breathed, in the accents of the Georgia Sea Islands, 'she treat that girl good?'

January nodded. Of course the woman assumed – as Neumann and every person they'd passed on Avenue B assumed – that January, neatly dressed and trailing respectfully at Hannibal's heels, was the fiddler's valet.

'She was here,' the Georgia woman went on, under Hannibal's closer questioning of the blandly uninformative

Neumann. 'Last week. Said her daddy a planter, an' she a free woman – your massa tellin' the truth?'

'It's her daddy who sent us,' murmured January. 'If you know who bought her, for God's sake tell me.'

'Pollack,' said the woman. 'Gideon Pollack. Got him a rancho northeast of San Antonio, next by Onion Creek in the hill country.'

'When?'

'Sattiday. Said he goin' up to Houston, then on up to Austin where he got kin—' She turned her face sharply away then, and slapped January's hand aside as if he'd tried to touch her. January, knowing that she'd been watching Neumann throughout their whispered conversation, drew back a little, apologetic, aware that the dealer must have turned his head and seen them talking.

'Danny, what're you doing?' demanded Hannibal in patient exasperation, and January replied in his most cotton-patch English.

'Nuthin', sir, nuthin' – just only this ol' wench, she was on Bellefleur Plantation when I was a little boy, sir.'

Hannibal sighed, and said, 'Go stand over by the door, Danny.' Then he shook his head as if to say, *Like children, all of them*, and returned to his talk with Neumann.

One doesn't comment, reflected January, as he obeyed him, on the random antics of a child – and he knew that to over-explain anything is to arouse suspicion. The conversation with the old woman was in any case over. Not for the world would he have exposed her to a slap and a reprimand – if nothing worse – from Neumann.

Gideon Pollack. San Antonio.

All the way along the Gulf coast on the French brig *L'Alouette* from New Orleans, January, Hannibal, and Abishag Shaw had pored over the map of the republic that they'd bought the day before sailing.

Mentally, January studied it now.

When Roux Bellinger had brought his daughter to New Orleans in December to enroll her in boarding school, the love he bore her had been clear in every word he spoke. Every glance he gave across the little parlor of the house on Rue

Esplanade where January and his wife Rose had established their little academy, spoke of how he treasured this pert, pretty, young lady. 'Her mama was what they call a placée,' the graying Scotsman had said, looking from Rose to January. 'The dearest, gentlest treasure God formed with His own hand, and the most beautiful. But *her* mama had been a placée also, and my Marie had got only the education that ladies then – and now, I might add – thought good for a girl of . . . of that class.'

He hushed his voice a little, as if he feared his daughter would be hurt. In fact, January had inquired of his various friends in the New Orleans demimonde the moment Rose had received Bellinger's letter inquiring about her school, and he knew that Roux Bellinger had kept Marie Pargette as his mistress in the small Cane River town of Cloutierville for the past twenty years. Bellinger had been married all that time to the daughter of a wealthy trader on the Spanish Trail, a fact of which his treasured Selina could not have been ignorant.

Tactfully, Rose had said, 'As the daughter of a placée myself, M'sieu, I understand perfectly the kind of education considered appropriate for a girl who is expected to do nothing but follow in her mother's footsteps.' The oval lenses of her spectacles had flashed as she tilted her head, a slim, rather gawky woman whose smallest smile January wouldn't have traded for a week of lovemaking with Helen of Troy. 'Since I was not suited for that kind of life, either mentally or in spirit, it cost me considerable struggle to take a different path.'

Bellinger's hard, lined face had softened. He'd set down his teacup with the air of a man who realizes he is in a safe place. 'I'm glad you understand, m'am. I want something different for Selina, something useful. The world's changing. Who's to say what it'll be like ten years from now, or whether my girl will have to make her own way? I'd like her to at least have the right tools, whatever choice she might make.'

'That is the act,' said Rose, 'of a father who is kind as well as wise, sir.'

But looking across the parlor, bright with the chilly winter sunlight through the French doors, January had seen the pretty Selina's expression of discontent at the sight of the well-stocked bookshelves, and her prospective school-mistress's old-fashioned headscarf. A girl, he had thought then, used to winding her doting father around her finger. He hadn't eavesdropped on their extended leave-taking, but through the windows he'd seen them on the gallery, Selina tugging at her father's sleeves with a desperate look on her face, shaking her head. When at last the planter had gone, the girl had rushed upstairs to the dormitory beneath the slanted roof, and two of the other girls had reported that she'd wept, the bitter tears of a thwarted child. In the weeks which had followed, she had made it plain that whatever her father wanted for her education – history, mathematics, botany and Latin as well as more stylish accomplishments like needlework and music – Selina was having none of it.

Dizzy with delight at the amenities of New Orleans – after a short, dull lifetime in Cloutierville – Selina saw no reason why she would ever need more than those things that had served her so well at her home: beautiful manners, bright conversation, considerable skill on the pianoforte (it was a genuine joy to teach her), and the ability to look like she was paying rapt attention to whatever was being said to her. She felt put-upon at the school, and she clearly considered the other girls – aged eleven to thirteen, and all of them darker of complexion than herself – beneath her.

Of course she'd fall in love.

January shook his head, half exasperated and half in despair.

Of course she'd believe any handsome young man – of her own octoroon complexion, so clearly 'available' (as a white man would not be) without being 'disgusting' (as many light-skinned girls described boys of even moderate brownness – much less January's coal-black hue). Of course the hand-some Seth Javel would find it child's play to work on her sense of grievance, her craving for romance, as well as her awakening senses.

Thirteen-year-old Germaine Barras had told Rose – when Selina's note was discovered, announcing her elopement – that Javel had bought Selina diamond ear-bobs, and a lace-trimmed hat such as women of color were not supposed to wear. He had met her secretly, when she'd slipped out at night after lights-out. Had taken her to masked balls and cafés. Natchitoches Parish lay five days up-river – January had borrowed as much money as he could raise that day, without jeopardizing the house and the school, had bought maps of Texas and fetched Hannibal from the Turkey Buzzard Saloon where he was dealing faro for the house. (Nobody in that part of town gave a tinker's damn about Lent.) They'd found Abishag Shaw at the Cabildo – where there was less demand for Lieutenants of the City Guard now that Mardi Gras season was over – and the three men had set forth for Galveston less than forty-eight hours after the fugitives.

The stevedores on the wharves, who knew January through the Underground Railroad and because of the work he'd done to help the blacks of New Orleans, slave or free, obtain what justice they could, had told him that Javel and Selina had taken the *Whitby*, bound for Galveston. One of them had spoken of Javel's earlier departures, with other girls.

On his bunk on *L'Alouette*, half-nauseated by the stink of the bilges and listening to the incessant creak of planking in the pitch-dark of the minuscule cabin, January had shivered at the thought of the Republic of Texas even as he'd gone over every inch of the map in his mind. He'd guessed already that they'd arrive too late to keep Selina from being sold.

Across the Exchange he could see Neumann shaking his head, and Hannibal jotting down in his notebook all the various places the dealer was suggesting the vanished 'slave-girl' might have been sold, though *he*, Andreas Neumann, had nothing to do with any of it. January wasn't surprised. He'd only been able to raise seven hundred and fifty dollars, and probably couldn't have gotten much more if he *had* been willing to mortgage the house. The effects of the country's financial collapse three years previously still reverberated. Field hands went for twelve hundred and light-skinned fancies could bring over twice that.

A rancher, the woman had said.

San Antonio. Deep inland, he recalled, on the map.

At least the man wasn't a professional pimp.

But he knew that what Shaw had said, outside the burning shack on Offat's Bayou last night, had been true. He shut his

eyes, thinking about that exquisite, willful girl who'd rolled
her eyes at Rose's headscarf – the *tignon* which had once been
mandated by law for all women of color in Louisiana – and
had begged her father not to leave her in the governance of
an old-fashioned blue-stocking.

Part of him wished Shaw had left Javel to burn. He wondered
if there were such a thing as a Catholic church in this very
American town, where he could go to confession for the
thought that wouldn't leave his heart.

THREE

H ouston lay a day's sailing across Galveston Bay,
through Trinity Bay and up into the bayou country
beyond. Knots of oak, and marshland thick with reeds,
alternated with flat prairies of head-high grass along its shores,
like the *vacheries* of the Sabine country, west and south of
New Orleans. As the small trading-schooner *Rosabel* worked
its way up Buffalo Bayou, January could see the cattle here,
too, the long-horned Mexican breed, peering like grotesque
deer from among the oak trees along the banks. Sometimes,
where the creeks widened into fertile bottomlands, he saw
cotton fields, and slaves chopping the first of the weeds in the
dense spring sun. The Constitution of Mexico had forbidden
slavery but the Americans who'd come in the twenties had
brought their bondsmen anyway: Mexico City was a long way
off. The terms of their settlement had stipulated they must
become Catholics, too, and January guessed there wasn't a
Catholic church in a hundred miles.

The Americans who had flooded into the country, who had
pledged loyalty to Mexico and obedience to its laws – who
had four years ago risen in revolt and declared their freedom
– had been concerned with one thing and one thing only: land.
Cotton land.

'Mr Mitchum, now . . .' A stringy man named Jack Ray,
who spoke with the accents of Virginia, nodded toward his

master up at the front of the boat, smoking and talking with
Shaw, the captain, and a pear-shaped little clerk with barely
a fringe of gray hair around the edges of a scalp as smooth
as an ostrich egg. 'He took up four leagues of land along
Greens Bayou when first he come to Texas in 1825 – that's
near twenty thousand acres. Got another ten thousand by
marryin' a Mexican wife.' Jack sipped thankfully at the bottle
of ginger-water January offered him, then – at January's gesture
of invitation and permission – passed it to the other slaves
who occupied the narrow strip of shade on the port side of
the little deck-house. These men were chained – Mr Mitchum
had purchased them the day before in Galveston – but Jack
and his fourteen-year-old son Jule had, January guessed, been
Mr Mitchum's property for enough time to be trusted. At least
trusted not to fling themselves into the flat shallow waters of
Buffalo Bayou and paddle for the shore.

And where the hell would they go? Free black men were not
tolerated in the republic. In New Orleans, at least, there was
some hope for a runaway, of disappearing into the *libré* commu-
nity, of finding work and going unnoticed, though that was not
as easy as once it had been.

'Many men do that?' January shaded his eyes against the
glare of the sun on the water beyond the sails' shadow. A
flight of pelicans skimmed across the path of the boat, brown
wing-tips nearly touching. Sky and silence seemed to fill the
world.

'Fewer now than ten years back. In the twenties, the government was desperate to get these lands settled up. They wanted
men who'd fight the Comanche, and they'd grant you a league
of range-land an' a *labor* – near two hundred acres – of farm-
land, just to hold it as a Mexican citizen, though why they
thought Americans was to be trusted beats me. I guess
they believed what they wanted to believe.'

'Mostly, Mr Mitchum buys up land now from them that had
it from the government.' Young Jule Ray handed January back
his nearly-empty bottle with a shy nod of thanks. Their fellow-
passenger on the schooner hadn't bothered to provide his new
possessions with water or food for the journey, figuring probably that they'd be in Houston by dark. January knew Hannibal

would re-fill the bottle for him, from the supply in the tiny
common cabin. Aside from considerations of sheer humanity,
it was an easy way to buy information.

'Or them that *claims* they had it.' Jack's mouth bent down
at a corner, wry and amused. 'Between land that was granted
to the church, an' then take away from them an' granted to the
big *hacendados*, an' men claimin' squatter's rights by farmin'
it for ten years, or signin' over this piece or that piece to a son
or a brother, it's turnin' into a lawyer's holiday here an' that's
a fact. Mr Mitchum's brother's a lawyer in Austin, an' he says
tryin' to figure out land-holdin' along the bayous an' around
San Antonio where the soil is good, is like playin' in a crooked
poker-game where everybody speaks Chinese. God knows
what's gonna happen if they ever do get the United States to
take Texas in.'

'*If*?' January raised his brows. 'My impression is the
Southern Congressmen are climbing all over each other trying
to convince President Van Buren – and the Northern voters
– that annexing Texas is worth going to war with Mexico.
Whoever the Democrats get to run in November—'

'My, you ain't been in Texas long, have you?' Jack shook
his head. 'Mr Houston – that used to be president – he was
all for joinin' the United States, mostly because the gov'ment
of this so-called republic can't afford to buy itself a pot to
piss in, much less pay an army or build a navy to keep pirates
off the shippin'. They claim the US could lick Mexico in a
week if they squawked about it. But the new president, Mr
Lamar, he say we don't need a bunch of Massachuser abolitionists tellin' the white men they can't have slaves. He say
we should go on as we are, wipe out all them Injun tribes – by
throwin' Texas paper money at 'em, I guess – an' claim all
the land west of here clear to the Pacific Ocean. It's Lamar
what moved the capital out to Austin last October – you shoulda
heard how Mr Mitchum went on about it!' He glanced toward
his master and grinned, again wry, hatred for the man as well
as amusement in his tired eyes.

'I guess Mr Lamar been workin' to borrow money from the
Queen of England an' the King of France, so's he can fight
the Comanche. The Mexicans, too, if they attack. He's tryin'

to pretend he didn't really say as how Texas is a "Republic of slaveholders" . . .'

'If he says that,' mused January, 'he's going to have a hell of a time getting England to give him as much as ten cents. They've started to campaign to abolish slavery altogether. I knew that Congress was just about ready to go to war about it,' he added, as both Jack and young Jule cocked their heads. 'When we were in Washington City – my master and I,' he added quickly, and glanced toward the front of the boat again.

And where, he wondered, *was* Hannibal? The fiddler had come on board with the confident aplomb which one presumably acquired at Balliol College, presented his card to the captain, and had looked down his nose at Lieutenant Shaw – whom he wasn't supposed to know, for purposes of the search for Selina Bellinger. He'd traded remarks with Mr Mitchum – a planter on Sims Bayou – and (inevitably) Mr Mitchum had tried to talk him into selling January ('Good Lord, no! You might not think it to look at him, but his way of starching my neckcloths is genius and it would take me years to train someone else . . .')

And then, just as the last passenger had hastened up the gangplank clutching his satchel to his bosom like a child, Hannibal had simply disappeared.

Presumably he was in the deck-house. But January couldn't imagine why anyone would sit in the cramped and smelly quarters with the cargo – which, consisting as it did of pine-apples, sugar, and tobacco would be alive with roaches.

Unless of course—

January returned his attention to the bald clerk with the satchel. Middle-aged and bespectacled, in his gray frock coat and checked trousers he had an air of meek respectability that was almost too pronounced to be true. January guessed that he might be an habitué of one of the back-of-town whore-houses where the fiddler worked in the summer times.

One never knew, he reflected resignedly. For all his own great height and breadth of shoulder, it was surprising how few white men noticed him. He'd heard visitors to New Orleans, at the Blue Ribbon balls, remark that they never could tell black people apart: they all looked alike. Meaning that slaves

– and those who in their opinion should have been slaves –
were equally beneath their notice: nobody that you'd ever
have to recognize again.

But even playing violin at the Countess Mazzini's House
(as it was politely called), the beauty of Hannibal's music
would have drawn attention to him. An educated man would
have taken note of it, the first time the fiddler expressed himself
with a Greek or a Latin tag. The more so, January was sure,
if his friend had been dealing poker for the house.

And in their pursuit of Gideon Pollack, the last thing either
he or Hannibal needed was some chance-met acquaintance of
their quarry remarking that a down-at-heels musician from a
New Orleans den of iniquity was claiming to be a gentleman
with an address on Bourbon Street.

Sure enough, once they put in at the wharf in Houston at
twilight and the clerk disembarked, still clutching his satchel
to his blue-and-yellow waistcoat, Hannibal re-appeared, to
shake hands and bid farewell to the captain and Mr Mitchum
(and Shaw, for good measure) with apologies for his attack
of dizziness. 'I'd thought I was done with these turns – No,
no, my doctor tells me it has very little to do with actual
mal de mer, though my wife teases me unmercifully
about it . . . *Multam ille et terris iactatus* . . . Come along,
Danny . . .'

'Yes, sir.' January picked up their two satchels and followed
him meekly ashore.

'I do beg your pardon,' said Hannibal quietly, as they made
their way along Main Street in quest of the Commercial Hotel,
which the schooner's captain had recommended. 'I thought it
best—'

'Our depilated friend with the satchel?'

'As you say,' the fiddler agreed. '*Ascende, calve.*' He checked
his steps, as two men burst from the door of a rough-built
saloon and slammed into the ground at his feet. Both were
armed with knives and both were bloodied. As others – presumably friends of the combatants – boiled forth from the doorway,
one of the fighters slashed the other across the belly.

'I'm killed!' yelled the man. 'Oh, God, I'm killed—'

January considered for one moment offering his services – at least to ascertain whether the wounded man was correct – and then stepped back as Hannibal touched his arm, and edged away from the affray. In New Orleans, even the American flat-boatmen and river rats knew that such things as free surgeons and physicians of color existed. Here, even the offer would probably get him beaten up – always supposing the spectators could take time away from savaging one another. The wielder of the blow had scrambled to his feet but had been surrounded and knocked down again by three others. The wounded man, curled in a fetal position in a growing puddle of his own blood, was gasping and screaming while his friends hammered the supporters of his enemy . . .

A shot was fired down the dark street. In the glow of the lanterns from the two other barrooms on the block, January saw a smallish dark man in the frock coat of a townsman running toward the fight, a long-barreled pistol brandished above his head and another in his left hand. Though he hadn't the faintest idea what the fight was about, January couldn't keep himself from looking over his shoulder as he followed Hannibal quickly away into the darkness. The wounded man – still ignored by his friends in favor of the battle – was sobbing, again and again, 'Dear God I'm killed – I'm killed . . .'

January wondered if he was.

'*This is no world/ to play with mammets and to tilt with lips*,' quoted Hannibal, his voice a little shaky. '*We must have bloody noses and cracked crowns.* In New Orleans one can avoid trouble by staying out of the wrong districts of town, but apparently the entire town comprises a wrong district.' He stepped aside again, this time to avoid a long train of horses, packed as if for a journey and surrounded by vaqueros – the equivalent of the mounted slaves in the vacheries of western Louisiana – trotting by in a jerking flare of torch-light. Some were clearly *meztisos* – descendants of the Spanish conquerors and the Indians they had subjugated three centuries before. Their long black hair was bound with silk scarves beneath wide-brimmed hats, and rawhide breeches, worn over under-drawers, protected their legs from bottomland thorns. Others were white men, in coarse shabby trousers and calico shirts, with bandanas instead of the scarves beneath their hats. Still others were black – almost certainly slaves.

January wondered what relations sere between bondsmen and masters were on the hill-country ranchos, where a slave could so easily escape to the native tribes that held the whole north of the republic as their own.

Or would the Comanche torture and butcher an escaping black man with the enthusiasm they turned upon whites?

He found himself wondering, as he followed Hannibal along the rutted dirt of the street, how near this Gideon Pollack's land lay to Comanche territory, and whether they'd be obliged to follow the man all the way there before overtaking him. 'With any luck,' he remarked, 'Pollack will be at the Commercial Hotel. He may even believe your tale of your wife's absconding maidservant, at least to the degree of accepting seven hundred and fifty dollars for her. Always providing,' he added gloomily, 'we can stay clear of our slick-pated friend . . . What is his name, by the way?'

'Gervase Hookwire.' Hannibal turned from flourishing his hat in greeting to a couple of young women in a second-floor window, clad – as far as January could see – in rather ill-fitting chemises and not a lot else. 'At least that's what the Countess Mazzini called him, though it's anybody's guess whether even that was a fabrication. *That which we call a rose . . .* We can but hope that he's taken lodgings at some lesser hostelry –' he looked about him as they crossed Commerce Street – the few, dim squares of lamplight that patched the darkness beyond the glow of Main Street's establishments didn't speak well for the size of the town – 'if there is such a thing in Houston. And pray he leaves town in the morning.'

'And that we don't run into any others of your acquaintance.'

Hannibal began to say, 'Surely—' when a female voice called delightedly from the porch of a building opposite.

'Hannibal! *Mi amor!*'

The streets in Houston were wide – enormously so, clearly laid out with wheeled commerce rather than foot-traffic in mind. Under other circumstances, and given sufficient warning, Hannibal could have ducked nimbly into any of the wide black gaps of darkness that yawned between the shabby buildings.

But even at this hour of the evening, there was wheeled commerce aplenty, and the woman who'd called out to him had been already three-quarters of the way across Main, hidden from the two men by a couple of drays piled high with sacks of flour. She came around the wagons with her hands outstretched, and Hannibal – though he'd flinched as if he'd been shot at – seemed to realize, in the next second, that flight would only draw more attention to himself.

And, January understood in that first instant, the fiddler would have realized from the woman's clothing that she was no street-corner tart whose comments would be ignored.

With no more than a split-second's delay as he calculated his chances for a clean escape – January suspected his friend had a great deal of experience in that kind of quick decision – Hannibal swept his chimney-pot hat from his head and bowed deeply. 'Mrs Dillard,' he said, and the woman's face beamed that he'd remembered.

Straightening, he kissed her hand.

January's first wife had been a dressmaker, so he recognized at a glance that this young lady's snuff-colored delaine dress was the attire of neither a whore nor a poor woman. It wasn't new, but had been carefully treated; the creamy lace that trimmed collar and cuffs set off the delicate peach-fair complexion, the red lips and the ash-blonde curls just visible under the stylish bonnet. Her gloves were reasonably new as well.

John Dillard – with whom the girl he'd known four years ago as Valentina de Castellón had eloped from her father's hacienda near Mexico City – must be prospering.

He saw she still wore her mother's sapphire earrings.

Her eyes sparkled up at him: sea-blue, for she was pure-blooded Spanish with no admixture of Indian blood, a tribute to her father's dedication to the *limpieza de sangre* so prized among the Mexican upper classes. 'And Señor Enero! But what are you doing in Texas?' Then her glance went to the tin slave-badge around January's neck, took in the three carpet-bags he was carrying, and flicked to Hannibal. The butterfly-wing brows tugged into a frown.

'My dearest Mrs Dillard—' Hannibal, still holding her hand, drew her a little closer to him and lowered his voice.

The young woman said, still in Spanish, 'It is not Mrs Dillard anymore, Hannibal.' Her chin lifted a little. 'John was killed, fighting—'

With a tiny shake of her head she thrust her lover's memory aside, and for an instant, in the reflected lantern-light from the nearest saloon, January saw the glint of tears that she blinked away unshed.

'After the fighting was over, my uncle Gael took me in – for I would not and will not return to my father! – and two years ago I married another American, Señor Taggart. It was of course Uncle Gael's land he wanted – he had a rancho of ten leagues of land and wanted the twenty leagues Uncle would give me upon my marriage. But he was – *is* –' she corrected herself, 'a man of . . . of kindness and decency.' Her lips tightened very slightly. 'My uncle was then very ill. And indeed, he died early in the following year. It is a hard country,' she concluded, 'for a woman alone.'

January remembered her, flirting with Generalissimo Santa Ana's military aides over her father's dinner-table. *She was flirting with the priest at her first communion*, a family member had said to him. Flirting, and scheming to get what she wanted, whether it was a new pair of slippers or the love of a man her father and brother detested: beautiful, laughing, and curiously intrepid. She had been, he recalled, affianced to another man at the time, and had blackmailed Hannibal into translating her love letters to her American swain. When her enraged brother had come close to killing Hannibal as a result, he remembered that she had not seemed particularly contrite.

She must be twenty now. There was a tiny scar – several years old, of the kind made when a bullet strikes rock-chips from a wall near one's face – on the corner of her cheekbone, and a velvety depth of shadow at the back of her eyes.

He said, 'I am sorry,' and she shook her head. While she'd been speaking a vaquero had emerged from the traffic on the street, a lean-flanked, craggy old desperado with a long white mustache and silver hair trailing from beneath his headscarf. He stood a respectful distance from her, watching with folded hands. Valentina did not give him so much as a glance.

'But you, Señor Enero . . .' Her smile flashed bright once

more. 'When last I saw you, you were a man of wealth, with a valet and a carriage and a maid for your beautiful Madame Rose . . .'

January set down the bags, and touched his finger to his lips. 'Señora,' he said softly, 'if ever you cared for our welfare – if ever either of us did you a service –' though Hannibal did not so much as flicker an eyelid, January could almost hear him sniff – 'I beg that you will forget such matters. We came here to find a young lady of color, one of the pupils at my wife's school. She ran off with a scoundrel and was betrayed by him, and sold as a slave.'

Valentina's splendid eyes flashed with shocked outrage and her mouth popped open, but January gestured her silent again. She whispered, furious, '*Bastardo!*'

'The scoundrel has come to a bad end,' Hannibal reassured her.

'Already?' Her expression brightened. 'That was quick of you!'

He made a deprecating gesture. 'My dearest Valentina, age cannot wither nor custom stale your infinite charms. You wouldn't happen to know of a rancher named Pollack, would you, *bella domina*?'

At the mention of the name, her eyes grew dark. Anger, bitterness, suspicion . . .

'We are acting on behalf of the girl's father,' said January. 'We have funds to buy her free.' The truth was more complicated than that – certain as he was that Roux Bellinger would reimburse every penny they spent, he had met an astounding number of men willing to sell their children of color – but now was not the time for a lengthy explanation.

'*Que tengas mucha suerta.*' Valentina's exquisite mouth twisted. 'Señor Gideon Pollack would, as they say, skin a flea for its tallow and hide, and his brother Señor Rance pays the very whores with worthless Texas paper.'

January and Hannibal traded a glance. *Damn it . . .*

'Their plantation – Los Lobos, and I cannot think of a better name to describe its owners! – lies close to ours. Ours is called Perdition, on the Pedernales River west of Austin. Up until October these Pollacks were my husband's enemies. They would steal one another's cattle, their men would beat up my husband's riders when they came into town. Now they are my husband's friends, and my husband lets Señor Pollack run his sheep on our hills.'

She didn't sound any too pleased about it.

'Have you been on Los Lobos, then?' asked January. 'Might you—?'

She startled then, and turned her head. Two women, followed by what were clearly bodyguards, were making for them with purposeful strides. Like Valentina, the women were dressed in the respectable challis and close round bonnets of planters' wives or sisters – not the garb of women one generally saw walking about the streets at night. They stared straight ahead, rigidly ignoring the ballyhoo of the saloons, and held themselves as if trying not to actually touch the dirt of the unhallowed street.

He said quietly to Hannibal, '*Hic venit Gorgones,*' – *Here come gorgons* – and stepped back, like a good servant, to stand beside the carpetbags, so that it would not appear that he was part of the conversation. Hannibal bowed once more over Valentina's hand.

'And might I chance to encounter you again before you leave the city?' he inquired, switching to English and glancing – without turning his head – in the direction of the advancing gorgons.

Valentina, likewise, gave no further sign of having seen the two women, save by a quick sidelong look in their direction – a caution which told January a great deal, even before the newcomers came close enough to speak. She herself said, 'I fear not, Mr Sefton,' also in English, as the taller of the advancing women quickened her stride to reach them.

'*There* you are,' said the gorgon. And, after a glance at Hannibal, added, 'dearest,' in a flat tone that ill concealed irritation and disgust. 'Where have you been?' She was trying to speak lightly, but January had the impression that she wasn't really capable of it. Her light-blue eyes, protuberant in a square, heavy-featured face, flicked from Valentina to Hannibal, and then to Valentina's silent bodyguard, hard with suspicion.

Given the young woman's history of flirtations, reflected

January, this wasn't an altogether surprising reaction. And bodyguard or no bodyguard, it wasn't usual for a married woman of good reputation to walk about at night.

January found himself wondering where she *had* been . . .

Not, he reminded himself, that it was any of his business . . .

The younger gorgon seized Valentina by the arm and jerked her away from Hannibal, fixing the fiddler with a disconcerting, insectile stare from behind thick spectacles. 'We have looked all over town for you!' Her gaze, too, flashed to the bodyguard: frightened, suspicious, and at the same time fascinated. A gaze that lingered too long, and too intently, before it transferred itself, first to Hannibal, then to January himself. 'And who is this?'

Valentina's chin went up. 'Mama, Aunt Alicia,' she said in a pleasant voice, 'please permit me to present Señor Hannibal Sefton. He was a friend of my father's in Mexico.'

January wasn't sure that 'friend' would adequately describe the relationship with a madman who had held Señor Sefton prisoner on his hacienda for five weeks, but couldn't think of a word that *would* adequately describe Don Prospero de Castellón.

'Señor Sefton, Madame Taggart, my husband's mother. And this is Miss Alicia Marryat, my husband's aunt.'

January, of course, being assumed to be merely Hannibal's valet, did not merit introduction of any sort, any more than the bodyguards – presumably free men – did.

'*Enchanté.*' Hannibal bowed over the hands of each gorgon in turn. Mrs Taggart – tall, stout, firmly corseted into subdued (but new and stylish) mauve faille – regarded him with narrow mistrust. Her mouth was heavy enough to suggest sensuality, but was closed hard as a bear-trap, deep lines of peevish anger grooved from nostril to chin. Aunt Alicia snatched her hand away when Hannibal bent over it – his lips never came within two inches of her kid-gloved knuckles – and backed from him, still gazing with that unwavering stare.

'He kissed me,' she gasped, clutching her violated hand. 'Amelia, he kissed me!' She sounded as if he'd seized her and stuck his tongue halfway down her throat.

Mrs Taggart gave her a glare that would have silenced rioters on the Paris barricades. The younger woman turned quickly away, and January saw tears in her eyes. For one moment his glance crossed Valentina's: *You're living with THAT?*

To Hannibal, Mrs Taggart lied, 'Pleased,' with barely a nod of her head. She went on, 'I'm sure you'll forgive my daughter-in-law her ignorance of good usage, Mr Sefton. She is Mexican, though she doesn't look it.' She made it sound as if Valentina's northern Spanish fairness were a deliberate deception. 'If you are acquainted with her father, you must be aware that her upbringing was somewhat neglected.'

Valentina opened her mouth again to protest, but Mrs Taggart turned upon her that same basilisk stare. January knew it well. It would have meant a beating to any slave, but he was surprised when the young woman – the tart and impertinent girl he had known – fell silent.

She's afraid . . .

And from the corner of his eye he saw, just for a moment, the white-haired old ruffian who'd stood behind her in silence all this time shift slightly on the balls of his booted feet.

Throughout the conversation, the gorgons' bodyguards had stood likewise, with arms folded like comic-opera eunuchs, just outside the rectangle of dim light thrown by the door of the nearest saloon. They were tall men, white, the older sandy and rather flat-faced, his dusting of freckles doing nothing to mitigate the meanness of his close-set, pale eyes and the small, ungiving mouth. The younger was bulky and powerful with barely a dusting of ginger peach-fuzz on his heavy cheeks. Given the fact that yet another fight had broken out across Main Street – men cursing, whores shrieking, the town constable in his black frock coat firing his pistol futilely in the air – January couldn't blame Mr Taggart for assigning protection to his womenfolk.

The senior Mrs Taggart went on, 'Now I fear that we must return to our hotel, sir. It would not, I am sure you must be aware, do for us to be out when my son returns. Good evening, Mr Sefton.'

Her glance at Valentina was a summons. And Valentina, to January's disconcerted surprise, obeyed without argument, only bobbing a curtsey to Hannibal and giving January a quick glance of apology.

'Alicia!'

The command had the force of a riding-whip slapped on a table-top, and the spectacled woman cringed. January wondered whether Mr Taggart backed his mother's arrogance with threats of his own, or whether she was simply one of those women so capable of making the lives of everyone around her hell that it was easier to simply knuckle under and obey. Her sister – as well as he could see her in the shadows and lamp-gleam of the dark street – seemed to be a woman in her early thirties, her features far more delicate but pinched by constant fear and suspicion. She glanced back repeatedly at January as she followed the older woman away up the street, obsessed and fascinated.

The three bodyguards followed them – clearly in the direction of the Commercial Hotel – the white men trading a *sotto voce* remark, the elderly vaquero silent as stone.

'Back in Mexico,' said Hannibal after a long moment of silence, 'I would have given almost anything to put that young lady over my knee and spank her. *Tempora mutantur, et nos mutamur in illis*, I'm sorry to say – and surprised to say that I'd ever feel sorry that Valentina would change with the change of times. Did you get the impression she was meeting a lover?'

'No,' said January.

'Nor I. And not because she had Briareus trailing about after her, either – he could easily have been disposed of. Maybe she was making plans with someone to flee?'

January asked, very simply, 'Where could she go?'

As Valentina had said, it was a hard country for a woman alone.

She had run away with a man once, four years ago. And Fate had led her, roundabout, to this place, barely better – it seemed to him – than she had been in her father's house in Mexico.

Where *could* a young woman go, without a protector, without money or land? Valentina was fortunate that she couldn't be seized as literally a slave, as Selina had been. But her options were little better.

Ahead of them, he saw her in the light of the lantern above the Commercial Hotel's door, as her mother-in-law and

Aunt Alicia preceded her up its shallow steps. It was the best hotel in town: he wondered what they'd do if the bald-pated Gervase Hookwire from the *Rosabel* were staying there also.

'All things considered,' he said, 'it might be best to get out of Houston at first light, before we encounter anyone else you know.'

'*Idem velle et idem nolle*,' agreed the fiddler, hanging back a pace to let January glance through the door into the lobby, to make sure the coast – as the smugglers said – was clear. '*Ea demum firma amicitia est*. Our thoughts chime together, *amicus meus* – the scum of the entire earth does seem to have gravitated to Texas, the lovely Valentina excepted, of course. I wonder if the good Lieutenant Shaw has managed to make arrangements for the purchase of horses at this hour?'

FOUR

Horses were cheap in the Republic of Texas. Shaw had, indeed, arranged to buy six for a hundred and thirty dollars, and three rather broken-down saddles for another sixty. This left the rescuers with far less than what anyone would have reasonably paid for a good-looking slave girl, but it was four days' ride to Austin and nobody in Houston – said the Kentuckian – was willing to rent to three strangers for less than that.

'By what you tell me this Miz Taggart says,' remarked Shaw, as the three riders left the town behind them in the clammy dawn, 'don't sound like this Pollack feller'd take even the whole seven-fifty for her, so likely it don't matter much.' He spit into the weedgrown ditch that bordered the road; Houston lay in the bayou country, where cotton fields alternated with long flats of head-high grass. Unlike the Louisiana sugar plantations, which could rely on corn, hogs, and pumpkins from Ohio and Illinois, the Texas holdings grew their own corn, their own wheat, their own vegetables and fruit as well as cotton. Baby jackrabbits peeked cautiously from among knee-high green stalks. Wild turkey and prairie-chicken burst from the young trees of orchards in flurries of feathers. Raptors circled, almost out of sight overhead.

The shadows of the riders lay far out ahead of them on the muddy track, but already the morning was hot.

'Most we can do,' the Kentuckian went on, 'I'm thinkin', is speak to him an' let him know there is a question 'bout the gal's freedom. Might be enough to keep him from sellin' her on. Nobody wants to find himself losin' a woman to a lawsuit, an' nuthin' to show for it. If the man's reasonable, he'll take earnest-money on our promise to bring whatever sum he names, soon as we can fetch it from her pa. It may even be enough to keep him from meddlin' with her, iff'n he knows he's gonna be answerable to her pa, though I wouldn't count on that.' He spit again, a world of comment implied by the action and by the dry silence that followed it.

Either he had found lodging last night at a cheaper hostelry than the Commercial or had – January guessed – slept with the local vaqueros among the corrals. He looked as he usually did, grubby, greasy, and surprisingly inconspicuous for one so tall.

He had also acquired – from heaven alone knew where – two six-shot Colt pistols, of the kind sometimes known as wheel-guns, the rear portion of the barrel being replaced by a revolving cylinder which could be loaded six times in advance. An enormous saving of time, January reflected, in the sort of brawls he'd witnessed in Houston.

He only said now, 'We can only see.'

They'd talked the matter over on the voyage across the Gulf, and neither had need to speak now of what was in both of their minds: that guilt still gnawed at January's heart, for not going to the bank and mortgaging the house to raise more money. Guilt that a dark cynical voice at the bottom of his soul whispered, *If her pa will pay . . .*

He might not.

Having seen the man, January would have bet – *Well*, he reflected, *bet seven hundred and fifty dollars anyway* – that to retrieve his daughter Roux Bellinger would gladly mortgage his acres, or sell . . .

Sell *what*, exactly?

Some of his slaves?

And putting aside the fact that January was fairly certain that in order to retrieve his daughter from slavery, the planter would take a husband from a wife, an adolescent boy or two from their families and friends and everyone they knew, and pass them along to dealers like Andreas Neumann . . .

Are you certain enough of his love for this child that you'd jeopardize Rose's school? Jeopardize the home of your sons and your wife?

If he had to whisper the truth into the ear of God, January had to admit that he followed the advice of that dark cynical voice at the bottom of his soul. He hated himself for it, but he had seen white men sell their children – children that they said they genuinely loved (not the children of their legitimate white wives, of course) – because they *really* needed the money. Sometimes, because they *really* needed the money to pay gambling debts.

He couldn't imagine how anyone could do this. Even an illegitimate child, even a *stranger's* child . . . As the horses trudged on through the flat heavy croplands under a monsoon sky, he saw the faces of his sons. Thin, grave, three-year-old Professor John, already sounding out the letters of the storybooks Rose read him. Golden Xander, who had just begun to stagger about the house, always underfoot and always trying to break into a joyful run . . .

How could anyone *sell a child?*

Men did it all the time. He knew that. His own father had come home from the fields one evening to the news that his wife and two children had been bought by a sugar-broker from New Orleans.

How could anyone say to a sixteen-year-old girl: 'I'm going to leave you here in slavery, with the man who has raped you every night for a week, because seven hundred and fifty dollars is all I can afford. Because I'm not willing to put my own interests in danger by borrowing more.'

Where would her father draw the line, of what interests of his own to give up?

He was again sorry Shaw had shot Seth Javel rather than letting him burn.

But that didn't solve the problem. Neither the one in his own heart, nor the one that awaited them in Austin.

And as the day went on, through those thick unchanging bottomlands between Buffalo Bayou and the Brazos, it became clear to him that he probably wasn't going to be able to confess his sin and hear Mass this side of New Orleans. Even had they been able to stay in Houston for more than the single night, he guessed there wasn't a Catholic church in thirty miles. The missions that hadn't been driven out by the Comanche had been shut down or abandoned during the revolution, their lands snabbled up into Mexican land grants or by Texas claimants who were still fighting over their provenance.

'What do the Irish do?' he asked Hannibal at one point during the day, and the fiddler's eyebrows had quirked up to the brim of his old chimneypot hat.

'You think any Irishman who's come to Texas is pining to confess his sins?'

The owner of the Brazos ferry – a tough, rosy woman whose husband ran the general store on its bank – confirmed this observation. 'No, I shouldn't think there's a Romish church closer than San Antonio,' she said, as she forked hay from a rack into the corral where the men led their horses. Nearly a dozen mounts were already penned there, and six mules. The ferry-woman's one-armed husband was fully occupied in the little adobe store building, pouring what January guessed to be truly horrible liquor for other travelers who'd chosen to pass the night rather than pressing on another twenty miles to Columbus. (Shaw told him the following day that his guess about the whiskey was accurate.)

'Back when the Mexicans ran this country we all had to be Catholics,' said Brazos Annie, wiping sweat from her fair, stringy hair with the back of her sleeve. 'They'd send a priest around every year or two – Father Gallagher, he was, and as good a man with a bottle as you'd care to see – to marry folks and baptize their children. I hear some of the Mexican ranchers will bring up a priest from San Antonio now and then, but there's never the money to build a church or a chapel or anything. And most of the local ranchers have had so much trouble with land-titles that go back to the missions, they sort of spit when they hear talk of Popish priests.'

Her scanty brows tugged together, and she helped the men hang the bridles they stripped from their mounts' heads on the fence, where the tack of the other horses was already draped. January wondered for about two seconds about the incidence of theft, but movement at the far side of the corral caught his eye: a couple of cowhands were building up a little fire under a grove of pecan trees. None was farther than a step from the rifles leaned up against tree-trunks or the back railings of the corral fence.

From what he'd heard of Comanche raids – and horse-thieves – in this part of the country, he knew he'd keep his own rifle close at hand, had he been permitted to carry one.

'Not the priests' fault,' the woman went on, and shrugged. 'But I never could see why a good Methodist preacher wouldn't do as well. At least they stirs up your blood.'

January guessed that a theological query about what stirred blood had to do with salvation would probably be considered 'uppity', and merely nodded. 'I guess people just feel most comfortable with the faith they were raised in, m'am.'

'Well, they shouldn't,' said Annie firmly. 'Mr Sefton, Mr Shaw, I charge ten cents for stew and bread, five cents for beer, or cook your own if you've got it.'

While Hannibal and Shaw played poker in the grocery with the other travelers – Hannibal managing to win back approximately half the cost of the horses and gear ('I could have taken more,' he said the next day, 'but thought moderation was called for . . .') – January sat by the campfire under the pecan trees and played penny blackjack with the cowhands, vaqueros, and drivers who hadn't the price of indoor accommodation, or who had been told by employers (or masters) to keep an eye on the stock. He himself maintained a surreptitious watch on the road leading down to the river's brim. There was no reason in particular to avoid further contact with Valentina Taggart and the gorgons, but the mere thought of calling attention to themselves made January uneasy. It would not help their cause with Gideon Pollack, to have Taggart say to him, 'Say, you know there's a couple men lookin' for you . . .'

But no band of outriders appeared, encircling the sort of heavy Mexican traveling-coach that January guessed must be in use to transport the formidable Mère Taggart and her sister, and he breathed a little easier as the night grew late and the gibbous white moon made a blurred shape behind thin clouds. The men talked politics, as men will who seek the comfort of talk but don't know those who share their campfire: politics, January had found, or guns, or horses. A dark-haired young Irishman named Finn, in between frying dough over the fire, showed him how to most efficiently cock his 'revolver' and switch the chambers while running, dodging, or hiding behind a tree.

'Bunch of damn cowards in Congress,' groused a heavy-shouldered Mississippi man named Wayne. 'Afraid of their own goddam shadows! America needs Texas, as much as Texas needs America! Hell, we're all Americans anyway, aren't we?' (The three Tejano vaqueros sharing the fire had nothing to say on this subject.) 'What the hell business is it of Bustamante or whoever the hell is president of Mexico these days, if we join the US?'

Not wanting to be beaten to a pulp, January forbore to point out that it was very much President Bustamante's business if the United States laid claim to a province that was, constitutionally, still Mexican and simply in rebellion against its rightful government.

'Hell, America could lick the goddam Mexican Army in a goddam week! You know how long it took us to whip the Mexes at San Jacinto? *Eighteen minutes*! What the hell those pussies in Congress are thinkin'—'

'What the hell do we need Congress for in the first place?' retorted the driver of the mule-wagon, chucking the stub of his cigar into the fire. 'With their goddam banks and their goddam abolitionists, tryin' to take away a man's property and keep him from earning a living? Screw 'em. Texas has the best cotton land on this continent, the best in the world. If true men, businessmen who see things as they really are, don't want to be pushed around by a bunch of milktoast Yankee abolitionists, let 'em come here!'

He folded his long legs to sit beside the fire, leaned across to stab a piece of flat-bread from the common skillet.

Another man said, 'Coop's right,' and wiped the grease from his mustache. 'What the hell do we need the US for?'

The young Irishman Finn pointed out mildly, 'Maybe to pay for an army to keep the borderlands safe from the Comanche?'

'Hell, Lamar took care of that last year!' blustered Greasy Mustache. 'Comanche an' the goddam Cherokee, too, which is more than that drunk Injun-lover Houston ever did!'

'Took care of it so well that Texas money is worthless these days,' replied the Irishman. 'You can't get but thirty cents on the dollar for it—'

'Just a bump in the road.' The tall man Coop waved a lazy hand. 'Soon as the country can get a trade-loan from England or France to get us on our feet, we'll have states like Louisiana and Mississippi askin' to join *us.*'

'When pigs fly!' Wayne was on his feet, knife in hand, enormous in the firelight. 'Lamar's a goddam crook, takin' bribes to open Texas land to speculators—'

'Like Houston never took a bribe—'

'Sam Houston never took a bribe in his life!'

'Only 'cause he was too drunk to count it!'

Under cover of the shouting, January turned to Finn – who continued to drop fry-bread into the skillet while gauging the fracas from the corner of one blue eye. 'Actually,' he said quietly, 'Texas redbacks are down to twelve cents on the dollar in New Orleans.'

'Are they, now?' The young man stirred at a pot of beans – to which all the men had contributed – bubbling gently on the coals. 'A pity, too, since the bank crash in '37, an' a poor man can't get credit to buy land no matter how much the stinkin' English mills are screamin' for cotton . . . but the British'll never lend Texas a ha'penny so long as they're workin' slaves. An' if that idiot Lamar thinks signin' a treaty with the French is gonna get him anywhere, well, the more fool he. An' nobody like to come settle in this part of Texas anyway, as long as the Comanche are there ready to cut out your lights an' liver just for the sport of the thing, an' be damned to your Texas Rangers. Though I will say,' he added, with a grin in the orange firelight, 'that the savages are a good sight tenderer o' heart than our landlord's agent back in Donaghpatrick.'

'I've heard that,' agreed January in a judicious tone.

'T'would be a joke on Lamar,' agreed the Irishman, 'if I hadn't seen the bodies the Comanche left last time they raided San Marcos, their guts spread over damn near three yards of ground. Children they were, not more'n what my daughter woulda been . . .'

Deftly he scooped up his own plate and retreated, January at his heels, as the shouting-match escalated into a full-on fight. January set his bowl down beside the corral fence, then dived back to rescue the fry-bread and the bean-pot from the fire.

'There's a man that's been to the wars,' approved Finn, settling rocks around the pot to support it. 'An' that's leavin' aside all the hoopla about where's the North gonna get a free state to balance Texas in Congress, if Texas *does* get in? Last time that happened they had to go choppin' up Massachusetts, which is where me sister lives. Ouch,' he added, as Wayne, inevitably, heaved his mustachioed opponent into the fire.

'That's got to hurt.' January wrapped his bandana around his hand and passed the bean-pot to one of the vaqueros, who had joined him and Irish by the fence.

'Not yet so bad,' replied the vaquero, 'as the fight last year in the Trinity Saloon. Remember that, Finn?' He picked a blob of fry-bread from the pan. 'When Wayne took on three of Vin Taggart's vaqueros, about Lamar moving the capital to Austin?'

'That he did,' grinned the Irishman. 'An' small blame to the man, given what it did to the price of town-lots in Houston, which is where his ma has a boardin' house.' His blue eyes danced as he looked back at January. 'Ain't seen the like of such a migration since me Aunt Maggie shifted twelve kids, two husbands – that's another story – a drunk brother-in-law an' the local preacher from her rooms on Elizabeth Street clear up to Sixth Avenue wi'out the rent-collector bein' the wiser. Archives, records, clerks, the very desks an' chairs—'

'Jalisco – that's Taggart's riding-boss – broke a barrel of beer over Wayne's head,' laughed the vaquero. 'Smash, like a pumpkin, and beer everywhere like a fountain and Wayne rising up out of it like Aphrodite from the waves!'

'Taggart of Rancho Perdition?'

'Himself,' agreed Finn. 'And a dear good pal of President Lamar in them days he was, and all for Texas rulin' the lands from the Sabine to the Pacific.'

'That was back when he thought Lamar was gonna clear the Comanche off that Mexican-grant land he got from his wife,' said the vaquero, dodging a thrown plate.

'No,' objected Irish, 'he just went over to the Pollacks when Pollack got a cotton-press—'

'Rance Pollack?' January moved his dinner out of the way as Coop, having finished his stew, waded into the fight and hurled Wayne over the corral-rails in among the horses.

'His brother. You know Gideon Pollack?'

'Only heard his name,' said January. 'From a lady who didn't think much of him,' he added, recalling what Valentina had said of the man.

'You would have to ride from sun-up to sun-down, señor,' said the vaquero expansively, 'to find a lady who *did* think much of Rance Pollack. It is the brother, Gideon, that has the brains – and the power. Rance . . .' He shrugged. 'A dog on a chain.'

'And the less dangerous,' said the Irishman quietly, 'of the two. Rance'll bark and bite. He's hot and red, like a rocket, that will go off anywhere. Gideon is a cold bastard, for all he's smooth as mother's milk an' has the ladies eatin' from his hand. He's the one you want to avoid.'

And he rocked back a little, as Coop the driver – who'd launched himself into the corral in pursuit of the burly Wayne – clambered neatly over the fence-rails and returned to pick up his own plate beside the scattered fire. The men settled down, leaving Wayne sprawled unconscious in the middle of the corral among the horses, where he remained, as far as January could tell, peacefully asleep for the rest of the night.

FIVE

Hannibal Sefton located Gideon Pollack two nights later at the Empire of the West saloon on Congress Avenue in Austin – a town up until last year known as Waterloo. The doors were open in the sticky darkness, which was fortunate, as slaves were not permitted inside. It was also fortunate, January reflected, that at least three other owners had left their human property outside in the dim puddle of lantern-light beneath the saloon's awning. Though he didn't really think slave-stealers would try to make off with the two grooms and the cowhand who shared the benches with him on either side of the door, his encounters with Valentina and the little clerk Hookwire had left him nervous.

He hated, these days, even being out of the French Town in New Orleans. People knew him there: specifically, white businessmen, white brokers, white planters who would cheerfully testify, *Hell, yes, Ben's a free man! One of the best! Known him for years . . .*

Freedom papers, January had learned long ago, were the easiest things in the world to tear up. He supposed that even if the French daguerreotype process were perfected to the point that such images could be made cheaply, any buyer would claim that the black man in the picture wasn't the man he'd bought – and the courts would believe him.

The courts in Texas, the self-proclaimed 'Slaveholders' Republic', wouldn't even check.

Bitterly and powerlessly, he hated the fact that this was so.

'My boss told me to watch his back,' he said, when the grooms who'd accompanied Mr Moore the cotton-broker and Mr Slater from the land office suggested a game of dice on their bench. 'I don't see the men that followed him back in New Orleans in there, but they hired a fella to go after him in Galveston, took us clean by surprise.'

'What'd he do?' asked the cowhand, who was loose-jointed and wiry and rejoiced in the name of Marcus Mudsill.

'Nuthin'!' insisted January, extemporizing freely. 'This Frenchman in New Orleans claims Mr Sefton – that's my boss – ran off with his wife, but it wasn't any such thing. Lord, if I'd been that fella's wife, I'd have run off, too!'

It got a laugh, and explained why he positioned himself with his back to the hitching-rail opposite the door, where he could see most of the room. Mudsill joined him. 'This town's lousy with Nationalists,' he groused. 'There's one or two that'd beat up any man that comes out for joinin' with the USA. Mr Pollack doesn't like to take chances.'

'Mr Pollack your boss?'

'Yeah.'

The twist of the man's mouth as he spoke brought back to January's mind what Valentina had said, about Pollack's main source of income being cotton. The prospect of being put in the fields was enough to make any enslaved cowhand nervous.

Within the dim gold lamplight of the room, Hannibal crossed from the bar to the table where three men sat. Two of them – by the similarity of their square-featured faces, the identical dust-brown of their hair and the shape of their outward-winging eyebrows – had to be brothers, and it was easy to guess which brothers they were. The third man – medium-sized and slim, with a handsome mane of prematurely silver hair and a dark, waxed mustache like the villain in a melodrama – glanced up as Hannibal approached, and for a moment January felt a lurch of dread accompanied by the desire to shake the fiddler in exasperation: *Not somebody* else *who recognizes him . . .*

But the man gave no sign of recognition, only watched the newcomer – and the door, and every corner of the room – with the wary eye of one who is making sure where every exit lay. January wondered if this was because he, like Pollack, was a Houstonite in this largely Nationalist new town.

Hannibal bowed, and gave Gideon Pollack – the slimmer of the brothers, smaller and more expensively dressed – his card. Pollack glanced at it, then up at Hannibal's face, as if trying to determine whether this was a trap or not.

If he thought it was, he also evidently didn't consider the

fiddler, upon perusal, much of a threat. He stood, gestured to his brother and their companion to stay where they were, and guided Hannibal to a quieter portion of the saloon: farther from the bar, closer to the door.

'How can I help you, Mr Sefton?' That was the first thing one noticed about him: the resonant beauty of his voice.

January had shifted over from the hitching-rack to the side of the door, and could hear, if not well, at least well enough to follow the conversation. Mudsill drifted over to join him, as a bodyguard should. *Just in case . . .*

'I've been asked to represent a man named Roux Bellinger, of Shreveport, Louisiana.' Hannibal produced a letter of introduction. He had written it himself, expertly copying the handwriting from the planter's letters found in his daughter's trunk, but nobody had to know that. 'I have reason to believe that the girl you purchased from Andreas Neumann in Galveston last week was his daughter, who had been seduced and kidnapped from her school in New Orleans.'

Pollack folded his arms. His sun-darkened features were craggily handsome, his velvet-brown eyes the eyes of a man who could smile like the sun and keep every thought concealed. He stood like a man who is used to being obeyed in all things. 'I bought no girl.'

'I'm sorry.' Hannibal dipped a slight bow. 'Mr Neumann seems to think that you did.'

In the dimness of the lantern-lit room his eyes glinted, like broken bits of bottle-glass. The beautiful voice grew soft. 'You calling me a liar, Mr Sefton?'

'No, indeed, Mr Pollack. It's very easy to be mistaken in cases like this. Mr Bellinger is of course deeply anxious to recover his daughter, and has empowered me to offer to reimburse whatever may have been spent on the transaction.'

'He is, is he?' Pollack held out his hand, and January saw his eyes shift again, thinking. Calculating how much he could ask? January wondered. Or just trying to decide whether he wanted to turn loose a pretty, fair-skinned, sixteen-year-old girl who was in his power?

The rancher glanced over the letter, which included – January knew, because he'd seen Hannibal write it – instructions for hiring a lawyer to pursue the matter, if necessary. Whether a suit for the recovery of a victim of kidnap in a case like this would even be admitted to a Texas court was anybody's guess, and January was inclined to believe that even should an American lawyer come to Austin to recover Selina, a Texas judge would probably find in Pollack's favor.

Would the threat of a lawsuit be enough to keep another buyer from purchasing her, if Pollack tried to sell her on?

Looking at that calmly untroubled face, he didn't think so.

Pollack handed the letter back. 'It is easy to be mistaken in a case like this, Mr Sefton,' he agreed. 'And I'm afraid you're the one who's mistaken. I bought no wench.'

Hannibal bowed. 'I'm very sorry to have troubled you, Mr Pollack.'

As he started to withdraw Pollack caught him by the shoulder of his coat, a quick motion, like an expert fighter gutting his opponent with a flick of his knife. His tone even, almost friendly, he said, 'Make sure you don't trouble me again.'

There was movement, very slight, along the wall near the bar, and for the first time January saw Abishag Shaw, sitting on a bench in the shadows with a glass of whiskey on the rough table before him. Whether it was he who had moved – he looked like any unshaven yokel adrift in his own thoughts – January wasn't sure.

This was because at almost the same instant, January felt Mudsill – standing at his elbow – step hastily back and aside, to get out of the way of three men who strode out of the darkness of Congress Avenue. The man in the lead – in a townsman's cutaway coat and silk vest – held a newspaper in one hand, and stepping through the door into the saloon, took Gideon Pollack by the arm and slapped him full-force across the face with it.

'You are a lyin' hypocrite pi-dog and a thief,' he said, in a voice that could be heard all over the enormous room, stopping all other conversation dead in its tracks.

Hannibal, no fool, slipped immediately from Pollack's loosened grip and was out the door and at January's side even as Rance Pollack, crimson with fury, surged to his feet and plunged to the rescue. The challenger's two friends intercepted him, and January noticed that the silver-maned man who'd been sharing the table with the brothers lost no time in vanishing through the inner door of the room. *Probably leads to the storeroom and out the back . . .*

Pollack's hand went to his side – he wore a knife the size of a young cutlass – and the newcomer reached for the pistol he wore, slung pirate-fashion on a ribbon around his neck and stuck into his belt. Five men started up from the tables and benches – one of them lunging at another and knocking him to the floor with a blow of his fist – and Pollack snapped his big hand into the air, commanding quiet.

Other friends pulled the new combatants apart, and there was momentary stillness in the room.

'And you, Burrell Stanway,' Pollack addressed his opponent in a voice like summer thunder, 'are a traitor. You're a traitor to this land of Texas and to our greater homeland of the United States. You name your friends, if you've got any.'

With cold calm he reached down to the floor and picked up the newspaper, and glanced at it. January had witnessed, or heard about, too many New Orleans duels which had come about through letters to various of the city's newspapers to be in the least surprised.

Pollack added, still calm and cold as marble, 'I'm surprised you could even read my letter, Stanway, much less figure out what all them big words mean.'

And he slashed Stanway across the face with the offending journal, signaled to his brother, and together they left the saloon, brushing past January and Hannibal, unseeing, in the doorway.

Being the state capital, Austin boasted two hotels, not counting two barracks-like establishments where lesser government clerks, day-laborers, and drovers put up and got their meals. January sat up late, in the yard behind Eberly's Tavern, a rambling hostelry on Congress Avenue, deeply grateful that the town was built on a bluff above the river and was less afflicted with mosquitoes than was low-lying Houston. But when Shaw slipped quietly out of the darkness at close to midnight he had nothing to report.

'I followed Pollack back to the Capital City – that's the fanciest hotel in town, meanin' it's been painted in the last six months.' Shaw spat into the weeds that grew along the back wall of the tavern. As usual his scrubby sand-colored whiskers were flecked with tobacco. 'I thought he'd take an' put the girl, if he's got her, in the regular jail over to Cedar Street for safe-keepin', but no. He stayed drinkin' in the barroom at the Capital City talkin' to one man an' another, then went upstairs. I kept a eye on the place til most of the lights was out.'

The following day – while Hannibal played poker and flirted with the handsome proprietress ('She's a nationalist in senti-ment but refuses Texas redback money . . .') – January scraped acquaintance with the stablemen and kitchen staff at the Capital City.

They of course knew all about the 'bright wench' Pollack was keeping locked up in Room 3-H ('That's her winder, right up there, see? The little one by the chimney . . .'). Pharaoh, the stableman he talked to, shook his head at January's tale of being Selina's cousin and said, 'No, he ain't gonna have her put in the jail, no matter who he thinks is lookin' for her. He an' Sheriff Quigley come near to knifin' one another four months ago, 'bout Austin bein' made the capital – an' mostly 'cause Quigley's one of the few men in this town that don't buy his sweet talk. If he let Quigley lock up any wench of his, he's afraid Quigley'd let her go, just to spite him.'

'Any chance I could see her? Talk to her?' The narrow window was on the third floor and didn't look wide enough to admit even a girl as slender as Selina, in the extremely unlikely event that January was able to acquire a three-story ladder and put it up to the sill undetected.

'See her? No.' Pharaoh – a blocky man with an R branded on his cheek, marking some long-ago attempt at escape – shook his head again. 'Be as much as my skin is worth, to try to even get the key to that room. I can get you up there to talk to her through the door, tomorrow, when everybody'll be out of the hotel, pretty much, to see if Pollack an' Bue Stanway are gonna put holes in each other over that letter

Pollack wrote to the *Texas Register* about Lamar's slippery land-deals.'

'I'll be here.'

The duel, according to Hannibal, would take place down by the river, at nine in the morning, Texans basically not caring who shot who on the Sabbath. It was Palm Sunday, and January was deeply conscious of this as he woke in the pre-dawn dark of the tavern's attic, where the housemen who cut wood and swept floors spread their pallets among the piled luggage of the guests.

His wife Rose – beautiful in her best pink frock and white headwrap – would be leading little Professor John, her pupils, and his nephew and niece who lived at the school, along the narrow brick banquettes of the French Town to the cathedral. A logical deist herself, she was conscientious in her duty to the parents of the girls in her school, and after Mass she would take January's usual place in instructing them in the significance of Holy Week, the reading of the heart of the Gospels.

No bell broke the silence for early Mass. He guessed there wasn't a Catholic church within sixty miles. But he whispered a prayer: for her, for his sons. For Selina.

For his own safe return . . .

At eight thirty, Pharaoh – suitably recompensed – guided January up the Capital City's narrow, stuffy backstairs, and along a dismal passageway on the floor allotted to the slaves of the guests, uncarpeted and smelling of chamber pots not frequently cleaned. The doorway of 3-H, at the far end, was locked, and Pharaoh stood near the head of the stairs, watching as January scratched softly at the panels. All the other rooms on the floor were empty, their open doors admitting a grimy light. The hotel below was silent.

Far off, now, a church bell rang.

In the stillness he heard a sharp creak, like the squeak of a very old bedstead. As if someone within were holding herself motionless in terror.

'Selina? It's Mr January.'

'Oh, my God!' The soft pat of feet, and, close against the

door now and constricted with tears, 'Oh, Mr J, get me out of here! Please, please, oh God, I'm sorry, I'm so sorry—'

'Hush,' said January, 'and listen. We haven't got a lot of time.' He glanced over his shoulder, gauging how much, if anything, Pharaoh could hear.

He didn't blame the man. Helping a slave escape, in Texas, would get even a white man hanged.

'I can't get you out right now—'

'Please!' He could hear she was crying. 'Please, Mr J, they . . . they hurt me. That man who bought me, he's . . . he's awful he—'

'Selina,' said January, 'listen to me. Listen.' From his pocket he brought out a cotton tobacco-pouch, containing all the coin Hannibal judged they could spare. He went to one knee, and pushed it carefully under the door. 'You can't cry. You have to listen. You have to be strong. Can you be strong?'

Her voice shaking, she whispered, 'I'll be strong.'

'I'm in town with Mr Sefton and another man, and if you see us on the street, if you cry out, or say our names, or show that you recognize us at all, in any way, the three of us will be hanged. Do you believe that? Do you believe me?'

Barely a whisper, choked with tears. 'I know that's true.'

'This money is in case you do get away somehow when we're not close by. Don't let *anyone* see it, don't let *anyone* know you have it. But we'll do what we can, as soon as we can. Are you physically all right?'

A thread of voice: 'He hurt me.'

'Can you walk? Can you run?'

'I can run.'

'Are you kept tied? Bound in any way?'

'No, sir.'

'Not when they take you out into the open?'

'No, sir. I . . . I tried to run away once and they caught me. And anyway there wasn't anyplace to run.'

The thought passed, very briefly, through January's mind: *Like Valentina . . .*

'All right.' He glanced over his shoulder towards Pharaoh again. 'I don't know what will be possible, but we're here. You're not alone. You have to be ready to run, the minute you have a chance. Don't get yourself hurt.' At one point last night he had considered slipping her something else – a razor, or something to put Pollack to sleep – but had decided against it. Both could too easily be used for other purposes.

'Did Daddy send you?' Her voice faltered again. 'Does Daddy know? Will Daddy . . .?'

'We've sent word to your father,' said January. 'We couldn't wait to hear from him, before coming after you. I'm not going to lie to you, Selina – I don't know what your father will do or say about this. But Mrs January and I will stand by you. You're not alone here. And you won't be alone when we get back. But you have to be ready. And you have to be strong.'

'Thank you.' The words were barely a breath. 'I'll be strong, I swear it. I'm so sorry, Mr J. Seth – I was so stupid, and Seth—'

'I know all about Seth,' said January softly. 'You won't be seeing him again. Ever.'

She whispered again, 'Thank you.'

'Do you know—?'

Clamor downstairs. Someone yelling for hot water, and sheets. Other voices bellowing about skunk-faced cheaters and lying traitors and coward suck-arse whores who'd sell out their mothers for a league of Spanish land. The shouting worsened at that, and January pressed his face to the door, said, 'Something going on. I have to go. You're not alone.'

Just as he and Pharaoh reached the top of the backstairs, someone two floors below hollered a question, and a voice rose above the general din with the reply.

'Pollack's been shot.'

SIX

*A*nd does that mean things just got harder, or easier? January rattled down the stairs in the stableman's wake.

If he's dead, does that mean Rance Pollack will get the girl?

If he hasn't bulled her already when his brother's back was turned?

Valentina had said, *He pays the very whores in Texas redbacks* . . . which didn't hold out much promise for coming to an understanding for the five hundred dollars January had left at his disposal . . .

The uproar in the lobby of the Capital City Hotel reminded January of the Place du Carousel in front of the Tuileries in Paris, when the second revolution had broken out, ten years before. Men shoving, shouting, waving their fists – a fight was already in progress in the street outside and several men in the lobby were pushing their way against the incoming crowd to join it. A wide-shouldered man with a broken nose and a rancher's sunburnt complexion stood beside the couch onto which others had laid Pollack, but turned toward the door and bellowed, 'Rance, you fucken imbecile, get in here!'

Another man, in the black frock coat of a professional over which blood was liberally splattered, crouched at Pollack's head, yelling, 'We gotta get that ball outta him! Somebody fetch me some whiskey! Can't do nuthin' til we pull the ball—'

'You goddam idiot he's bleedin' like a pig already—'

'You, nigger,' said – unexpectedly – Shaw's scratchy voice, suddenly hard with authority, and from out of the crowd the tall Kentuckian jabbed a crooked finger at January. 'Wasn't you the doctor's boy at Chalmette?'

January had been nothing of the kind – he'd been behind the cotton-bales with a rifle in his hands, like the rest of the Free Colored Militia – but he replied promptly, 'I was, sir.'

'Thought so.' Shaw wriggled out of the press, grabbed the doctor – if he *was* a doctor – at Pollack's head and pitched him aside like a man breaking up a dogfight. 'What you need? I saw your master at the fight—'

January dropped at once to his knees beside the couch where Pollack lay. Behind him, the manager of the hotel was wailing and wringing his hands about upholstery and blood. Somebody had already torn away the wounded man's coat, waistcoat, and shirt, and it was clear the subclavian artery had been grazed. 'Kerchiefs, cloth, anything – a lot of it—'

'You gotta take the damn ball out first, you blockheaded

nig—' began the former would-be healer, and Shaw thrust him toward the door. January smelled liquor on the man's clothing as well as blood and weeks' worth of stale sweat.

'Somebody get him outta here,' said the Kentuckian, and with the authority of a white man behind the request, two or three of those present obliged. Had January said the identical words, he guessed he'd have been lynched while Pollack bled to death on the couch.

'Cravat,' said January, packing more and more cloth against the spouting wound, pressing it closed, pressing it tight. Pollack gasped, and cursed, though his eyes were rolling back in his head and January could tell the man was barely aware of his surroundings. The hotel manager whipped off his neckcloth and put it in January's free hand.

'Can somebody support him – gentle – like that, yes, thank you, sir . . .'

A Tejano rancher with a face like lumps of broken granite eased Pollack forward a little, and kept him steady while January slipped the cravat around his back, and tied the thick pad in place. 'Another,' January said. 'Please . . .?'

Three other cravats were proffered, and two glasses of whiskey.

When he'd tied the pad more firmly into place January took one of the whiskey glasses, and carefully dribbled the liquid between Pollack's lips. The rancher swallowed, and some of the rigidity went out of his back.

'He needs to be kept warm,' said January. 'Right away, feel how cold his hands are.' A touch on Pollack's wrist was enough to tell him his pulse was sinking away, going fast and thready. 'Put something under his feet. My master always said, when a man goes cold like this, you got to put his feet higher than his head. Could someone watch him, in case he starts to vomit – has he eaten?'

'Just coffee.' The broken-nosed man bent over the back of the couch, his crystal-blue eyes curiously cold, as if he were thinking of something else. Calculating something. For a moment January wondered where he'd met him before. Then he realized that the shape of his strong chin and wide lips were those of Valentina Taggart's elderly gorgon. The eyes

– clear, pale blue and drooping a little at the corners – were the same as well.

This must be Vin Taggart. Valentina's husband.

At the same time, somebody in the mob – which was still pressed up around the couch like medical students watching a dissection – said, 'I seen my cousin puke up, after he been shot at San Jacinto . . .'

Blankets were passed over and through the crowd.

'Hell,' said somebody else, 'the food we got in Houston's camp, you didn't have to be shot to puke . . .'

'That doctor was right, sir,' said January, with a quick glance around the crowd. Three of the blankets he folded up, and put beneath Pollack's hips, then elevated his feet to the arm of the couch. 'The ball needs to be drawn, and soon. But the bleeding had to be stopped, sooner than soon. He sure would have died, else. Sir –' he turned to the hotel manager – 'might a room be made up for him, as close to here as you can get? He shouldn't be moved at all for most of the day . . .'

'He can have mine,' said a gawky Frenchman – obviously one of those who'd surrendered his cravat, for his collar stood open around a throat like a couple of lengths of bamboo. 'It's just down the hall there. That was smart work, sir,' he added, with a nod to January.

'An' smarter work,' said a rough-looking unshaven man in a preacher's collar, 'chuckin' Doc Parralee outta here.' He turned to hold out his hand to Shaw, who had hovered quietly at the foot of the couch. 'I don't think Parralee's drawn a sober breath since God left for Cincinnati, an' you probably saved Gideon's life, kickin' him out. Fancy you recognizin' the surgeon's boy from far back as Chalmette! I fought at Chalmette, an' I couldn't pick my captain at that battle out of a line of men today, not if I was to be hanged—'

'An' I bet your captain wasn't six an' a half feet tall neither,' returned Shaw, and spit on the blood-soaked carpet. By the look of the carpet in other parts of the room, January guessed that he wasn't the only person to have neglected the spittoons in the corners. 'Damned if I can remember his name, but I was in the sawbones' tent durin' the fight, an' I never seen no man, black nor white, so quick an' resolute with wounds.'

'My name's Ben, sir,' said January, inclining his head respectfully, just as if any of Shaw's story had been the truth. 'And I thank you kindly, for remembering me after all those years. I haven't been with Michie Drake for near to ten years. This man should be seen by a . . . a reliable surgeon . . .'

'Well, that for sure ain't Parralee,' sighed the preacher, and at that moment there was a stirring around the outer door. The crowd parted to admit a brisk, rotund man with a face like a friendly gorilla in a great ruff of brown beard, carrying a doctor's satchel. Doc Parralee followed him, still maunderingly insisting on the necessity of immediate extraction, but the newcomer – whom the hotel manager greeted as 'Doc Meredith' – took a competent look at January's work, apologized to the company at large for having been in church, and said to January, 'Good job on your part – Ben, is it? Very nice work! Even elevated his feet . . . No, good God, if you tried to draw the ball now you'd kill him. Now, Luke,' he said gently to Parralee, 'you're quite right in your diagnosis. Al –' to the manager of the hotel – 'can you stand Dr Parralee a couple of drinks at the bar and charge them to me? Thank you. Yes, by all means leave him where he is for the next few—'

More commotion around the door. Belated – and covered with the dust and blood of a fist fight – Rance Pollack surged into the lobby, trailed by Marcus Mudsill and two other ranchhands. He cried, 'Gideon!' and flung himself at the couch, and caught Doc Parralee by the sleeve just as Al the hotel manager was leading him toward the bar. 'He gonna be all right, Doc?'

'No goddam thanks to you!' Vin Taggart stormed over to the younger Pollack, and fetched him a stunning whack with the back of his hand across the face.

It was like striking a boulder. Taggart stood six feet tall and was built like a coach-horse, but Pollack, two or three inches taller, was a mountain walking on thighs like oak trees. Rance Pollack let out a Minotaur bellow, and though he'd clearly just finished a major battle out on Congress Avenue, launched himself at Taggart.

The room erupted into chaos, and January, Shaw, Al the

manager and Doc Meredith swiftly dragged the unconscious Gideon Pollack's couch behind the counter where the clerk ordinarily sat.

'Idiots,' fumed Meredith, in the accent of an educated Englishman.

'What the hell happened out there?' asked January of Shaw, remembering to add, 'sir,' since he wasn't supposed to have met the Kentuckian since the battle of Chalmette. 'I thought Taggart was part of Pollack's camp. By what I've heard.' He glanced at Al the manager and Doc Meredith, both checking bandages and pulse.

'Taggart was Pollack's second,' explained Shaw. 'Stanway got off his shot a good second 'fore Parralee dropped his hankie, an' Rance went after Stanway. Stanway's a banker an' lively in the Nationalist Party hereabouts. Ten fellers jumped on Rance, includin' Sheriff Quigley, an' Pollack's ranch-hands all joined in on Rance's side—' He moved out of the way as a hurled chair splintered on the front of the counter.

'Then all the way back here, every time the fightin'd sort of die down, Taggart went after Rance, yellin' at him that he was a coward an' a pup an' too stupid to work as a shoe-shine boy let alone a man's second, an' Stanway would chime in on that opinion, an' Rance would go after Stanway again – Stanway bein' the party that actually cheated in the duel, you understand. Sheriff Quigley arrested Rance two or three times durin' the course of all this, an' got hisself thrown into a couple of horse-troughs, an' I must say I'm a little surprised Gideon Pollack didn't bleed to death 'fore they got him up here.'

'I am, too,' agreed Dr Meredith, ducking a thrown spittoon. 'Al, might I trust you and your good wife to nurse Pollack, once the battle dies down and he can be moved into a room? He should have nothing but liquids – and a lot of them – for the first twenty-four hours. After that I'll see about removing the ball—'

'By the bruising on his back it looks like it deflected off the left scapula,' provided January. He flinched as someone flung Doc Parralee, with great violence, against the counter, but evidently the medical man was too drunk to notice. He leapt to his feet and re-joined the fray. 'I think I could feel it, about two centimeters immediately south-east, you might say, of the bottom corner of the shoulder blade, but I was too concerned with getting pressure on the wound to make sure. But I'm fairly certain you can cut for it through his back without coming anywhere near the artery, sir.'

'Thank you, sir,' said Meredith. 'That will help very much indeed.'

In the main body of the room, Taggart managed to get a double handful of Rance Pollack's shirt-front and slammed him up against the wall by the counter. Both men were covered with dust and blood; both were gasping for breath. 'You're a fool and a coward!' yelled Taggart, in a voice that carried effortlessly over the din. 'An' I spit on the day I ever had to do with you or yours! You can shove your cotton-press up your brother's arse and get your damn sheep off my land—'

He flung Pollack from him like a sack of meal, then turned, and jabbed a finger at the grizzle-haired Sheriff Quigley, who was just picking himself up from a corner, blood streaming from his mouth and from what remained of the ear of the man collapsed, howling, before him.

'And you!' Taggart shouted. 'God damn the suck-arse lot of you! I'm giving orders to my men to shoot the first outsider they see ridin' across my land, an' I don't care who it is!'

Turning, he strode from the lobby and into the street, nearly colliding with Hannibal Sefton in the doorway.

Hannibal looked around him at the ruination – chairs and couches overturned, blood and tobacco soaking into the rugs, every lamp and picture shattered. '*As o'er their prey rapacious wolves engage,*' he quoted mildly, and crossed to the counter. '*Man dies on man, and all is blood and rage.* Benjamin, I've been looking all over town for you, to take care of – ah, you did!' He leaned across the counter to look down at Pollack. '*Head to foot/ now is he total gules; horridly tricked with blood . . .* Is he alive? Just as well.' He added, in Latin – after a glance to make sure that Meredith was fully occupied with the wounded man. 'I never thought to say so, but I think we'll actually be better off dealing with Gideon than with Rance.'

'*Nihil est ab omni parte beatum*,' said January. 'I'm not sure if "better" is a term we can apply here.'

Dr Meredith removed the pistol-ball on the following afternoon – Monday – with January's assistance. By that time January had had time to read the letter to the *Texas Register*, and agreed that if he'd been a white man, he'd have sought out its author and slapped him in the face in public, too. In it, Pollack accused the National Party of not only treason to the United States (the original rebellion against Mexico, which could also be construed as treason, went unmentioned), but of cowardice, theft of public monies, manipulation of the National Bank of Texas for the profit of President Lamar's cronies, and illegally removing the government offices, archives, land office records, and armory from Galveston to Austin, to the detriment of the former city and of many of its employees.

'Demented, the lot of 'em.' Dr Meredith shook his head. He had a light clear voice, like a teenaged boy's, incongruous in so powerful a frame. 'And Vin Taggart – I'd have thought he was a steadier man than to go re-openin' his quarrel with the Pollacks, when they'd finally made peace between 'em.'

Gently, he and January arranged pillows – every pillow the Capital City Hotel possessed, by the look of it – behind Pollack's back and shoulders, to keep both the incision in his back, and the tightly-bound wound in his chest, from irritation or pressure.

'How long til he can ride?' Rance Pollack reappeared in the doorway, where he'd been hovering, on and off, throughout the brief procedure. *Nervous*, January thought, glancing back at him. Frightened for his brother, of course. But he wasn't pale with the pallor of shock, and whenever he'd disappeared from the room, January had heard the murmur of voices in the hall, and booted steps that came and went.

'Good Lord, man,' said the physician irritably, 'he's lucky he isn't dead! He'll be abed for a week at least, or risk killing himself. More, if I have anything to say of it. That'll teach him to fight duels on the Sabbath.'

The bulky man sidled into the room as January bundled the

bloodied linen up to carry it away. 'Can he . . .? When'll I be able to talk to him?'

'Talk to him?' Meredith stared at Rance. 'Let the man rest, for God's sake. I've given him pretty much as much paregoric as he'll hold. Here, Ben, you don't need to clean up! Get one of the hotel servants—'

January relinquished the task to one of the housemen, noticing as he did so that the cowhand Mudsill lingered in the hall. Watching the door of Pollack's room, he thought . . . *Does he really expect Stanway to be back with his nationalist friends, to murder Pollack in his bed?*

And if he expects it, why?

Evidently, however, he expected *something*. Two of the Pollack cowhands, in addition to Mudsill, had been loitering in the Capital City's yard all day yesterday and through the night – even at three in the morning, when January and Hannibal had slipped quietly up in the blackness, to see if there were any chance of pilfering a ladder long enough to reach the third-floor window, men had been there, playing cards by lantern-light.

There were still men out there now, smoking and yarning with Shaw – who would at least, January guessed, get out of them what their plans were. Los Lobos – the Pollack plantation, Valentina Taggart had said – lay mostly in the creek-bottomlands near San Antonio, two days' ride from Austin. A mail-coach traversed the route several times a week but Doc Meredith forbade the injured man to take it ('Good Lord, man, d'you want your wound to open in the first thirty feet?') and recommended a horse-litter. 'And not for a week or ten days, you hear me?'

'You watch,' predicted Mudsill, when January encountered him in the dingy hall. 'He'll be on his feet inside two days an' in the saddle on the third. You can't stop that man, when he's got an idea in his mind. Yes, sir,' he added, springing to his feet as Rance Pollack put his head out the sick-room door.

'You get Shaughnessy up here,' said the big man. 'Tell him we need to hire three more riders, to take the stores and the new niggers down to the farm tomorrow. Taggart's been claimin' for years that he owns that Bonner's Prairie land along Onion Creek east of the road, and it'd be just like him, to hold us up an' make us go 'round.'

Mudsill said, 'Yes, sir,' in a perfectly expressionless voice, and started to head for the kitchen quarters – cowhands were permitted to cross through the hotel's lobby but not, January had observed, if they were slaves.

Rance added, 'You tell him he's going to be in charge of making sure there's no trouble.'

Mudsill looked surprised, but made no comment. Rance went on, 'My brother wants me here for a couple days – take care of some things for him. An' Gideon says to tell you, you keep an eye on things, too.'

Mudsill said, 'Yes, sir,' as Rance turned and went back into the bedroom, his huge shoulders blotting the light from within as he passed through the door. 'Lyle Shaughnessy's an idiot,' he added quietly, as soon as the door shut. 'You ever get stuck with keepin' an eye on some white man an' makin' sure he don't screw up, in spite of all his best efforts to do so? An' then he kicks the shit out of you if you tell him things like, *Let's put extra guards on the train* when there's been Comanche in the neighborhood? Mr Pollack always pats me on the shoulder an' says, *Good boy! I knew I could rely on you!* But he don't fire the stupid son-of-a-bitch.'

January shook his head. 'I thought you knew,' he said gravely. 'Gettin' kicked is part of our job. *Would* this Taggart fellow have his men keep your store-wagon from crossing his land? Is he that cussed?' He thought of Valentina, and of the calculating coldness in Vin Taggart's light-blue eyes.

A coldness curiously at odds with his fury when he'd proclaimed that no outsiders would cross Perdition. Valentina had said he was reasonable . . .

But she also said that he drank. Here in Texas, that frequently meant, drank at breakfast. And January had found, in his journey to Mexico four years before, that the cattle-ranchers – like the American owners of the larger plantations of the Mississippi Valley – tended to regard themselves as kings of their territories, and treated others accordingly. Valentina's father, he recalled, had ruled his own thousands of acres like a tribal sheik, and had seen nothing amiss in imprisoning

Hannibal for no better reason than that he'd wanted his company.

Being twenty miles from town, and in command of a half-savage band of vaqueros, gave scope for any amount of arbitrary behavior.

'Oh, hell,' said Mudsill. 'You shoulda seen the pair of 'em back before him and Pollack buried the hatchet. Once up on Elbow Creek, when I was huntin' for some of Mr Pollack's sheep, I got caught by that wall-eyed lunatic that runs his riders, got beat up an' my boots an' horse taken, an' had to walk ten miles back barefoot, an' I don't give a crap whether Texas joins the US or not. Jake Sorrel got horse-dragged by some of Taggart's men – though I will say, him and Shaughnessy beat up Lope, another of the Perdition vaqueros, in back of Eberly's Tavern. So, yeah, Taggart's that cussed. More so, I'd guess, now that he's got his mother and that crazy sister of hers livin' in the house. Enough to make any man cussed.'

January located Hannibal at Eberly's Tavern – where he was engaged in a small-stakes poker game with several of the locals – and relayed to him the information that Gideon Pollack's wagonload of supplies, plus his newly-purchased slaves, would be on the road to San Antonio in the morning. 'I presume including Selina,' he said quietly, during one of the frequent bouts of chafing and joking between hands, when the dark-haired, handsome proprietress came over to replenish the beer and Hannibal's discreetly disguised ginger-water. 'Given what Madame Taggart said about Pollack, I doubt he'd leave a woman he'd bought for himself in his brother's keeping. It may be one reason he's sending everything down to Los Lobos tomorrow, since Rance is staying here in town.'

Hannibal's dark eyebrows pinched. 'That's odd, isn't it? That he isn't sending his brother to look after the ranch?'

'From what I hear of Rance,' returned January quietly, 'it may be that Pollack feels that things will be better run with his brother here where he can keep an eye on him. Particularly if there's a chance of fighting breaking out with Taggart's men.'

Just as well, he reflected, an hour later when, after an early dinner in the kitchen, he and the fiddler returned to the Capital City. He wanted to hear of Pollack's condition, and also to get a final look around the yard on the off-chance that Pollack's men were absent.

Not that it was likely, he thought. He wondered if Selina had seen him and Hannibal in the yard earlier in the day – Hannibal whom she knew as the teacher of Greek and dancing at Rose's school.

Wondered if she'd been told at all why she'd been kept locked in that tiny room for the past thirty-six hours. Did she pray that Pollack would die? Or did she know things about Rance, even on short acquaintance, that made her pray that the older brother would live?

I'll have to find out from Pharaoh if she's been let out at all . . .

'How is he?' he asked of Mudsill, meeting him as they came through the back door.

The man blew a line of smoke from his corn-husk cigaretto. 'Tough as prairie sod.'

'Dr Meredith with him?'

'Just got in.'

They passed the kitchen quarters, and the short passageway to the lobby, where the carpets had been stripped and two house-slaves were holystoning the puncheon floor in the vain hope of getting the bloodstains out.

Meredith had clearly changed the dressing on Pollack's chest, and was in the process of tidying up when Hannibal edged around Rance Pollack's heavy bulk in the doorway. January followed him, stepped aside with the physician and asked quietly, 'There anything further I can help you do, sir? Does he look to be getting better?'

'You Americans never cease to amaze me.' Meredith glanced across at his patient. An oil-lamp had been lighted next to the bed, for the daylight in the room had begun to dim. The sulfur stink of the Lucifer-match still hung in the air.

Pollack looked up from his pillows at Hannibal, then across to January, dark eyes drooping with laudanum but still holding the echo of their sharpness. 'What the doc tells me, Sefton, I owe you my life. If that boy of yours hadn't been on hand here at the hotel, that idiot Parralee woulda killed me. I do owe you for that.'

'Then might you reconsider,' said Hannibal, 'the matter we spoke of Saturday night? I'm delighted that Ben was able to help a fellow human being—'

The lamp was just bright enough, that January could see the way Pollack's eyes shifted. That slight contraction of the brows was perfect: genuinely sad to disappoint a benefactor. 'I wish I could oblige you, Sefton.' The deep voice, even, seemed to slur a little more, mimicking a more profound intoxication than was actually the case. 'But I was telling the truth the other night, when I said I bought no wench in Galveston.' He frowned as if struggling against the drug. 'My guess is, Neumann gave you my name because he'd sold your gal to somebody else, and wanted to put you off his trail. He knew I was leaving town and figured you'd chase me half across Texas. I wish you all the luck in the world, findin' her.'

He turned his head, as Rance – who had stepped into the hall to speak to Mudsill – re-entered the room. 'The men set to leave in the mornin', Rance?'

'They are, Gideon.' The hulking man gestured back toward the hall. 'Shaughnessy an' Mudsill's in charge, an' everythin's set here for—'

Pollack raised an impatient hand, his face creasing briefly, as much with annoyance as with pain. 'Good,' he said, cutting off his words.

But his glance flickered past his mountainous brother, towards the doorway into the hall, and January had a brief impression, in the shadows, of a shock of silver hair, an extravagantly waxed mustache . . . The man from the saloon?

The one the Pollacks had been talking to, at the beginning of the fracas Saturday night.

Set for what?

'I should be on my feet by Friday,' whispered Pollack. 'No matter what this Tory sawbones says.'

And Meredith retorted, with only half a grin, 'You'll be on your feet Saturday and in your coffin Monday, at that rate.'

But Gideon Pollack's glance crossed the rather porcine gaze of his brother, and Rance gave a nod.

Set for something, reflected January, as he followed Hannibal from the hotel. Revenge on Stanway and the Nationalists?

Something to do with the reason Pollack had had Marcus Mudsill following him around Austin, guarding his back?

A gaggle of Pollack riders were gathered outside the Capital City, waiting for Rance. January recognized most of them as men who'd been stationed in the hotel yard last night.

Two men stood a little apart from this group, though clearly watching the door for Rance's re-appearance. One of them was the young Irishman Finn, last seen on the banks of the Brazos, friendly and lazy and chatting up one of the local señoritas in execrable Spanish.

The other, unobtrusively watching the street around him, with two Kentucky long-rifles on his back and a couple of wheel-guns in his belt, was Abishag Shaw.

As they passed him, January dug into his trouser pocket and brought out a bandana, which he fumbled and dropped to the splintery planks of the hotel porch. He bent to pick it up, using his left hand.

Shaw spit, but made no acknowledgement of the signal.

Right hand meant, *He said yes.*

Left hand meant, *We'll have to do this the hard way.*

SEVEN

From Onion Creek the trail south of Austin lay through the bottomlands of the Guadalupe River, toward Plum Creek to eventually swing east to reach the ranger station at Seguin. In the open grasslands between the trees, January glimpsed more long-horned Mexican cattle, and several times, near town, he'd see the smoke of a farmhouse, or the darker green of cotton fields. This was farming country, the good cotton land that both Nationalists and Houstonites were counting on to bring in American planters, their money, and their slaves.

But as they rode west the farms and plantations grew more

sparse. Unlike the Cherokee and Tonkawa, whom President Lamar had simply ordered exterminated, the Comanche still raided these lands that had once been theirs, stealing horses and killing by torture any invaders they encountered. Riding in the chill of the morning, January strained his ears, listening behind and around him, and remembering every tale of horror he'd heard since coming into this disputed land. Born in the flat green bayou country near New Orleans, he had spent his early manhood in Paris. The countryside he knew in those years was the tame sweet realm of the Ile de France: orchards, meadows, hedgerows and cropland. He was reminded, as they rode south-west, of Mexico, in the winter before the Texas Revolution; rugged hills of pale-gray rock, lush bottom-lands thick with cedar and juniper, dry savannahs now blue with wildflowers. But even in the green monotony of the Louisiana bayous, as a slave-child (and the brother of one of the most troublesome runaways in the quarters) January had acquired a sharp sense of camouflage and cover. He set his ambush in a cedar brake beside the southward trail, amid an area of plentiful creeks and even more plentiful trees, near a stretch where the creek ran through high gray rocks which (had said Marcus Mudsill back in Austin) boasted a number of caves.

It was an hour's ride from the town itself. With luck, Pollack's supply-train would reach it before there was much traffic on the trail. 'And if the Fates truly smile upon us,' added Hannibal, as they walked a few paces from the brake to make sure their horses couldn't be glimpsed from up the trail, 'Mr Mudsill won't think it worth his while to risk being shot to keep a slave-girl from escaping.'

'Don't bet on it,' said January quietly. 'As one of Pollack's cowhands Mudsill has a lot of freedom, but he knows damn well he can be bought and sold. Or that his wife can, or his child.'

Hannibal was silent at that.

'Men get funny about women they think they own – black men as well as white,' January added. 'And a white man'll see red at the thought of anyone taking any slave away from him, let alone a woman he's paid upwards of two thousand dollars for – which is what I guess Pollack paid for a fancy like Selina. Pollack knows someone is interested in getting Selina away from him and he may suspect you didn't believe his story. I'm guessing Mudsill's been told it's his hide, if the girl gets away.'

He led the way back to the brush-festooned rock he'd picked out that overlooked the trail, checking the 'revolver' in his belt as he went. Hannibal followed, carrying both rifles and two pistols of his own. Ravens cawed at them from the thicker trees along the creek.

'I did wonder,' remarked Hannibal, 'about the black cowhands I saw in town. It seemed to me that escape would be easier here on the frontier.'

'Then he'd be a hunted man. As a cowhand, a slave is in a privileged position. It's hard work, and dangerous work, but it's not soul-killing, like picking cotton. Mudsill is wed to one of Pollack's housemaids, he told me. They have a child, a son. He runs, he loses them, the same as if Pollack sells him, or them. Either way, if Selina gets away, Mudsill's life is going to be hell.

'He'll come after us,' he finished, and stretched himself out on the rock behind the thick tangle of rabbitbush.

Hannibal said, 'Hmn,' and crouched beside him. 'He's also smarter than Rance. The same could be said of my horse, of course. Damn Stanway,' he added. '*Manus, caput, pedes vermes interet* . . . And damn—'

He turned his head sharply.

Hooves up the trail.

January cast one quick glance behind them, in the direction of the horses. The purchase of another two, with tack, had reduced their working capital to barely more than would cover passage out of Galveston, provided they could find a boat bound for the United States before Pollack put two and two together and gave Hannibal's description to the port authorities. Yesterday afternoon he'd noted Mudsill's horse, which was of that golden hue that the Mexicans called *palomino* (and which most Frenchmen likened to the color of an old cheese). Flickers of sunlight caught the golden coat through the dust. January counted the riders as they came into view around the bend in the trail, though he knew their number already from Mudsill: five cowhands, two drivers for the wagon, and a ginger-mustached riding-boss – presumably Shaughnessy – to look after the five slaves Pollack had purchased in Galveston.

Four of these slaves – men – walked alongside the wagon, collared with iron rings joined by a chain. Their wrists were likewise shackled. January reflected that if Marcus Mudsill should need a reminder of what would happen to him if his master's chosen concubine got away, those dark faces, gray with the dust of the horses before and around them, would be it.

Selina rode a mule among the men, and January could see, by the way she held her hands, that they were tied to the horn of the stock-saddle on the mule. Her print cotton dress, blue and white, didn't quite fit her. He'd seen similar frocks on the other women at Neumann's. Her headscarf was simple, not the defiant fantasias the free women of New Orleans concocted in scorn of the custom that said that women of color must keep their heads covered. Back in New Orleans, he had seen her roll her eyes in contempt at just such a covering on Rose.

Her face, a symphony of delicate ovals, bore bruises on cheekbone and the point of her jaw. She kept looking around her at the trees, and January hoped to hell that Mudsill thought this was just fright, or curiosity about her new life, or anything but hope of rescue. *She's sixteen*, he told himself, *and scared out of her mind. Of course she's on tenterhooks . . .*

Mudsill was up at the front of the line, his back to her.

The man closest to her, riding with a lazy slouch in the saddle, rifle across his arm, was Abishag Shaw.

January hated to do it – as he hated any act which harmed the innocent, human or beast – but this was a situation that admitted no leeway. He took aim and shot Mudsill's palomino through the head. The beast went down and Hannibal fired – and missed, because with that first shot the train erupted into a chaos of confusion – and January shot again, taking down the near leader of the wagon team. In that same instant Shaw grabbed the bridle of Selina's mule, spurred his own horse into the trees south of the road, and as the men broke and scattered in all directions January managed to shoot two more horses. The four chained slaves headed for the trees and Shaughnessy deliberately took aim and shot the last man of the line, bringing the third man down with his weight and pulling the other two up short.

January fired at the riding-boss – whose horse he'd already shot – but the man had ducked behind the wagon. Hampered by the dead weight of their comrade, the three surviving slaves dragged the body towards the trees. Praying the Colt wouldn't blow up in his hand, January fired over the heads of the two cowhands, making them duck flat behind a dead horse. He could hear Hannibal moving off among the trees in an effort to make it less obvious that there were only two men attacking. *Come on, Shaw . . .*

His next shot was also at Shaughnessy but he missed that time, too. Pollack's riders were keeping under cover. A sharp whistle told him Shaw was at the horses (*That was quick . . .*), and he fired once more, then dashed back to the brake where the Kaintuck was helping Selina into the saddle. Presumably the mule and Shaw's own horse were making tracks away on the other side of the road. The girl was ashen with shock and struggling not to weep; when she saw January and Hannibal crash through the trees she burst into tears, and would have called out to them had not Shaw clamped a hand over her mouth. 'Silence or we's dead, Miss.' He practically threw her onto the horse's back, swung onto that of the one beside it.

January, mounted already, spurred to her, caught the bridle, and zig-zagged away at a hand-gallop among the trees, the other two men riding off fast, together, in another direction. Men's voices clamored behind him: not a second to be lost. He spared a glance back at Selina, who clung to the saddle-horn and seemed to be gasping for breath. He whispered, 'Don't you faint,' and she shook her head, though she still wept.

She'd never seen Abishag Shaw in her life, he realized. Until the moment he, her schoolmistress' husband, had appeared she hadn't known for certain whether she'd been rescued or just stolen by somebody else.

He took the horses down through the brush to a creek, walked them through the water, pushing downstream, away from the hills and the caves. His heart was in his throat when they crossed the road – he could still distantly hear the men's voices in the tangles of the bottomlands – and he dismounted, found a deadfall branch to sweep out the hoof-tracks in the road's dust, and led the way on south of the road where the ground was stonier and there was less obvious cover. It was two days' ride to Columbus and two beyond that to Galveston – bypassing Houston – always supposing the map was correct – and January had only the name of a woman connected to the Underground Railroad. She might be dead by this time, or moved on . . .

Let's deal with that, he reflected, *when we have to.*

He checked the silver compass he wore around his neck on a ribbon. Stopped once, long enough to load his pistol and all six chambers of the revolver, and his rifle. Listened, to the great silence of the deep-grass prairie, the scrubby woodlands.

Not even smoke smudged the blue of the sky.

Good.

Virgin Mary, Mother of God, protector of women, please *keep the Comanche on their own side of the hills today . . .*

After another couple of miles they came on the ruin of an adobe plantation-house – a fresh ruin, walls black with the charring of fire – and the burnt-out snaggle of out-buildings. What had been cotton fields, and corn-fields, lay along the creek. Skeletons, and the bones of dogs, lay among what had clearly been the quarters of three slave families, now half-choked in elephant-ear and scuppernong. Selina whispered, sickened, 'What happened?'

'Comanche, probably.' January led the way towards a clump of pecan trees a hundred feet from the quarters, where the brush was thick enough to conceal the horses. 'Somebody came along and fetched the whites' bodies soon after it happened. You all right?'

She nodded. 'Thank you,' she whispered. 'Thank you – I was so stupid . . .'

'Don't thank me yet,' he replied quietly. 'We've got a long way to go.'

*   *   *

They rested the horses among the trees for two hours, January slipping as cautiously as he could to the ruined house, to draw up water from the well. But it smelled foul, and he guessed the Comanche had thrown corpses into it, to thwart any whites who tried to return to this place. He found the overgrown trace of a path behind what had been the quarters, which led him to a spring. After he'd shared the pones and jerky he'd brought from Mrs Eberly at the tavern with Selina, and watched and listened in every direction (*No birds flying up startled from the trees, no sign of riders . . .* He tried to think of other telltale signs people had told him about one time or another and couldn't.) he took his courage in his hands and led the horses down to drink.

When he got back, he found Selina had changed her blue-and-white cotton dress for the boy's clothes they'd bought for her in Austin. She offered him back the little bag of silver he'd given her. 'Hold onto it,' he said, 'in case we get separated. We're going to need every cent of it, to get out of Texas alive.'

He took his knife from his boot, asked, 'You want me to cut off your hair, or would you rather do it? Watch out,' he added, as she extended her hand, 'this is sharp.'

'I'll do it.' Her voice was barely a whisper, and he noticed how her fingers avoided contact with his as she took the blade.

'You think my daddy's going to be very angry with me?' Her eyes told him that she already guessed the answer to that one.

And how would he not?

January said, 'You know your daddy better than I do, Miss Bellinger. If you were my daughter I'd be sick with terror, and ready to strangle you. But I saw him with you, when he came to the school to leave you off, and it looked to me like he loves you very much.'

'Miss Claire . . .' Her voice stumbled a little on the name. 'Daddy's wife might make him . . . might not let him come for me. That's . . . I think she's the reason Daddy sent me to go to school in New Orleans. He married her two years ago when M'am Marie died, but she only just found out about me last Christmas.'

She spoke without raising her eyes to his, carefully intent on cutting through those beautiful bronze-gold curls of which she had been so vain. Outside the dense little green world of the thicket's shade, January watched and listened, watched and listened: the dry scrub of the overgrown fields, the black jumble of adobe and torn-up boards that had been a man's dwelling-place. In the ruins as he'd passed them, January had seen the broken bisque head of a doll, and a woman's shoe. He wondered if the man who'd been father and husband had whipped his cottonhands, or raped the girls who did the wash and the sewing. If the woman who'd worn that shoe had urged her husband to sell off the children as soon as they could do a little work, because the family needed the money.

He thought about what the Comanche did to whites they caught.

About what the whites did to men who helped slaves escape.

Virgin Mary, Mother of God, get us out of here safe . . .

Gently, he said, 'Your daddy said your mama and you had a house in Cloutierville.'

Selina nodded. 'He used to stay with mama and me, before he married Miss Claire. Even when he was married to M'am Marie. When he married Miss Claire he told us – told me and Mama – that he couldn't come in as often, and I cried and fussed and acted like *such* a little bitch.' She shook her head, as if trying to thrust the memory away. 'Now I look back I think, how'd poor Miss Claire feel, knowing her husband had a . . . a lady-friend, and a daughter? *I'd* be mad, if a husband did that to me. I didn't think about that, then. Or about what Daddy felt. And when Mama died last year, Daddy hired Lella – Mrs Jowett – to come live with me, and I . . . I want to cry, thinking about how I treated her, being so snippy and mean and her so patient. I was even mean to Daddy, when he'd come in to see me . . .'

'It's all right,' said January softly. 'A lot of girls act like mean little bitches when they're unhappy, and they turn out all right.'

She raised golden-hazel eyes to his, bruised with sleeplessness and tears. 'I'll bet Mrs January didn't.'

'Mrs January is perfect,' replied January gravely. 'And has never done wrong in her entire life.' As he'd hoped, the girl was surprised into a giggle.

'But my first wife – who was perfect also –' and he smiled at the thought of Ayasha, spitting-mad at the iniquities of Madame Barronde who had lived on the ground floor of that tall old house they'd occupied on the Rue de l'Aube. Who had died of the cholera, the same day that Ayasha had died – 'she told me she used to make spell-dolls of her father's wives and stick pins in them and smear them with grease and leave them where rats would eat them. And I won't even repeat some of the things my sister did when she was fifteen.'

The girl clapped her hands over her mouth, to stifle another giggle, followed almost at once by tears again. After a time she said, 'It would serve me right if he just left me—'

'Nothing would serve you.' January hushed her with an admonishing finger. 'Nothing excuses – nothing justifies – what happened to you. If your father doesn't come through with help, for whatever reason, you'll stay at the school and help Mrs January and Zizi-Marie with the house, to pay your own way. Later we'll figure out where you're to go from there, when you're ready. Until then,' he finished, 'you do what I tell you – the instant I tell you, without asking questions – and we'll work on getting out of Texas alive.'

She laid the cut-off hank of hair on the ground between them. Her shorn head looked awful, longer on one side than the other and sticking out in all directions. Still he made no move to touch her, to even it up. Her disguise included an old cap, which, he reflected, would help. But though she was visibly thinner than she'd been three weeks ago in New Orleans she did not make a convincing youth. He doubted anyone seeing her up close would be deceived, and men looking for two riders in this lonely country would descend on them no matter how she was dressed.

'You could get killed, Mr J,' she murmured. 'And poor Mr Sefton, who I know isn't well – and the man who grabbed me when the shooting started . . . Is he a friend of yours?'

'That's Mr Shaw,' said January. 'And yes – a very good

friend. And we'll manage,' he concluded. 'Stay quiet here while I have another look around, then we'll move on.'

He gathered up the cut locks, and buried them in the soft earth of the vegetable patch behind the ruined quarters, like the miniature grave of a child who was no more.

When he'd discussed the ambush with Shaw, in the darkness beyond the Capital City Hotel's corrals last night, the Kaintuck had vetoed the idea of travel by night. 'They's plenty moonlight, but you don't know the territory. Head for Columbus an' we'll try an' pick up your trail there, an' from there we'll sort out what we can do.' Shaw didn't know the country either, but January had little doubt that the lanky policeman would be able to find shelter – and additional food beyond the bare minimum they carried in their bulging saddlebags – a good deal more easily than he could himself.

So they pushed on east-south-east through the dry, gently rolling hills, skirting the fields of cotton and corn in the bottomlands, and slept that night among the oak trees of a creek-bottom, January mildly surprised that they'd made it til sunset without sign of pursuit.

Or sign of pursuit that he could see. Shaw had been right – the moon was too young, and set too early, to be of much help in escaping, but it was inconceivable that Pollack's riders wouldn't guess that an escapee would head for Galveston via Columbus – where else could you go to get out of Texas? – and that they wouldn't know the ground between. So he sat awake for as long as he could, before gently waking Selina to take her turn at watch. And when he opened his eyes a few hours later, when first the birds began to sing, it was to see the girl, her shorn head bent on her shoulder, wrapped in the saddle-blankets, sleeping like an exhausted child.

The creek ran eastward, towards the Colorado River (Shaw had told him there was another Colorado River west in Mexican territory – 'They does that just to fool with you'), but they were coming out of the rolling lands and January's instincts told him to follow the shelter of the trees as long as they could. They rode in the stream itself, to cover the horses' tracks, but towards noon he began to think they might be followed. An hour later he was sure of it.

'What do we do?' Selina glanced in terror at the open country to the south beyond the trees.

'We'll never outrun them,' said January quietly. 'We don't even know if it's Pollack's men, or if Pollack happened to tell Mudsill that he'd been approached by a great big nigger trying to snatch his wench away from him. They've seen Shaw, they haven't seen me.'

He tried to judge, from the few distant sounds he'd heard (or thought he'd heard) – the click of a hoof on the stream-bed rocks, the sharp rustle of foliage thrust aside – how far behind them pursuit (if there was pursuit) lay. An oak tree bent its branches over the stream a few yards ahead: it would have to do. He guided the horses into the stream again, brought them up close enough to the oak's roots to dismount onto one, then held out his arms for the girl. She came down awkwardly into his grip, and he boosted her into the lowest branches – 'You ever climb trees when you were little?'

She shook her head. 'Mama said ladies didn't – and I didn't like to get dirty.'

'Think you can get around to that branch behind you and go up to where the leaves are thick?'

She looked scared, but managed it – helped by the boy's clothes she wore – with January glancing back up-stream all the while.

What do I do? What do I say if it's Mudsill?

Did Pollack tell his slave – or his riding-boss – about the attempts to get Selina? He remembered Shaughnessy shooting the last chained slave of the line, and sweat crawled down his ribs. He had meant it, sincerely, last Monday night when he'd expressed his regret that Shaw hadn't left Seth Javel to burn alive in that wood-shed, but the thought of keeping silent about Selina's whereabouts were fire to be put to his own flesh made him sick. *Hail, Mary, full of grace, the Lord is with thee . . . Help this poor girl stay free and for God's sake help me keep her free by not getting caught myself . . .*

'Stay here,' he whispered, when she was out of sight among the branches. 'I'll come back for you, I swear it.' He walked back along the root, re-mounted and rode off down the stream, trying to think of some plausible reason to be leading a saddled horse: *Gosh, this old nag? I found him in the woods* . . .

A mile downstream, where the bank was stony, he turned his horse's head and went ashore, taking refuge in the thickets of hackberry and native holly. After ten minutes' waiting in silence he heard them, the soft distinct click of a hoof on stone, then the creak of saddle-leather. A man said, 'They came along here, I'm sure of it,' in Spanish.

Shit . . . January crouched back deeper into the thicket, and made sure his pistols were where he could get them.

'The stream comes out onto Barnsell's prairie in another two miles. We should see them, then, señora.'

'When we do,' said a woman's voice, 'you stay back, Ortega. Father Monastario himself told me this.'

'The Comanche, madame—' began the man protestingly, and as they came into sight, January stood up among the underbrush, hands raised to show them empty.

EIGHT

'Señora Taggart!'

The man Ortega – three-quarters Indian, by the high bones of his face, despite the faded cottons and high boots of a white cowhand – whipped around to face him, his rifle trained.

Valentina's face blossomed with relieved joy. 'Señor Enero, I thought we'd never find you in time!' She dropped from her saddle and threw the rein to her bodyguard, who stayed, disapproving, beside the stream while his employer's wife scrambled up the stony bank. Her fair hair was braided up under a wide-brimmed hat such as the vaqueros wore, and her boots and plain blue riding-skirt were dusty. The horses looked as spent as his own.

Only when she got close to him did she ask in an under-voice, 'The girl – they said you'd taken the girl Pollack had bought. She was the one you were seeking when we spoke in Houston?'

'She's well. I left her in an oak-tree upstream. I thought you were Pollack's men—'

'Good for you!' She reached out and clasped his hands impulsively. January could see why men fell in love with this young woman at the drop of a hat. 'Borrachio – one of my husband's vaqueros – came to me yesterday saying Pollack's men were insisting they must search our land. My husband has given orders that no one ride into our land, for any reason – an idiot command!'

'I was there.' January matched her whisper, with a glance toward Ortega, still sitting on his rat-tailed roan like a dilapidated Don Quixote beside the stream.

Valentina shook her head, and sighed. 'Back when my husband was still a nationalist he would often have his men shoot the Pollacks' sheep and cattle, who came over onto our land, and also beat up Pollack's riders. Father Monastario—'

January glanced at Ortega again, and asked, 'Who is Father Monastario?'

'My confessor.' She hesitated, as if considering what to say. 'My . . . my anchor, in all of this. It is he, whom I was seeing, when we met in Houston. When Madrecita Taggart went out to look for me, as if I were a felon.'

'Your husband permitted you to keep your religion, then?'

'He did and he didn't.' She sighed. 'It was understood between him and my Uncle Gael that I would "convert" to the Lutheran heresy for the sake of the marriage. But Father Monastario – he is a priest at Mission San José, in San Antonio, though he travels to other towns sometimes, Protestant towns – he said that this was done under duress. I would be forgiven for it, he said, and God would not consider me apostate. My uncle knew he was dying, you see, and having no son, he arranged for his land to go to me. But with *norteamericanos* pouring into Texas, every Tejano land grant – every grant given the *nortes* by the government before the rebellion – would be fought over, and questioned. Taken away if they could manage it. My uncle knew I had to marry a *norte*, a man who would be listened to in the Texas courts.'

A lawyer's holiday, the slave Jack Ray had called it, on board the *Rosabel*.

'Father Monastario understood this. He rides up to Austin, twice a month, to hear confessions and say Mass,' she went on. 'It is he who sent Ortega –' she nodded back toward the elderly ruffian – 'to be my bodyguard, for these trips. But since Madrecita Taggart and Aunt Alicia – and my husband's young brother Francis as well – have been at Perdition, they have pestered my husband that in doing this he is insulting God and endangering my soul – *idiotas*! So now the good father is kind enough to delay going back to San Antonio, and will meet me early Monday mornings, at an old *jacal* in one of the canyons, to hear my confession, and give me blessing. It is a great comfort to me.'

Then she quickly shook her head, and made a gesture as if putting her own concerns aside. It was something she had never done when January had known her in Mexico.

But then, he reflected, she had been a girl of sixteen. Spoiled, as Selina had been spoiled . . .

'And are we still on your husband's land?' He glanced at the rising ground beyond the stream, calculating cover and distance. 'How far—'

'They rode north,' said Valentina. 'Pollack's men. I rode out with Borrachio to speak with them, to keep there from being a war right there, and I told them that you had been killed by the Comanche, that Ortega had seen it done. The girl, I said, had escaped, and ridden north.'

'Did I not fear violence at your bodyguard's hands,' said January, with a respectful bow, 'I would take you in my arms and kiss you, Señora Taggart.'

'Better you fear violence at the hands of your Señora Rose.' The old teasing sparkle returned to her eyes.

'That, too,' he agreed. 'How many riders were there? If we can make it to Galveston—'

'You can't. Not now.'

He thought that if it had been four years ago in Mexico, she would have seized him by the sleeve.

'I have said, this Pollack is the devil. With his angel voice and his pretty eyes, but he will not let go of what he considers

his, nor be "made a fool of", as he says, by a woman. His
men fear him as they fear the devil. More, some of them – the
ones that he owns as slaves. They will soon return, when they
cannot find tracks. Listen. Follow this stream to the river. Cross
it, and hide in the woods on the other side. I will send Ortega
to the Swedes who have settled in the hills north of town.
They are Lutherans, and abolitionists. Señor Ekholm has
worked with Father Monastario on these matters. He will send
someone to meet you, and I know they will shelter you and
this poor girl, until the next trading caravan goes south to
Galveston. You can trust Señor Ekholm – and even more so,
his good wife – to make sure that none of you is recognized,
and to get you on a safe boat back to New Orleans.'

Trust. The word touched January's mind as the young woman
used it: *trust. Safe.* Trust Ortega. Trust Ekholm. Men about
whom he knew nothing. Trust Valentina, for that matter . . .

Everything hinged on those words, even as his thoughts
fleeted to the danger of betrayal, the horrible consequences
– to himself, to his friends, to the girl whose headstrong spirit
and trust in a handsome man's promises of love had gotten
them all into this mess in the first place. To his family back
in New Orleans: Rose a widow, Professor John and sunny-
hearted Xander fatherless and poor.

Trust.

His friend Judas Bredon, the yellow-eyed 'conductor' of the
New Orleans branch of the Underground Railroad, had been
betrayed twice by people he'd trusted – people he'd helped. It
had never stopped him from walking into danger again.

And one of the names Bredon had given him, before he'd
left for Texas, had been Torvald Ekholm.

'Very well. Tell Señor Ekholm, whoever he sends to bring
us north, when he comes to the river, to carry a red bandana
in his right hand.'

Selina wept, and clung to him, when he told her the plan, and
she, too, used the word: 'How can you trust them? How can
you be sure they won't go straight to Mr Pollack and tell him?'
She was exhausted, and shaking with terror after two hours
sitting in her tree. Betrayed by the man she'd believed loved

her, the man she'd loved enough to run away with, loved enough to marry, she was mentally and emotionally spent, physically exhausted. She had been rescued only to be told that there were more miles to flee, more days to spend waiting to be captured again.

The terror in her eyes told him everything he needed to know about Gideon Pollack, and be damned to his look of grieved disappointment that he just wasn't able to help the men who'd saved his life.

'It'll be all right,' he told her, and held her, letting her have her cry out. (*The horses need rest anyhow . . .*) 'It'll be all right.'

And, when she was calmer: 'There's nothing we can trust right now. But Pollack will have men watching the wharf at Galveston, and his men will be watching the road between here and there. We stand a better chance with help than we do on our own.'

She shook her head, shuddering as if with high fever, but consented to mount. She spoke little as they followed the widening creek down into the bottomlands of the Colorado, listening, as January listened, to the brief bird-songs, the intermittent hiss of the wind in the trees. They reached the river an hour before twilight, and though there was no ford there, the current wasn't strong.

January left Selina with the horses on the south-west bank and swam across, his knife and two of his pistols wrapped in a square of oilcloth on his head and praying (to Saint Barbara, the patron saint of firearms) that the powder wouldn't get wet. On the far bank he checked the brush-choked gullies, scanned the wet pebbles along the water for tracks. Then he swam back, dressed, and fetched her and the horses across. The tortillas and jerky that Valentina had given them got soaked with river-water in spite of their oilcloth wrapping, but Selina devoured the evening's ration as if it were *boeuf marchand de vin* and angel-cake. From where they hid among the trees of the largest gully January watched the river, and just as the last light was fading, a man rode out of the trees on the opposite bank, holding a red bandana in his right hand.

It was Hannibal Sefton.

*   *   *

Neither Hannibal nor Shaw – who'd been covering him from
the trees – had seen pursuit all day, though they had been
assiduous in avoiding anything resembling a track that led
toward Houston. 'It's a big country,' observed Shaw. They
made a cold camp in the hackberry thickets of the gully, and
January felt a great deal safer with the Kentuckian back in
the party. Glancing across at January, the lawman added,
'Most recent sign of Comanche I seen was a month old.
When he hired me on, Rance Pollack said there was a
Comanche raid back the beginnin' of March, so that'd be it.
I don't wonder your Mrs Taggart kept her bodyguard by her,
ridin' back to Perdition. She the little lady what threatened
to tell her brother you'd raped her?' He turned inquiringly to
Hannibal.

'She was trying to get herself out of a very bad situation,'
put in January.*

Hannibal sniffed. 'Easy for you to say, *amicus meus*. But I
think Benjamin is right,' he added, looking back to Shaw and
Selina. 'I think the lovely Valentina can be trusted – and I will
say for her she's a damned clever girl. I am sorry to hear of
her current situation – a sentiment I never thought I'd hear
myself express. Did Benjamin tell you about Miss Valentina's
lunatic father, Miss Bellinger? A man whose habits make her
own conduct almost understandable . . .'

In an undervoice, as darkness settled on the river, he enter-
tained Selina with his account of his imprisonment by Don
Prospero de Castellón at that gentleman's isolated hacienda
– leaving out the certainty that the mad old *hacendado* had
murdered Valentina's mother and at least two other women
– and though the drawing-room lightness of his conversation
was incongruous in the extreme, January saw Selina relax, for
the first time. Once she even laughed. When she slept, it was
without tears and very clearly without dreams.

They kept to the camp in the gully all the following day.
Shaw went out to scout, and reported seeing two parties of
riders – both of which included men he recognized as Pollack's
– across the river to the south. If they'd gone north hunting

for Selina, they'd evidently drawn a blank in that direction. January reflected that Valentina seemed to have been right in her estimate of Pollack as a man who would not tolerate being made a fool of by any woman, least of all by a slave.

On the following morning, with the threat of rain blowing gray over the green hills, two riders appeared from the wooded gullies northeast of the river, and as they drew nearer, January – crouched in the thin stand of black-oak at the top of the stream-bank – saw that they were tall fair men, each carrying a red bandana in his right hand. Shaw, scouting again, would almost certainly have picked up sight of the newcomers; January slid quickly down to the camp, and had Hannibal move two of the horses out to another thicket of willow a dozen yards up-river, and conceal himself with a rifle in the trees. (*Not that Hannibal could hit the broad side of a barn.*)

But the men, when January went out to meet them, identified themselves as Torvald and Lucien Ekholm, and produced – rather to January's surprise – a sort of wax theatrical blacking which quickly transformed Selina from a not-very-convincing 'high yeller' boy to a much darker lad at whom, from a distance, searchers probably wouldn't look twice. They then rode north for most of the day – Shaw and Hannibal joining them – and at twilight reached the solid, wood-walled farmstead inhabited by the Ekholm brothers, their wives, and an assortment of small children and tow-headed cousins who'd come to Texas to avoid military service in Sweden.

They stayed there four days, while the moon waxed full, and the Pollack riders combed the countryside to the south.

Torvald Ekholm had a small saw-mill by San Marcos Creek, and Shaw and January contributed their labor to their hosts' timber business, rifles at hand, and listening always for signs of a Comanche raid. Two other families inhabited that part of the hills – Gabriel Olendorff of Hesse, and Jeremias Mueller and his brother Karl, of Holstein – who worked also felling trees, and at the end of the week Karl was scheduled to take a little caravan to Galveston to trade. 'They should have give up watching the wharves, by then,' said Torvald. The little colony, isolated from the Americans in Austin and the Mexicans down in the flat-lands, were, as Valentina had said, Lutherans, and firm opponents of slavery in any form. Torvald knew the woman in Galveston whose name Bredon had given January, and assured him that yes, Fru Holland was still in business there and would have no hesitation at arranging passage for them back to New Orleans. Fru Ekholm taught Selina to milk cows and make potato dumplings, and clipped her hair evenly with her dressmaking scissors. In the evenings, Hannibal played Herr Olendorff's fiddle and the three households gathered at Ekholm's, to listen and to dance.

When a message was sent to the 'conductor' – as the Underground Railway called its operatives – in Galveston, January sent a note with it, to Rose. *So far, all is well. The bird that I thought I had lost, we have found again, injured by her misadventures, but whole and learning to sing again a little.* On Friday, when Sheriff Quigley and a party of men rode up to the compound, January and his companions took refuge in the saw-mill loft. Peering around the edge of the loft door, January could see the gray-haired lawman gesturing as he questioned Torvald, but when the posse rode away, the Swede said no, they were not seeking the runaway. 'There is politics in town,' explained Torvald. 'Nationalists say, Houstons have done some frightful thing, and now the sheriff is seeking them all over the county.'

January wondered how much of that had to do with Gideon Pollack's meeting with the silver-haired, mustachioed gentleman who'd been so concerned not to linger in the Empire of the West saloon. Or with why Rance Pollack had not ridden to Los Lobos with the plantation's supplies.

He wondered also if Mr Stanway the banker was still alive.

Sunday – Easter – a German pastor rode up from Austin, and January reassured Selina that the God who'd forgiven the misdeeds of Mary Magdalene and had told Simon Peter that both clean and unclean animals were alike appropriate fare was certainly going to hear their own prayers no matter who was leading the worship. In the big western room of the 'dog-trot' timber house, January whispered thanks to God and Christ and the Blessed Mother Ever-Virgin, protector of women, for watching over them so far.

They were still a long way from Galveston, and a longer way yet, from New Orleans.

And meanwhile, the stockpile of trade-goods grew at the other end of that big western room: the skins of deer and otter, fox and beaver and raccoon, trapped in the woods by the Olendorff boys or traded from the Tonkawa; tobacco grown in the small field east of the house; cider from the orchard. Boxes, packs, and pack-saddles were lined up across one side of the walled yard. Sven, one of the Ekholm cousins, came back early Tuesday evening from a little discreet scouting along the trail that led to Houston and Galveston with the news that he'd seen none of Pollack's riders.

'And the Comanche?' inquired Ekholm, and the youth shook his head.

'None in sight, nor sign of them.'

Outside in the yard dusk was just beginning to gather, the fresh smell of the rain which had fallen that morning breathed through the open windows like a promise: *Everything will be all right.* The children – Ekholm's three, and a ten-year-old girl cousin whose parents had died on the voyage to Texas – were setting the table. Another cousin brought in the lighted lamps.

Someone shouted something from the yard, and the household's three deer-hounds scrambled leggily to their feet and raced out into the yard to see what was going on. January heard a woman's voice speaking German, and the jingle of stirrups and bits.

Then, 'Oh, thank God!' in Spanish, and the light clunk of swift boots on the step. 'Señor Enero, I have prayed all the way here, that you had not gone!'

It was Valentina Taggart.

She held out her hands to him, caught his fingers in a grip like a drowning woman's when she clutches at a floating branch.

'My husband has been killed,' she said. 'Murdered, shot in the orchard near the hacienda yesterday morning.' Her words choked momentarily, and she turned her face aside. Then, 'His mother, and his aunt, and his brother all swear that I did this thing. Please.' She tugged at his hands, like a child. 'Ortega was not with me – my husband sent him away on Wednesday, when he came back from taking my message to Ekholm . . . I went to meet Father Monastario yesterday but he did not come! No one was with me! I was shot at – someone tried to kill me . . .'

Again she struggled to keep her voice even. 'And now, no one believes that I did not kill him.'

January had always believed that God did not hold a person responsible for their first thought in any given situation – only for what they did after it.

This was a good thing, because his first thought was, *Shit.*

NINE

'He was a good husband.' Valentina's hands were shaking so badly, as January guided her to one of the bent-willow chairs beside the hearth, that she had to clasp them together to keep them still. 'A good man, until his mother and his sister came from Virginia.'

Outside, Cousin Sven was putting up shutters over the unglazed windows. Fru Ekholm entered, bearing the first of the supper bowls from the kitchen behind the house – January had heard all about her opinion of the American idiocy of putting the kitchen in a separate building and had explained to her that not all Americans did this. Torvald went to meet her, glancing tactfully at January and the young woman beside the hearth.

'Pooh,' said the matriarch. '*Dumheter.*' *Nonsense.* She beckoned behind her, to Selina and Cousin Elsa, similarly laden. Shaw, entering with Lucien and one of the hired men, hands and faces damp from washing, paused on the threshold, but Signe Ekholm gestured them all briskly to take their places on the benches, and gave her husband instructions in no uncertain terms.

Torvald came over to the fire, and explained in German – which was better than his English – 'My wife says, madame, that you are to join us for supper before you give long explanation to Herr Januar.'

Haltingly, Valentina returned, 'Please, it is not—'

The Swede shook his head. 'I am not permitted to take *no*

for answer,' he said. 'My wife says, she sees your horse has been ridden long and hard, all the way from Perdition today, and there are no saddlebags, and there is no place between where you could eat. Please,' he added. 'She will do violence to me if you do not come and join us, and you will feel very much better afterwards.'

Valentina laughed, and disappeared into the curtained lean-to that Cousin Elsa showed her, to wash her hands and face – and tidy her hair, it turned out, for when she emerged it had been taken from its braids and twisted into a fetching chignon. Even facing hanging for the murder of her husband, Valentina was still Valentina. She allowed January to take her hand and lead her to the long table, where she sat between Hannibal and January and devoured dumplings and ham, greens and pickles, like a starving woman. She smiled, and chatted with Selina in her halting French, but January saw the apprehension in the younger girl's eyes as she watched her. When Valentina turned her head, to praise her hostess for her cooking, he caught Selina's glance and made an open-palmed gesture: *Don't worry. It's going to be all right.*

While thinking, *Shit, shit, shit . . .*

Because he already knew he'd have to go.

Without Valentina's help he, and Hannibal, would almost certainly have been hanged days ago (Shaw would almost as certainly have managed to get away). Selina would have been in a far worse case than she'd been before his arrival. Whether Valentina had shot her husband or not, he couldn't desert her.

At the end of the meal he took the girl, Shaw, and Hannibal aside, as the Ekholm men, instead of retreating to the fireside with their pipes, gathered around a lantern at the far end of the table, and Fru Ekholm signed to the girl cousins to help her clear away.

'Can you get Miss Bellinger back to New Orleans without me?' he asked softly. 'Whatever is happening here, I can't—'

'Don't be silly, Benjamin,' broke in Hannibal. 'I'm not going to leave *my valet* –' he looked significantly at January – 'to wander around Texas by himself.'

'We'll do fine,' said Shaw. 'If'fn Miz Bellinger's agreeable. Ain't like we'll be ridin' alone.'

'Finer without the necessity of looking after me, I daresay.'
Hannibal bent, and kissed Selina's hand. '*Per aliam viam
reversi sunt,* like the three Wise Kings . . . And someone needs
to protect Benjamin from Madame Taggart, if nothing else.'

'And who's going to protect *you* from her?' retorted January
with a grin at his friend. Then he caught Valentina's eye, and
the five of them gathered again around the hearth. Selina
looked a little uncertain at being included, but January said
in a low voice, 'You should know what's happening, in case
there's trouble or questions later. And also, you may have
heard something about Vin Taggart that will help us.'

'I doubt it,' said the girl, but looked gratified at not being
told to run along. She still retained her boy's clothing, but the
dark stain was fading from her skin – Fru Ekholm had declared
she would renew it in the morning. The Swedish matron's
matter-of-fact welcome, and the unobtrusive gentleness with
which January, Shaw, and Hannibal had treated her, had done
a good deal, January was glad to observe, to restore some of
Selina's shattered self-confidence.

Which she'd need, he reflected, when she returned to a city
and a society that would regard her as 'fallen'. He prayed that
Rose would be able to further counteract the horrors that had
been done to the girl.

Valentina, he had noticed during dinner, had never once
asked for an account of Selina's experiences, but had treated
her woman-to-woman, with tact and acceptance. *For that alone,*
reflected January, *she deserves my help . . .*

'Tell me what happened,' he said.

Valentina sighed. For a time she stared into the fire, gathering her thoughts and putting them in order, like a bookkeeper,
he thought, sorting through a mass of some dead relative's
letters and bills.

Then she said, 'I don't . . . I don't really know what
happened. Only what happened to *me.*

'Before all else,' she said, after a time, 'please believe that
my husband is – was – a good man at heart.' She spoke as if
she expected to be contradicted. As if she were waiting for
January to point out the fresh bruise on her left cheekbone,
the small, swollen cut on her lip.

But in her silence, January read also the puzzled wonder he himself had felt, along with the savage grief of his own bereavement: *Really? Gone? Never – not EVER – again?*

'I never loved him,' she went on after a time, her voice barely audible. 'But he – was – a reasonable man. At least . . .' She stopped herself, and shook her head, dismissing a thought.

What thought?

'He came to Texas because there was good land here, where cotton will grow well, and he did not want to stay in the United States. The Yankees in the north, he said, will eventually get enough strength in the Congress to forbid slavery, and that, he said, he would not endure. This was in 1834, before the Texas Rebellion, when he arrived. He was granted a *labor* – about two hundred acres – of lowland, to grow crops and cotton, and a league of range-land for cattle in the hills. Later he bought another two leagues from the ranchero who had been deeded them from the old San Saba mission grant, that goes back to the King of Spain. All this he called Perdition.'

Outside, the night was deepening. The men went out, to look after the milk-cows and the mules for tomorrow's caravan. Moonlight shone in the dooryard; January heard the hoot of an owl. At the end of the table, around the candles, the women talked softly in Swedish, like the distant cluck of a stream.

'My husband's father had a plantation in Virginia,' Valentina went on, her voice steadier, as if she were delivering a report about someone else's family. 'His father was a drunkard, and a quarreler – my husband would not speak much of the household he had left. He was in a quarrel with his father when his father died, and he was not much surprised to learn that he – and his younger brother Francis, whom their father despised because he is a cripple – had been left nothing in their father's will. All of it went to the oldest brother, Jack. Jack was a brute and a drunkard also, and my husband, who had left the plantation – Elysium, it was called – years before, did not contest the will. The soil was worn out, and his father had sold off most of the slaves to pay his gambling debts. My husband was a lawyer by that time, in Richmond, and he knew that had he gone to law, all the rest of the patrimony would have been eaten up.'

'Your husband was a wise man,' remarked Hannibal. 'There are property cases in England that started in the last century and are still being fought over.'

'My husband was a . . . a *clever* man,' agreed Valentina, with a catch of hesitation in her voice. 'Wise . . .' Her brows pulled together into a frown. 'That I do not know. He told me once – when he was drunk – that there were memories there that he did not wish to see again.

'Like his father and his brother, he drank, and he would keep away from me at such times. But his drinking worsened when last Fall his brother died also, and the plantation went all to debts. Then his mother, and Aunt Alicia whom she had raised from the age of five, and his brother Francis came to Texas to live with us, because they had nowhere else to go.'

'Ah,' sighed the fiddler. '*The bold intrusion of the suitor-train/ Who crowd his palace, and with lawless power/ His herds and flocks in feastful rites devour* . . . And believe me, drinking would certainly have been *my* reaction, had any of *my* family turned up on my doorstep – always supposing I possessed a doorstep – with luggage in hand.' And he rose and bowed as Fru Ekholm appeared beside them, with a small tray bearing cups of thick Mexican coffee.

'For my part,' continued Valentina, as she dropped sugar into the tarry liquid, 'I knew Señor Taggart for . . . for over a year before we wed. His lands bordered ours, and my uncle Gael often used the wharf that he built. I knew he drank, but not to excess . . . not then. When Texas became free – when my year of mourning was finished – he spoke to my uncle, asking for my hand.'

She fell silent again, and January saw in his mind that tall, flat-shouldered man in the lobby of the Capital City Hotel: the broken nose, the wide mouth both sensual and strong, and the eyes that seemed so blue.

'He was not a kind man.' Valentina seemed for a time, also, to see him in the black ink-bowl of her cup. 'But before his family came he treated me with respect.'

Her eyes darkened, with bafflement as well as pain. 'Then

last Wednesday, when Ortega came home from taking my message to Señor Ekholm here, my husband met him before the doors of the hacienda, accused him of . . . of being my lover . . . and dismissed him, without a word to me. I did not hear of it until some hours later. When I protested, and said that Father Monastario had vouched for him, my husband – who was drunk by then – shouted at me that he could not be certain that I was not . . . was not lovers with the good Father as well. I was *speechless*!'

Hannibal raised his brows – January had never known Valentina to be speechless – and murmured, '*Entirely?*' and the young woman blinked aside her tears of remembered rage with the ghost of a grin.

'Well, no. Indeed, far from it. We quarreled – oh, horribly!'

January glanced again at the bruise on her cheek. It looked to him fresher than that.

'On Easter morning he rode out by himself, without a word to anyone. He had ridden out so every day since our quarrel, because the men not only had their work to do, but also to guard the borders of our land and drive away Señor Pollack's men, who would come to try to get back Señor Pollack's cattle and sheep. In the evenings my husband would come in late, and lock himself into his library, for of course Madrecita Taggart and Aunt Alicia were *incensed* that he had broken with Pollack. They are supporters of Houston, Madrecita and her sister, and whenever they saw my husband they would pester him and nag about how he must return support for the man, because the United States *needed* Texas.'

'I'd hide, no question,' put in Shaw, folding his long arms. 'An' a damn sight farther off than the library.'

Selina, on the bench at Hannibal's side, asked, 'Wasn't there anyplace *you* could go, Valla?'

'Not away from the hacienda. Not without a guard of some kind, because there is indeed danger of the Comanche. Ortega was gone, and with the men all patrolling like soldiers to keep Pollack's men away, I kept waiting to hear that the Comanche – or the bandits, the Comancheros – would come in, to steal horses or indeed to attack the house. So my husband would leave *me* to dine with Madrecita, and Aunt Alicia, and they would argue with *me*, as if I gave a rotten fig about Texas. And because my husband was not there, Madrecita came to table half-drunk and poor Alicia fuddled on laudanum, and Francis kept to his study with his maps and his books.'

'Swine,' commented Hannibal dispassionately.

'Could you ask for another bodyguard?' suggested the girl, and Valentina shook her head.

'None could be spared. And he . . . my husband avoided me. And when he was home, he was locked in his library, or was drunk. Or both.'

Selina looked as if she would have asked something else, then stopped herself. Seeing this, Valentina smiled a wry, bitter smile.

'There is a little boudoir next to our room. I slept there. Sometimes – when I heard him shouting at Enoch – that's our butler – or when he would hit the serving-men – I would lock the doors. But he never tried them. Then on Easter morning, though she had barely spoken to her son – either of her sons – for a week, Madrecita Taggart chose to become enraged that my husband wouldn't ride into town with them to go to church. She said that it was not right for a Christian not to worship on Easter Sunday, and that he would go to Hell. But when I asked, might I go into town to attend the Mass that Father Monastario holds in the back room of Eustacio Pardo's *botica*, for the sake of the Catholics of the town, one would have thought I had proposed to spend the day at a tavern! I could only accompany them, she said, if I attended a "real, Christian" church.'

'Personally,' remarked Hannibal, 'I'd sooner spend Easter having tea with the Devil in Hell than sit in a carriage for six hours with your husband's relations, with all due respect. No wonder he drank.'

She shook her head, a small, despairing gesture. The men came in from the yard, except for Cousin Sven, who had the first shift of guard-duty that night. Fru Ekholm went to the kitchen, and returned with more coffee. The dogs paced in circles, then curled up at the feet of the men. The smell of tobacco drifted at that other end of the long room.

'Then when Madrecita, and Aunt Alicia, and Francis

returned from town, very late in the afternoon, Francis told me that in town he had seen the woman who had been my husband's mistress. She had returned, Francis said, and a man at church had told Aunt Alicia that my husband was keeping her again, and had bought her a house on Franklin Street. That was . . . that was the last I could stand.' Her red lips tightened, and again tears filled her eyes. 'I lost my temper.

'After what he had said, about me, about Ortega, about Father Monastario – after he had been gone all those days, and come home to sit and get drunk and leave me to be pestered and scolded by his mother – when he finally came home, after dark, I confronted him and we quarreled again, worse this time, terribly. He struck me, and locked himself in his room, drinking, and I pounded the door and cursed him. Locked into my boudoir that night I wept, and counted the hours until I could ride out to meet with Father Monastario in the ruined jacal in Arroyo Sauceito, as we always did. I needed him. Needed to tell him, to have him pray with me. To have him advise me what to do.

'I have been a good wife! I really have!' She raised her face to January's in the firelight, her eyes now swimming with tears. 'When I was a little girl in my father's house I was a dreadful pagan, as he was. I knew no better. I cared for nothing but how to fix my hair, and tales of romance, and making men fall in love with me. John – my first husband, my true husband – never asked me to change my faith. I went with him some-times to his church in San Antonio, not as a communicant, but so that I could see what his faith was like. To see what it was that drew his heart. To understand. And he sometimes came to mine. And since his death, I have found such comfort in Father Monastario's care and teaching. Since I have lived with Señor Taggart – since I have lived with his terrible family! – I have so needed such comfort.'

Selina leaned across to her, and took her hands, and Valentina clung briefly to the younger girl's strong fingers. It crossed January's mind to wonder if the priest was young and good-looking, but he pushed the thought aside. What mattered was her need.

'And did you ride out?' January inquired gently.

'At first light. I slipped down the backstairs, caught my own mare and saddled her behind the sheds, for Malojo – our stableman – had been ordered not to give me a mount. I took my pistol – two of my pistols, all I could find in my room. With our riders patrolling the bounds of Perdition land, I felt I should be safe from the Comanche, and even if this was not so, it was worth the risk to me. Anything was worth the risk.'

'And was Father Monastario waiting for you there?'

'I don't know,' she whispered. 'I reached the place, dismounted and hid my horse in the deep brush of the gully. But as I was halfway to the hut someone shot at me. The jacal – or what is left of it – stands among thick brush and trees. I ran inside, and crouched between the window and the door. I shot back, but they shot twice more, whoever they were. I had to keep moving back and forth between the door and the window, trying to load and fearing every second that they'd rush the house. Fearing, too, that Father Monastario would arrive, and be killed as well. They ceased shooting but I dared not come out. I was afraid they were waiting for me to do just that. I thought they'd come up through the brush behind the jacal. It was two hours before I dared come out, and then another two, to walk back to the hacienda. And when I reached the place I found that my husband had been shot. Killed.'

'Shot how?' asked Shaw.

'Through the heart.' Her voice shook a little: maybe not love, maybe not grief, but shock and exhaustion. They had been husband and wife, thought January, for three years. Had known each other as only those who live together can know one another. 'From close up, close enough that his clothing had been burned by the gunpowder.'

'What time?'

'I don't know. I kept asking and they kept insisting that I had done it.'

'This happen indoors or out?'

'Outside.' Again, the re-telling of simple facts seemed to steady her. 'His body was found in the orchard behind the house. My mare was found wandering near the corrals. She'd been tied by the reins, and had broken free, I suppose at the sound of the shot. The dead branch was still tangled in her rein.'

Shaw glanced at January, expressionless but with a glint of calculation in his eyes.

'Who else was in the house at the time?' January asked.

'Aunt Alicia. Madrecita. Brother Francis. Enoch, our butler. Malojo the yard-man, and TA the cook, certainly. Melly – Melanie – Madrecita's maid. But Madrecita Taggart, and Aunt Alicia, claim that they saw me in the orchard in the middle of the morning, before they heard the shot – at the time when I was in the jacal in the arroyo, being shot at myself! And one of my pistols was found near the body, along with one of my shawls! Francis ordered Enoch, and Noah – one of the house men – to lock me in my room. Malojo, and Davy – the other houseman – had already taken my husband's body away to Señor Firkin the undertaker in town, and sent for the sheriff.'

'Sure enough sounds fishy to me,' said Shaw. 'They get claim to this rancho if you's hanged?'

'I think so, yes!' The young woman flung out her hands in despair and rage. 'My husband made no will, but if I am hanged for this thing – this thing that I did not do! – they will have the portion of the land that was mine, that had been my uncle's, as well as that belonging to my husband! They had the servants lock me up, for Aunt Alicia was having hysterics . . . Madrecita – to judge by her voice – spent the rest of the afternoon drinking in the parlor, and then started to quarrel with Francis. The sheriff did not come. In the evening I heard voices down below in the yard – the bedroom is at the front of the house, you understand – and Enoch told me, when he brought me food a little later, that Sheriff Quigley had not been in Austin when the men took my husband's body there. There was some political trouble between the Nationalists and the supporters of Houston. Enoch was not clear what it was.'

Some frightful thing, Cousin Sven had said.

Stanway's murder?

'Enoch said that Malojo had remained in town, to wait for Señor Quigley's return, while Davy brought the wagon back. All last night I sat awake, waiting for the sheriff to come, and listening to them quarrelling: Madrecita, and Francis, and

Jalisco, the *jefe* of my husband's vaqueros. I don't know what
about.' She passed her hand across her forehead, and shivered
at the recollection. 'Then in the morning, when the house was
quiet, Juana – Enoch's wife – brought me coffee at first light,
and did not lock the door of the room when she left. When I
slipped out to the guest-room at the back of the house, whose
window overlooks the roof of the kitchen, I saw that someone
had left a horse saddled on the far side of the orchard, just
visible.

'The house is mine,' she finished simply, thin desperation
in her voice. 'The land is mine. Juana, and Malojo, and Jalisco
and most of the vaqueros – they were Uncle Gael's servants.
I had told Jalisco about you, and I think he understands,
that I cannot just ride away and disappear. That is what
Madrecita, and Francis, want me to do, I'm sure. They may
even have told Juana not to lock my door – I don't know.

'But without the land I am nothing. I will have nothing. I
will . . . I will be one of those girls you see on the docks of
Galveston, or in the saloons of Houston and Austin . . . I will
not do that. *I will not.* I will have my land – I will have my
name – or I will hang.'

She made a move, as if, again, she would have taken
January's hand, but stopped herself. 'I need your help, Señor
Enero,' she said softly. 'Please.'

TEN

They rode all night by the waxen glow of the full moon,
and reached Perdition with the sun well into the sky.
Ekholm, when he lent them spare horses to speed their
travel – as well as Lucien and Cousin Sven, to ride with them
until the walls of the hacienda were sighted – suggested they
wait til sun-up Wednesday to depart, but January demurred.
'Taggart was shot on Monday morning,' he said. 'If we don't
arrive until dusk Wednesday, that means by the time I can get
a look at the ground – in the orchard and in the arroyo where

somebody obviously wanted to keep Madame Taggart pinned down so that she'd have no alibi – it'll be Thursday. Maybe Shaw can read three-day-old signs.' He nodded toward the tall Kentuckian, who was saddling up January's big roan gelding by torchlight in the Ekholm corral. 'I can't.'

Selina, who had followed the party out to the corral and stood leaning her chin on the top cottonwood pole of the fence, had suggested hesitantly, 'Might it be better if Mr Shaw went with Valentina – Madame Taggart—' she corrected herself – she and Valentina had gotten onto first-name basis almost at once during dinner.

'The thing we need most to do – and most quickly,' January replied, 'is to get you out of Texas. Of the three of us –' he had gestured, from Shaw, to Hannibal – carrying saddlebags from the house – and to himself once more – 'Mr Shaw will give you the strongest protection. Any danger you run into will be greater than any danger we'll come up against, riding back to Rancho Perdition with Mrs Taggart.'

He was later to remember those words with eye-rolling amazement at his own naiveté.

He would in fact rather have had Hannibal ride with the caravan to Galveston and return to New Orleans; for the fiddler, though cheerfully willing to ride all night into whatever the hell situation awaited them, was not a strong man. By morning the drawn look had returned to his face, and January several times heard him trying to stifle the rasping, consumptive cough that spoke of exhaustion.

But he and the fiddler both knew that he dared not leave him behind. Legally, there were no free blacks in Texas. Any man of African parentage who couldn't account for himself – or who didn't have whites to speak for him – was likely to find himself in the Houston bayous picking somebody's cotton in short order, if he wasn't simply shot for being someplace he wasn't supposed to be.

The rolling country north of Austin was largely empty, and due to the danger of Comanche raids, for most of the night the party rode without speaking. January saw no horsemen, but that, he knew, meant nothing. The gullies lay in darkness. Across the hills he heard the wild yikking of coyotes, and now and then the ghostly screech of an owl. Movement flickered in the corner of his eye: a prairie fox? Or a man burning with the hatred of centuries of injustice and warfare, who would like nothing better than to stake him down and skin him alive? Sven and Lucien turned their heads. Identified and dismissed the shadows.

But though January burned to get an exact account of the Taggart household, even when they stopped to rest or change the horses, they did so in listening silence.

Shortly after first light riders appeared, vaqueros in leather breeches and short jackets, riding down the slope of a hill to their left. 'Your husband's men?' asked January, and Valentina nodded.

'That's Jalisco on the pinto,' she identified a wiry, medium-sized man in the lead. 'My husband was always having to smooth things out between the Tejano vaqueros and the Nortes . . . and between the Yankee Nortes from the north and the Texians and the men of the South, Tennessee and Georgia and Carolina.' She shook her head. 'And between the Tejanos and the Nortes and the slaves . . .' January had already seen that two of the vaqueros were black.

'How many men did your husband employ?'

'Twenty-eight. Sixteen Tejanos, two slaves, four Yankees and six other Nortes, not counting the house servants and Malojo. It became very complicated. *Buenos dias!*' She nudged her horse forward, raising her hand as the men drew near; Jalisco swept his low-crowned hat from his head, bent from the saddle in a bow. Like Ortega, he would have been called *indio* by any aristocratic Mexican of Mexico City, swart and thin and amazingly ugly, with wide, mobile lips and one large, coffee-dark eye turned disturbingly sidelong.

'*Doña.*' His good eye flickered from January's face to Hannibal's, then past them to the two blonde Swedes. 'You didn't run into *El Jerife*, then? Just as well. And these two Nortes are your friends?'

'Don Hannibal Sefton.' She introduced, of course, the white man first. 'And Benjamin Enero.' She did not, January noticed, specify his legal status. 'Did Señor Quigley never come to the hacienda at all, then?'

The vaquero shook his head. 'He had not come when we rode out this morning, and I think he has not since. Brother Francisco –' his deep voice slid over the name with just the trace of scorn – 'gave us orders that his brother's command is to be upheld: no strangers are to be permitted on Perdition land.'

Valentina said, '*Qué demonios . . .*' and Hannibal's comment, though in Homeric Greek, was considerably stronger.

Jalisco spread his hands, and January slid from his saddle and set about helping Lucien and Cousin Sven – with the aid of two of the vaqueros – sort out the horses, unsaddling and returning the Ekholm re-mounts to their owner, saddling those that remained of Hannibal's little stock. Behind him, he heard Jalisco say, 'The young señor says that *El Jerife* Quigley is a nationalist and a traitor, and probably had something to do with the murder himself, because Señor Taggart went over to the Houston men last October. I think he thinks you have fled for good, Doña, for we received no orders concerning yourself.'

'*Mierda!*' Valentina flung up her hands. 'Don't tell me this concerns that stupid lost silver mine that Francis thinks is somewhere . . . *Madre de Dios!*'

'There's a lost silver mine on the property?' inquired Hannibal, dismounting.

'There's a lost hole the size of a silver mine between Francis's ears!' retorted Valentina. 'He is—' She turned in her saddle, as Cousin Sven and Lucien drew near; extended her hands, and smiled a smile that left the two young men breathless. '*Herrar*—' She pronounced the Swedish word clumsily, but by the expressions on their faces, her listeners could have been hearing angels sing. '*Tack sa mycket.*' And, in German scarcely less awkward, she added, 'Thank you more than I can say.'

They bowed deeply in their saddles, took her hands as if they never wanted to let them go. Whatever else she'd been through, reflected January with an inner smile, even in shock and confusion and exhaustion, Valentina was still Valentina, and couldn't keep the warmth of genuine pleasure from her eyes.

It wasn't until they were on their way west – the two Swedes and their little string of horses disappearing into the oak-gullies among the hills – that Valentina returned to the subject of the lost silver mine.

'My husband's brother is an imbecile,' she informed them matter-of-factly. 'He has never been to school – *la Madrecita* thought him too delicate for such things, and had him schooled entirely by tutors – and he has lived most of his life among books, and hidden in his room. And indeed,' she added, with the air of one doing justice to a foe, 'he was probably safer in his room. Aunt Alicia, who worships the ground on which he treads, says that his father and Brother Jack would beat him, when they were drunk. But she . . . sometimes what she says cannot be counted on, on account of the laudanum she takes for her headaches. My husband told me that she will mix up that which actually happened, from that which she dreamed.'

'*Weave a circle round him thrice/ and close your eyes with holy dread,*' murmured Hannibal. 'I know the feeling well. Upon a time I dreamed that I had a wife and a child, and woke to find that it was nothing of the sort . . . Not to speak of the many times I have dreamed I was in love.'

'Well,' said Valentina, 'at least she has the excuse of laudanum to be crazy. Francis is the only one of the family who doesn't drink, and he will ply you with medical tracts as to why this is unhealthy—'

'I don't wonder his father and Brother Jack beat him,' Hannibal remarked.

'He will give anyone information about anything. He is very learned, my husband's brother – but an imbecile all the same. But when he came to Perdition last October, he heard the stories of the lost San Diablo Mine, and became utterly convinced that it lay somewhere near. He has a study attached to his room and he has collected dozens of old maps and old land grants. Half of them he cannot read, because he doesn't understand Spanish, but he spends all his time with his door locked anyway, studying them or poring over his Spanish dictionaries and grammars. Yet I cannot believe he would . . . would instruct Jalisco and the men to keep Señor Quigley away, only for fear that he would discover it—'

'Possibly,' said January, 'he's ordered it in the hopes of giving *you* time to flee the country, so as not to contest his claims.'

At this, the young widow's eyes flashed blue fire.

January leaned a little to Hannibal, and instructed, in Latin, 'Ask her if she's certain, that her husband left no will.' It would not do, even here in these empty hills, for the one white cowhand of Jalisco's party to hear a black 'valet' asking questions of a white woman. The men who rode the ranges, Tejano and Norte alike, were men to whom observation of what went on around them was not only second nature, but a matter of life and death. They missed little, and his ride from Houston to Austin had taught January that they gossiped among themselves worse than the girls in Rose's school.

Obediently, Hannibal inquired, 'Did your husband leave a will, madame? And, would your uncle's land also go to your husband's family in the event of – er . . .'

Valentina shook her head firmly. 'My husband left no will. Uncle Gael deeded his land to me on my marriage, as my own, not my husband's. But since my uncle held it through a land grant from the Church rather than from the King of Spain, I am not certain of its transmission, should I myself . . .' Her voice trembled a little, and she raised her chin, as if in contempt of the word, *hang*. 'Should anything happen to me. And as a married woman, I was not able to make my own arrangements for its disposal, and my uncle's nearest relations are now in Spain, I believe. My husband made no will.'

'You're sure of that?'

'He was young, señor, only thirty-two. No man in Texas, I think, truly believes he will be killed by the Comanche or by anyone else. But as a lawyer himself, he hated the thought of wills. He hated the thought of giving over to others the property that he had fought and sweated to achieve. He said there was plenty of time for that, when his mother would pester him about it.'

'And did she pester?'

Her lips tightened.

'It was almost the first thing she asked him,' said Valentina, 'upon coming here in the Fall. Had he made a will? *This is a dangerous land, what will happen to us when you die*? I think she wanted to make sure that her beloved son, her precious Francis, would not be cut out a second time.'

'I can understand her feelings,' January could not help himself from murmuring – but in French, not English, so that only Hannibal understood.

As indeed, he thought, he could understand those of the pretty young woman riding beside them. With her mother's nearest relatives in Spain – if they were alive at all – Valentina, too, was very much a stranger in a strange land. She had spoken truly when she'd cried, *I am nothing! I will have nothing*!

Without the resources that land could provide, she would have no one to turn to.

'*Quod si vivere in aeternum vive tibi destinatis.*' Hannibal agreed. And then, continuing in Latin, 'Should we perhaps make a detour to look at this hut-and-gully arrangement first, where someone took pot-shots at the fair Valentina?'

'Better we start at the house,' returned January in the same tongue. 'Whatever sign might have been at the gully, it may or may not have survived the past thirty-six hours. A wiser course would be to first establish where we stand.'

'You speak truly, my lord.' Hannibal just stopped himself from bowing in the saddle. '*Vera decam tibi, domine mi.*'

In the event, it was just as well that they chose to ride first to the Taggart hacienda. In the course of the last six miles, January and Hannibal acquainted themselves, so far as they were able, with the events of Monday: none of the little band of Jalisco's vaqueros had been at the hacienda, to observe who had been present at the time of Taggart's death.

'Mr Enoch tell me Noah an' Davy – the housemen – had took the wagon down to the bottomlands to pick up the wood the men'd cut Saturday,' provided Missouri, one of the black cowhands, in English. 'Malojo – the yardman – woulda been in the tack-shed that time, fixin' saddles or polishin' the rust off bits. Mr Enoch's wife Juana woulda been in the laundry, an' the housemaid – Clytie – with her.'

'Who else in the house?'

The cowhand shook his head. 'Melly – Old M'am Taggart's maid – takes her mendin' out to the kitchen, to chat with TA – that's the cook – while she's doin' it. The house is an adobe, with the kitchen sort of stuck on the back like a tail. Old M'am Taggart was all over Mr Taggart to have bells put in, like she had back in Virginia, 'stead of havin' to yell or ring a hand-bell out the window, but Mr Taggart, he had other things to think about.'

'Time enough to be puttin' in bells,' agreed Twenty-One, the younger of the two slave vaqueros, 'when we could be sure the whole place wasn't gonna be burned down by the Comanche next week.'

'That ever happened?' asked January. 'Not burned down, but attacked . . .?'

'Not in twenty-seven years, it ain't,' added Missouri, whose wiry blackness contrasted sharply with his youthful friend's walnut complexion and European features. January guessed his parent or parents had been smuggled into Louisiana straight from Africa, in defiance of American law and the British navy. 'The house used to be M'am Valentina's uncle's hacienda. The Comanche'd raid the horse-herds an' the mules, old Malojo says, but they never attacked the house. It's got walls on it like a fort. When Mr Taggart come out from Virginia in 'thirty-four, and got bottomland along the Pedernales, he set to growin' cotton. He had fifty acres in cotton, an' thirty in corn, an' built him a cottage near the river, where the overseer lives now, near the quarters. First thing he did, when he married M'am Valentina in 'thirty-seven, was move up to the adobe, where the mosqui-toes don't come. Down in the bottomlands where the cotton fields is, they 'bout eat you alive.'

After trading a few observations about New Orleans mosqui-toes, and horror stories concerning the Texas varieties of the pest, January led the conversation back to the events of Monday morning. 'How close is the orchard to the house? Who reached Mr Taggart's body first, after they heard the shot? Was he dead when people got to him?'

'Well, sir . . .' Missouri pushed his wide-brimmed hat forward, to scratch his close-cropped head. 'That's the thing.

By what Enoch told me, him an' Melly an' TA was all in the
kitchen together when they heard the shot. They froze up, an'
listened for more. Like I said, we never had the Comanche
raid the house, but there's always a first time. Then again,
with Mr Taggart's orders that nobody was allowed onto the
place, it coulda been a warnin' shot—'

'Were any of the men posted that close to the house?'

Missouri shook his head. 'Mostly we was down by the San
Antonio road. Enoch said, he an' Melly walked round to the
front of the house to see if there was anybody ridin' off, but
didn't see nobody. The orchard's a big one – three acres – with
one edge about eighty feet from the back of the house an' the
back edge maybe a half-mile beyond that. Enoch an' Melly
walked clear around the house an' didn't see nuthin'. Juana
an' Clytie just stepped outta the laundry to make sure it wasn't
Comanche an' then went back to work – Juana don't take no
account of Comanche an' Clytie's a darn sight more scared
of Juana than she is of any Indian ever born. Musta been near
two hours later, that Malojo saw M'am Valentina's mare
standin' outside the corral, saddled, with her reins tangled
around a piece of branch, like she'd broke free after bein'
tied.'

January nodded. He remembered the walled quadrangle of
Mictlán – the hacienda of Valentina's father – and also the
isolated plantation on which he himself had spent his earliest
years. A shot in the countryside, even fairly near the house,
wasn't like a shot heard among the crowded houses of a city.

'Did Malojo know Mrs Taggart had taken her mare out?'

'He says he didn't.' The vaquero shrugged. 'It ain't like
back east, where the horses is kept in a stable, see. If Malojo's
doin' somethin' inside the tack-shed, or checkin' on the pigs,
you can lead a horse outta the corral an' saddle him behind
the sheds, easy enough. An' I will say for M'am Valentina,
she don't need no help tackin' up a horse.'

Recalling some of the girl's exploits back on Mictlán,
January nodded. And if the young woman had been slipping
away to rendezvous with Father Monastario, it was a safe bet
the other Catholics on the place kept their mouths shut, whatever they saw or guessed.

'Anyways,' Missouri continued, 'Malojo says the mare wasn't sweated-up or dusty like she'd been wanderin' in from the hills. He put her in the corral an' looked out toward the woods an' the orchard, rememberin' the shot he'd heard, an' saw the hawks an' buzzards above the orchard.'

'So no one missed Mr Taggart in – what – three hours?'

'All of that.' The vaquero looked surprised at the question. 'He'd rode down to the bottomlands that mornin' like he usually does, to talk to Mr Vabsley. The folks down there grubbin' the crop, an' Mr T liked to keep a eye on things.' By the flex of Missouri's non-committal voice he might have been discussing a construction project in China. January had encountered this before among the *librés* of New Orleans, this careful distance between the light-complected *gens du couleur librés* and the slaves cutting cane in the fields. *Nothing to do with us.* Free colored owned slaves, and never seemed to want to see how easily, these days, they could become slaves themselves. *Like Selina . . .*

There seemed to exist the same division between slave cow-herders and the mere grubbers in the soil.

'Nobody was expectin' Mr Taggart back til evenin',' put in Twenty-One. 'His horse was there, tied up in the orchard, saddled, maybe a quarter-mile from the house. He was layin' in a sort of clearin', where two trees died a long time ago, an' the grass is deep. Malojo said he looked to been dead three hours, by the way his eyes set back in his head. He'd been shot in the chest, an' the gun – one of M'am Valentina's pistols – was layin' near the body, with one of M'am Valentina's shawls.'

ELEVEN

S heriff Quigley – last seen biting the ear off one of Gideon Pollack's supporters in the lobby of the Capital City Hotel in Austin – stood on the shallow steps of the Rancho Perdition adobe as Valentina Taggart and her supporters rode up to the house.

The house itself was, as the cowhand Missouri had indicated, a fortress-like adobe structure, its main section two storeys high plus (January judged) an attic which could double as a blockhouse at need. The white plaster of its walls looked well maintained – vital in such constructions. The windows of its ground floor were stoutly barred with wood. Built on high ground a few miles from the rise of the surrounding hills, it faced south, toward the oak groves and tall-grass meadows along the Pedernales River. On its west side a wing extended – probably kitchens, January guessed – and walls enclosed a courtyard, glimpsed through an open gate that reminded him strongly of the portals of a medieval castle.

Quigley, in his town frock coat and low-crowned beaver hat, was dust-covered, mud-splattered, and, as Valentina and her riders approached and he turned toward them, looked exhausted and vexed. He was a short man, stocky-built so that he reminded January of an oak bollard, graying brown hair thin over a high forehead and gray eyes piercing under a pale shelf of brow. A fading black eye remained from the hotel fracas of the preceding week.

In the doorway before him were grouped the gorgons – both clothed in black – and a tallish, slight, rather twisted figure whom January identified immediately as the young Francis Taggart, not quite boy and not quite man. An ephebe, the ancient Greeks would have called him – *that most charming age*, as Homer said, *when the beard first begins to grow*, though January guessed that few Athenian erastes would have had much to do with this particular specimen. He moved clumsily – severe scoliosis, January diagnosed as he dismounted. Lateral pelvic tilt and dysplasia, complicated by kyphosis. Pale-blue eyes, disconcertingly like Aunt Alicia's, blinked from behind thick spectacles and his thin, straight line of a mouth was already bracketed with lines of disapproval.

These lines deepened sharply as he recognized his sister-in-law, and beside him, Madrecita Taggart exclaimed, 'The *nerve* of the girl!'

'How much nerve do you think I need, madame?' Valentina drew herself up like a soldier in her saddle. 'This house is my house – this land, my land. Fearing that I would be accused falsely, I sought a man who could be trusted to put my interests before his own – or those of anyone who might offer him reward.' She turned her scornful gaze for one moment in Quigley's direction, then looked back at her mother-in-law. 'Madame, Aunt Alicia, surely you remember my father's friend Mr Sefton, of New Orleans?'

Waxen and haggard with fatigue, Hannibal dismounted, and made a profound bow over the hands of each lady in turn.

Quigley said, 'Your boy was the one helped Doc Meredith fix up Pollack.'

Hannibal bowed again. 'It was my privilege and honor to be on the spot with the means to assist.' January, as befit a slave, continued to unfasten saddlebags from their horses and made no acknowledgement of the remark, since it wasn't directed at him but at his 'master'.

The sheriff sniffed. 'Asked for what he got, if you ask me. An' lucky not to get as much as he deserved.' Both Aunt Alicia and the elder Mrs Taggart, January noticed, bridled fiercely at that remark.

'Mrs Taggart . . .' The sheriff turned to Valentina, whom the fiddler was now assisting from her mount. 'I'm afraid it's my duty to place you under arrest, on suspicion of the murder of—'

'Have you a warrant?' inquired Hannibal politely.

Spots of color darkened under the lawman's heavy tan.

When he didn't reply, the fiddler continued, 'As Mrs Taggart's representative, I feel impelled to ask what constitutes "suspicion" in her case that does not equally apply to everyone else in the house at the operative time. Has the operative time been determined, by the way? I presume that any arrest will include both these ladies, and this gentleman—'

The gorgons looked horrified and Francis blenched.

'We were together,' announced Madrecita Taggart, her chin coming forward.

Francis opened his mouth to protest and then shut it. Aunt Alicia, blue eyes seeming even bluer because their pupils were contracted to pin-points, exclaimed hazily, 'You're always telling *me* not to tell lies, Amelia! You were . . . Oh!'

Her elder sister silenced her with a glare.

'Yes,' Alicia gasped, turning back to the sheriff and nodding. 'Yes we were all together. All together all morning—' Then she slapped her lace-mitted hand over her mouth, burst into tears, and ran back into the house.

'We were together,' reiterated Madrecita Taggart firmly. 'In the parlor. All morning.'

'I was in the study,' added Francis. 'Newspaper accounts had just come in regarding Captain Wilkes's interesting voyage to the Antarctic . . . I mean,' he corrected himself hastily at his mother's glare, 'I'd *been* in the study and had just come into the parlor.'

'And I was in the Arroyo Sauceito being shot at by Comanche,' Valentina retorted. 'Though I neglected to ask their names, so cannot bring them as witnesses.'

'We saw you,' claimed her mother-in-law. 'We all saw you walking in the orchard. You were wearing your red-flowered shawl.' She looked furious, and a little disconcerted.

They really did mean her to flee, reflected January. Whoever actually committed the crime . . .

'How did you see me in the orchard, Madrecita? The parlor is in the front of the house, its window looks out into the yard.'

'Your shawl was found beside my poor son's body!' Madame's heavy mouth hardened like the mouth of a Japanese mask. Her eyes, January noticed, were completely dry, though her son had been found murdered not forty-eight hours before. 'Your shawl, and your pistol. Sheriff –' she turned like a lioness upon Quigley – 'how can you hesitate? I told my son – I warned him of this girl, a hundred times!'

'Indeed you did,' returned the younger woman. 'You warned him not to trust me – told him to put me aside! While eating the corn that was grown on my land, and the beef that was raised in my hills, and sleeping under the roof that my uncle—'

'Ladies!' Hannibal stepped forward, lifting his gloved hands, at the same moment that Quigley raised his own hands in the same placating gesture.

'Ladies—'

'I fear, sir –' Hannibal turned to the sheriff, with another slight bow – 'that I cannot permit you to arrest my client on evidence so questionable, without proper warrant. You are, however, welcome to accompany me in a search of the premises—'

Francis Taggart and his mother both cried, 'No!' and stepped forward. Behind him, January heard the faint clatter and creak among the vaqueros, and glanced back to see Jalisco and the others unshipping their weapons. Not pointing them at the sheriff – and neither Missouri nor Twenty-One had touched the guns they carried – but making their presence felt.

'I'm afraid I can't permit that, sir.' Francis Taggart collected himself, and limped down the remaining steps to face the lawman. 'My brother left written instructions that no intruders were to be permitted on Rancho Perdition land, in the event of his incapacity or death. Not until after the reading of his will.'

'Vincent made no will,' snapped Madame, startled. 'He told me—'

'According to the document I found in his study,' replied her younger son hastily, 'it sounds as if he did.'

'You mind if I see this document?' Quigley's sharp pale eyes flickered to the young man's face. Then he looked back at the elder Mrs Taggart, who was hastily re-making her expression of astonishment into one of determined agreement.

'When you return with a properly executed warrant, sir,' asserted Francis, a trifle smugly, 'you certainly may.'

The sheriff looked back at the vaqueros with their guns, then turned in frustration to Hannibal, who nodded wisely – just as if he'd studied law at the Inns of Court instead of wasting four years at Oxford in pursuit of Latin poetry and the local light-skirts. 'I'm afraid he's within his legal rights, sir.'

January had already formed his own opinions about who had ordered the servant to leave Valentina's door open that morning, and why Francis Taggart and his mother would rather have the house un-searched – considerations of lost silver mines entirely aside – and the young widow un-arrested. He held his peace, watching the glances that passed between them before Francis turned to Hannibal again.

'And that –' the youth concluded smugly – 'includes you, sir.'

'Mr Sefton –' Valentina regarded her brother-in-law with an expression usually reserved for unwashed mongrel dogs – 'is here at my request, to assist in protecting my interests. As this is my house, and my land—'

Francis's eyebrows snapped down over his nose. 'It's nothing of the kind! After murdering my brother—'

'There is no evidence—' began Hannibal.

'—held in trust –' Valentina placed a protective hand over her trim belly – 'for the child that I carry.'

This was the first that Hannibal or January had heard of a child, but Hannibal didn't miss a beat. 'Nothing can be decided,' he declared, with the smooth authority of a barrister, 'until Mr Taggart's will is located and his wishes ascertained. Mr Quigley, I give you my word that Mrs Taggart, having returned to her home of her own free will, is unlikely to abscond. Indeed, to do so would jeopardize her own position with regard to her husband's portion of the estate. But until some firmer evidence is found pointing to one or another person in particular—'

'I saw her!' protested Madame Taggart. 'I saw that wretched hussy in the orchard, minutes before she murdered my son!'

'If it was minutes before Señor Taggart's death,' pointed out Valentina calmly, 'why did you not go out to the body at once when you heard the shot fired? Why was it three hours before—?'

'You be silent!' Her mother-in-law spun angrily and January had the impression that she only barely restrained herself from slapping her. January could almost see the snakes of the gorgon's hair flaring out from beneath her black lace house-cap. To Quigley, she raged, 'This girl quarreled with my son – the whole household heard it! You find her pistol beside his bleeding body, the shawl with which she concealed it from him only feet away, she comes tripping up to the house with the most preposterous tale of being chased by Indians, and you still refuse to believe in her guilt? What is wrong with you, sir?'

'I doubt he was bleeding,' pointed out Valentina, 'three

hours after his death – unless you saw his body immediately after the shot was fired and for reasons of your own went back into the house and told no one—'

The elder Mrs Taggart lunged at Valentina that time, hand upraised. Quigley had evidently been brought up not to lay a hand on respectable women and Francis Taggart could only bleat, 'Mama!' Like the sheriff, Hannibal had been 'raised right', as they said in America. He had, however, spent ten years playing the violin in venues where women regularly engaged in fisticuffs and hair-pulling matches, and caught Mama Taggart's wrist before her blow landed.

The older woman spun in his grip and fetched him a stunning swat on the jaw that nearly knocked him off his feet, but Hannibal didn't release his grip. Francis again cried, 'Mama!', Valentina drew back, Sheriff Quigley strode forward, and the vaqueros – like January – wondered what the hell they were supposed to do in a situation like this. Their guns – or the threat of them – obviously wouldn't serve, and January had no intention of being hanged – or at the very least beaten to a pulp – for laying a hand on a white woman, no matter how belligerent.

But Madame, weighed down by Hannibal's weight on her wrist, drew back, boiling with rage. She wrenched her arm free of Hannibal's grip, glared at Quigley and spat the words, 'I will have your job for that,' and, turning on her heel, stalked back into the house.

Valentina turned to Sheriff Quigley, the picture of martyred dignity. 'It's true that I quarreled with my husband Sunday evening,' she said. 'But on Monday morning I was in the hills along Sauceitos Creek, where I was shot at, and my horse either stolen or ran away. I did not reach this house again until mid-afternoon.'

'Why'd you run away yesterday mornin'?' The sheriff's eyes narrowed again.

'Isn't what you just saw sufficient explanation for that?' The young woman flicked her hand toward Francis, and the door behind him through which her mother-in-law had vanished. 'I knew I could expect no justice – not even a hearing – if she, and the son whom she hopes will inherit the rancho, have their way.'

'Enough of this!' Francis thumped his ebony cane on the ground. 'As my brother's executor—'

'By what authority?' demanded Hannibal.

'—until such time as you bring a properly executed warrant, I'm afraid I'm going to have to ask all of you – Sheriff Quigley, and you, Mr Sefton – to vacate these premises.'

Jalisco and the vaqueros stirred again, looking at one another uneasily, not knowing whose orders to follow. But Valentina looked past her brother-in-law to the still-open door of the house, and called out, 'Enoch?' Under the near-certainty, January reflected, that every servant in the house was clustered around the doorway just out of sight, listening . . .

And indeed, a straight, handsome, middle-aged butler appeared instantly in the aperture, with the expression of a man who would not lower himself to eavesdrop even with the fate of humankind at stake.

'Yes, M'am Valentina?'

'Please show Mr Sefton's man to the north guest-room.'

'Yes, M'am Valentina.'

January was a little disappointed that he wouldn't hear the final stages of the sheriff's dismissal – at this point Francis couldn't very well permit Valentina's arrest without allowing a search of the house as well – but knew that it was most important right now to establish that Hannibal, and incidentally himself, were not going to be chased away. Francis, left before the house's great doors, looked uncertain as January passed him. For his part, January did his best not to look as if he were listening behind him, for the young man's voice calling them back.

He followed Enoch through the wide, tiled central hall of the ground floor. Beneath the main stairway, its risers and adobe balustrade handsomely tiled in orange and blue, a narrow door let into a pitch-dark, enclosed flight of backstairs. The ill-nailed wooden risers creaked under their weight as they ascended and a loose one caught the toe of January's boot and nearly tripped him.

'You'll have to excuse us,' apologized Enoch, in the soft accents of the Virginia tidewater. 'We were not expectin' company, an' everythin' in an uproar followin' on poor Mr Taggart's death—'

Emerging into the upstairs hall, a spacious duplicate of the downstairs and, like most Mexican dwellings January had seen, nearly bare of furniture, they passed a thin woman in the plain blouse and skirt of a servant emerging from a door at the end of the hall. She said to Enoch, in Spanish, 'I've made up the bed,' and his severe face broke into a brief smile.

'Knew Mr Francis wouldn't chase 'em off, did you?' To January – switching back to English – he said, 'The guest-room opens off the back gallery here.' He led the way through a double French door, into a bare chamber, windowed across the back of the house, between two small rooms which in New Orleans would have been called 'cabinets'. 'My wife can make up a pallet for you here, or in your gen'leman's room, whichever your gen'leman would prefer.'

'The gallery would suit me fine, if you'd be so kind.'

Was that the Juana who left the door open yesterday morning?

'Your gen'leman's a lawyer?' inquired Enoch, as they passed through the gallery – which overlooked the corrals to the north of the house, and offered a view of the orchard beyond – and into a small chamber to the left. 'Poor Marse Vincent was a lawyer back in Richmond.'

The little room was furnished (or semi-furnished, to an American's eye) in the sparse Mexican style with a bed, a chest, a small table below the windows, and not much else. In the downstairs hallway January had noticed a number of new-looking lithographic prints of Biblical subjects – absent, apparently, in the upper regions of the house. At least the Mexican-style room lacked the gory, primitive crucifix that had seemed to be a feature of every bedroom he'd seen in Mexico itself. Absent also were the pieces of American-style furniture – chairs, whatnots, small tables – that he'd glimpsed downstairs. *Madrecita Taggart's contributions to the household?*

As he arranged Hannibal's shaving things on the table he replied, 'There's all different kinds of lawyers in England where he comes from, sir – Chancery court and Queen's Bench court and solicitors and barristers. I never can keep straight which kind Michie Sefton is.'

'I heard that.' Enoch checked the room's other door, which presumably led into another room in the interior of the house, and made sure it was locked.

'He was a friend of her father's down in Mexico.' January skated neatly away from telling a lie that he could be later taxed with. 'M'am Taggart ran into him in Austin last week, and knew where he'd be stayin'.' He had no reason to distrust the butler, but the scene on the front steps had been enough to clinch his suspicion that he had to pick his steps carefully. There was no telling, at this point, who was on whose side. 'I know it's not my place to ask,' he continued diffidently, 'but I couldn't help overhearin' some of the talk, an' I wondered – when will Mr Taggart be laid to rest?'

And is there any chance I can get a look at his body – or at least the contents of his pockets? Even as he framed the thought he guessed there wasn't a hope.

'He's being put to rest today.' Enoch's face – inscrutable with the family's secrets, like that of any good house servant who didn't want to end up picking cotton – seemed to harden.

'Of course, it isn't usual for white women to attend funerals, though I understand they do in some places. But Mr Francis . . . well, he said it was more important for him to be here.'

He was silent a moment, straightening a corner of the fine linen cloth that covered the dressing-table, as if by this small action he might tidy up some of the dark and pullulating mess that was the family which Valentina had described.

'He's a cold man, Mr Francis,' the butler said at length. 'But he cares for Miss Alicia, in spite of all she near drives him crazy. I'm thinking he didn't want to leave Miss Alicia alone.'

Or didn't want to be away from Perdition when the sheriff arrived to search the house?

'She's torn up somethin' terrible by all this. She never cared for Mr Taggart. Sometimes, when she'd had maybe a little too much headache medicine . . . when she wasn't quite herself it was as if she were afraid of him. But to have this happen . . .' He shook his head. 'It's a bad business. A bad business.'

And it would be a bad business, reflected January, for any

house servant who'd sided with the wrong faction, when the master died. He'd never encountered a slave-owner who didn't owe thousands – usually tens of thousands – of dollars, and the master's death was frequently followed immediately by a sell-off of slaves to cover them. The death of a master always meant trouble, even in a family that was not as divided as this one. The whole issue of wills and heirs could take on terrifying implications for those whose bodies were not their own.

He forbore to ask further questions on the subject, however – aware that Enoch had his own jobs to do – and after a brief orientation regarding such important matters as, where were the slaves' latrines (behind the stables), when the household staff got its meals (an hour before the white folks, in the long room that separated the kitchen wing from the dining-room) and was there anybody a newcomer needed to watch out for ('M'am Amelia's mighty strict with them who don't look like they're workin'.'), the butler left him to unpack the rest of Hannibal's slender belongings.

Instead of doing this, January returned to the upstairs rear gallery and looked out one of its wide windows, to get a better idea of the layout of the home-place of Perdition. The biggest of the corrals lay closest to the rear of the house, and he recognized his own big, rather clumsy-looking bay gelding being unsaddled by a grizzle-haired Mexican, in conversation with someone who stood too close to the house for January to identify.

But the three horses still hitched – saddled – to the corral fence were those of the Tejano riders who'd escorted them to the house, including the black-and-white paint mare ridden by Jalisco. January turned, hurried down the backstairs, and out through the shaded downstairs piazza at the rear of the house to find, indeed, Jalisco and two other vaqueros, chatting with the stableman in Spanish.

In that language, he said, 'Señor? A word with you, if I may?'

The vaquero raised a shaggy eyebrow and followed him a little ways along the house wall (cowhands clearly being discouraged from lingering in the piazza itself).

'Correct me if I'm wrong, señor.' January glanced back to
the doors that led from the piazza into the house, through
which the voices of Hannibal, Valentina, and Francis could
still be faintly heard. 'My impression is that young Señor
Taggart may consider it in his own interests that Madame
Valentina be unable to prove where she was at the time of her
husband's death. For this reason, my master and I would like
to have a look at this Arroyo Sauceito as soon as may be –
immediately, if possible, before further time passes that would
obliterate whatever signs may remain.'

A slow smile twitched the man's wide lips. 'Not much
remains as it is.'

'I'd still like to see the place – my master would,' he
corrected himself. 'And the orchard as well, if that's possible.
I understand it would be wiser to visit Sauceito Creek with
an escort.'

'We've seldom had Comanche this far east on the ranges,'
replied Jalisco. 'But a man would be a fool to do otherwise.
I've had a look—'

Footfalls thumped in the central hall of the house. January
turned his head and saw the door into the piazza open, and
Francis Taggart limp through, followed by the tall, sandy-
haired cowhand he'd seen in Austin playing bodyguard to the
gorgons. Young Taggart's spectacles flashed as he gazed at
January and then Jalisco: 'What are you still doing here,
Jalisco?' he demanded in English. 'You know my brother's
orders. You should be out keeping watch on the San Antonio
road. You never know who might try to come onto the property.
And those *were* my brother's orders.' He glanced at the other
two Tejano vaqueros, loitering near their horses, then returned
his attention to January.

'Your master intends to ride out to look at Sauceito Creek
in half an hour, though I assured him, there's nothing of interest
out there. I'll have Malojo saddle horses for you –' he gestured
toward the gray-haired stableman – 'and Creed here –' the
slightest of nods indicated the sandy-haired cowhand at his
back – 'and two men will accompany you, though I assure
you no Comanche has come anywhere near the spot in twenty
years. Creed knows the way.'

.

January bowed his head. 'Thank you, sir.'

And Creed, he judged, has his orders to see us off Taggart land the minute we're out of sight of the house . . .

Leaving Valentina here alone.

His glance crossed that of Jalisco. In Spanish, the vaquero agreed quietly, 'Yes, it would be as well not to ride alone.'

Turning, the man swung up onto his pinto mare, and he and his two bravos left the corrals in a scattering of pebbles and dirt.

TWELVE

'You all right?' January glanced behind him as he stepped through the door from the upstairs back gallery into the guest-room, where Hannibal lay stretched out on the bed like a dead man, his face chalky with fatigue.

'I stand ready to imitate the action of the tiger,' whispered the fiddler, struggling up onto one elbow. 'My sinews stiffened, my blood summoned . . . it's on its way, and will be here in a moment, never fear . . . my fair nature disguised with hard-favored rage . . .'

January waved aside this parody of *Henry V* and came to his side. 'Brother Francis informs me that horses will be ready in half an hour, for us to ride out to Sauceito Creek.'

'That was his idea.' Hannibal sat up, and coughed. 'And I can't well quarrel with the notion. I estimate that we have about forty-eight hours before Sheriff Quigley returns from San Antonio – which, according to the beautiful Valentina, is the closest place where a nationalist judge can be found – with a warrant to arrest Valentina and search the house and grounds. Evidently the Honorable Justice Long in Austin was a Houston appointee – the president, not the town – and can be recalcitrant. *Why* would Francis seek to keep Valentina from being arrested, if in the same breath he and his mother are accusing her of murder? What was all that business about, "Come back with a proper warrant—"?'

'Because he wants me to run away.' A key rattled in the lock of the door which Enoch had taken such care to fasten, and it opened to admit Valentina, still in her riding-dress. 'After you went up the stairs, Señor Sefton, Francis stopped me in the hall, and told me – not very convincingly, I must say! – that with the case against me, my only chance is flight. He even offered to give me horses, and money. My own horses! And *my* money, money from my lands—!' Her blue eyes were sparkling with rage.

'He knows the case against you won't stand in court,' said January.

'No wonder Madrecita looked so shocked when we rode up,' Hannibal remarked, and began to straighten the elaborate folds of his voluminous linen neckcloth.

January added quietly, 'They were counting on you fleeing, as an admission of your guilt.'

'And this is an admission of his!'

'Not necessarily,' he pointed out. 'Your husband could have been shot by a total stranger – or one of his own men, for that matter – and if Francis, or his mother, found the body, the best thing they could do was run back to the house for your shawl and your pistol. Particularly if they knew there was no will.'

'Bastards!' gasped the widow. 'Lizards! And like as not they will set the sheriff on my trail as soon as I—'

'I doubt it,' said January. 'Whoever actually killed him – whether the evidence against you was planned or opportunistic – Francis has to know that his claim on both his brother's land and what you got from your uncle will be a great deal safer if you're not around to dispute it. You said you have no kin nearer here than Mexico.'

Hannibal glanced up from the unraveling Gordian knot of his recalcitrant neckcloth. 'And here I thought he was just trying to keep the sheriff from finding his maps to the Lost Mine.'

'It could be.' Valentina sketched a gesture of vexation with one hand. 'With Francis, one doesn't know. He lives in terror that someone will find the mine before he does – or that one of the servants – Noah or Davy or even poor Enoch – will steal the map and sell it, as if such things aren't being peddled to fools all over the county! He trusts no one, except maybe Aunt Alicia.'

She sank down, rather suddenly, on the chair that January brought up for her, and passed her hand across her forehead. Like most white women in Texas she'd worn veils around the wide brim of her riding hat, and her face, always delicate of complexion, seemed suddenly pallid with exhaustion. She had, January recalled, been in the saddle for almost twenty-four hours with only the briefest of rest.

'She would defend him, you know,' she said after a moment, 'against his father, and his horrible brother Jack. And from my husband, too. My husband told me once that Jack was always pushing him to join him in his acts of violence and mischief. He said—'

She broke the thought off quickly, and shook her head. Hannibal got creakily to his feet, defeated by the neckcloth, and went to finish the process with the assistance of the room's small shaving-mirror. 'And is she one of the reasons he locks his doors?' he inquired, keeping his scratchy voice light. 'I had an aunt like that. She loved all her nephews and nieces, but when she came to visit she'd drive all of us insane, knocking on our doors or coming into our rooms to "see if we need anything".'

'*Dios*!' She sighed. 'Yes, that . . . And the laudanum makes it worse, because she forgets that he's told her to go away. And some days – after spending the whole of the day in the library, reading novels or political newspapers – she'll wander around the house at night. "Checking" on him. "Checking" on us. More than once I've wakened to see her standing in the doorway of our room – mine and my husband's – staring at us as we sleep.'

And she shuddered, though the morning was balmy with springtime. 'And she'll search the house – search our room, even—'

'Like living in a Gothic novel,' remarked the fiddler. 'All one needs is a bricked-up vault in the cellar—'

'Don't laugh,' said January. 'Can Francis ride?'

'Yes, quite well, though I don't expect he could saddle his

own horse. He rides into town every few weeks, to look at the State Archives, for records that might lead him to his Lost Mine.' She made a wry mouth. 'Only he won't tell anyone that's what he's looking for, so he just pokes around. He and Aunt Alicia came up with a scheme of searching for it themselves – they got Jalisco to teach them how to tell directions by the stars, and how to read animal tracks, and shoot. But they quarreled about who was going to saddle the horses and look after the pack animals, and how they were going to divide up the silver from the mine—'

'Francis obviously has no idea how much it costs to operate a silver mine.' Hannibal turned from the mirror. '*Are* you *enceinte*, by the way, my dear?'

'*Dios*, no!' She looked shocked at the very suggestion. 'But I had to say something, you see. And it makes my position stronger if Madrecita and Aunt Alicia should believe me to be.'

'If worst does come to worst,' said January thoughtfully, 'it might keep you from being hanged. But it was a dangerous thing to say. My personal opinion is that Francis wants to keep everyone away from the house until he has time to forge a will, which he will conveniently "find" before Sheriff Quigley reappears. He's assigned Creed and two other men to "guard" Mr Sefton and myself when we ride out to look at the jacal.'

Valentina's eyes flared with alarm. 'Creed? Creed is his minion, his *arrastrado*. He will have given orders, to throw you off this place—'

'If he hasn't given orders to shoot us, as soon as we're far enough away from the house that it won't be heard. Or shoot Hannibal, anyway,' he added dryly, 'and take me to Galveston to sell.'

'*What profit is it if we slay our brother,*' quoted Hannibal, '*and conceal his blood? Come, let us sell him to the Ishmaelites.*'

'*Bastardo*! I will come with you—'

'You will stay here quietly,' said January, 'and rest. Jalisco and a couple of his men are going to double back and intercept us. Can't be too careful,' he added gravely, 'in Comanche country. But until we return, watch yourself. Don't eat or drink anything that doesn't come out of a dish you can see others eat from.'

She stared at him in alarm.

'I don't know who's behind this,' said January. 'Though I have my suspicions.'

'It's obvious—'

'It is,' he agreed. 'But I don't want to take the chance of you being hurt while we're all chasing the obvious suspect in the wrong direction. Don't get yourself into a room that doesn't have two exits. And while we're gone,' he finished, as he bowed over her hand, 'you might put together a list of who in the household we can trust.'

Jalisco, Lope, and a very young vaquero named Ajo were, in fact, waiting for the little party in the first of the heavily wooded gullies that led up toward the hills. 'Madame Valentina considered three men too slender a guard, in such country as this,' explained Jalisco, as he turned his scrubby pinto mare to follow Creed's horse, and the sandy-haired bodyguard grumbled, but couldn't really argue the point.

'They must indeed have intended to murder us,' murmured Hannibal in Latin. 'Look at the disappointment in their faces.'

'I hate Texas.'

'A rose by any other name would smell as sweet, *amicus meus*. In Louisiana it would be the same.'

January sighed. 'Can't argue with you there . . . Master.'

Before they had gone down to the horses, Valentina had quickly sketched a map of Arroyo Sauceito, marking the ruined jacal – the thatched peasant hut common to Mexican and formerly Mexican territory. Once there, January had little trouble finding the tree where she'd tied her mare, and, close by it, a pale scar where a pistol-ball had glanced off a boulder. Though not nearly up to Shaw's skill as a tracker, January knew enough about pistols to follow the trajectory of the shot. It had come from the thickest tangles of mesquite and rabbitbush where the creek-bed bent west, a snarled wall of grayish-green not twenty feet from the tree and thirty, at most, from the doorway of the hut.

As January suspected – and had feared – after two days

there was no trace of tracks on or around the stony creek-bed itself, though some distance down the rain-swelled watercourse he found horse-droppings that didn't look more than two days old. Someone else had poked them apart with a stick – the crotted twig lay where it had been carelessly tossed about three feet away – but having never made a study of what half-digested oats looked like, as opposed to half-digested grass and seeds, January could draw no inferences of his own.

'It does tell us that someone checked out her story, though,' Hannibal remarked, as they picked their way back up toward the jacal.

'Someone who didn't think his evidence would be believed or accepted.' January put a hand out, stopping his friend when they drew near the thicket where, he guessed, the attacker had hidden. 'That would probably be Jalisco.' The cowhand body-guards were grouped around the hut, the Tejanos smoking corn-husk cigarettos, the Nortes muttering together and spitting tobacco.

There had been, January had noted, no tobacco-spit on the rocks by the creek-bed.

'Could you hit someone between that tree and the hut?'

'Drunk or sober?'

'Sober, I hope, that early in the morning.'

'You clearly,' reproved the fiddler, 'have a very limited notion of how to spend a night on the tiles. I've never tried to ambush anyone,' he went on modestly, 'but I can't imagine even I could miss at this distance.'

January nodded, and led the way into the jacal itself.

The adobe walls were crumbling from neglect and a decade of spring rains, rafters long ago vanished to looters in quest of solid timber. Tangled mats of brown, decaying foliage that had once served as thatch hung like an ogre's filthy laundry over the walls. Rabbitbush and bullweed grew thick in the corners. On what had been a wall-bench – an adobe shelf or step, rather like a high divan, which January had seen only in the poorest jacals in Mexico – a space had been recently cleared and dusted, and he guessed that this was where Father Monastario set up a portable altar, to give Valentina what spiritual comfort he could.

He turned to the front wall of the jacal, with its two apertures – window and doorway. Both had, at one time, been framed in with wood, to hold shutters, hinges, and a door. That wood, too, had been cannibalized long enough ago to leave the exposed adobe darkened, damaged, and beginning to disintegrate.

From his pocket he took Valentina's account of her miniature siege in the jacal. *Crouched between window and door – had to keep moving back and forth between window and door because I was afraid they'd rush the house* . . .

The brush certainly grew thick enough on both sides of the jacal to make that a possibility. The dark green tangle started a dozen feet from that wall of the hut, and formed a semi-circle in front of the little building itself. 'Go stand in that brush opposite the door, if you would,' he said. 'Tell me if it's as heavy as it looks.'

As Hannibal moved toward the doorway, January disengaged a half-decayed wooden slat from among the leafy debris in one corner. 'Better take this.'

'If I get bitten by a tarantula I shall come back and haunt you.'

'You'll have trouble doing that, since a tarantula's bite isn't poisonous.'

'*Volenti via est.*' The fiddler crossed the open patch and waded into the brush, vanishing almost instantly from sight.

'Raise your staff,' called January, and the stick poked out of the glossy snarl of green brier.

When Hannibal returned to the jacal, January said thoughtfully, 'Well, it wasn't Comanche who attacked her, anyway. I'm not sure we can even call that an attack.'

The fiddler raised his brows, and poked a finger in the bullet-hole in the thick adobe of the window's side. 'I am at a loss as to what else to call it. Enlighten my darkness.'

January took a twig from the debris, and very gently inserted it into the hole. What remained above the surface of the wall pointed at an oblique angle out the window. 'That's barely more than someone yelling "Boo!" to make you hide behind a chair. Whoever was shooting could have circled easily around to the front of the house and fired straight in through the window. Or, as Valentina observed, come all the way around to that side of the house and rushed the door. Look where the other bullet-hole is.' He crossed the room in a stride, pointed to the other fresh pock in the back wall and, using the same twig, measured again the angle of its penetration.

Hannibal pressed his back to the wall between window and doorway, and looked out, as Valentina must have done Monday morning. 'Well, you certainly can't see where she tied her horse, from here. It doesn't look like a very serious attempt at murder, does it?' he added thoughtfully. 'Particularly when everyone in the county knows that it would *have* to be someone in the household, given the *cordon sanitaire* Taggart put around his land.'

'It makes sense if it was in fact Francis and Madrecita Taggart who did the murder, yes.' January walked carefully all around the jacal, poking in the matted leaves and mud on the floor, though he didn't really expect to find anything.

'You don't think it was?'

'I don't know. But it does relieve my mind of the fear that I – and you, through the kind office of your friendship – are being made a dupe of by Valentina herself. If she'd fired those shots in an effort to corroborate her own story, she'd have fired straight through the windows, not obliquely like this. And I'm guessing she'd have fired more of them.'

Hannibal sighed. 'I wouldn't put it past her, at that.' He coughed as a drift of harsh tobacco-smoke wafted through the window, and tried to wave it away with his hand. 'Although honestly, I think if the lovely Valentina were going to murder her husband in such a way as to prove herself elsewhere, I think she'd have done a much better job of it than this.'

'I think you're right.' January passed his hand again across the crumbling adobe of the wall, the sharply-angled twig where it emerged from the bullet-pock. 'Someone could have come in from the outside – either down from the northwest through Comanche country—'

'I don't know about you, *amicus meus*, but I'd need some tremendous incentive to get within stone-throwing distance of even the *possibility* of meeting Comanche.'

'We don't know what incentive the killer might have had.

It might have been tremendous. Or tremendous in his opinion, anyway. Or, he could have come up through the bottomlands. They're heavily wooded, where they aren't planted in cotton, and there isn't much chance an intruder would be seen. But on the other hand, an outsider would be less likely to have known that Ortega had been sent away the previous Wednesday. Whereas someone in the household could have engineered the dismissal with a couple of well-placed lies.'

'Myself,' remarked Hannibal, following January to the door of the jacal, 'I'd be hard-pressed to believe any of the three of them if they told me Rome had fallen. And by the sound of it, Vin Taggart shared my opinion.'

'Men can be talked into nearly anything,' murmured January, 'if it concerns a woman they consider their property.' He stopped, to let the fiddler precede him through the doorway, as was proper for a slave. 'And anyone in the household would know Valentina comes here on Monday mornings, to meet with the priest. Any one of them could have arrived here early, before her.'

'And someone in the household would be able to set up a rendezvous with Taggart in the orchard.' The fiddler dusted the dirt of the window-sill from his hands. 'I'd say someone he knew and trusted, given the fact that he'd recently insulted his most powerful neighbor.'

On the way back down the arroyo they rode stirrup-to-stirrup, Hannibal waving Creed and the Nortes to ride ahead. Quietly – and in French, because the vaqueros were close behind them – January continued, 'Whoever it was fired a few shots, enough to keep Valentina inside and afraid for her life, took the horse, and rode back to the hacienda to murder Taggart.'

'Or had a confederate do the actual shooting.'

January nodded, squinting against the sun that hovered over the rolling wonder of the Texas hills. *The most beautiful land God made*, John Dillard – the young Tennessean who had been Valentina's first husband – had told Rose once . . .

From the wooded gullies to their right he heard the skreeking of scrub-jays, and the rich warble of a vireo. The crystal brightness of the afternoon had softened, beginning to turn gold. Blue rims of shadows edged the hills.

'But why *now*?' persisted Hannibal. 'Why not wait until Taggart got over his pet and let his men get back to their proper work – so that attention wouldn't focus so particularly on the household.'

'Why indeed?' January agreed quietly. 'What changed? What's different?'

'Is that a way of telling me we'll have to search the house? Serves Francis jolly well right,' the fiddler added, 'if the Comanche *do* ride down and lift half the horses on the place, while he's keeping the men all standing guard. Surely the silly boy doesn't actually believe he can keep the law off the place while he hunts for his lost silver mine?'

'So your money's on Francis?'

'Who else could it be? I can't see Aunt Alicia plugging her nephew and galloping ten miles out to the back of beyond just to prove to Valentina that all Catholics deserve to come to a bad end.'

'Can't you?' asked January quietly. 'We know nothing about Aunt Alicia except that she spends her time fogbound on laudanum and wanders around the house in the middle of the night – and dotes to idolatry on Francis. We know nothing about Creed, for that matter.' He nodded ahead of them to the lanky cowhand, with two rifles in his saddle scabbards and a wheel-gun at his belt. 'We know nothing about Jalisco, or Enoch, or TA the cook – or any of the cowhands who come and go around the house. When it comes to murder – even a complicated and well-thought-out murder – *why* is the silliest question you can ask.'

He rubbed thumb and fingers together, like a man counting out coin. 'And sometimes,' he went on, 'you don't even need that. Though personally, I find it hard to believe that Francis would trust a confederate –' he nodded up ahead of them at Creed – 'to saddle a horse for him. Whoa!' he added, as his horse flung up its head with a startled snort.

Every man of the party – who had been watching all corners of the compass like cats in a kennel-yard – swung his attention to what had clearly spooked the animal. A coyote plunged through the long grass at the head of a gully, with a huge gray-black buzzard diving down on him, snatching with his claws. The coyote dodged, doubled, then apparently gave up and dropped whatever piece of carrion it bore in its mouth. The buzzard settled on it, the little gray wolflet trotted away. Jalisco nudged his horse at the bird and the bird, in its turn, flapped aloft again, hissing.

January saw the vaquero draw rein, looking down for a moment, and then cross himself.

Creed called out, 'Whatcha got there, *compadre?*'

It was a man's hand.

THIRTEEN

'White man.' A ruffianly Norte named Maddox dropped out of his saddle as the rest of the party drew near.

Creed said, 'Shit. I'd'a swore there been no Comanche closer than Elbow Creek since last year.'

January, too, dismounted. Behind him, and for the benefit of their bodyguards, Hannibal called out authoritatively, 'Did Dr Kerr train you to identify – er – *disjecta membra* like that, Ben?'

'Yes, sir.'

With a white man's blessing, the cowhands were prepared to let January investigate. He wrapped a bandana around his fingers, picked the horrid thing up. The wrist had been chopped through with an ax or a heavy knife, and by the look of the flesh, had remained half-attached to the arm until the coyote had torn it loose. Even this early in the year, the maggots and larvae in the wound looked healthy and plump. *Little bastards grow up fast.* Pupae, too: pale, glistening little ovals in the sour meat. The fingers flopped limp.

No calluses, no sunburn, no hair. Ink-stains on the index and middle fingers, and the edge of the hand. Clean nails, unbroken and tended. No scars, no wounds on the palm or heel, such as a man might get if he defended himself in desperation against edged steel.

He carried it to Creed first. (*No harm laying it on with a trowel.*) 'Does this look like the hand of anyone you know, sir?'

The cowhand drew back with a noise of disgust, then thought about it a moment and asked, 'You mean like scars or marks?'

'Yes, sir.' He kept his voice carefully diffident. *You're so wise and important, I'm asking you first.* 'I know it's not something a man usually notices—'

'No, no, you're right, Ben.' He bent – carefully keeping his distance – and studied more closely the intricate miracle of engineering and flesh. *How can something that practical, that well-designed – powerful and delicate, capable of wielding a pen or guiding a horse, of constructing the intricate machinery of a gun or a watch – or of comforting a child with a touch on her cheek – just grow, like bananas on a tree?*

The sandy-haired man shook his head. 'Don't look like it belongs to anybody I seen.'

'Did you see where the coyote came from, sir?' January had already spotted the area, but knew better than to lead the way, and again Creed looked gratified at being consulted.

'There.' Jalisco rose in his stirrups and pointed. 'He first came out by that oak. Witch Cave Canyon – there's caves, all the way back along the stream.'

January wrapped the hand in his bandana, and tucked it into his saddlebag. Hannibal said, 'Best if we spread out,' and, though January knew he wanted nothing but to return to the hacienda and sleep, dismounted. They both knew that none of the Nortes would stand to let a black man take the lead in the investigation.

'Lope – Maddox,' Jalisco added, 'best you keep an eye around us, though it looks to me that hand is a few days dead.'

Past the oak tree, Witch Cave Canyon was a thickly wooded cleft winding back between the hills. 'They's near a score of caves, big an' small,' Creed informed Hannibal, pointing to the uneven silvery rim of the limestone escarpment. All his wary resentment at being outjockeyed by Jalisco seemed to have vanished, in his interest in the puzzle. 'Come sundown, you'll get bats pourin' outta the ground like the smoke of Hell.'

'We lost two cows last summer, back where the canyon

ends,' put in the youth Ajo. 'There's a pool before Witch Cave, and more within it.'

'There.' Jalisco pointed to a shallow lozenge of blackness six or eight feet up the canyon wall. 'And there, see? Another, further along . . .'

'*Coyotes allá,*' put in Lope, and indeed there was a flicker in the brush of the canyon. Outside the mouth of one small cave, clear against the bright blue of the air, January saw the glitter of flies.

A lot of flies. And, the next moment, the familiar whiff of decaying flesh.

'Keep back a little, if you would,' said Hannibal, as January put a hand under his elbow to help him up the slithery slope of talus below the dark cave-mouth. 'Tracks may tell us something.'

'Maddox, Brawny.' Creed waved to his two Norte companions. 'You keep an eye down the canyon by the old road.' He broke a limb from one of the mesquite trees that grew so thick where spring floodwaters periodically nourished them, stripped it of twigs and leaves, then wrapped the end in his bandana. 'Lemme have your kerchiefs, boys . . .'

Jalisco, who had dismounted also, added his bandana to the end of the torch, along with handfuls of dried bark, bound on with the other cloth.

With Hannibal – supported by January – supposedly in the lead, the four men scrambled up the seven feet or so of slope, to the mouth of the cave.

There was scratching within. January saw the glow of coyote eyes, deeper in the cleft, where the scavengers had taken refuge from the humans.

The stink was worse, here.

Creed said, 'Shit,' in pity and disgust. The naked torso staked to the sandy floor of the cave had been slashed, across and across, and the vermin of the hills had feasted – messily – on the organs. '*Fucken* Comanche.' The body lay spread-eagled, and the bones of all four limbs had been hacked with an ax. The man was missing a foot, as well as the hand the coyote had taken. Whether the man's eyes and ears had been removed by his killers or by the local foxes and coyote, January couldn't tell, but weirdly, he didn't need them – or the rest of what remained of the face – to know who this was.

He said softly, emphasizing the servile tone of his English, 'That there look like the bald feller we saw on the boat, doesn't it, sir?' Hannibal had shut his eyes and looked away, struggling not to be sick. Not, reflected January, the persona of a masterful investigator that they needed to project. 'Comin' up from Galveston?'

The tone of his speech seemed to remind the fiddler of who and what they were supposed to be. He managed to open his eyes, though without being obvious about it – fortunately they were far enough into the cave that his effort not to vomit or faint didn't show – he didn't actually look at the body. 'You're right,' he said faintly. And then, more steadily, 'Gerry Hookwire.'

Without turning, he went on, in a voice perfectly steady, 'Mr Creed, could I get you to have your men make a litter or a travois of some kind, so we can take this man back to the hacienda? The least we can give him is a decent burial.'

'*Fucken* goddam Comanche,' repeated Creed, as Hannibal relieved him of the torch.

'Jalisco, go with him.'

The minute the two cowhands were silhouetted in departure against the light, Hannibal passed the torch to January, and sank down onto the nearest boulder like a man who'd been shot. January knelt beside the body, held the torch close. Skin color, bloating, maggots but no beetles yet. Rigor mortis mostly gone. Ants, despite the chill of the spring weather.

He glanced over his shoulder to make sure Hannibal hadn't passed out entirely, then turned back and examined the wounds. Quickly, because he didn't know how long the cowhands would be . . . then examined them again. Then, with another glance at the cave-mouth – he could hear the men's voices below, as they cut saplings, argued about whose horse and saddle-blanket were to be pressed into service – he moved further back into the cave, studying the mix of sand and fine gravel of the floor. The ceiling sloped down sharply as he moved deeper. Again he caught the glint of canine eyes.

He knelt by the body once more, and removed the rawhide thongs that bound wrists and ankles to the short stakes that held him. Checked the dirt beneath the body, around the stakes.

Twilight stained the air beyond the cave mouth. Creed, Jalisco, Brawny and Lope came scrambling up the slope, carrying a saddle-blanket for use as an improvised litter. Hannibal got to his feet and tried to look as if he, and not January, had been perusing the gruesome remains. As they carried the corpse of Gervase Hookwire down to the horses, the men told Hannibal a dozen anecdotes about Comanche outrages on women and children, on priests and traders, and speculated on how long it would take the president to send in the militia again and wipe the Comanche from the face of the earth.

While they were tying the body to an improvised travois of cottonwood saplings, January touched Hannibal's arm to draw him aside, murmured, 'That's all very well, but it wasn't the Comanche that killed him. *Tace*,' he added – Latin, for with the men so close he didn't dare touch his lips for silence, at the fiddler's startled look.

The torch was quenched in the stream. Ajo – who had evidently lost the card-cut or finger-count or however the matter had been decided – led his horse, which drew the sorry burden. January and Hannibal mounted, but followed the rest of the party slowly through the long grass of the prairie clearings at a little distance, their voices reduced to a whisper.

'You're sure about that?'

'His throat was cut,' said January. 'So far as I can tell, every other wound was inflicted after death. You've heard the mountain men talk about what the Blackfeet do to prisoners, as well as the stories about the Comanche here. But whoever mutilated that body left the genitals alone. That's what a man will do who isn't used to torture – a man who doesn't do it either as his job, or his way of displaying vengefulness, or to deliberately frighten other men into submission. The body was cut up, and chopped with an ax, to make it look like the Comanche did this, but the killing itself was done elsewhere.'

'*Why?*'

January shook his head. 'Beats hell out of me. But there wasn't enough blood under the body to have come from the cut throat. Very little blood at all, in fact. And no sign that the man had fouled himself, in terror, or pain, or death. Those stakes hadn't been driven into the ground nearly deep enough to hold against a man in real agony. The dirt around them hadn't even been disturbed. Nor the dirt under his heels.'

He turned in the saddle, glanced back along the canyon at the darkness gathering among the rabbitbush and oaks. The moon would rise in an hour or so, waning now but still bright. Nevertheless, he shivered, knowing he'd have to come back here. 'But by the blood pooled under the skin of his back he was brought here – and cut up – within an hour or so of his death.'

Looking a little greenish in the twilight, Hannibal opened his lips to speak, then closed them again. Overhead, as Creed had promised, bats were pouring from the caves behind them in the gully, like the smoke from Hell.

'What's going on?' he asked at last.

'I don't know,' said January. 'But I'll take oath he hasn't been dead more than four days.'

'Sunday, or maybe Monday.' The fiddler did a little mental arithmetic. 'But it was over a week ago that Taggart ordered his men to turn away anyone from riding across his land.'

January said, 'Yes.'

'So there's a good chance we're going to spend tonight within a few hundred feet of whoever did this. *Gloria in excelcis.* Unless of course he's out riding picket-guard by the road.'

'No,' said January mildly. 'Actually, we're not.'

'I was afraid you were going to say that, *amicus meus.* What are we going to be doing instead?'

'Searching the other caves along that canyon. The killer knew that the Comanche strip their victims. He also knew that burying the man's clothes and effects – even hiding them in a hollow tree – would be too risky. I looked to see if there were tracks leading farther back into the cave and there weren't, but given the thickness of the foliage in that gully, I don't expect he carried him far. I'm hoping it won't take us too long.'

'And I'm hoping,' said Hannibal gloomily, 'that we won't be seen sneaking horses out – either by whoever did this, or by whoever might be in his pay.'

*　　*　　*

But as Petronius had once observed, there is little point in expecting much of one's projects, when Fate has projects of her own.

It was well and truly dark by the time Gervase Hookwire's makeshift cortege reached Perdition. Because they were traveling at walking pace from the rolling limestone hills, Lope had been sent riding ahead with the news that they'd found a dead white man, tortured by the Comanche, and that the danger from that tribe was in fact greater than everyone supposed. When they reached the hacienda, they were met by Francis, limping on his ebony cane. He took one hasty look at the half-covered corpse, blanched in the light of the cressets in the courtyard, and detailed Noah, Malojo, and January to dig a grave and get him buried at once.

'We'll send for the Reverend Willet . . .' He stopped himself, calculating – January could almost hear him ticking off pros and cons in his mind – whether whatever plan he had for the production of his brother's 'will' would be derailed by the arrival of a minister on the morrow. 'We'll send for the Reverend Mr Willet tomorrow,' he finished, in a tone that told January, at least, that he had no such intention and didn't much care whether this stranger's soul went to Hell or not.

January could almost hear him thinking, *The man's dead already, why bother?*

Hannibal looked as if he would have protested, but January caught his eye, shook his head slightly. 'It makes no nevermind to me, sir,' said January, in the most cheerful-nigger voice he could muster. 'If it's all right with you, seems to me right, that the poor gentleman should have a decent grave.'

The fiddler, who like January had had several hard days in the saddle and no sleep last night, looked deeply grateful. 'You just wake me betimes in the morning, then, Ben.'

January nodded. '*Primo levis equitare*, like your old granddad used to say,' and Hannibal chuckled, as if the Latin had been an actual classical tag instead of, *We'll ride out at first light*.

January had, in fact, been wondering how to get a more detailed account during the servants' dinner, of who had been where at what times on Monday morning. According to the list that Valentina had slipped to Hannibal, Madre Taggart's maid, Melanie, carried tales to her mistress of everything that was said and done in the house. But though he winced at the thought of spending until after midnight digging a grave – and probably until almost dawn shoveling dirt back into that same hole – he knew there was no better way of unlocking a slave's lips than sharing with him a disagreeable task.

And in any case, he reflected uneasily, Hannibal looked like he would indeed be better for a night's sleep.

As would he himself.

Provided, of course, that Hannibal hadn't been right about spending the night within a few hundred feet of the man who'd slit Gervase Hookwire's throat, carried him to the cave in Witch Cave Canyon, and carved up his body.

Am I looking at one crime, or two?

Vin Taggart had land to leave, a family who detested and distrusted his young wife, and a powerful rancher reasonably near-by whose brother he'd called a coward and a pup ten days previously in front of witnesses. In Texas (or in New Orleans, for that matter) that alone constituted grounds for retribution up to and including homicide.

But why kill Hookwire, who had only arrived in Texas two weeks before?

And, re-phrasing the question: what, if anything, was there about Hookwire that someone considered worthy of murder?

Juana came down from the house as Noah and January were filling, with billets of wood, the two iron cressets that had been set in the little burying-ground. January had noted the roughly-fenced little plot between the orchard and the corrals earlier in the day, and had meant to investigate it after thoroughly looking over the scene of the murder itself. At that time – mid-morning – riding out to Arroyo Sauceito and back would leave him an hour or so of full daylight before the servants' dinner.

As it was, the handsome laundress bore a basket of tortillas and a pot of beans and beef left over from that meal, better rations than most Louisiana field-hands got.

During this makeshift supper, by the light of the flames, and afterwards for most of the remainder of the night, January had little trouble learning from his fellow gravedigger every-thing he cared to know about the household at Perdition.

'Ran all the way from Virginia to get away from 'em,' said the houseman Noah, unwrapping the loose bundle of picks and shovels. Malojo, his back to the cressets' glare, checked the loads on the two rifles he'd propped against the fence at his side. January had heard Jalisco giving orders, for Lope and Brawny to stay close to the house, and had caught the word, *Comanche.*

We probably couldn't have slipped away to search the canyon anyway, he thought, not altogether displeased. Though he had wanted to avoid anyone on the rancho learning how much he guessed about Hookwire's death, he had also had doubts about conducting such a search by torch-light.

Is Quigley riding down to San Antonio tonight to get his warrant, or will he wait til sun-up, like we'll have to do?

Damn it. Damn it.

'I thought he was gonna choke, when they came drivin' up from town with all their trunks an' plunder.' Noah shook his head, and shucked off his shirt. Though barely five-foot-five, he was muscled like a fighting-dog. 'It'd be funny, if they hadn't moved in. Elysium, their place was called back in Virginia. Enoch tell me it's a fancy word for "Heaven", an' you'd never see a place less like Heaven if you walked til your toenails bled.'

'You were there, then?'

'Born there. Worked in the stables when I was a pup, an' then in the house when Ole Marse gambled away the boys' valet, like the idiot he was. Best day of my life, when Marse Vincent took me an' Enoch, in exchange for not goin' to court over that stupid will. An' given how Marse Vincent got when *he* was drunk,' he added grimly, '*best day of my life* ain't sayin' much.'

'I heard,' said January tactfully, 'as how Old Michie Taggart drank.'

'I wouldn't mind a man drinkin', if he didn't take it out of his niggers when he was jaggered.' The small man drove his shovel into the soft earth. 'But he was mean as poison an' stupid to boot, an' Marse Jack was just like him. An' myself,

I personally wouldn't give Mama Taggart a litter of rats to raise. When Ole Marse was in Richmond, she'd thrash whatever of the housemaids he was bullin' that week – I remember when she pulled the earbobs right outta one gal's ears, left the meat hangin' bleedin', drippin' blood down on her shoulders. Texas was about as far away as Marse Vincent could run, for all the good it did him.'

'Still,' said January, 'a man can't turn away his kin.'

'Oh, can't he?' Noah sniffed. The flickering light threw the shadows of the two diggers against the other crosses in that handkerchief of consecrated ground; names and death-dates already faded to nothing. 'First thing M'am Amelia did, when they came, was tell Marse Vincent to fire all the Mexicans, 'cause they's Catholic an' takes orders from the Pope. Like the Pope got nuthin' better to do than send Jalisco letters tellin' him to murder us in our beds.'

'I got letters from the Pope,' put in Malojo, not taking his eyes from the darkness. 'I got a whole stack of 'em. But I can't read, so I don't know what they says.'

'They're probably written in Latin anyway,' pointed out January, and the older man chuckled. 'I take it Mr Taggart gave his mother some good reason why he couldn't fire three-quarters of his cowhands on short notice?'

'He coulda told her God hisself sent him engraved instructions not to, an' she'd *still* pester him about them bein' Catholic. She hates Catholics like poison. Freemasons, too. She was on after him to have us dig up Sancho an' Chapo here –' he nodded toward the crosses nearby – 'an' plant 'em over by the tack shed, rather'n leave 'em lay in the same dirt with a good Protestant like Jayce over yonder . . . who'd ride into town, get drunk, an' bugger the boys who worked at the livery-stable. White people . . .' Noah shook his head.

'But they wore on him, on Marse Vincent. M'am Amelia, an' Miss Alicia. From the start of comin' here, back when he was livin' down by the river 'fore he married M'am Valentina an' got this land, Marse Vin was for President Lamar an' Texas takin' its place among the nations of the world – *A shinin' single star in the West*, he'd say. An' Gideon Pollack been courtin' him for months, when they wasn't stealin' each others' cattle an' beatin' each others' men in town.'

'Over Texas nationhood?'

'Hell, no! Over land. In Texas, it's always about land.'

January looked around him in the darkness. 'Like there's a shortage?'

'Good land,' amended Noah. 'Meanin', land you can raise cotton on. Pollack's got three *labor* of bottomland by Onion Creek – that's not quite six hundred acres – an' the rest of his land lies too close to the Comanchería for it to be much good to him. He was maneuverin' to get Don Gael Valenzuela's share of the old San Domingo land grant – that was originally part of the San Saba Mission lands – but Don Gael deeded the whole caboodle over to M'am Valentina. Pollack kept tryin' to make up to Marse Vin, to get him to let Pollack sheep run on Perdition ranges, so Pollack could then put *all* his land into cotton.'

And if he got it, that explains what he was doing buying slaves in Galveston, thought January. 'So Michie Taggart blockin' him out of his lands was a real blow.'

'He'd have talked his way around it in a couple of weeks.' The slave gestured the problem aside with a wave. 'Gideon Pollack can talk anybody into pretty much anythin', if he gets the chance. He'd got M'am Amelia eatin' out of his hand. Let me tell you, *that's* a wonder to see! Her brother's a Congressman, see, though I didn't notice *him* offerin' her an' Auntie a room in his house when Jack the Idiot managed to lose the plantation. But she'll go along with any Texan who'll support Houston an' join the United States, so's the slave states in Congress won't get pushed around by the factory-owners an' abolitionists up North. He – Pollack – even got Aunt Alicia all in a flutter.'

'I think,' said Malojo, 'he is the only man of whom poor Doña Alicia is not afraid – with his voice like a caress, and his tender eyes.'

Did he think she'd inherit part of her nephew's lands? Or that she'd convince Francis to sell cheap?

He couldn't imagine a man that smart being that deluded.

'Taggart was Pollack's second, when some banker in Austin called him out last week.'

'Doesn't surprise me,' said Noah. 'M'am Amelia made eyes at him like a spoony schoolgirl.'

'There's a picture I can live without . . .'

'You an' me both, brother. Pollack would come here – without that wife of his – bringin' copies of the *Southern Patriot*, an' him an' M'am Amelia an' Aunt Alicia would sit out on the gallery, slangin' Daniel Webster an' John Quincy Adams, an' goin' on about the abolitionists an' how the United States needs Texas. For Pollack, politics, an' all their bullshit arguments about slavery, are more important to him than livin' every day. An' I swear Pollack was the feller behind the State Archives bein' stolen—'

'The *State Archives* was stolen?'

'Oh, hell, yes. Just this last week. Where you been?'

Hiding with an escaped slave of Pollack's . . . January saw again Quigley and his men, arguing with Torvald Ekholm before the doors of that rambling wooden house.

There is politics in town . . . Nationalists say, Houstons have done some frightful thing, and now the sheriff is seeking them all over the county.

'Why the *hell* . . .?'

'First thing President Lamar did when he took office,' provided Noah, '– well, other'n slaughterin' every Cherokee he could lay hands on – was move the capital from Houston to Austin, lock, stock, an' barrel. Mostly barrel: Houston – the town, not the general – has been hurtin' for the loss of trade an' business ever since the move. An' ever since, Houston's supporters – the general, not the town – all been sayin' how the capital ought to be moved back, so's they can be close to New Orleans an' the US trade. So just a week ago, somebody up an' broke into President Lamar's brand-new Records Office in Austin an' stole three wagon-loads of archives, tax-records, property records, government accounts goin' back to the King of Spain, an' fuck-all else, an' everybody in town's sayin' as how it was Gideon Pollack that was behind it, an' how they'll show up any day now in Houston.'

'So what's General Houston going to do with them when they arrive?' asked January reasonably. 'I mean, he can't pretend they're not there. Certainly President Lamar is going to have something to say about it.'

'Beats hell outta me. Who knows what white folks can talk theirselves into believin'? But M'am Amelia been goin' around callin' it "a blow struck for true democracy", an' Miss Alicia's been hoppin' up an' down, she's so pleased with it. I'm thinkin' that kind of finished the job of openin' Marse Vincent's eyes, as to what kind of people the Houstonites are callin' to 'em. You want some of this?' He reached up out of the grave for the gourd of ginger water that Juana had brought down from the house, and January accepted it gratefully. Though the night was deeply chilly, he was sweating.

Torch-light gleamed in the direction of the house. A moment later, a wave of stink told January that someone – it turned out to be Davy and Missouri – was carrying the remains of Mr Hookwire down to his final resting-place: evidently nobody wanted him in the courtyard anymore, and no wonder.

'*Man*,' gasped Noah, 'we gotta get that poor bastard put away . . .'

Gold eyes gleamed from the orchard trees, where every carrion-beast in Travis County seemed to be lingering beyond the light of the cressets, disappointed but hopeful.

'Best dig that hole deep,' said Malojo.

'He's all yours,' said Missouri.

Noah sighed. 'Gonna be a long night.'

FOURTEEN

For the next several hours, until the iron tongue of midnight tolled twelve (as Shakespeare – or Hannibal – would have put it), January encouraged his fellow gravedigger in his gossip about the folks at the Big House: their histories, their personalities, and where they'd been and what they'd been doing Monday morning.

It wasn't difficult. White people said slaves gossiped about what wasn't any of their business, but January knew from bitter experience, that whatever was going on in the Big House *was* the business of people who could be sold off like horses, if Daddy lost too much money at poker, or Miss Susie wanted to be sent to school in Paris. Nothing, he had learned, could be kept from the servants, to whom even small decisions made upon a whim could become matters of life and death.

So he heard how M'am Amelia, while berating Old Marse George about his drinking, always made sure there was plenty of liquor about the house. 'It kept him out of her way, see, so's she could run the place.' How Jack Taggart, from the age of fifteen, would force himself on the girls in the quarters and would dare and bully his younger brother Vin into joining him in these expeditions. 'You couldn't keep him off the girls. Abby – headwoman on the place – told me, he even bulled poor Miss Alicia when she was young. He was the same age as her, see. Had her, not once but a dozen times, *an'* pushed Marse Vincent into joinin' him.

'Alicia always was queer,' he added. 'I don't know whether it started with that, or if she was queer before it. She used to sneak out early in the mornings, saddle her own horse and ride down to the cotton fields, to stare at the men while they worked. When Old Marse'd have one of the men stripped an' whipped in the yard, you could see Alicia, peekin' around the curtains of her room, watchin' like she couldn't look away. Yet she'd run a mile, any man spoke to her. Still will, though that was a long time ago.'

A long time ago, January well knew, had nothing to do with rape. He recalled that disconcerting stare, fixed on him in the lantern-light of the street in Austin. That combination of fascination and dread. 'I take it Ole Marse George wasn't about to put up a dowry for her big enough to interest anybody in the county?'

'Marse George?' Noah's short laugh held no mirth. 'I'd have paid to see that. By the time that poor gal was fifteen, Marse George couldn't have come up with the money to give to his own daughters, let alone his wife's sister. His own daughters at least got out into society, an' did make marriages, eventually. But M'am Amelia kept a grip on her sister –' he paused, demonstrating with the hard dark knob of his fist – 'so

she never did learn how men and women talk to each other.
Just what she read in novels. No wonder she's 'fraid of men,
an' makes up stories about 'em in her head.'

Noah's account of Monday morning was substantially the
same as Missouri's had been, earlier that day (though it felt
like weeks before).

'Now that story 'bout how the three of 'em – M'am Amelia,
Aunt Alicia, an' Francis – was together in the parlor an' seen
M'am Valentina down in the orchard through some window
or other . . . That's just nonsense. You seen yourself the parlor
don't look out onto the orchard nor anywheres near it. And
yeah, there's times when the three of 'em will be playin' cards
in the parlor an' slangin' everybody they know, but not this
past week, they weren't. M'am Amelia an' Aunt Alicia weren't
speakin', on account of M'am Amelia chewin' into her sister
that Aunt Alicia had a lover . . .'

And he laughed, as January's eyebrows shot up.

'Yeah, just what I said myself when Davy told me 'bout it.
He'd got it from Melly—'

'*Could* a woman meet a lover in secret around here?' asked
January.

'Oh, hell, yeah.' Noah drove his shovel into the earth, and
paused to stretch his back. It was late in the night by that time,
the lamps in the Big House darkened except for a glow at the
northeast corner of the upper floor, where Mr Francis – Noah
said – had his 'study'. 'Most days, M'am Valentina would
ride out – cause she couldn't stand bein' stuck under the same
roof with M'am Amelia – or else do sewin' in that little boudoir
of hers, an' that suited M'am Amelia just fine. She'd sit in
the parlor, goin' over the plantation accounts or readin' the
newspapers an' drinkin'. Sometimes Aunt Alicia'd be with
her, readin' newspapers or novels or whatever, an' sneakin'
into the library where she had her laudanum hidden behind
the books. But often as not, she'd be in the library, or wanderin'
around the house searchin' it like she does, or walkin' in the
orchard . . . She coulda been anyplace, really.'

And Francis, reflected January – perennially in his 'study'
with the door locked against his aunt's befogged good inten-
tions – could in fact have been anywhere as well.

'Damn!' Noah reached up to the edge of the grave for a rock – the surface of the ground was slightly higher than his armpits by this time – and flung the missile in the direction of the still form, covered with saddle-blankets, that lay in the corner of the burying-ground farthest from the side of his prospective resting-place.

There was a frantic scurrying and two or three somethings – rats or weasels, by their size – bolted out from beneath the coarse coverings and vanished into the dark.

'Hate those goddam things. Missouri, you gotta be keepin' a better eye on our friend over there—'

'You want me to watch him, or watch for Comanche?' retorted the cowhand.

The big adobe house, pale in the moonlight, had gone dark.

And what would become of them now, January wondered. Noah, and Davy, and the cowhands Missouri and Twenty-One? What would become of the cottonhands in their tiny hamlet in the bottomlands near the river, where Vabsley the overseer locked them into their cabins every night? ('He's a Yankee from Providence, Rhode Island,' Noah had said. 'A teetotaler, an' mean as a rattlesnake. He steals the food from the plantation stores an' sells it in town.') Did Francis intend to keep Perdition, once he forged a will leaving it to himself? Or did he plan to sell the land, and the people on it, for what they'd fetch?

When Noah spoke of the cottonhands down in the quarters, something in his voice had made January wonder if he, and Enoch, and Davy, and the two cowhand slaves who had access to horses, were making plans of their own. On the frontier, as Hannibal had remarked, would it be less difficult for a black man to escape bondage? Though the risk of running into the Comanche made January's blood run cold.

It was slightly less than two hundred miles to Mexico, where slavery had been abolished in 1824 – not that the slave-owners in Mexican Texas had cared. A long way to run, and anybody's guess what would happen to you, if you were caught.

'Do you think she did it?' asked January after a time. 'M'am Valentina?'

'Not my place to think anythin'.' Noah's dark eyes glinted as he bent again to his work.

'They'd fought.'

'Wasn't the first time. Like I said, Marse Vincent drank. Hell, with M'am Amelia an' her kin there, I'd drink, too. Even before they came, he'd get morose. Shut himself up for days. It was him takin' up with that woman in Austin again, after turnin' Ortega off, that made M'am Valentina go after him the way she done Easter night. He came in late, an' dead-tired, it looked like, an' covered with dust. You think that's deep enough?'

He measured the level of the ground, which was now almost to the top of his head.

'I've never seen coyotes dig down this deep,' January agreed. He scrambled up out of the grave, holding down his hand for the shovels, and then to drag the smaller man up. The waning moon had passed its zenith. In another three or four hours, he calculated, it would be dawn. His back and shoulders felt as if he'd been beaten with a hoe-handle, and the thought of getting up before sunrise to investigate Witch Cave Canyon made him want to scream and bury his head in a cotton-sack.

But he made himself lay lengths of rope around the wrapped form of Mr Hookwire (*may he rot in Hell*) and pray over him, translating what he knew of the Mass for the Dead. 'Our help is in the name of the Lord who made Heaven and Earth . . . May Almighty God be merciful to thee, and forgiving thee thy sins, bring thee to life everlasting . . . Thou, O God, will turn again, and bring us to life, and Thy people will rejoice with Thee . . .'

'Them's Catholic prayers?' asked Noah, when they had lowered Mr Hookwire – whoever the hell he was, whatever the hell he'd been doing in Texas, however the hell he'd actually died – into his nameless grave. January had placed the detached hand in the folds of the old saddle blanket, leaving it wrapped in his bandana. *I'll buy another bandana . . .*

'That's them.'

'They don't sound so bad.'

'They're not.'

Putting the dirt back into the hole took less time than taking it out, but each shovelful, now, was like a red-hot knitting-needle jabbed into January's back.

Noah went on thoughtfully, 'Anybody can steal a shawl an' a pistol, you know. M'am Valentina had about four pistols – Ortega was teachin' her how to handle a wheel-gun. She kept 'em all on the top shelf of her armoire. An' anybody coulda made an appointment with Marse Vincent, to meet him in the orchard.'

He shrugged. 'She have reason to kill him? Depends on how you feel about gettin' hit by your husband, or havin' him turn off your servants, or buy a house for another woman in town. M'am Valentina's a proud woman, a ranchero's daughter from Mexico – you say your master's a friend of her daddy? Most of this land by rights is hers. Depends on how you feel about the promises a man makes to his wife.

'Anybody else have reason to kill him?' Noah cocked an eyebrow at January, and stomped the mound of loose earth above the grave. 'Hell, white folks kill each other in Texas all the time.'

Returning at last to the house, January washed himself first in the courtyard pump, then, more thoroughly, in the laundry-room (where it was warmer and where lukewarm water could be dipped from the copper). Barefoot and damp, he stole through the kitchen, the dining-room, and the big central hall, and thence up the backstairs (tripping again on the loose step) and into the long rear gallery – unheated and with its barred windows open into the night – where his pallet lay unrolled, just outside the guest-room where Hannibal lay.

Softly he opened that door, and saw his friend, barely a suggestion of a skeleton form beneath a pile of striped trade-blankets, in the thin slats of moonlight that leaked through the shutters. Closing the door, January stripped to his shirt, then paused to look out the gallery windows to the dim shape of the orchard, visible as a dark tangle in the moonlight. He could see the burying-ground, the final embers burning to extinction in the cressets. The dark rectangle of Gervase Hookwire's grave.

A middle-aged, chubby, bald man in a gray frock coat and

spectacles, clinging to the rail of the schooner *Rosabel* with one hand and clutching his satchel to his bosom with the other. January had not spoken a word to him, had barely noticed him, save to wonder why his appearance on the deck had caused Hannibal to vanish so precipitously below. *The Countess Mazzini always called him Gerry . . .*

Buried by strangers, in a foreign land.

Virgin Mary, Mother of us all, bless him in his stranger's grave. Whoever he was, whyever he came into this country. Give him rest.

He lay down on his pallet, which was no more than a tick stuffed with cotton flocking and covered with two trade blankets. It was warmer and more comfortable than the bedrolls he'd occupied on the ride from Houston to Austin. He knew that many planters still, in this day and age, had their valets unroll such pallets in their bedrooms, as a matter of course, and sleep beside their beds on the floor like dogs.

I suppose it beats getting out of your blankets on a cold night to look for the chamber pot . . .

His back and shoulders had begun to stiffen and he knew he'd be in agony when he woke in the morning – *far* too soon, now . . .

Movement at the door which led into the main hall, from the gallery where he lay. For a moment he saw her, standing in the half-open French doors, the gleam of her spectacles catching the moonlight as she gazed at him.

Though he couldn't see her expression, January felt the hair on his scalp creep. In her black dress, the only things visible were her thin face with its shiny round lenses, the fingers of her lace-mitted hands.

Watching him.

Trying to understand something of an alien species, a creature she feared? Trying to figure out how to negotiate with some strange and terrible creature, as she saw her sister and other women negotiate, manipulate, control?

Or . . . What?

She stood there in the doorway for perhaps five minutes, silent as a ghost not yet dead, nearly invisible in the darkness. Just looking.

Then she turned away. He didn't even hear her footsteps as she left.

After what seemed like a long time, he heard the rattle of the well-chains near the corrals, and the muffled hoof-beats of the night-riders coming in. Birds in the orchards cried their territories, answering the crowing of Juana's chickens. Someone was singing a corrido about a desolate lover and a crow. The smell of pre-dawn kitchen fires gritted in the air.

FIFTEEN

Getting Hannibal Sefton out of bed, upon those occasions on their travels when it became necessary to do so, was not, January reflected, markedly more difficult now that he was sober than it had been in the days when the fiddler had lived on a steady diet of laudanum and sherry. Rose said it was the Irish in him, and wisely scheduled his lessons to her scholars in music and Greek for late in the afternoons.

January took the precaution of stealing down to the kitchen and trading gossip with the cook for a cup of coffee. TA – a man almost as tall as himself and vastly heavier – had heard all about the dead stranger and was gratified to get the details of his discovery ('You remember to toss that hand into the grave 'fore you filled it up?' 'That I did . . .'), and generously offered the shards of two broken jars, to bury in the loose earth around the stranger's grave to keep the witches away.

('What's TA for?' 'Titus Andronicus. Used to be just Titus, but my old marse, he stuck on the other. Said it was a guy famous for his cookin'.')

Hannibal groaned and struggled when January woke him, and, sitting up in bed, coughed like a dying horse for about five minutes, his long hair draggling in his eyes. January listened with the ears of a physician and a friend, torn between genuine concern for a man who was dear to him and genuine concern for his own safety. Though Hannibal's health was better these days, he knew that no one ever really recovered from consumption of the lungs.

Pneumonia would finish him. January knew that, as surely as he knew his name.

And were Valentina in fact arrested for her husband's murder, no matter how temporarily, it would be a long way to Galveston for a black man on the run.

First things first. Hookwire's murder may have nothing to do with the person who killed Vin Taggart . . .

And pigs may fly.

Gamely, Hannibal downed the coffee and dressed, in his threadbare coat and long, elaborately-wrapped cravat, such as dandies had worn in Beau Brummell's day, his graying hair queued in a tail down his back. He followed January down the stairs and out into the cindery gray of a cold pre-dawn. In fact, as Valentina had said, it was an easy matter to get their horses from the corral, their saddles from the tack-shed, and ride out without anyone being much the wiser, with the exception of Valentina, who came hurrying from the house wrapped in a long cloak and a manga – an embroidered rain-cape, rather like a large and heavy shawl. Her soft, fair curls were hastily pinned up and January guessed that she wore little more than a night-rail and dressing-gown beneath the cloak. *Enough to give Aunt Alicia a seizure.*

'Where are you going?' Her eyes had a wildness to them, like a hunted deer.

'Witch Cave Canyon,' returned January soothingly. 'The man we found wasn't killed by the Comanche – I'll explain to you when we get back – and I want to find his things.'

He saw her eyes go to the back of his saddle, and then to Hannibal's. Noting the lanterns, the coil of rope quietly pilfered from a tack-shed. Looking, he guessed, for saddlebags, which would have told her they were running away and deserting her. As others had, he thought, leaving her alone . . .

Gently, he removed the hand she'd laid on his sleeve. 'We'll be back,' he promised. 'Within a few hours, I hope. Don't tell anyone you've seen us, or where we've gone. I don't trust your brother-in-law and I don't trust his men.'

She stepped back, trying to put a brave front on herself, but he could see the fear in her eyes. 'I'm sorry—'

He shook his head. 'We'll get you out of this, madame. But let everyone go on thinking the man we buried last night was killed by the Comanche. Let everyone think we think so, too. See if you can get word to your Father Monastario, that we'd like to meet with him, and hear what he may know of all this.' (*And have a look at him, to see if he* is *young and handsome* . . .) 'Now don't hold us up.' He stepped up into the saddle, and Hannibal, too, mounted with a light sureness that belied his bedraggled appearance.

'*He feels each limb with wonted vigor light,*' proclaimed the fiddler, with an extravagant salute. '*His beating bosom claimed the promis'd fight!*'

They headed off, at a hand-gallop, for the hills.

At least, thought January, *we won't have to be worried about the Comanche ourselves.*

Yet he kept glancing over his shoulders, and around him, at the stands of oak, and the long grasses of the prairies through which they rode. In the pocket of his jacket he carried the list Valentina had written out for Hannibal, of who could be trusted, and under Eli Creed she had written, *Came to work in October when Mdre Taggart insisted white vaqueros. Obeys Francis rather than me.*

Does Francis trust him? he wondered. *Enough to make him accomplice to murder?*

Somehow he couldn't see it. Or was it in fact the other way around? Was Francis *Creed's* minion?

And as he rode – trying to make sense of landmarks he'd only seen once, going the other direction, with night coming on – his mind counted and shuffled dates and times.

Sixty miles to San Antonio. *If Sheriff Quigley started riding Wednesday night when he left here, he'd reach the old Spanish town this morning.* How long to find his nationalist judge? What if the man had left town? *How long do we have then?*

How long before Francis finishes forging Vin Taggart's will, if that's what he's doing? How good a forger is Francis? Surely Valentina has samples of her husband's handwriting.

Is there anyone in Austin who knows enough about handwriting to credibly dispute it?

Cattle raised their heads from the shoulder-high prairie grass, horns like the bizarre limbs of trees. A rabbit bolted in panic from the approach of the hooves.

A list of people he needed to talk to: Father Monastario, Ortega, Vin Taggart's banker (*would that be Stanway? A job for Hannibal . . .*)

Taggart's mistress, if possible.

No time, he thought. *No time.*

Vin Taggart's family arrives from Virginia in October. In October also, Taggart turns his back on his long-professed hopes for Texas as a free nation and joins forces with Pollack, a man he formerly hated. Likewise in October, Taggart forbids his Catholic wife to ride into Austin on Sundays to hear Mass, but turns a blind eye on her Monday-morning rendezvous with the priest until April. How are these things related?

Was Valentina in fact Ortega's mistress?

Was she Father Monastario's?

Where is Ortega now?

He remembered the shape of the oak, where the coyote had first appeared. Found the original cave without trouble. Hannibal remained down on the canyon floor with the horses, where the remains of an old road made the ground level by the stream. January didn't like the way the fiddler's dark brows stood out on a face still chalky with exhaustion, and in any case his chief job, really, was to make sure January didn't encounter anyone who thought he could get away with kidnapping a black man to sell.

He thought again of what he'd said yesterday, about the size of Perdition, and the fewness of the men tasked with keeping 'outsiders' away. Surely Comancheros, bandits, and slave-stealers would know this. Would guess that one only had to ride north through Comanche country, or come up stealthily, one at a time, through the cotton lands along the river.

Gideon Pollack would know this, too.

Yet Gervase Hookwire – last seen alive on the deck of the *Rosabel*, clutching his satchel to his chest on the eighth of April – had died, probably in this canyon, eleven days later

– Easter Day. Eight days after Vin Taggart had ordered his men to keep all outsiders off his land. He had trouble picturing that tubby, soft-handed little man, blinking behind his spectacles, riding north through Comanche country to come down into Perdition land from the north-west.

What the hell was in his satchel?

Did Taggart know he was here?

Is this a part of Taggart's murder? Am I looking at two crimes, or one?

Enough time had passed between Hookwire's death and the discovery of his body, that January couldn't find tracks or traces in the talus-slope beneath the cave. From his satchel he took Rose's spyglass, and from the cave's mouth, scanned the eastern wall of the canyon opposite him. Then he scrambled down a little distance to get a view of the western canyon to the left, upstream of where he stood. Even for a man of his own great strength, he wouldn't have welcomed the chore of bearing a dead man's body any great distance through the thick growth of oak and juniper that choked the stream-bed.

Not Francis. Or either of the women.

Well, he reconsidered, *Madrecita, maybe. Or maybe if Hookwire had been a smaller man.*

Creed would certainly know the canyon well enough to get a man from one cave to another. Following whose orders?

There was a sort of a trail along the top of the talus slope, above the thickness of the trees. January worked his way upstream for a distance, and he thought he could have carried a body along it if he had to. Down below, he could glimpse the rusty green of Hannibal's coat, as the fiddler followed with the horses along the old track. The cliff bulged, and the slope descended; he saw a small cave some eight feet above him. Though he was fairly sure nobody could have got a body down from there (*And what would Hookwire be doing* up *there to begin with?*), he scrambled up to check.

Nothing.

What would *Hookwire be doing up here?* The thought re-phrased itself again: *what would he be doing on Perdition in the first place?*

Two crimes or one?

Slithering down to the top of the talus was ten times more difficult than climbing up, and the rock debris clattered and slipped beneath his boots. Somewhere close by he heard the dry, deadly buzz of a rattlesnake, but couldn't see where it hid. Above the canyon rim, full light had come into the sky. Everybody on Perdition would know by this time that he and Hannibal had ridden out someplace.

He knew the second cave he saw was the one he wanted, by the green glitter of flies that still hummed around its mouth. Not nearly as bad as the swarms that had attended Hookwire's mutilated corpse, but enough to be noticed. This cave-mouth was larger, and lower down, tucked behind another shoulder of cliff. The cave, when January stepped into it, was higher than the others, and deep in its dark throat he could see the gray shapes of stalagmites and stalactites, such as he had encountered in the south of France.

The flies were thicker there.

He scrambled down the slope to where Hannibal waited. 'This is the place. Want to come up? I'd welcome a second pair of eyes.'

The fiddler tied the horses ('I'm going to be very cross if someone comes along and steals them . . .'), removed the lantern, torches, and the coil of rope from behind his saddle, and scrambled up after January, panting like a bellows but shaking his head at the offer of assistance. In the opening of the cave January scratched a Lucifer-match from the tin tube of them that he always carried, and kindled both lantern and brands.

The green-black bodies of the flies glittered eerily against the dark. As they walked toward the cluster of gray, melted-looking columns that half-screened the black interior from the cave's outer chamber, January heard the scratch and scramble of small vermin – *foxes? Weasels?* – deeper in, and wrinkled his nose against the whiff of old garbage and stale human waste.

Gold eyes winked in the dark, close to the ground and resentful at the intrusion.

'Here.' The dark stain lay a few feet beyond the stalagmites.

Flies hovered around it, drawn by the smell of it, soaked into the pebbles of the cave floor.

Several days old. Nearly black.

January lowered his torch, to better illuminate the stain. Hannibal stayed behind him, aware at first sight – as was January – of the cryptic tangle of scratches, gouges, and scuffs on the gravel and sand.

'Table there, it looks like,' said January after a moment, studying the marks. 'Those four little dints. He must have been sitting in a camp-chair. See where the legs scraped.'

The fiddler murmured, 'Must have turned over when he was – um – interrupted. Look there near that crack in the wall . . .'

January looked, and then, very carefully, stepped to pick up the object Hannibal had seen.

There were two of them, actually . . .

'Brings back my schoolroom days,' mused Hannibal. 'My tutor was an absolute fanatic about cutting them. He'd only use – and would only permit *me* to use – swan-feathers, and only the first three on the wing.'

'The masters at St Louis Academy would crack our knuckles with a ruler if we didn't prepare our own.' January turned the two quills over in his fingers, while Hannibal held the torch close. 'A woman named Zalie used to sell them on the Rue du Levée, ready stripped of the vanes. I think he could smell them and tell whether we'd cheated and bought them.' He rubbed his knuckles reminiscently, thinking of that outsize, too-black-for-polite-society boy he'd been, laboring over his penmanship lessons at the back of the class.

'But these are fresh,' he added. 'I didn't think anybody used quills anymore.'

'Fresh indeed.' Hannibal lowered his torch, to where another stain – free of flies, much smaller, and darker – blotted the cave floor. He knelt, carefully, to sniff. 'There's the ink. You said our friend's fingers were stained.'

The two men moved back into the darkness. His experience in caves – both in France, and in the horrible hollows of the old pyramids at Rancho Mictlán – told January to carry his lantern low and step carefully. Close to the bloodstain, and the scraped marks on the cave floor, he saw the hollows where a place had been scooped to lay out a bedroll; he guessed where the man's food-waste had been disposed of, and was fairly sure that the place would have been used as a privy as well.

He was right. The passageway at the back of the cave narrowed and twisted, the ceiling lowering until January and even Hannibal had to bend to avoid the toothy spikes. Around a curve of the passageway a pit gaped, some thirty feet deep, and the damp air that rose from it bore the smells of a short term of human residence. When January held his lantern down, its light glinted on broken glass.

'Inkwell,' guessed Hannibal. 'Look, there's another quill.'

'What was he writing?' January looped the rope around the stoutest of the stalagmites, jerked on it several times, then dropped it over the pit's edge. It wasn't a sheer drop, and the rock had been much soiled and smeared from its usage as a privy. January studied and counted for a moment, then said, 'Looks like he was here three or four days. Somebody must have known it, since he had food – not to speak of a table and a chair and a bedroll . . .'

'Why not dump his body down here as well?' Hannibal held both lanterns out over the rim of the pit as January, hanging onto the rope, edged down the steep slope.

'Not deep enough. Coyote could get down – and back up. Somebody was bound to notice, if scavengers started prowling around the cave. It's Jalisco's job, and Creed's, and the job of every man on the place, to notice if it looks like some living thing has died back in these canyons – or maybe hasn't died, but has just gotten itself trapped. A man's body would have to be accounted for.'

He balanced on the steeply slanted floor, where the pit narrowed to a very uneven cone. The table – a light camp-table, such as military men used on campaign – had been thrown down first, along with the folding camp-chair, the bedroll last. 'Trade-blanket.' He picked it up – then dropped it as a dozen white, gelatinous-looking little spiders scrambled wildly out of the striped wool.

'Like the blanket on my bed back at the hacienda?' inquired Hannibal.

'Just like those very ones.' Wishing he'd brought a stick
with him, January prodded with the toe of his boot at the ruins
of the chair, flipping it aside to reveal a man's blood-crusted
shirt and piss-crusted drawers, and beneath them the gray coat,
blue-and-yellow waistcoat, and checked trousers he remembered seeing on the *Rosabel*. 'And I might add,' he continued,
'like the ones on every other bed we've slept in since we
reached Texas: in Galveston, in Houston, on the trail, at
Eberly's Tavern, and at the Ekholms'.'

Boots and socks lay close by. A pair of spectacles clinked
and fell out of the coat, like the skeleton of a murdered pixie.
Underneath all that – lying on top of the garbage and the
sewage – a pair of saddlebags.

January put those over his shoulder, shook out the clothing
very carefully and rolled it into a bundle which he tied into
the end of the rope, and climbed back up, thinking every foot
of the way that he felt more of those nasty little white spiders
creeping around the back of his neck.

They sat in the daylight at the mouth of the cave – the sky
bright now above the canyon, though shadow still filled it, all
save a sharp line of gold on the rocks above their heads – and
opened the saddlebags.

One contained three shirts and four pairs of drawers, one
still clean, three obviously worn. There were socks, shaving
gear, soap, and a toothbrush, as well as a copy of Dryden's
Aeneid and four twenty-dollar gold pieces.

The other bag held the satchel that Hookwire had been
clutching on board the *Rosabel*. Opening it, January found
half a dozen trimmed quills, three pen-knives, three bottles of
ink, two steel-nibbed pens, a box of spare nibs, three candles,
five sticks of sealing-wax in various colors, and several packets
of paper.

No, thought January, turning them over in his fingers. *Not
paper*. Or not all of them paper. 'Parchment?' He ran a testing
finger along its edge. 'And this is vellum – who writes on
parchment?' Two other bundles *were* paper, old, yellow, stiff,
and blank. A little further exploration at the bottom of the
satchel unearthed a half-dozen small glass jars, which
contained what looked like lamp-black, powdered ochre, the

soft brown pigment known to artists as umber and another
of the redder dust called sienna, and a slightly larger jar of
powdered chalk.

There were also four small blocks of wax, wrapped carefully
in blue paper; some soft enough to be molded with January's
powerful fingers, but one harder, almost like the modeling clay
his friend Carnot had used back in Paris.

'He was an artist,' he said softly.

Hannibal sniffed, almost a derisive laugh. 'Oh, I'd say so,
yes,' he agreed. 'But not the way you mean.'

January looked at him in surprise. 'I thought you said you
didn't know him.'

'I didn't – bar having seen him at the Countess Mazzini's
bagnio a time or two. But I know what all that paraphernalia
is, because I use it all the time myself. At least,' he added,
taking the packets of yellowed paper and unfolding the sheets,
'I've used some of them.' He held them up to the light for a
watermark, examined the edges where they had been scuffed
and browned. 'And old Bridemere, who tutored me at Oxford,
God bless his sticky-fingered soul, in things Balliol College
never knew of, had the whole kit: papers of various ages and
colors, inks of different strengths and consistencies, quills of
different sorts that could be trimmed and shaped to match
whatever tricks of handwriting any given don of the college
– or any father or banker to my friends, I daresay – could
come up with.

'The powders are a nice touch,' he added approvingly. 'He
can discolor any document when he's finished with it, to any
degree of age or decrepitude desired. And I'll bet . . . Yes.'
He picked up one of the little knives, which turned out to be,
not a penknife as January had thought, but a very fine-bladed
scalpel. 'For carving seals,' he explained. 'Or removing them
from one document, to be placed elsewhere. Very pretty.

'I'm not sure what our friend was doing here,' he added,
into January's astounded silence, 'or why someone thought it
a good idea to murder him. But whyever he was here, just
off-hand, I'd say our friend appears to have been a professional
forger.'

SIXTEEN

L ike Hannibal, Gervase Hookwire possessed seven sets of visiting cards, each set bearing a different name and a different city of residence, ranging from Paris to Chicago. January had not heard enough of the bald man's speech to guess at a point of origin, but he was interested to note that three of his bogus addresses were in the upper South: Lexington, Kentucky; Baltimore; and Richmond, Virginia. The box of Lucifer matches which was in his coat pocket with them was also marked as coming from a manufacturer in Virginia.

Nothing in the clothing, or the saddlebags, provided information as to who had brought the dead man from New Orleans – where Hannibal had seen him – to Texas, or for what purpose.

The man was, after all, January reflected wryly, *a professional.*

'I don't suppose there's any way of proving where Eli Creed was on Monday morning, when Madame Valentina was being shot at,' he said thoughtfully, folding the clothing into a bundle and stowing it – and the forger's kit – in the saddlebags. 'Or on Easter Sunday, when I'm guessing Hookwire was killed. We'll need to find some way to ascertain Creed's movements Sunday and Monday without letting him know we're asking. But any of the three – Francis or his adoring mother and aunt – could easily have brought Taggart to the orchard with a note.'

'And gotten close enough to him to shoot him point-blank,' agreed the fiddler. 'Which I'm not sure Creed could have done. But if Hookwire were forging a will for Brother Francis—' Hannibal leaned his back against the rocks of the cave-mouth, and pressed his hand to his side to still another spasm of coughing. 'What's his customer doing cooped up in the study? Unless Francis knew of Hookwire's death before we arrived . . . But if Francis was paying Hookwire, why have a hand in his brother's murder before those "written instructions" – let alone the will – were complete? This was obviously planned days – if not weeks – before Taggart was actually killed.'

'Somebody's certainly playing a double game.' January frowned into the tops of the oaks below the cave-mouth, each emerald leaf now edged in morning light. 'It might not be Francis, you know.'

'Who else *would* it be, then?'

Again, January shook his head. 'According to Valentina, there isn't much Madrecita Taggart wouldn't do to guarantee her son four hundred thousand acres of Texas land, but it's a far cry from adoration to murder . . .'

'Farther for some than for others,' remarked Hannibal. 'Shall we keep the gold, at least? We're going to need getaway money if Valentina's arrested—'

January buckled the saddlebags, stood up and slung them over his shoulder, and held down a hand to pull his friend to his feet. 'I think we'd better leave it as it is for now. We're going to need this as proof for *someone* – or against someone – and right now, we don't know what the presence of the gold proves.'

'I'd say it proves that God helps those who help themselves,' sighed Hannibal, 'and we may regret your devotion to due process when we're trying to talk our way onto a ship without a penny to pay its captain, but have it your way. That cave back there that you had to climb up to?'

'Should do.'

Hannibal scrambled cautiously down to the horses, while January re-traced his steps along the top of the crumbly debris slope to the higher cave he'd earlier visited. He concealed the saddlebags in the rocks far at the back, where the passageway narrowed to barely a foot in diameter, then nearly broke his neck when he lost his footing climbing down the talus to the bottom of the canyon.

'Would a tracker like Shaw be able to guess you'd been up there?' asked Hannibal, helping him to his feet and dusting him down.

'I am *not* going back up there to move the satchel.' January flexed his arms, scratched the gravel out of his close-cropped hair, and picked up his hat. 'Shaw could probably guess where we'd been and what we'd been doing if we'd done all this by hot-air balloon.' He mounted, and they rode down the canyon. The sky was clear, sharp blue above, the line of gold daylight halfway down the canyon's western rim.

In Texas, everything is about land, Noah had said.

Last month, someone writes to Gervase Hookwire in New Orleans, bringing him to Texas to do a job . . . unless of course Francis met him by chance in Houston. But how would he have done that?

In either case, Francis brings him to Perdition, presumably to forge Vin Taggart's will, preparatory to murdering his brother in such a way as to put the blame onto his Tejano wife. He comes after *Vin Taggart has put up his men around the property to keep Gideon Pollack's riders away. So he would need the connivance of* someone *on the property . . .*

Then either on Easter Sunday, or on Monday while Taggart is actually being murdered, Hookwire is killed . . .

To cover up his role in the forging of the will?

Did he demand more money? A share of Perdition?

And what the hell was he doing, performing his task in a cave halfway up Witch Cave Canyon anyway? To judge by the dead man's figure, and the probable cost of his clothing and linen, he'd have preferred the warm, clean comfort of the Capital City Hotel in Austin.

To keep him from prying eyes? *Probably.*

January frowned into the sharp morning sunlight as they passed from beneath the limbs of the oak tree and into the long grass of the prairie beyond.

What else is going on?

From a distance, he could see no scrum of horses around the hacienda which would have warned that Quigley had turned up with a warrant and a posse earlier than expected. Smoke curled from the kitchen chimneys, reminding him that he was ravenous. The tortillas and coffee he'd cadged from Titus Andronicus in the pre-dawn blackness had been a long time ago.

They approached the house from the north-east, and tied their horses at the edge of the orchard, though January had little hope of finding anything of use three days after the murder. He knew roughly where the killing had taken place – the place where two trees had been hit by lightning was an obvious rendezvous.

'I don't suppose anyone would write a note, *Meet by the seventy-third tree from the left in the twenty-fourth row,*' Hannibal remarked, as they waded through the orchard's long grass to the spot. The open area around the stumps of the two dead trees was visible ahead of them as a sunnier patch among the green shade. Bees already swarmed among the white and pink blossoms overhead.

Taggart's horse, Noah had said, had been found, saddled, tied at the far side of the orchard; the same horse he'd had out earlier that day, when he'd ridden down early in the morning to talk to the overseer of his cotton lands. A note would easily have brought the rancher to this place at some specified hour.

But a note saying what?

How many of the vaqueros, or the house servants, could write?

What excuse would someone in his household – his mother, his brother, his aunt – have to arrange a rendezvous here, in secrecy, when they could meet just as comfortably in the house?

January could guess. *'They're forging your will – they plan to murder you. I don't know who's in on it, so meet me in the orchard.'*

Maybe even a less intimate acquaintance could have gotten away with it, but probably no one from outside of Perdition.

And whoever it was, had been able to step up close to him and put a pistol against his chest.

A double game again. Played against whom?

The long, springy grass around the two dead stumps bore no trace of the body that had lain there, or of footprints coming or going. January searched the ground without any real hope of finding anything, and wasn't disappointed. That Valentina's shawl had been found 'nearby', along with a pistol known by the household to be hers, he disregarded. Evidently the entire household knew where she kept such things.

'Any thoughts?'

Hannibal shook his head. 'I did try two or three times last night to get into Brother Francis's "study",' he admitted. 'It's that little "cabinet" chamber off his bedroom, at the opposite end of the upstairs gallery where you sleep—'

'When have I ever slept there?'

'Don't be a sissy, Benjamin, you got two whole hours last night. He keeps it bolted from the inside, and I couldn't well pick the lock on his bedroom door and get through that way unobserved. Even in the middle of the night, when I woke I could hear Aunt Alicia walking about the house in pitch darkness, humming to herself – "The Harp of Love", I believe it was.'

He turned to look back in the direction they'd come, where the hills were just visible above the new-leafed tangle of the trees. 'But if it isn't Francis behind it – or his mother – why else would someone murder Taggart? Ones political or social enemies would presumably do so in a duel, à la Pollack . . . *Is* there a lost mine on the property?'

'If there is,' said January, falling into step behind him as they waded through the deep grass back toward the horses, 'Valentina will be able to tell us.'

'Not lost, exactly,' said Valentina, when they put the question to her a half-hour later in the laundry-yard behind the kitchen. She had clearly been watching for their return – or had assigned Enoch or one of the housemen to tell her when they rode in – and had come hurrying out to them as they turned their horses over to Malojo among the corrals. Had listened in startled bafflement to the account of the finding of Hookwire's personal effects, and of the deductions which could be inferred from them. Francis, she had reported, had come to breakfast looking tired and haggard, but had brushed aside the anxious urgings of his mother and aunt about what he should eat, or the medicine he should take, or which doctor he should send for from Austin ('I have no need of a doctor and I will not have my brother's last orders violated until I find his will!'). He was, she informed them, back in his study now, with the door locked.

'No surprise there,' remarked Hannibal.

She hadn't seen whether there was ink on his hands or not.

She went on, 'There's an old Spanish copper mine in Witch Cave Canyon, but it ran dry years ago. Everyone knows about it. It's the first place – I think the only place – Francis actually visited. That's why there was a road at one time, going up the canyon.'

'What about the other mines?' asked January. 'Your uncle owned this land . . .'

Valentina thought about it for a time, then shook her head. 'There were rumors, of course, about the San Diablo Mine, northwest of here and deep in the hills. I've never been that far, and my husband said it was all nonsense. The land, he said, had been controlled by the Comanche even when the Spanish ruled. No one could have gotten workers in, or brought silver out. Jalisco would know.'

'Jalisco knows this territory?' On Valentina's list, Jalisco's name had been marked, *Confianza. Trustworthy.*

'Jalisco worked for my uncle, and for Grandfather Valenzuela when he first got this land from the king. Well, the land had originally been part of the San Saba mission grant, but the Comanche destroyed the mission back, oh, I don't know how long ago. In any case, Jalisco has about six blood-brothers in the Comanche and three among the Comancheros. He would know if there's actually a mine up there or not.'

Valentina called out across the dusty mazes of corral to Malojo, to saddle fresh horses for Don Hannibal, Enero, and herself. 'He'll be down on the road in the bottomlands today,' she said, as they walked back to the house for her to change into riding clothes. 'It drives him mad – Señor Creed, too, the first time I've ever seen those two agree to anything between them – that they and their men are patrolling the property lines against imaginary intruders, when the cattle are wandering about getting themselves tangled up in the canyons, or for all they know Comanche are sneaking down from the north and helping themselves to the mules and the horses. And Francis, of course, is no help, and swears he will fire the first man who doesn't do as he is ordered.'

She stopped in the hall at the foot of the stairs, her face suddenly hard. '*He*, to be giving orders! I have not even been convicted of this stupidness! Yet the men – even Jalisco and his Tejanos! – they think I will be hanged for it, and Francis come into the whole of the rancho. Or maybe,' she went on, still more softly, 'they think that I will flee. Men!'

She turned with a swirl of dark skirts, and hurried up the stair.

But when she came down, less than ten minutes later, clothed for riding, Madame Amelia stepped into the hall from the parlor, tall and strangely jagged-looking in her mourning black and smelling of bourbon whiskey over the heavy reek of perfume. 'And where do you think you're going?'

'Riding.' Valentina's chin came up. She seldom spoke English – all her conversation with January and Hannibal was in Spanish – but her command of the language, though heavily accented, was crisp and pure. 'And why should you have objection to that, madame?'

'You know perfectly well why, girl. You walk around here, as if you think it doesn't matter that you murdered my son! As if you consider yourself free to come and go as you please! Well, let me tell you, when that spineless traitor Quigley comes back, you'll be lucky if you aren't strung up from the nearest tree instead of arrested and made to stand your trial!'

The young widow's eyes blazed. 'I want to stand my trial!' she snapped back. 'I want my husband's true murderer – or murderers – to come to justice, the person – or people – who seek to slander my name and steal my property!'

Behind Madame Taggart, Aunt Alicia emerged from the library, which was – January craned his head to look past her – a sort of back-parlor containing about a dozen books and many boxes and shelves of newspapers. Behind their spectacles, Alicia's eyes were bruised from weeping and hazy with opium, but she stared at Hannibal, and then at January, with her usual unwinking intentness.

'They're going to hang you,' she said. 'Why don't you just ride away, like Amelia says? Amelia will have them give you a horse.'

Valentina turned and made for the front door, but her mother-in-law strode to intercept her, caught her by the arm, and jerked her around to face her. The two women stood, furious, face to face, the younger shaking with rage, the older with the look of a dog about to bite. Then Valentina pulled her arm to free herself. Madame's hand tightened – big hands, January noted, strong as a man's – and without a word Amelia slapped her.

'Ladies—' began Hannibal, and Aunt Alicia scuttled forward into the hall, flapping her hands at her sister.

January – with instinctive tact (and the self-preservative instincts of a slave-child who'd be beaten for overhearing what he wasn't meant to overhear) – stepped back into the library.

'Riding,' Alicia giggled, tugging at Amelia's sleeve and rolling her blue eyes at Hannibal. 'She's going riding with a *man.*'

Amelia turned and slapped her across the face. 'Shut up! You have a mind like a sewer, Alicia; I'm sick of the sight of you.' And to Valentina, as Aunt Alicia cowered away and began to weep again, 'Don't make me call Enoch and have you put off this place like the hussy you are, girl.'

'This is *my* house—'

'Don't tell me it's *your* house, I'm purely sick of hearing that puke about it being *your* house. Enoch!' yelled Amelia. And, raising her voice to a bellow that could be heard in the kitchens, '*Enoch!*'

January heard the swift clip-clip of Valentina's boot-heels ascending the stair, Hannibal's diffident, 'Please excuse me for intruding—'

'There's no excuse for your intruding and don't think I don't know what you're up to,' snapped Amelia. 'All that bush-wa about being a friend of her father's and how you just *happened* to meet up with her on the street – *tcha!* Just *happened* to meet with her, and now her husband is conveniently dead and you're here with your hand-kissing and your French poetry—'

'He tried to kiss me, too,' babbled Alicia desperately. 'He's tried a dozen times, to get me alone! Just like—'

'Mesdames, I assure you—'

'*Enoch!*' Amelia had a voice like the crack of doom.

January heard the swift, light tap of boots on floor-tiles, and the creak of the outer door.

'He did,' persisted Alicia. 'He's tried to get me alone. Last night he tried my door . . .'

'Don't be a dunce,' said Amelia shortly. 'If the man was out to ravage someone in the night he'd have raped Valentina, not you—'

'He's violated her already,' whispered Alicia. 'Watch the way he looks at her. I daresay, he and that great black savage of his, both. I saw them. I saw them last night. And she reveled in it. For men like him . . .'

January backed from the door, disgusted and thoroughly alarmed.

He wasn't sure how seriously anyone would take the accusation, or even if the woman would remember making it, an hour from now. But he knew also that if Brother Francis, and Madrecita Taggart, wanted to get rid of himself and Hannibal, they could certainly find someone to believe it.

The library windows were curtained, and the chamber dim. There was a square bottle on the library table which January recognized as Kendal Black Drop, a notoriously potent 'elixir' good for the cure of everything from headaches to typhus and recommended highly for female complaints. By the sweet, slightly vinegar smell of the glass beside it, she was mixing it with very little water.

Books and newspapers strewed the table. A volume of the letters of John C. Calhoun, that great proponent of slavery and states' rights. A book on the cranial capacities of various human groups explaining why white men should have control of all resources and social power. The *Federalist Papers*. A collection of what appeared to be treatises on United States trade. Copies of the Richmond *Enquirer*, the New Orleans *True American*, the *Southern Patriot*. Southern newspapers going back at least four years. The few shelves contained little beyond the statutes of the Republic of Texas and of the State of Virginia, plus several volumes of American and Mexican law, and a Spanish lexicon.

Outside in the hall, Madame Amelia's voice rose in fury, shouting names at her sister. *Bitch. Whore. You asked for what you got . . .*

In moments, January guessed, the younger woman would flee back to the library for a refill of her Black Drop cocktail. *Not* the moment for a *great black savage* to be discovered waiting for her.

He beat a quick retreat across the back gallery, and down to the corrals. Hannibal was already there, gossiping with Juana and Malojo. Completely apart from forged wills and murdered forgers, January had a former slave's instinctive dread of drunkards in power, knowing how swiftly things could get out of control. Whatever violence had been done to Alicia in her girlhood, she seemed ready now to confuse memory with fears – and that, January knew, would be easily enough to get him hanged.

The sooner we figure out what the hell is going on here, and get the hell out, the better.

SEVENTEEN

'Ah.' Jalisco's good eye slid momentarily to January, seated stirrup-to-stirrup with him in the warm shade above the roadway. 'The San Diablo Mine.' Beyond the tangle of woodland, the noon sun glared hot on the cotton fields. The air was filled with the sharp, monotonous chink of hoes, and the smell of turned dirt.

Everyone in Galveston, Houston, Austin and all points between had spoken of how perfect Texas soil was for cotton; how long the growing season, how valuable the land was and would be soon. As soon as the Comanche were completely extirpated, as soon as the threat of Mexican re-invasion was settled. ('And how they're going to do *that*,' Hannibal had remarked, 'if every landowner refuses to pay the taxes that the government hasn't the money to enforce, in order to maintain an army, I am most curious to see.') But what it came down to, for the men, women, children obliged to actually participate in the cultivation of cotton-plants, was endless chopping of the weeds that flourished in the semi-tropical climate.

'Is there such a thing?'

'Of course.' The sardonic smile widened one corner of the vaquero's ugly mouth. 'I've even visited it – or a mine that

one map claimed was it.' Below them on the road the dust
was settling. A small chain of mules had passed, drovers and
outriders glancing nervously up at the half-seen shapes of
Jalisco and another vaquero named Yanez – and now January
and Hannibal – among the trees.

And no wonder . . .

'Don Gael sent four of us to see if stories of the mine were
the truth. And there was, in truth, a hole in the ground round
about where the rumors said there was a hole in the ground:
fifteen miles from here, up the west fork of the Pedernales
and into the hills a ways. One man had his shoulder shot to
pieces by a Comanche bullet and never regained the use of
his arm.' Jalisco took a cigaretto from his shirt-pocket without
taking his good eye from the road, offered it to January – who
shook his head – then lit it himself.

'We were fortunate we weren't all killed. The mine was
on Don Gael's land, yes – if you believe that the king actually gave that part of the hills to Don Gael and not to the
Franciscans who were going to establish a mission at San
Diablo. There's some question about that. But it didn't look
to me like the mine had been worked for more than a few
weeks. God only knows how the Spanish got a few weeks
out of it, the Comanche must have been off fighting the Apache
that month. Certainly not enough to produce the thousands
of silver ingots the stories all talk about. So maybe it wasn't
the San Diablo Mine after all.'

'Has Francis sent anyone out to investigate?'

The vaquero chuckled. 'Señor Francis has maps to eight
different mines – or maybe the same mine in eight different
places. He keeps them locked up and won't show them to
anyone, yet he fears to ride out himself and see what's there.
It's why he quit asking me to teach Señorita Alicia to ride
and shoot: she spoke of wanting a share of the "treasure" so
that she could hire a companion and go back to live in the
United States.'

January remembered the raised, shrill voices in the hall.
The strew of American newspapers across the library table.

'White people always say,' he murmured, 'that it's hard to
get good help.'

'Did he suggest that he blindfold her, when they went treasure-seeking?' inquired Hannibal, and Jalisco's grin widened.

'Who do you think killed Taggart?' January asked suddenly.

'I think it was the Pollacks.'

'Any idea how? Or why?'

The ugly man shrugged. 'That I don't know. And in truth it could have been anyone. This is the stupidity of what we do here, sitting watching the road, as if Pollack is going to send in his men to invade us. Riding the hills along the Arroyo Ciervo to the west of here, or Sauceito to the east. Perdition land is huge, señor. It isn't just that anyone could ride north-west along Chato Creek and come down here through the lands where they might meet the Comanche – because I promise you, none of us patrol more than ten miles in that direction. But all anyone needs to do is slip between us—'

He nodded westward along the road, where a flicker of sunlight through the trees caught the red coat of Brawny's horse, a hundred yards further on.

'Once they're inside this silly line, with all of us riding the boundaries, you could march the Mexican army up to the hacienda and nobody would see it. Austin – this whole countryside – is filled with men who come and go. *Nortes* who come for the cheap land, who seek work – as overseers in the cotton lands, or cattle-hands here in the hills, or muleteers, or smugglers – because nobody in their right mind will hire them in lands where law is enforced. Men who have fled from Mississippi or Louisiana or Alabama – or indeed Mexico – because they have broken the law.'

He turned his head sharply, at the distant *tuff* of hooves from the direction of Austin. The banks of the road were steep here – the main trace that led to Hacienda Perdition lay just past the cowhand Brawny and his party – but anyone sufficiently determined, January judged, could push their mount up the slope. Thin stands of woodland surrounded the cotton fields, enough to cover a single rider heading for the higher ground.

With what aim? he reflected. *To secretly pasture Gideon Pollack's sheep?*

Hide in a cave? Meet Brother Francis – or Madrecita Taggart

– for instructions about forging Vin Taggart's will? Wait beside
Sauceito Creek to shoot at Valentina? Ride to the orchard
where Taggart would arrive in response to a note from someone
he knew – someone he trusted (or more or less trusted) –
saying: *'There's a plot against you and I don't know who's
in on it . . .'*?

Two riders came into sight, a man and a woman. The
woman's clothing was the sort that January had seen on the
poorer sort of Mexican women, in Austin and Houston and
Galveston, and even up in the high country, far beyond the
frontier. A wide, brightly-colored skirt, a satin bodice over a
white chemise, a short red jacket heavily laced with embroidery. A shawl rather than an American bonnet covered her
thick gray hair. The man wore a wide-brimmed, flat-crowned
Mexican-style hat, and the short jacket often seen on Tejanos,
but his boots were American, and January had seldom seen
Mexicans or Tejanos wearing checked trousers. The man signed
to the woman to wait where she was, out of sight of the road
that curved northward into Perdition lands, then nudged his
horse to a quick trot.

January heard young Mr Brawny hail him in his Alabama
drawl. A moment later, the bark of gunfire. Jalisco and Yanez
spurred away through the trees, January and Hannibal behind
them. On the Perdition road, Brawny and young Ajo had closed
in on the rider. Brawny shouted to him that if he tried that
again they'd plug him before he got ten feet. The horses were
jittering, Ajo trying to circle the other two. Jalisco rode out
of the trees, calling out, 'What's your hurry, then, amigo?'

'I got to see Mr Taggart's next of kin,' returned the man,
and entered into a protracted argument with the guards,
protesting that he was damned if he'd tell them his business
or who sent him, and quoting the US Constitution about why
he had the right to ride anywhere he damn well pleased.

'Does he know we're not in the United States?' asked
Hannibal softly, and January shrugged.

'Few of them seem to.' Sitting in the shadows of the trees,
January studied the rider's face, wondering where he'd seen
him before. Medium-sized, slim, with a handsome mane of
coal-black hair, but it was the mustache that caught January's

attention. Long and waxed and curling up slightly at the ends, like a villain's in a melodrama. Yet there was nothing of melodrama in the way he watched behind him, and around him, even while declaiming a rambling analogy about a man not being obliged to explain himself to the dogs chained up outside a man's house, even though the dogs themselves were admirable creatures who did their work surpassingly well.

Watched in all directions, as if marking out a course of flight. That, too, touched a chord in January's memories of the past two exceedingly crowded weeks.

In the midst of his discourse the stranger referred to Ajo as a greaser, which drew the young man into furious argument. The stranger apologized – at length, and with a long explanation about how 'greaser' wasn't a term of opprobrium, but rather a comment on the differences of Mexican culture and cuisine.

'He's stalling,' said Hannibal softly.

Jalisco told Ajo to be quiet and the stranger used the opportunity to get into another extensive diatribe.

January reined his horse around, and he and Hannibal trotted back over the slight rise of ground and around the curve of the road, to the place where the Mexican woman had been left.

She was gone.

It was almost an hour's ride back to the hacienda. The oaks along the road screened the good black bottomlands soil where the true wealth of Perdition was generated. Further on lay a belt of cornfields, green ears showing in the tall plants and small black children standing guard against the birds. Beyond the cornfields the land rose, to the rolling prairie-lands, the deep grass and scattered stands of trees. Now and then to their left the white trace of the road appeared and disappeared like a chalk-mark, but January saw how right Jalisco had been.

Anyone could have slipped past Taggart's guards. And, once past, could have ridden with impunity – or driven a line of elephants, for that matter – unseen.

He glimpsed no sign of the Mexican woman, but knew she had to be riding from grove to grove, or following the wooded course of Bruja Creek.

'Think she's going up to the caves where we found our friend?'

'That's my guess.' January frowned, and squinted at the hills. It would be another hour's ride to the head of Witch Cave Canyon, and in the thick woodland of the canyon bottom it would be easy to lose even an inexperienced quarry. He was, moreover, tired and very hungry – his earlier plans to get sustenance from TA having been interrupted by Valentina's appearance, and his shoulders still smarted from a night of grave-digging. 'Shall we see if we can get some of the men from the house? We may be hunting her all afternoon.'

'*Ecce cor meum quid gaudet.* Whatever she's looking for, let's hope it'll be of some use to us before Quigley and his Merrie Men turn up with a warrant. Incidentally,' the fiddler added, 'do you think – before Quigley and his Merrie Men *do* turn up – you and I could make enough of a diversion to permit the lovely Valentina to search the rooms of her mother-in-law and her aunt? I could have another go at Francis's study – for all we know, there's a letter there from the President of Mexico, offering a thousand gold pieces for Taggart's murder, with nothing said about forged wills or lost mines or stealing shawls and pistols from Valentina's room to make it look as if . . . *What* kind of horse was our quarry riding?'

The two men were making the turn of the path to the back of the house and the corrals. Hannibal half-rose in his stirrups to get a better look.

And January said, 'Damn.' He didn't have to answer, though he recognized the big, sleek buckskin tied outside the courtyard gate.

The men put their horses to a trot, and reached the gate in time to hear the shrill clamor of speech through the open doors of the house.

'*Oway! Oway!*' sobbed a beautiful contralto voice. '*Mi oorpay arimay! Edday, anish'dvay – avhay ittypay, adylay, egopray, egopray!*'

Entering at Hannibal's heels, January saw the gray-haired woman on her knees before a confused but concerned-looking Valentina, and a deeply disapproving Madrecita Taggart. Since the visitor was crying at the top of her lungs, Francis had been brought, limping, down the stairs, and Enoch stood in the doorway that led to the back gallery of the house.

'What on earth is she saying?' demanded Amelia Taggart. 'Here, you, speak English!' She reached down and shook the woman by her shoulder.

'*Oway!*' sobbed the woman, and clutched, first Madame Taggart's wrist, then Valentina's skirts. '*Ittypay sur ovrepay iddoway! Egopray!*' She began to weep, tears running down the handsome bones of her too-strongly-featured face. '*Egopray!*'

Helplessly, Valentina turned to Hannibal. 'Do you know what language she speaks?'

'I do,' said the fiddler, and walking over, put a gentle hand on the woman's back.

And in pristinely clear pig-Latin – the encrypted English mixed in with a word or two of encrypted French – he asked, 'What the hell are you doing here, Cornelia?'

EIGHTEEN

Cornelia Passmore – confidence trickster, thief, gambler and sometime madam – gazed at Hannibal with wide, violet-blue eyes filled with bogus tears that barely hid the surprise she must have felt – almost as much as January felt at seeing the woman.

She made a swift recovery, clutched the fiddler's wrist, and said – still in pig-Latin based in English, French, and the smattering of Italian that all well-educated girls were expected to learn – 'Bugger me, Hannibal, are you still pretending that Benjamin here is your slave?'[*]

Gently, Hannibal assisted her to her feet. To the two ladies – and Francis, who by this time had reached the bottom of the stair – he said, in English, 'The lady Fatima here is Turkish, a language which I learned while working for the Foreign

---

[*] See *Drinking Gourd*

Office in Constantinople. If you would be so good as to permit me, I think I had best speak to her in private.'

January half-expected Aunt Alicia to emerge from the library and accuse the fiddler of plotting to ravish 'Fatima' – possibly with January's assistance – but no such interruption occurred. Hannibal guided the lady – who had commenced to weep again, softly – into the parlor across the hall, saying over his shoulder, 'Benjamin, if you would assist me . . .?'

January followed him in, and closed the door.

'What the hell are you doing here?' asked Hannibal again, in plain English, and stepped back from Mrs Passmore's attempt at a welcoming kiss.

The woman, brushing the shawl from her hair – which January saw had been whitened up with flour from her usual lush (and not entirely genuine) brunette – pouted at the rejection. 'Don't tell me you're still holding a grudge over me trying to sell Ben?'

Hannibal opened his mouth – probably to ask her if *she'd* accept a friendly kiss from someone who'd attempted to kidnap and sell one of her children – then clearly recalled to whom he was speaking, and closed it again.

January asked, 'Who was your friend down on the road?'

'Joe?' She shrugged artlessly. 'Just a friend.'

'Who's working for Gideon Pollack? Who met him – when were we in Austin, Hannibal? – in the Empire of the West saloon on Congress Avenue, a week ago Saturday night. And was lurking in the corridors of the Capital City Hotel a day or two later, if I'm not mistaken.' He folded his arms and regarded her: a handsome woman rather than a pretty one, and, he guessed, older than she looked.

'We may have another few hours before Sheriff Quigley turns up with a posse and a warrant,' he went on. 'After Brother Francis's obvious jiggery-pokery I'm guessing it'll be sooner rather than later, so if you have anything you're trying to accomplish here before the law takes charge, I suggest you speak up and let us pool our knowledge. What the hell is going on?'

Mrs Passmore sank into a chair and cocked her head. 'Aren't you even going to offer a lady a drink?'

'I would if one were here. M'am.'

Hannibal crossed to the cabinet, attempted to open it, said, 'Just a minute,' knelt and picked the lock.

'You want me to get that, dear?' asked Mrs Passmore, digging in the pocket beneath her voluminous skirt.

'Rum or brandy?'

'Oh, the brandy,' she said. 'Vincent told me it was smuggled in from France.'

Hannibal removed the stopper from the bottle and sniffed it. 'Vin was cheated.'

'I knew I should have gone with him to the pick-up.'

Hannibal brought her back a glass. 'Will you have any, *amicus meus*?'

January shook his head. 'You wouldn't by any chance be the mistress Vin Taggart swore he'd dismiss?'

'Well, he did dismiss me.' Mrs Passmore arranged her gray-and-white rebozo more becomingly around her splendid shoulders. 'When he married Miss de Castellón – or Mrs Dillard, I suppose I should call her. That's when I went back to the States in '38. I had no idea she was so pretty – and such a sweet girl, she seems. Did she really shoot Vin?'

'So far as I know, no. But she's going to be hanged for doing so unless we find what really happened – and what's really going on.'

'My money's on the old bitch in black. You're quite right, Hannibal, Vincent was cheated – the man had no palate.' She frowned, thinking it over – or perhaps, reflected January, merely deploring her former lover's taste in liquor.

'And "Joe" is . . .?' January prompted.

The woman sighed, and took another sip – palate or no. 'Silver Joe Fleam. As far as I knew, he was doing a job of work for Gideon Pollack – have you met Pollack? Voice like poisoned cream, and would sell his sister to the Comancheros – after seducing her first, I daresay. And he's the *good* brother of the pair.'

'We've met. What kind of work?'

Mrs Passmore shook her head. 'It could have been almost anything. He smuggled slaves in from Cuba, until the British Navy started making things tight in the Caribbean. Later I heard he and his men were kidnapping Mexicans from villages west of San Antonio and selling them to the Comancheros. Not a nice man.' She smiled as she said it.

'The thing is, he told me Vincent had *also* hired him and his men – ten of them, altogether – for some kind of job, which completely precluded their collecting the second half of Pollack's money. Then Vincent died and they never got paid for *his* job.'

She might have been speaking of the man who drove the grocery-van. *You'd think the purchase of a house on Franklin Street would warrant at least a sniffle, or a little break in that lovely contralto voice.*

As Valentina's voice had broken, when she'd spoken of the man whose blows had marked her face. *He was a good husband*, she had said. *A good man at heart.*

'When they brought Vincent's body into town Monday night,' Mrs Passmore continued casually, 'Joe rode out here to try to put in his claim, but that lemon-puss Creed turned him back. Joe came to me because he was pretty sure Vincent had the money. It was a thousand dollars in gold, and it took him awhile to put it together.'

'How long of a while?' asked January thoughtfully.

She thought about it for a moment, then shrugged. 'Christmas at least. Anyway, at Christmas he was already working at this little thing and that little thing – mostly with the smugglers – to get gold together without anybody knowing about it. Christmas was when I came back to town, you know. He gave me the house on Franklin Street the first of January – and believe me, I've had better. But if Lamar stays president I can sell the place for a fortune.'

Hannibal looked puzzled at that, and January provided, 'If Lamar stays president, Austin will stay the capital. If the capital's moved elsewhere – Houston, or Galveston – land values in Austin will collapse, since there's really no reason to have a town here at all. I suspect that may be behind some of the . . . *impassioned* . . . nature of the Nationalists' quarrel with the Houstonites. Did Taggart own other land in Austin?'

'Oh, a dozen lots, at least.' Mrs Passmore sounded a little surprised that January had to ask. 'Vincent kept the gold at my place – and counted it like a Scotch Jew, damn him. Then he'd give me a little and take the rest away. He said he didn't dare keep it here at the hacienda because his crazy aunt searches the house. Usually in the middle of the night, he said, but he thought she'd do it in the daytime, too, when he was away.'

Hannibal said, 'Ah! This explains many things, including the locks Francis put on his study door.'

She shrugged again. 'I'd put locks on my door if I shared a house with her, that's for certain.'

And January remembered the pale face, the pale hands in the darkness. Moonlight gleaming on round spectacles, like an insect's eyes.

'Looking for money?' he asked, remembering, too, what Jalisco had said about the aborted expedition to search for the lost mine.

'Oh, God yes. That's what all three of them are after, really. Vincent was pretty sure Aunt Alicia has a cache of money someplace that he never found. And his mother – was that the old bitch in black? His mother was always trying to keep the books on this place, to make it earn more. She did that with his father, too, he said – and bought the old man as much liquor as he wanted, to keep him out of her hair while she did it. But Auntie just wants money.'

She spoke of wanting a share of the 'treasure', so that she could hire a companion and go back to live in the United States . . .

And who could blame her?

I am nothing! I would have nothing! Valentina had cried. Amelia Taggart and her sister – and her youngest son, a youth of eighteen without physical strength or formal education – had already lost one home. Without doubt they knew themselves to be unwelcome in this one, and nothing beyond its walls but the turbulent wilds of an alien land. Silver mine or no silver mine, if Texas became a part of the United States, the value of land would rocket sky-high. (*As if President Van Buren is going to be stupid enough to risk war with Mexico and a revolt in Congress by adding an enormous slave-state to the Union . . .*)

With land, they would be safe.

And the hacienda was so isolated, so far from town. The crime could indeed have been done by anyone. Even if that sandy, broken-nosed man with the cold blue eyes had been murdered by, as the lawyers said, 'person or persons unknown,' it would still be much to Francis's advantage – or Madrecita's – to run up to the house for a quick rummage in Valentina's wardrobe for shawls and pistols.

But he knew it wasn't that simple. *Valentina was targeted. Valentina was followed to Arroyo Sauceito, dismounted, and delayed.*

'Did you know a man named Gervase Hookwire?' he asked.

'Gerry the Hook?' Mrs Passmore looked surprised. 'Little fat party with a head like a billiard-ball? Best forger in Washington City. Made a fortune drawing up – er—' She had the grace to look embarrassed – or the grace to pretend to it, anyway. 'Drawing up fake sales papers, for the kidnapping rings that stole slaves. With a side-line in fake toll-road shares, and bogus identity papers that he sold to Irish just off the boat.'

January closed his mouth hard. *Was that who you would have used when you tried to sell me?* Such a question would not have advanced the conversation. He suddenly felt less sorry for the little man he'd buried last night.

'Why do you ask?'

'You didn't know he was in Texas?'

She shook her head, genuinely ignorant – or looking genuinely ignorant, anyway.

'We found his body yesterday.'

Her eyes filled with tears, which in her case might or might not have meant anything. 'Dear lord,' she whispered. 'Poor Gerry.'

'He'd been dead four days. His throat had been cut – here on this property, a few miles from the house. You didn't know of any job he had going here in Texas?'

'I thought he was still in New Orleans.' Then her strong black brows tugged down over her nose. 'What the hell was Vincent up to? Hiring Joe Fleam – hiring Gerry the Hook—'

'We don't know it was Taggart who hired him,' said January, though the gold pieces in Hookwire's saddlebag offered a trenchant hint. Unless Hookwire had . . . What? Found Taggart's cache? Been paid by someone in the household who'd been pinching gold from Taggart's cache?

'Joe says it was Vincent who hired him,' returned Mrs Passmore. 'Well, Pollack hired him first, and then Vincent got this second job that would take him away from Pollack's. What did either of them have in mind, that they'd need ten men for, for God's sake? The Pollack boys have thirty of their own on Los Lobos; Vincent had – what, twenty-six? Twenty-seven? – on Perdition, even if you didn't count Creed and Maddox. They were working for Pollack,' she added, seeing Hannibal's look of surprise. 'Or anyway were awfully thick with Pollack when they'd come into town. Creed for sure always spent more money at Theodora Fischer's saloon and knocking-shop than he would if he was just making twenty-five Texas dollars a month.'

'And he didn't say—' January began.

In the hallway someone – Enoch, it sounded like – exclaimed, 'My God!'

Hannibal turned, quickly, and opened the parlor door, in time to see Francis standing at the bottom of the stairs, a document in his hands and a look of smug, blazing triumph on his thin face. Enoch had gone to the door of the front parlor across the hall, and knocked imperatively on it. Francis, limping behind him, called out, 'Mama, I've found it! I've found Vin's will!'

Very quietly, Hannibal said to Mrs Passmore, 'Get a look at it if you can. I think it's forged. Ben, watch the stairs . . .'

January followed Hannibal through the discreet door of the backstairs, and up to Valentina's boudoir above. Leaving January at the top of the main stair, the fiddler strode quickly across the hall, slipped through the open bedroom door – open for the first time since January had been in the house. With one eye on the stairs, January noted the monastic severity of Francis's room, the neat stacks of books on the small table, and the door open into the study beyond. Hannibal stepped into the study and returned a moment later bearing a thick stack of what looked like letters and invoices.

These the fiddler shoved into January's hands. 'Hide these. There's pens and paper all over the desk in there. These are samples of Taggart's handwriting – and of Francis's. And about six half-finished drafts of the will. Enough to get it thrown out of court.'

They'd passed through the upstairs rear gallery even as Hannibal was speaking, and into the guest room. One glance told January there was noplace in the sparsely-furnished chamber that wouldn't be obvious to a searcher – the shaving-stand contained one drawer, and instead of an armoire there were only a few wall pegs and a chest. January pulled one of Hannibal's spare neckcloths from his saddlebag, tied the bundle of papers up firmly in the long band of linen, and led the way through Valentina's boudoir again – she had long ago unlocked the door between it and the guest room – and thence into the backstairs. One of the steps, he knew from coming and going, was loose . . .

Yes, the fourth from the top. It had been repaired not long ago where the wood had cracked, and the new wood was already warping. He wedged the blade of his knife into the crack, pried it up just enough to admit the bundle of papers – the gap opened easily – then punched it back down with the hammer of his fist.

They went up the backstairs, through the gallery and the upstairs hall, and listened at the top of the main staircase to make sure there was no one in the hall below to see them descending the stair. Voices echoed, muffled – *outdoors*?

January and Hannibal traded a look. A lot of voices . . .

'Of course,' Francis was saying, 'you are correct insofar as the principles of English law go, but your warrant is a moot point because I have discovered my brother's will . . .'

'Quigley,' Hannibal mouthed. They came downstairs swiftly, and saw through the open front door that yes, Sheriff Quigley stood on the front gallery, along with Francis, Valentina, Madame Taggart, Enoch, Noah, and a group of rather grim-faced men in town coats. At the foot of the steps, near the horses of the posse, stood Jalisco and several of his cowhands.

Mrs Passmore was nowhere in sight.

No surprise, reflected January. *Even with her hair grayed and got up in Tejano garb, men from Austin would recognize her.*

Valentina looked around a little desperately, and caught sight of January and Hannibal in the hallway behind her. Hannibal touched his finger to his lips, turned and strode down the hallway to the house's rear gallery, and so out and around the side of the house, to come to the group from outside, rather than inside, the house.

No sense in getting Francis suspicious of where we've been. He'll notice soon enough that some of his papers are gone . . .

'What is this?' demanded Hannibal, arriving on the scene just as Francis and his mother were ushering the posse into the house. 'Sheriff Quigley.' He bowed. 'I'm delighted to see you. I trust you located your nationalist judge in Austin?'

'I did,' said the sheriff grimly. 'And I have a judge's warrant here, for the arrest of Mrs Taggart on a charge of murder.'

She said, quietly, 'I wasn't here.'

'Hah!' retorted her mother-in-law. 'And that wasn't your shawl, I collect, that was on the ground beside my poor son's body! Oh, no! Nor your pistol . . .'

'It sounds like an awfully silly thing to drop,' pointed out Hannibal. 'I mean, something that large – wouldn't a killer of average intelligence have noticed it?'

'In any case,' put in Francis, 'it scarcely matters.' His spectacles flashed in the light from the open door as he threw back his head. 'I mean, obviously, this woman thought to murder my brother as a way of seizing control of Rancho Perdition—'

'I had control of it already!' Valentina stamped her foot on the red tile of the hall. 'Three-quarters of it is mine! My land!'

'Not according to my brother's will.' Francis held up the slim sheaf of extremely fresh-looking papers that he held. 'I found this this morning, Mr Quigley, slipped into the back of one of my poor brother's account-books. It's dated—'

'It is a forgery!' Valentina whirled on him, blue eyes snapping with fury. 'Ask anyone who knew my husband! He hated the very thought of making a will. And he hated his brother. Any of his friends will tell you this. This . . . this cowardly milk-toast has been shut up for the past two days in his study, trying to write in my husband's hand—'

Francis's face twitched in hatred and alarm, and he stuck his ink-stained hand into his trouser pocket.

'That's certainly what *you'd* think of, you Papist hussy!'
Madame Taggart shouted, and Quigley raised his hands.

'Ladies—'

'You only want me out of the way,' stormed Valentina, 'to
make way for your precious son—'

'Ladies,' repeated Quigley, more firmly. 'That's as may be,
and that'll be for the courts to decide. But in my opinion, and
that of Judge Ananias Kendrick, there is sufficient evidence
for me to arrest Mrs Taggart, to take affidavits for all possible
witnesses and to search the house for evidence—'

Francis blenched, and threw a quick glance up the stairs.

*Probably remembering that unlocked bedroom door and the
papers on his desk.*

'Mr Sefton, you'll be representing Mrs Taggart's interests—'

'I'll work through a local colleague,' said Hannibal
smoothly. 'As I'm not licensed to practice law in the Republic
of Texas.'

January privately doubted whether any lawyer practicing in
the republic needed a license to do so, but kept his mouth shut
about that, too.

'But yes . . .'

'Mrs Taggart,' said the sheriff, 'with your permission I'll
have Doc Meredith here –' he signed back through the open
doors, to the physician, who stood among the men of the posse
– 'accompany you upstairs, if there's anything you'll need to
collect. Mrs Taggart –' he bowed to Amelia Taggart, like a
harpy in her mourning frock and ablaze with spiteful triumph
– 'Mr Taggart –' to Francis – 'if there's a place we could go
to take your statements. I'll need Miss Marryat's statement as
well, about the finding of the shawl and the pistol.'

'I'll get her,' said Francis. 'She's been indisposed . . .' He
bolted up the stairs.

Well, reflected January, *he can't very well make an outcry
about the rough drafts of his forgery being missing from his
study at this point.*

NINETEEN

Between riding out to look at canyons in the hills, searching caves, burying bodies, and collecting information from servants, this was the first occasion on which January actually heard the evidence as Madrecita Taggart and her corroborators presented it.

'I never trusted that girl.' Amelia Taggart sank into a bergère chair whose pink brocade upholstery contrasted sharply and awkwardly with the spare white plaster and simpler furnishings of the adobe hacienda. January had noted, when he'd earlier passed the door of the large main parlor, that this was clearly the place that Vin Taggart's mother and aunt had taken for their own when they'd turned up on his doorstep last October. Unlike most dwellings January had known in Mexico – and indeed, unlike the French Creole houses in New Orleans – the parlor was cluttered with bandy-legged chairs, a breakfront cabinet embellished with Corinthian pillars, a mahogany cellaret, three small occasional tables with clawed feet and marble tops, several patent Argand lamps with pink roses painted on their chimneys, a carved wooden clock inlaid with far too much brass, and heavy swagged curtains of teal-blue velvet and gold that 'puddled' fashionably on the tiled floor. (*Wait til they're here in the summer when the tarantulas come out . . .*)

Not-very-good Biblical scenes adorned the walls, (January, having lived for sixteen years in Paris, was a terrible snob about art) alternating with portraits whose stiff, expressionless faces were offset by intricate portrayals of every detail of the sitters' lace and brocade costumes.

On the cellaret beside Madame Taggart's chair stood a half-empty cut-crystal decanter and a glass, which she refilled to the top and took a revivifying sip. Her pale eyes narrowed as they regarded her daughter-in-law. 'Oh, poor Vincent was taken with her pretty eyes and her fawning ways, I daresay, but from the first I saw her for what she was.'

Valentina came in at this point, rigid with anger, and at these words stamped her foot. 'That is not—'

Quigley raised a finger. 'You'll have your say, Mrs Taggart.' He settled on the chair opposite, hard and shiny black horsehair, and spread open a dusty memorandum-book on his knee. 'Right now we just need the facts about what happened last Monday.'

'Sunday.' Madame set her glass down and re-filled it with barely a glance at what she was doing. The 'finding' of the will having settled who'd get the land – in her eyes, at least – she seemed ready to have Valentina put out of the way once and for all.

'Easter – the Lord's Day – which my poor son felt himself unable to honor because of the work that needs to be done on this place. Even on such a day, because of the laziness, the wastefulness, the thievery of that Yankee trash overseer, those Mexican good-for-nothings and the sheer stupidity of the field hands, Vincent was in the saddle before sun-up. And when he returned, as night was falling, exhausted, that wife of his lit into him, screaming accusations that he'd been with a woman! Well! Maybe where *she* was brought up men could be expected to spend the Sabbath – and Easter Sunday, of all days! – consorting with their mistresses—'

'I did *not*—'

'M'am.' Quigley lifted a hand again, then turned his attention back to his notebook.

'I was here, in this room.' Madame's mouth was a tight line of anger. 'I heard their voices and came to the door. My poor son had not even come inside yet when she started in on him, and him covered with dust and bowed, bent, he was so tired. He said only, "Leave me alone, woman!" but of course she didn't. She followed him up the stairs, ranting and shouting, and goaded him so that he shouted back at her. Ask poor Francis – ask poor Alicia – the whole house heard them! And *she* should accuse him of infidelity, after his patience in bearing with her adulteries, the way she carried on with that swinish priest from San Antonio, and then later with one of the Mexican cowhands!' Her eyes blazed with the spiteful anger of the self-righteous. 'She was angry because my poor son had finally had enough and sent the man away last week. Don't try to deny it, Miss!'

'I do deny it!' protested Valentina angrily. 'My husband trusted Ortega – he himself told him, to ride with me! He himself warned me never to go out riding without Ortega—'

'Then why did he turn him off?' demanded her mother-in-law.

'I don't know!'

'Huh! He finally had his eyes opened to what was going on between the two of you!' She turned back to Quigley in triumph. 'When she sneaked out of here Monday morning – and don't think I wasn't aware of what you were up to, girl! – I daresay it was to meet with that Mexican, instead of to kiss the feet of that heathen priest of hers.'

'You saw her leave?' asked the sheriff in a patient voice.

'I heard her. I don't sleep well.' She raised the backs of her black-mitted knuckles to her forehead, and sighed deeply. 'Not in this terrible place. I heard my son take his departure, well before the sun was up – as he always did, so hard-working as he was, and with Vabsley and the men needing a firm hand. I'd barely turned over and closed my eyes, when I heard her creep down the stair.'

Valentina opened her mouth to protest again, but Quigley waved her silent.

'After that I finally got some sleep. I'd been up half the night, unable to sleep because of the terrible threats she'd uttered.'

'She threatened him?'

'She did,' said Madame decidedly. 'I heard her clearly shout, "I will kill you!"—'

'I said nothing of the kind!'

'Then in the morning,' she went on firmly, 'I came down and had breakfast—'

'What time?' asked Hannibal mildly.

'Oh, heavens, I don't know. Nine o'clock? Ten o'clock? It takes that wretched girl of mine forever to bring up hot water, and then when she does it's usually stone cold. I went over the account books with Enoch – this place would go bankrupt, the way my poor son managed it. Not that it was his fault,' she added.

She took another sip of her glass, and re-filled it again. 'At ten o'clock my sister came into the parlor and said, "My goodness, what on earth is Valentina doing out in the orchard?" I got up – I was here in this parlor – and she and I went into the dining-room—'

'That's down the hall and into the main dining-room, or into the smaller work-room beyond the pantry?' inquired Hannibal.

Madame looked nonplussed, and her eyes shifted, mentally – January assumed – counting windows and calculating angles and realizing that neither from the main dining-room, nor from the work-room beyond it, could any portion of the orchard be seen. 'The room beyond,' she said after a moment. 'And we saw my daughter-in-law – er – come around the corner of the house from the direction of the orchard, hurrying and holding her skirts up.'

'Which direction was she going in?'

Another swift calculation. 'The corrals. She was going to the corrals. We all saw her! Alicia, and Francis, and myself—'

'So Francis was with you in the parlor?'

'Yes. No. That is –' she glared at Hannibal with a sort of envenomed annoyance – 'Francis was in the library next to the parlor, and joined Alicia and myself.' Then she shrugged again. 'Well, I didn't think a thing of it, and went back into the parlor. But I had a terrible premonition of dread,' she added, a little contradictorily. 'Luncheon was served at one – I insist upon punctuality, because there's no bearing it if the household isn't run properly, not that *Mexicans* –' here she glared at Valentina – 'have the smallest idea of such a thing. And it was just after luncheon that that scoundrel Malojo came running up to the house, shouting that my poor son . . .'

She sniffed, and turned her face aside to dab her eyes. 'My poor son . . .'

Her description of the body matched the one January had already heard from Twenty-One and Missouri: that Vin Taggart lay on his back, dressed in his riding-clothes of wool trousers and a rough tweed coat; that he had been shot once, through the chest, at a range so close that the gunflash had burned the

cotton of his shirt. His horse had been found tied at the far
side of the orchard.

Valentina's red-flowered silk shawl had lain a foot or so
from the body, and half beneath it, one of the several pistols
that Taggart had given his bride. 'It was horrible,' she whispered. 'Horrible. He had . . . bled . . . a great deal. Poor Alicia
fainted – the poor girl has *no* stamina – and when she was
brought round, went into strong hysterics. The men said they'd
found that woman's mare near the stables, with its reins tangled
in a broken-off branch, and well over an hour later that . . .
that *hussy* herself walked in off the prairie as cool as you
please, with some cock-and-bull tale of being shot at by Indians
and having to take refuge in a convenient hut.'

Quigley nodded, deliberately turned a page of his
memorandum-book, then took from his pocket a penknife,
with which he sharpened the point of his pencil. Enoch tapped
at the parlor door, and asked, would maybe the gen'lemen
outside like to have some beer sent out from the kitchens?

'Absolutely not!' Madame glared at him. 'I don't know how
many times I have to tell you, beer costs *fifteen dollars* a barrel
in town – fifteen dollars *American*! – and how they *dare* charge
that for it I cannot imagine! And no man needs beer. There's
a well in the courtyard, and I assume your men –' she turned
haughtily to Quigley – 'know how to operate a bucket.'

Patiently, the sheriff said, 'They do that, m'am.' He added,
'Thank you, Enoch. That was a kind thought.' And turning
back to Valentina, said, 'Now let's hear what you have to say
about all this, Mrs Taggart.'

As a child, January had early mastered the skills of remaining
quiet and unnoticed, no small feat for a boy who'd always
been taller than every other child of his year on Bellefleur
Plantation. The plantation's master had been a violent drunkard,
and every child, he suspected, who had grown up in that toxic
compound had learned how to stay either out of sight or at
least away from the notice of anybody white. Before the age
of six January had had two ribs broken for "What're you
lookin' at, boy?".

He didn't draw attention to himself now by taking physical
notes, but as he listened to Valentina's account of descending

from her room – 'I went down the backstair, as I always did . . .' – and riding out to Sauceito Creek it occurred to him to wonder where the hell Francis had gone. And what he was telling Aunt Alicia. The young man had taken the 'will' away with him, and probably also the 'written instructions' allegedly concerning his older brother's incapacity or death.

How good a forger is Francis?

And how would Francis have learned of Hookwire's death – if it was he who'd hired him? (*And who else would have?*)

I'll have to speak to Juana – she was another on Valentina's list as trustworthy – *about when Madame actually got out of bed. Get a better idea of where she, and Alicia, and Francis really were Monday morning, and what they'd been doing.* Had they had visitors? Letters?

He cursed the rush of events (and the night of digging) that had prevented him from checking these things.

And why was Ortega turned off? The fact that Valentina hadn't murdered her husband (if it *was* a fact – he reminded himself that four years ago she'd been as adept a liar as Mrs Passmore) didn't mean that she hadn't been having an *affaire* with Ortega. The man was decades too old and not nearly handsome enough to fit Valentina's tastes . . .

But tastes change . . .

And am I ever going to get a decent meal in this place? He had, he realized, been in the saddle since before daybreak, and it was now halfway to sunset . . .

And where the hell did Mrs Passmore get to?

Quigley finished taking down Valentina's account, then he, too, frowned, and looked first at the overly-elaborate clock, then at the door to the hall. He rose, and went to put his head through it, listening. Hannibal stepped quietly over to him and January, standing in his corner, heard the fiddler murmur, 'If I may make a suggestion, sir . . .'

Quigley raised his brows.

'When young Mr Taggart and Miss Marryat *do* arrive, you may want to get their stories of Monday's events separately.' Hannibal turned aside to cough, bracing himself against the door frame. 'And keep them from talking to Madame Taggart until you've gotten both of their stories.'

The lawman considered him with thoughtful gray eyes. His voice, like the fiddler's, was pitched low, to exclude the two women – who were too busy reviling one another anyway to have heard a word. 'You sound like you think they might not match up, sir.'

'I fully expect them to be identical in every particular, sir.' Hannibal inclined his head respectfully. 'But surely you've had the experience of one witness to an event remembering different details than—'

The door at the back of the house banged. Francis's voice gasped, in the hall, 'My God!' and both the sheriff and Hannibal plunged through the parlor door, followed immediately by January, with the two women, their quarrel postponed though probably not forgotten, at his heels.

Francis stood in the dining-room door, clinging to the door-jamb, mousy hair falling over his forehead and his eyebrows – even behind his spectacles – standing out against a face pallid with shock. 'My God,' he gasped again. 'Aunt Alicia . . .'

Enoch appeared behind him in the dining-room door and steadied him as he tried to step forward. In one hand he carried something, a bulky wad of white cloth, crumpled tight. By his hands, and the knees of his trousers, he had fallen several times outside already. January dodged back into the parlor and snatched up the rum bottle and glass from the cellaret. These he thrust into Hannibal's hands and scooped up the shaken boy, carried him into the parlor.

'What is it?' Quigley demanded.

Francis sobbed again, 'Aunt Alicia. Dead. In the orchard—'

January laid him down on the parlor sofa; the boy clutched at his mother's hands, his own shaking like twigs in a high wind.

The bespectacled blue eyes went to Quigley's, and Francis added, 'This was in her hand.'

He opened his fist, to display one of Hannibal's old-fashioned white neckcloths.

January stepped back as silently as a cat while they were all still staring at the evidence, slipped into the hallway, and scooped his satchel from the side-table. Knowing they'd all go running out to the orchard via the dining-room and the back of the house, he went out through the front door, walked down the steps – the posse, as Quigley had hinted, being gathered in the courtyard where it was shady around the well – selected the largest of the horses tied to the porch-rail, and headed at a gallop for the hills.

TWENTY

From the oaks on the high ground, January looked down with Rose's spyglass at the house. The images were tiny, but clear. He saw, as he'd expected, the sheriff in his black frock coat, Hannibal like a dilapidated scarecrow, Valentina and her mother-in-law – like a birch-tree and an oak, both painted black – and the wizened sable shrub that was Francis limping ahead of them, shaking off Enoch's efforts to help. A few moments later the rear door of the hacienda opened again and spurted forth Noah, and then the seven men of the sheriff's posse, the square, squat bulk of Doc Meredith striding in the lead.

Clothed in the light, preliminary foliage of spring, the gray jackstraws of the orchard's branches couldn't quite hide the tiny wink of black that had to be Aunt Alicia's body.

Why Alicia?

January remembered the intent blue eyes behind the thick lenses. The desperate unhappiness in the hunched shoulders, the wary turn of the head, like a nervous hare.

Noah saying, *He was no good, Marse Jack. You couldn't keep him off the girls . . . he even bulled poor Miss Alicia when she was young . . . an' pushed Marse Vincent into joinin' him . . .*

He wondered how long she'd been dead.

And how long it was going to be before Francis or Madame Taggart shoved Hannibal's old-fashioned linen neckcloth under Quigley's nose again and pointed out that Valentina's 'lawyer' and his 'valet' had been absent all morning. Madame Taggart's statement, and Valentina's – and the bitter argument between them – had occupied over an hour, plenty of time (to put the most generous interpretation on events) for Francis to find the body, go back to Hannibal's room, steal a neckcloth from his saddlebag and . . .

He wouldn't even have to go back and put it in her hand. Just say that he'd found it there.

Damn it, damn it, damn it.

Is this heavenly retribution for assisting in Seth Javel's death?

The wet scent of last night's rain seeped from the earth beneath his elbows. Clammy wind swept down from the hills, smelling of more rain in the canyons.

Who would kill her?

What had she seen? What did she know?

A pang of grief went through him, for that poor, scared, half-crazed woman, bound by insolvency and loyalty to – or fear of – her sister to stay in that poisoned household.

No wonder she wandered the place at night, seeking for money to flee.

And what the hell do I do now?

Just east of the orchard he could see the yellow-gray grass of the burying-ground, the brown rectangle of the grave he'd dug.

Was that only last night?

It felt like months ago.

He still hadn't had anything to eat.

The sun was just touching the rampart of cloud in the west when the little procession emerged from the orchard again. Two men carried a makeshift litter – saplings run through the sleeves of three coats, the men's white shirtsleeves bright against the dimming light. Another coat covered the face and upper body of the woman they bore, her black skirts trailing the ground. January wondered if there were any chance at all of seeing the body. By the time they left the premises it would be too dark to investigate the orchard itself.

I can do that in the morning.

He was thirsty, as well as desperately hungry, and knew he wasn't thinking as clearly as he should have been. Men were riding in from several directions to the hacienda, coming in off the cattle ranges: January recognized Maddox and Creed, Lope and an elderly vaquero named Téo. No sign of Jalisco's faded red shirt and scrubby pinto mare. Yet he was certain the vaquero had been part of the group that had escorted the posse back to the house, to ask for orders . . .

If anyone could figure out who was giving orders now, on Rancho Perdition.

Two men ran ahead of the cortège, one to the house, one to the corrals. Even before Alicia Marryat's body reached the place where she'd lived her final six months – still under the shadow of the sister who had dominated her life – January saw Malojo drag the wagon from its shed, then go into one of the corrals to catch and harness a couple of horses.

Alicia's body was placed in the wagon. This was led around to the front of the house – which January couldn't see – while everyone went into the back door. Lanterns were lit. Malojo went back to the stables – accompanied by one of the posse – to saddle more horses.

January counted. He couldn't see, at this distance, whether the saddles were the Mexican stock-saddles or the sidesaddles of ladies, but ten mounts were readied: they must be taking in all the house servants as well as Madame, Hannibal, Valentina, and Francis. No surprise, if Quigley were smart enough – as January was certain he was – to guess that nobody in the household was telling the truth. In Louisiana – or anywhere in the southern United States – the servants would have walked into town under guard, linked by a chain. But night was drawing on, and Austin was a good twelve miles away. The moon would rise late, and if the wind turned the clouds would come over . . .

Better to make the servants ride – their hands, if necessary, tied to the saddle-horns – than to risk an escape. There'd already been one ambush and escape on that road recently, though at the moment Selina's rescue felt like the memory of another lifetime.

No lights came up in the house. After a time, January saw a thread of glowing dots wind away from the front of the house towards the road.

In his mind he heard Hannibal's scratchy voice: *And leaves the world to darkness, and to me.*

And though his body ached with hunger, he waited another hour, long after the torches had disappeared, watching. Once he saw, near the corner of the house, the flare of a match, the movement of something in the shadows. They'd left a guard.

As far as he could tell, after long observation, only one.

With infinite caution he returned to his stolen horse, mounted, and rode down to the dark hacienda.

His first stop was the kitchen. Enough moonlight leaked through its windows to show him the water-jar, and the covered bowl where the leftover tortillas were kept, almost the only food in the place that was already cooked and available to eat. He had observed, during his conversation that morning (*this morning?!?!*) with Titus Andronicus, where the butter and cheese were kept, in a jar buried in the floor, and a little cautious searching yielded it. Another bowl held dried apples and peaches, wrapped in paper. These he stuffed into his satchel.

So far, so good.

Feeling much better, January slipped from the back door again, and cautiously circled the house. He ascertained that yes, there was only one guard he could see, sitting in the blackness of the front terrace, smoking, his horse tied at the foot of the steps.

Good. The likelihood of anything being hidden in the front parlors, or the little 'cabinets' that flanked the terrace like miniature towers, was negligible. In the lamp-room next to the kitchen, the household lamps had been cleaned and filled but not set out yet. From several pieces of writing-paper in the library he made a shade for one of these, giving the effect of a dark-lantern. With this to guide him he crept up the stairs to Hannibal's little chamber, and slung the fiddler's saddlebags over his shoulder – after ascertaining that either Hannibal or someone else had taken every penny of the money that had been in them (as well as Hannibal's deck of marked cards).

Aunt Alicia's room was next. It contained a small writing-desk, whose surface bore ample evidence of an extensive correspondence in the form of ink-blots and old stains of sealing-wax. Three pens and at least a dozen steel nibs. The stubs of five sticks of sealing-wax. Seven pink ribbons, of the

sort that January's wife Rose – and the girls at the school –
used to tie up correspondence in.

But the only letters he found were three short notes – barely
two lines apiece – from Francis, carefully bound in ribbon.

> *Dearest, thanks so much for the book. You must have*
> *searched for weeks to find it! Your beloved, Fr.*
> *Auntie, many thanks for helping me out! Your*
> *beloved, Fr.*
> *Dearest Aunt, many thanks again. I knew I could count*
> *on you. Love, Fr.*

Old – the paper yellowed, the ink faded. On two, the handwriting was the careful script of a child. Yet she'd kept them.
Because he called her, 'Dearest'?

And where were other letters received?

He searched, and found more newspapers – mostly the
Southern Patriot – tied up in another of the pink ribbons and
mostly folded open to articles and letters relating to the admission of Texas to the Union, and the vicious battle in Congress
over the issue of slavery.

Three books of sermons. More tellingly, a stack of novels,
hidden under the mattress of her bed: *Pamela. Thaddeus of
Warsaw. The Old English Baron. The Monk.* A scientific work
of comparative anatomy that classified the races: Asian,
African, white, Indian.

*She used to saddle up her horse and sneak off to watch the
men at work . . .*

Who was this, who'd been so casually killed?

Wretched, intelligent, struggling to achieve her own life and
taking refuge in political questions. Disregarded and scorned
as mad. Drowning her fears in laudanum and dreaming of
freedom. Hiding the memory of rape and living in the household of one of her assailants.

He found a bottle of liquor – comprised, by the smell, small
quantities of rum, brandy, and bourbon all poured together
into the same container – hidden on top of the armoire. Another
was cached behind a false back in the drawer which held
her chemises. The false back was made of cardboard and

held in place with sealing-wax; in addition to the liquor, the narrow space was filled with empty and half-empty bottles of Female Elixir and Kendal Black Drop.

No letters.

Even more curious, given what Mrs Passmore had said, no money.

Francis's room, on the other hand, was crammed with correspondence, all neatly bundled in red ribbons, not pink. More than could possibly be explored, particularly by the shaded gleam of a candle-lamp. January's nerves fizzled with the knowledge that if anyone came up the stair – if the guard set on the terrace had instructions to walk the house, for instance – he was trapped. He was now legally a runaway slave, and his very flight would be considered a suspicious circumstance, in the eyes of whites who were one and all outraged by the fact that slaves didn't trust them or their laws.

Hannibal had clearly judged aright about Francis forging the will. The desk was littered with quills as well as more modern steel-nibbed pens, and he found one sheet (which he stuffed into Hannibal's saddlebag) of practice letters and words, trying to adjust the shape of the letters to match those of another hand, presumably that of his brother.

He also found a small kit of geologist's tools, presumably assembled during the phase of preparation for an expedition to the lost San Diablo Mine. One of the thick packets of papers on the desk seemed to be maps of varying ages. January took a hammer and chisel from the kit (and the pistol and bullet-pouch that lay in the drawer beside it) and pried off the top of the fourth stair from the top of the backstairs, where he'd hidden the papers that Hannibal had judged would prove Francis's attempt at forgery.

The papers were still there.

Beside them – January recalled that he'd only pried up the board enough to slip the packet of papers inside – lay another packet of what looked like letters, and a carved ebony music-box which, when opened, proved to contain a hundred and seventy-seven dollars in gold and silver coin.

Vincent was pretty sure Aunt Alicia has a cache of money someplace . . .

Auntie just wants money . . .

No, he reflected. *Auntie wants her freedom.*

As do we all, Mrs Passmore. As do we all.

And, he reflected, *I thought that board came up rather easily this afternoon . . .*

The letters bore no address or superscription. The top one began, *Beloved Alicia,* and was signed, *Ever yours, Gideon.*

And the line immediately above that signature was: *As you love me, burn this letter.*

Being Alicia, of course she hadn't.

January shoved them into his saddlebags, along with the money and the papers collected by Hannibal.

Pollack . . .

A voice like poisoned cream . . . He can talk anyone into anything . . .

He even got Aunt Alicia all in a flutter . . .

M'am Amelia chewin' into her sister, that Aunt Alicia had a lover . . .

The only man of whom poor Doña Alicia is not afraid.

The way the woman's voice had cracked when she'd gasped, *He kissed me!*

Aunt Alicia and Pollack. Aunt Alicia who was desperate for some way out of her sister's household, the household of the nephew she had never ceased to fear.

She used to stare at the men while they worked . . .

He would have seen the terrified fascination that interlaced her dread. Would have known how to use it.

Run. Run now, before that guard comes in . . .

Instead he went into the room that Taggart had shared with Valentina.

On the top shelf of the larger of the room's two armoires he found, shoved roughly behind some clean shirts, a calico shirt fouled with dust and sweat whose right sleeve bore crusts of dried blood. More blood had dribbled on the back – where blood would leak from the cut throat of a man carried from one cave half a mile to another. A pair of wool trousers was there also, shoved in carelessly, as if the man who'd stripped out of them had done so with his furious wife pounding on the bedroom door.

And behind these, yet another bundle of papers. It was larger and thicker than the others: some parchment, some vellum, some old brown paper, cracked with age. Pot-hooked and abbreviated legal Latin and antique Spanish. Land deeds, January realized. Definitions of grants. Locations of boundaries. From the King of Spain, from the Mission San Saba, from the Viceroy of Mexico and the Emperor Iturbe and Anastasio Bustamante.

'Oh,' said January, as he understood. 'October,' he said. 'Ortega.'

Everything seemed to drop into place, with the disconcerting suddenness of a dream.

Some frightful thing . . .

Quietly and rather thoughtfully, he uttered the most scatological curse he could think of, because the whole thing would have been funny, had three people not died and had he not been frightened almost out of his wits and in near-immediate danger of enslavement.

No time for that now. He shoved shirt, trousers, and papers into the now-bulging saddlebags and turned his attention to the little 'cabinet', a sort of dressing-room in one of the stumpy towers that flanked the house's upstairs front gallery. It was the twin of Aunt Alicia's room on the other side of the house and the gallery would shield its window from the eyes of the guard on the front terrace – if he remained on the terrace.

The little room was locked and, at a guess, Taggart had had the key on him when he'd been killed. *Unless the killer took it, in which case it's on its way to Austin by this time . . .*

The adobe walls were thick. How well would sound carry?

He took a pillow from the bed, inserted the thin end of Francis's geological chisel into the lock, muffled the thick end, and dealt it a smart blow with the hammer. The sound rang – to his ears – like doomsday in the silent darkness. With a feeling of stepping into a trap he entered the little dressing-room. Another armoire in there, and a shaving-stand. He pulled open the bottom drawer of the armoire, yanked it all the way out and yes, there was a false back on it and yes, there was an iron strongbox in the hidden rear compartment.

He caught it up – it was heavy enough to contain a thousand

dollars in gold, but iron strongboxes weighed like stones even empty – started to turn . . .

'Get your hands up,' said Mrs Passmore's voice. 'Or I'll blow your head off.'

TWENTY-ONE

January dropped the box, hammer, and chisel, and flung himself sidelong at the door which led to the front gallery. This was bolted rather than locked, and he had a good idea of what Mrs Passmore would do before she'd fire at him – not with a guard downstairs, she wouldn't.

But on the gallery, he saw torches below and flattened at once against the wall.

Peering down, he saw them: men with torches dismounting in front of the house.

The guard stepped from the porch and flicked away his cigaretto. January thought he recognized the man's blue flannel shirt and the next minute his voice, with its drawling Mississippi inflection, confirmed it.

'Not a soul stirrin', Mr Pollack,' Creed said.

'Good.' Gideon Pollack allowed his brother Rance to help him from the saddle, but afterwards shook off his supporting hand. His voice sounded as strong – as beautiful – as ever. 'Rance, you take four men and search the barns. He's got to put those wagons someplace.'

January slithered back through the door to the dressing-room, where Cornelia Passmore, who'd been bent over the strongbox, had just risen to her knees in alarm.

'Pollack's men,' said January in an undervoice. 'Searching the house.'

Mrs Passmore uttered an expression that would have made the Devil blush in Hell.

January shoved the drawer back into the bottom of the armoire, caught Mrs Passmore's hand – the last thing he needed was her sending them after him as a diversion – and darted through the bedroom (leaving the dressing-room door open in the hopes that, in the darkness, these new searchers wouldn't see the lock had been forced), through Valentina's boudoir, through the guest-room where Hannibal's plundered luggage still lay on the narrow bed.

The window above the bed looked down onto the roof of the work-room, which in its turn backed up against the kitchens: the escape route, in fact, that Valentina had taken on Tuesday morning. Since the men – assured by Creed that not a creature had come near the place since Quigley had hauled away the family and servants – had simply entered the house through the front and hadn't surrounded the place, nobody remarked their egress, though flickering orange reflections fell through the windows of the downstairs rear rooms almost at once. Mrs Passmore was clearly of two minds whether she should reveal herself to Pollack's men – surely most of them would recognize her from Austin, where she'd been pointed out as Taggart's mistress. She followed January with quiet agility, out the window and across the roofs, still clutching the heavy strongbox to her side, to the dark mass of the kitchen chimneys.

Behind these they crouched, as – by the sound of it – men went thoroughly through the house. Torches moved in the darkness around the barns and corrals as well.

'What are they after?' breathed Mrs Passmore.

'At a guess,' lied January, 'exactly what we're after. Either one of your friend Fleam's men blabbed that Taggart was stockpiling gold for a pay-off, or Pollack's got a friend at the bank. Pollack got wind of that gold somehow – and it may be more than a thousand dollars; we have no idea what Taggart was up to. Unless,' he added, 'we're both idiots and Francis was right about having found which was the correct map to the lost San Diablo mine.'

She whispered, 'Mother of . . . You don't think so? That little weasel . . .'

'I don't know. I know there were a dozen maps in his study and a list of what he'd need for an expedition into Comanche country—'

'Including bodyguards like Fleam?'

'I certainly wouldn't go in that direction by myself. I take it that "will" Francis was waving around gave the whole of the property to him?'

'Lock, stock, and the living-room carpet.' She brushed a loose strand of gray-dyed hair from her forehead. 'Not a half-penny piece for Mama, not a bottle of rum for Auntie, not a spavined horse for his wife to ride back to Mexico on . . . nothing. Didn't even pass along title of Mama's maid to her. And some of the clumsiest forgery I've seen in my life, though I'm not the expert that Hannibal is. A good lawyer will tear it to pieces in ten minutes – or he would in the USA. God knows what would happen in a Texas court.'

They were silent for a time, as two men came back from the corrals, lanterns swinging in their hands.

'Where'd you leave your horse?' he asked softly.

'Far end of the orchard. Well, it wasn't mine, it was one I grabbed from Quigley's posse . . . Where's yours?'

'In the corral, saddled. See how they're searching the barns? They'll probably miss him in the darkness. Did you ever hear anything about Pollack and Aunt Alicia?'

Again she was silent, and the damp wind breathed down off the hills, bringing the faint thread of smoke. 'Why do you ask?'

'Something I heard from one of the men,' said January. 'And I found one of his love letters.'

Cornelia Passmore sighed. 'He did that kind of thing,' she said at length. 'Got people to spy for him, I mean. I'm not surprised that when Madrecita and Aunt Alicia showed up, Pollack set about romancing one or the other of them. He'd obviously have a better shot with Alicia. She wasn't as clever as her sister – even making allowances for rum and dope – and she was desperate to get out of her sister's household. Who wouldn't be?'

'Did Pollack want a spy in Taggart's household on general principles?' January recalled the noblewomen and society ladies in Paris, who routinely bribed the maidservants of their social foes – or the foes of their husbands' political rivals. 'Or did he suspect that Taggart was up to something from the start?'

'Well, Vincent was pretty outspoken in his support of
President Lamar and the Nationalists before he went over to
Pollack's side. It might have been a genuine change of heart.
He had one, you know,' she added. 'At least, when he wasn't
drinking. Then in October – must have been a couple months
after Lamar sent his troops after the Cherokee, killed their
chief who was a friend of Sam Houston's, and tore off his
skin for souvenirs – Vincent started making up to Pollack.
That was just before Madrecita and her party showed up. I
think Pollack didn't quite believe the about-face.'

'Did you?'

'Oh, God, no. Vincent thought Pollack was a dungball and
Houston an incompetent drunkard who'd tie Texas to the US
to cover up the fact that he couldn't govern a pig-farm and
his precious republic was going bankrupt. I think that was
how Vin put it. No,' she went on with another sigh, 'Vincent
was up to something. Whether he thought he could prove title
on the three *labors* of good cotton land that Pollack had – that
Vincent said had belonged to *his* original purchase from the
San Saba grant – or whether he was trying to split that idiot
Rance from his brother so Vincent could get him to sign over
some of his water-rights to one of the creeks in the hills, I
don't know. But he made a good hard pitch at Pollack.'

'And Pollack didn't trust him.'

'Not entirely. I'd heard about Pollack making eyes at Alicia
back in October, almost as soon as she arrived. Pollack has
. . . I don't know how to describe it. Probably a man wouldn't
understand.' She shrugged again. 'When he talks to you in
that voice of his . . . But he's married. And even Alicia has
to know that married men don't leave their wives for their
mistresses.'

January said nothing to that. He knew that too many
desperate people – particularly those with limited experience
– have a terrible, tragic inclination to believe what they hope
will come true.

Whatever they were looking for, Pollack's men searched
the house from top to bottom for nearly two hours. The men
came back in from the barns – another group was sent out.
January heard the rancher's voice float up from the yard below,

'. . . can't have disappeared into thin air . . .' Terror that he'd
be caught – impounded as a runaway slave or, worse, claimed
by Mrs Passmore as her own property – made January's hands
shake as he lay on the tile of the roofs, in the dense shadows
of the chimney. Otherwise, exhausted as he was, with barely
three hours of sleep last night and none the night before, he
guessed he would have passed out where he lay.

Smoke drifted on the wind, and he wondered if that was
Jalisco and his men, up in the hills.

Or Comanche.

Or Comancheros, waiting to loot the place as soon as
everyone was gone.

The men rode out with the moon still four hours from
setting. January saw Creed walk the perimeter of the house
and the courtyard wall, once, trailing the smoke of his cigaretto.
Mentally timed how long a second circuit would be, but
the cowhand didn't appear again. He wondered if, during the
search of the house, he'd appropriated some of the contents
of Madrecita's cellaret.

In time he tapped his companion's shoulder, helped her over
the tiles of the kitchen roof, to one of the sheds. He slid down,
knowing she wouldn't release her hold on the heavy strongbox,
held up his hands for her. 'I've got you.'

Cautiously and awkwardly, she turned her back and slithered
after him.

Allowing him to remove the pistol from her waistband
and twist one of her arms behind her back even as her feet
touched the ground.

'Inside,' he whispered, pressing the gun-barrel to her side.
'And don't think I wouldn't blow a hole in you, because I
don't have a single thing to lose.'

'Ben—'

'Not – one – word.'

He marched her into the house – Pollack and company had
obligingly left the rear door open – up the stairs, and into
Francis's room, which, he knew, had locks on all its doors.
Still holding his prisoner's wrist, and watching for the obvious
move of attacking him with the iron strongbox, he set the gun
quickly down and extracted a candle from his pocket. 'Put

that box down and light this.' He picked up the gun again, and released her wrist.

'What are you going to do?' She managed to sound innocent and hurt. Terrified, as if any man in January's predicament would take the time for even the speediest of rapes.

'Avoid killing you – if I can.'

'Ben, I wouldn't—'

'You would – in a heartbeat. Although I will remind you that slave-stealing is a capital offense in Texas, so if you still have those forged ownership papers from last time they'd better be good. Now light the candle.' And, when she still hesitated, 'I'm only going to take a hundred dollars of your gold.'

She lit the candle. 'Ben, I have always regretted—'

'I'm glad you have.' By the candle's flickering light – gun still pressed to the woman's side – he made sure all the doors into the study and the upstairs rear gallery were locked, then dug one-handed into the geologist's kit for a length of light rope. 'I'll sleep better at night, knowing of your repentance and regret. Because selling me into slavery in Vicksburg two years ago would have shattered the lives of my wife and children; it would very likely have ended my life within a year or two, and would have left my dearest friend stranded, ill, and quite possibly dying in a strange town with no one to make sure he wasn't murdered by the ham-handed idiot they had as a doctor.'

He set the candle on the corner of the shaving-stand, and backed her up against the foot of the bed.

'Now, I could choke you until you passed out,' he said. 'I can do that one-handed. My hands are big. But as you probably know, it takes an experienced strangler to judge how much is too much pressure and I'm not inclined to err on the side of caution. Or, you can accept my promise that I'm only going to take one hundred dollars of that gold – I saw you slam that strongbox so I assume you picked the lock and that the gold is in there – and you can let me tie you up without any trouble. It's just to keep you from coming after me – I assume there are guns all over this house – until I can make a clean getaway. I'm going to blindfold you, leave this key –' he brandished the key to the door that led into the hall – 'in the lock of the door – there's paper on the table here, and you can use one of Brother Francis's stick-pins to poke it through and pull it back under the door. I'm going to hide the gold somewhere in the house. Then I'll come up, untie your hands, and make my run for it.'

'What, you're not going to promise to marry me as well? That's what the last man I believed promised.'

'Mrs Passmore,' sighed January, 'do you believe that it would be much, much easier for me to kill you?'

'Pig.' She heaved the strongbox onto the bed, and extended her arm to one side of the bedpost.

'A pig is an extremely intelligent animal, m'am. More so than most dogs.' Moving swiftly, and keeping the side of his waistband where he'd thrust the pistol turned away from any chance of being grabbed, he knotted the rope around her wrists on either side of the bedpost, then for good measure passed the bond under and through the stringers that held the posts together. He pulled the knots tight, cut off the slack, and used a yard of it to tie her feet to the stringers of the footboard as well. He felt in his pocket for a bandana, remembered he'd used it to wrap up poor Hookwire's severed hand (*Was that only yesterday?*), swiftly fished two handkerchiefs from Francis's carved mahogany bureau (*And how much did that cost, to transport here from Virginia?*), and used one to blindfold her, the other to gag her.

'The hundred dollars,' he said, opening the strongbox – and yes, it contained an assortment of ten- and five-dollar American gold pieces, plus a great deal of American and Mexican silver, and a paper with a list of names on it. The first of them was *Fleam* – 'is partly for my inconvenience, partly to buy me dinner when I get to Austin, and partly to get me the hell out of this godforsaken republic. You can keep the rest.'

She made a noise behind the gag, probably telling him what he could do with the hundred dollars.

He pocketed the list and ten ten-dollar gold pieces, then carried the strongbox and the candle from the room. Four more ten-dollar pieces he laid on the floor of the hall just outside the door of the room, then proceeded to move swiftly through the house, concealing some of the money, leaving other little piles where she would be sure to find them – to remind her to keep searching. His last stop was the kitchen, where he filled three canteens with water and crammed the remainder of the tortillas and cheese into the overstuffed saddlebags.

'You probably have three hours,' he said, when he returned to the bedroom and untied her hands, 'before anyone comes to search the house again, so you should find the gold fairly easily. I've hidden Francis's stick-pins, just to give myself a little more time, but I doubt that'll slow you down much. But be quick,' he added, retreating to the door. 'Unless you trust Mr Creed.'

She said something else behind the gag.

Will I regret not killing her? How is a woman selling a man into slavery different from a man selling a girl?

No difference.

He would have watched Seth Javel burn without a qualm.

He still couldn't do it.

He closed the door, locked it, left the key in the lock, and descended the stair as lightly as he could. The gold-pieces on the floor, the hall table, the dining-table winked in his candle-light as he hurried from the house. The big bay horse he'd stolen earlier in the day – had its owner appropriated one of the Taggart herd in compensation? – was still in the farthest corral, still saddled. *What's the penalty for horse-theft in Texas?* He slipped the bit into its mouth, mounted, and rode to the far end of the orchard, where, in fact, a stringy dapple-gray gelding was tied.

It was hard not to break into a gallop, but he knew that the sound of two galloping horses would carry a long way on a still night. It was another three hours before he reached Witch Cave Canyon, and the moon had passed out of sight behind the rim. He lit one of the lanterns he'd taken from the house, and by its bobbing, uneven light, walked the horses until he came to the pond that Jalisco had described, where Arroyo Bruja bubbled and trickled down from the cave itself.

There'd better not be a bear in that cave . . .

Saint Francis, friend of animals, was in a good mood that night. The cave was empty.

He watered the horses, led them up the tangle of rocks, and

through the damp arch of stone to a rocky hollow that bore signs of being an old camping-place for *somebody*, clearly many years ago. It was dawn before he'd unsaddled the animals and rubbed down their backs – they'd been worked all day and he felt considerable sympathy for them – then rolled himself, finally, up in the saddle-blankets and went to sleep.

Virgin Mary, Mother of God, let me know in the morning what I owe you for getting me through these past two days . . .

His last thought was of Rose, and his children.

I'll get back somehow, I promise.

TWENTY-TWO

It was full daylight – gray and cloudy – when January woke. He had dreamed of Bellefleur Plantation, where he'd been born. Of the grinding, sickened fear that he'd lived with all his childhood, tied to the household of a man who liked nothing better than to drink himself into raving fury, secure in the knowledge that neither his wife, nor his sons, nor his slaves had the power to either raise a hand against his behavior, or to leave.

Michie Fourchet had called this, 'being free to live as I choose'. Most white men did.

As far as January could tell as an adult, looking back, drunken rage was the only joy the man had, not caring that it was at the expense of everyone around him.

In his dream January had been trapped in the house, where no black child was allowed. He ran in terror from room to room, knowing if he was found he'd be tied to a post in the barn and clubbed with a broom-handle. He'd later learned that there were laws in Louisiana against beating slaves to death but he knew also that these laws weren't often enforced. In his dream – in his child-self – he knew only that he'd seen his nine-year-old friend Cal beaten to death with a wagon-chain.

And he couldn't find his way out.

Instead of opening onto the galleries, front and back, the

ten rooms seemed only to open into each other. Somewhere he could hear Michie Fourchet's heavy footfall, hear his drunken voice bellowing, 'You listen to me when I'm talkin' to you!' The smell of the man – the reek of liquor that seemed to come out of his sweat – hung in the air, clogged his nostrils when he breathed. He saw a girl running, too, darting through doorways glimpsed from the corner of his eye. A tall girl, vaguely pretty, with a wide, sensual mouth and sky-blue eyes. Sometimes she was a child, as young as he. Huge blue near-sighted eyes – she stumbled on the edges of rugs, or blundered into the sides of doors in her clumsiness. Soft brown curls bounced when she jerked her head around to listen, like a nervous hare.

Sometimes she was older, fifteen, sixteen, seventeen.

I was sold, he thought. *She couldn't even be that.*

Once he saw her in her bedroom, sprawled on her bed with her skirts turned up to her chin and a boy her own age standing at the bed's foot, buttoning up his flies. 'You tell an' I'll say you begged me to.' He had rough sandy-brown hair that fell over his forehead, and her same pale-blue eyes. A strong chin, a half-familiar face.

'I'll say it to Pa an' I'll say it to every man an' boy in this county. That you was a whore an' you pestered me. Go ahead, Vin,' he added, turning to the boy that January hadn't seen until that moment, standing in the doorway, looking on. 'What's the matter? Can't get it up?' He laughed like a neighing horse and bent over the weeping girl again.

January woke, hearing rain on the trees outside the cave, and the wild purling of the stream below. He remembered how Michie Fourchet would take a fancy to this woman or that in the quarters – quite young girls, some of them. He remembered looking out the door of their cabin once, seeing his mother cleaning herself in a bucket in the half-light before she'd come in, not just bruises but blood.

One of his aunties had said, *You just have to put up with it, til he gets tired.*

He wondered if Jack Taggart had ever gotten tired.

He shut his eyes again. *Virgin Mary, Mother of God, what can I do?*

Virgin Mary, Mother of God, rest her poor, battered soul.

Tiny and far-off, like a single blink of glass in sunlight, he saw his own parlor on Rue Esplanade, and Rose in her dress of faded pink calico, standing behind Selina Bellinger's chair. Saw old Roux Bellinger come in the door and run, weeping, to clasp his daughter in his arms.

Is this only something I'm *desperate to believe?*

When he woke again the rain had stopped. The stream below the cave-pool still sounded loud. *Couldn't I have had a dream vision of Bellinger writing Rose a bank-draft to pay me for all this?*

He led his stolen horses down to drink, and fashioned halters out of what was left of the rope, tying the beasts where the grass grew thick. The smell, and the sound, of the water were like a song, quiet in his heart. He sat on the rocks by the pool to keep an eye on the horses, tossed them slices of dried peaches and dried apples from the Perdition kitchen. Ate stale tortillas and salty white cheese, and read Gideon Pollack's love letters to Alicia Marryat.

Beloved . . .

In the first of them it was, *Miss Marryat.* He worked up to *Beloved* later.

How the Hell *could she believe this?* Knowing what she knew, of the man's distrust of her nephew?

But it was obvious that she had.

Did anyone ever call her 'Beloved' in her life? Or say the word to her that he and Rose so casually passed back and forth, with smiling kisses and the touch of treasured hands?

The letters spoke of meetings. Of time snatched among the oak-woods of the bottomlands, in the deep shade beyond the prairies where *'by your kind efforts'* Pollack's sheep and cattle grazed on Alicia's nephew's land. Of *the lovemaking that brought me within touching-distance of ecstasy . . .*

I stand in awe of the gift you have given me. The memory of your limbs entwined with mine makes my heart pound even now . . .

January thought of Selina, locked in a back room of the Capital City Hotel. Of her tiny whisper, *He hurt me . . .* And the hair prickled on his scalp.

Pollack might have had charm, but he laid it on with a trowel. And obviously, Alicia devoured it.

Why not? The poor woman was starving.

You have no idea what relief it is, after all these years of beating my head against the stone wall of indifference and stupidity, to talk with someone who truly understands politics . . . Meaning, January gathered, the necessity of Texas joining the Union. Like threads of indigo in a tapestry, loyalty to the United States twined around the crimson dialog of passion: *I could not love thee, dear, so much/ loved I not honor more* . . .

I count the days until I dare sever the poisonous bonds that hold me, and take you to be my wife.

So the payment for spying on Taggart was the promise of marriage. The promise of freedom. The hope of love.

Then towards the end, rage and fear, that her nephew had betrayed her lover. *He has lied about a great and patriotic undertaking. He has, I have come more and more to fear, betrayed a secret of which I cannot speak, even to you* . . .

The pain of my wound yesterday was as nothing to the joy I felt at seeing you, as you ran to our meeting-place . . .

Clearly, he'd ridden to meet her at some point after the duel. *He* must *be tough as prairie sod,* as Marcus Mudsill had said. And what Taggart had done – what Taggart had paid Silver Joe Fleam a thousand dollars in gold to do – was important enough to him, to endanger his life.

Have you learned anything, come to know any way by which he, and that spitfire wife, and all within the house can be got rid of? You must *help me clear away those imbecile guards he's posted, all around his lands. This is imperative, my love. The house – and the grounds – must be emptied, for reasons I cannot – dare not – reveal. He has committed treason, and will commit a greater unless I can stop him. Like Eurydice I must beg of you, trust you – do not ask questions. Do not look back. Do not speak of this to a living soul. You are stronger of soul than the Thracian singer was. I know I can rely on you* . . .

Every one of the letters ended, *As you love me – as you hope for our love and our future together – I beg you, burn this letter.*

Had he meant for Alicia to murder her nephew?

It was hard to tell. And hard to guess what he might have said to her, in the hot, clammy shadows of the bottomlands. As Cornelia Passmore had observed, it might not even have made sense to someone who wasn't a woman desperate, and in love.

It was certainly a stupid solution to the problem. But who could tell what Pollack had whispered to Alicia when they'd met on the Friday before Taggart's death? (*It could scarcely have been earlier, given the amount of blood the man lost . . .*)

Not a difficult meeting to arrange, if Creed was in his pay. The bottomlands, in the trees not far from the cotton fields, would be easy to reach from Los Lobos, and an unlikely place to encounter Comanche.

The final note was short. *My darling, I must see you. Tomorrow at nine, in the orchard. Creed will be keeping watch.*

Was that so she wouldn't flee when she saw Creed waiting there? Or had the cowhand kept guard on their meetings before?

Had she kept all these letters – the last note tucked loosely into the ribbon at the bottom of the pile – only because he called her *Darling*? Because she couldn't bear to burn paper that bore his handwriting? Or had she had another reason?

He cached the letters in his shirt-pocket, pulled from the saddlebag the thick bundle of old deeds. They were difficult to read – the clerks who'd written them didn't know Latin (or, in some cases, Spanish) very well, and they were full of abbreviations and clerical pot-hooks. But the same names cropped up in all of them. Sauceito Creek. Elbow Canyon (*Cubitus Amnis*). Mission San Diablo.

It looked like – sounded like – the boundaries of the same stretch of land, granted to the Valenzuela family 'in conditional usufruct under the absolute title granted to the Order of St Francis at San Saba . . .'

It would take a lawyer – or several lawyers – or a series of court decisions beside which the English Courts of Chancery would appear as simple as nursery-rhymes – to figure out who actually owned the land between the Little Colorado, the Pedernales, San Diablo Hill, Elbow Canyon (or Creek) etc. etc. January recalled with a shudder the English case Hannibal had spoken of, which had been going since 1798 with no decision in sight.

And as he considered this, his fingers took in the textures of those old documents: hard, rough parchment. Smoother, paler vellum. Thick paper, stiff and brown with age.

The different hues of the faded ink. And most particularly, the pale red stains where seals had been winkled off the documents with a hot knife. *To be affixed elsewhere . . .*

By that time the sun was high. The creek had come down a little, though its voice still babbled strong. January led the horses back up into Witch Cave, tied the dapple at the back, and saddled the bay. He took the saddlebags with him: *No sense taking chances.* It took a bit of searching to find the remains of the old road up the narrowing canyon, but it wasn't so overgrown, he judged, that ten or eleven determined men (with the prospect of being paid a thousand dollars in gold) couldn't have taken a couple of wagons up it.

He wondered what they'd done with the horses and mules.

Not left them at Perdition, anyway. Even with Taggart's men keeping intruders away, somebody was bound to notice and talk.

The overgrown road was flooded, right across, in three places. But it rose as the canyon shallowed and the stream-bed was left behind. The mouth of the old Bruja copper mine was overgrown, too, and barely larger than the caves further down the canyon. Someone had taken the trouble to scratch out the tracks of wagon-wheels in the tunnel, but he found the sticks of three Lucifer matches, flicked to the side where he flicked his own when he lit his lantern.

And fifty feet down the tunnel, there they were.

Three wagons, loaded with goods-crates – many of them still stamped with the names of Houston and Galveston warehouses. *That should make them easy to trace . . .*

The stolen government archives of the Republic of Texas.

They were lined up doubletree-to-tailboard: Fleam and his men must have unhitched them and man-handled them up the tunnel. He guessed that Taggart had dictated the order in which they were stored, because the one nearest the mouth of the tunnel – and easiest to get to – was the one in which one of the goods crates had been later pried open, and documents extracted.

And replaced. Taggart had put slips of plain note-paper to mark the place in the crate – and no wonder, the box was filled with other deeds, other grants, other land-holding documents within that section of the archives. He'd wanted to make damned sure that he got every grant and deed and document that related to his own land, and to that transferred to his wife by her Uncle Gael, and replaced them with grants and deeds and documents which proved his own title to those lands unquestionable beyond shadow of doubt. None of this 'usufruct' or 'absolute title granted to the Order of St Francis' nonsense.

January pulled out one of the documents, and compared it with its twin in the bundle in his saddlebag.

Gervase Hookwire had done his job well. Every word, every letter, every pot-hook – the very ink and parchment – were identical. Except that the title was granted, absolutely, in perpetuity (a lawyer himself, Taggart must have spent months looking up what to say), and at the sole discretion of, Alejandro de la Vega, who thirty years later in another document transferred them absolutely, in perpetuity, and at the sole discretion of Cosimo Valenzuela – the grandfather of Uncle Gael . . .

'You fucking bastard,' sighed January. He wasn't even sure to whom he spoke. Vincent Taggart. Gideon Pollack. All white men. (Though he knew dozens of black ones who'd have perpetrated the same hoax if they'd had the power to do so and thought they could get away with it . . . starting with Seth Javel . . .)

The entire Republic of Texas, of which he now hated every square inch.

He could, he calculated, reach Austin by dark, riding east to the Colorado River and then south into town. Following the Pedernales would be quicker, but would take him through the bottomlands where men grew cotton. More people, and every one of them on the lookout for a runaway slave.

Either way he ran the risk of encountering Pollack's men.

By this time they'd be criss-crossing Perdition land looking for someplace where three wagonloads of the republic's archives could have been cached. A bodyguard would help, but riding around looking for Jalisco and his men would put him in greater danger of being caught by the Pollacks, not something he wanted to risk. He was almost out of tortillas and cheese, though his sparing consumption of them at breakfast had left him profoundly unsatisfied.

Would Quigley ride out today to have a look at the house, and at the scene of Aunt Alicia's murder?

Or had he combed through the long grass around those two stumps in the orchard yesterday evening, and found whatever there was to find?

If they're hunting, he thought, *they'll be hunting by daylight. And with the stream high and the canyon half-flooded, there's every chance they won't come up here til tomorrow.*

He led the horses back to the Witch Cave – being careful to scratch out his own tracks in the mine-tunnel, and pick up the match-sticks – and from there picked his way on foot to the small, high cave where he'd cached Hookwire's spare pens, papers, pigment-pots. Remembering the precise artistry of the fakes that Taggart had inserted into the archives, he had to shake his head in admiration. The clerkish little bald-pate had truly been an artist (and he was almost certain Hannibal was going to try to make off with the implements of forgery when this was all over: in his way, Hannibal was an artist, too).

(That is, provided either of us lives through this . . .)

The larger, lower cave in which Hookwire had worked – and died – was more comfortable to lie up in for a day, but January remained where he was. He read through Pollack's letters to Alicia again, piecing together fragments of their conversations – of the way the rancher had used the desperate, miserable woman as his spy – and wishing he could read what Alicia had written to Pollack. Twice Pollack referred to poems she had written.

At least Selina could be rescued. At least people would believe her, when she said, *I was raped*. Would understand why she wanted to escape.

You asked for it, Alicia's sister – the sister who had raised her – had shouted.

Fifteen years. And then to be bullied into accompanying her sister to the house of another perpetrator.

No wonder she lived on laudanum and novels where everything ended happily.

He read through, also, the papers Hannibal had collected from Francis's study. Words had been ticked with pencil in the seemingly random bundle of letters, account-books, bills. The young man had noted how his middle brother had formed the words 'give' and 'will', 'absolutely' and 'brother', 'Rancho Perdition' and, in one place, 'bequeath'. He'd had a couple of Taggart's signatures to copy, and those of men from Galveston and Corpus Christi – men who, if they existed at all, probably couldn't be looked up at this late date, to testify whether they'd actually witnessed Vincent Taggart's will or not. There were four practice drafts of the will.

Provided Valentina wasn't convicted of her husband's murder, this would amply pay her for the help she'd given him. Then he remembered the young woman's kindness to Selina at the Ekholm farm, her matter-of-fact acceptance that had restored the shattered girl to confidence.

No. Nothing can ever repay her.

Later he slept again – a childhood spent in slavery had given him the ability to fall asleep even though gnawed with hunger – and he dreamed of Rose, and his children, back in New Orleans.

When the shadow of the opposite canyon rim fell chillingly across the cave-mouth and he woke, he hid Pollack's letters, Taggart's bloodstained clothing, and the true land documents relating to Perdition, in separate nooks at the far back of the cave, well away from Hookwire's forgery kit, and ate the last of his rations. In the advancing twilight he returned to Witch Cave, watered the horses again and staked them for awhile outside to graze, then saddled the bay and rode northeast up the canyon, until he found one of the steep-sided gorges that led up and out onto the hills.

The moon was rising. The day's clouds had broken, showing him enough of the hills to orient himself – more or less – toward the Colorado River, ten miles – more or less – north-east.

I can do this, he told himself.

And then I can turn the whole thing over to Sheriff Quigley, and get myself and Hannibal the hell out of Texas.

Always supposing Hannibal hasn't been hanged already for murdering Aunt Alicia.

But he guessed that Quigley was smart enough to realize that a woman couldn't just tear off a man's old-style cravat – which wound several times around the wearer's throat – while he was in the process of strangling her. *And if he isn't, Hannibal's smart enough to point out that this is a rather longer procedure than simply tearing off a bandana.*

Even if Quigley doesn't want to listen – if for whatever reason he wants to push Hannibal onto the gallows – I doubt he could do it that *quickly . . .*

But the thought of being stranded in Texas, three days' travel from any seaport, turned January cold.

The Texas hills were full of more than long-horn cattle and Comanche. January had seen Comancheros in Austin, men who traded with the tribes for stolen horses, stolen mules, and slaves to sell, either deeper into Texas or, if they were women or children, north to the Navajo. He had also seen bandits, who would trade anything with anyone and would certainly be delighted to encounter an unclaimed black man – free papers or no free papers.

I will never – not ever *– help anybody in trouble again. Nor will I ever leave the French Town again except possibly to move to Massachusetts . . . or to Canada, for that matter . . .*

Movement on the hillside to his right. Cattle grazed there, moonlight sliding along those grotesque horns, but they rose and moved off, startled, wild as deer with the sudden appearance of two riders from a stand of oak.

One of the men shouted, 'You, there!'

Damn it . . .

A white man could probably have talked his way out of 'What the hell you doin' on this land?'

In Texas, a black man by himself at night was assumed to be a runaway.

January jabbed his heels into the bay's sides, and took off for the nearest gully where trees offered the shelter of darkness. Hooves thundered behind him. 'Pull up, goddammit!' and a shot. January flattened on the bay's neck, tried to form a plan – *how far does that gully go? Which direction?*

Another rider emerged from the gully, and moonlight glinted on a rifle-barrel. January veered, sent the bay slithering down the steep side of the gully, heard the men curse as they plunged down after him. It was black down there, like riding into a cave. January dropped from the saddle, pulled the saddlebags off and slung them on his shoulder, slapped the horses to send them running and doubled back in the direction he thought he'd come, down the gully, praying he'd be able to find his way once daylight came. He heard a rider pass him in the dark, the man cursing fit to peel paint off a gate. A thread of moonlight winked ahead of him and to his right; his foot slithered on a stone, crunched softly in last year's dry vegetation.

How long will they keep looking?

That probably depends on who they think they're looking for.

He followed the moonlight, feeling his way from tree to tree. It was too dark even to find a place to go to ground. The ground was rising, and he moved closer toward the moonlight, nearly breaking his leg where the rocks dropped off suddenly in an old water-course. *There's got to be a tree I can climb. Or a deadfall I can hide in . . .*

That isn't inhabited by rattlesnakes?

Movement again beyond the trees. The next minute, another blink of moonlight on cattle-horns. The glint of reflective eyes.

Something that felt like an oak in front of him, a gnarled trunk and – as he felt upwards – branches he could reach, that seemed thick and strong enough to bear his weight. Leaves like black clouds—

'Got you, boy.' A hand on his shoulder and a pistol-barrel in his back. 'Next move you make gonna be your last.'

TWENTY-THREE

'You're that feller Sefton's boy.' Gideon Pollack rose from the chair in the Perdition hacienda's dining-room. He held out his hand to January as the ginger-haired Shaughnessy and Mudsill brought him in through the back door. 'One who helped Doc Meredith save my life.' In the light of the lamp on the table Pollack looked awful, his eyebrows standing out black against waxen features, his face drawn with pain. From two feet away January could smell the wound, a smell he knew from years working the clinic at the Hôtel Dieu.

'You need to get that wound looked at right away, sir.'

When the man's hand clasped his, January could feel it dangerously hot. All his fear, all his disgusted rage at the man, could not, for the moment, eradicate the healer's instincts that had ruled his life for as long as he could remember.

Pollack coughed, the wet, heavy sound of pleura filling with fluid. 'When I'm done here,' he said. 'Rance, get me some whiskey.'

His brother lumbered out to obey.

Pollack sat, flipped open the saddlebag that Mudsill had dropped on the table in front of him. 'What'd you run away for?'

'If you was a black man in this country you wouldn't be asking that question, sir.'

The man grinned, and pulled out the little bundle of gold pieces, wrapped in one of Alicia's handkerchiefs. The grin faded as he weighed the coin in his hand. 'Where'd you get this?'

'It was hid under a board in the backstairs, sir. The hand-kerchief was with it.' (It hadn't been, but January wasn't going to go into how thoroughly he'd searched the house or who else had been there, unless he had to.) 'I think it was Miss Marryat's, sir. One of the other men here said as how she pinched money, from her nephew and whoever else was in the house – I think from my master as well.'

His anger at Pollack surged back under the man's hard gaze. And with it, disgust at himself for the pity he'd felt. This man had raped Selina Bellinger – and Heaven only knew how many others among his bondswomen. He had used, and betrayed, Alicia Marryat as coldly and deliberately as Seth Javel had used Selina. At least Javel hadn't pushed Selina into killing a man.

And Javel hadn't ordered anyone – probably Eli Creed – to kill Selina when he was done with her.

Yet January couldn't keep himself from saying, when Rance returned with a bottle half-full of whiskey and a glass, 'You're feverish, sir. And if you'll permit me to say so—'

Pollack poured himself a glass and gave January a crooked grin. 'I'll not permit you to say so, son. This is just enough to loosen me up a little. Rance?' He glanced up at his brother, inquiring.

'Not a thing yet.'

'Keep looking. He's got to have done something with it.' The rancher shook his head, as if to clear a buzzing from his ears, and returned his gaze to January. 'So you thought you'd run away in all the confusion?'

'No, sir,' January returned. 'When I came back from the corrals, and saw Sheriff Quigley leading off my master and everyone else in the house, I–I was afraid of what was like to happen to me, if I got taken, too. In Vicksburg and Natchez, and places like Baltimore, you get slave-stealers comin' through the jails, pickin' every likely man an' boy, an' payin' the jailers to look the other way when they says, "Oh, that man's a runaway".'

He saw Pollack's eyes shift. He'd heard that story, too.

Maybe from men he'd bought.

'Beggin' your pardon if he's a friend of yours, sir,' continued January, with the assumed diffidence he had all his life been forced to practice. 'But I didn't know a thing about Sheriff Quigley. Nor about his deputies nor his jailer. My master's ill, and he knows no one in Texas. I stayed back in the darkness til everyone was gone, then snuck in and searched the house for this money they said Miss Alicia had hid. I knew I'd need it, if I was to get back to Austin and see what I could do for Michie Sefton.'

Pollack sniffed. 'You didn't need to worry, boy. Atticus Quigley's a bone-headed jackass and a traitor to his country, but he's got his honor where the law's concerned. I'll give him that.' As he spoke he stacked the gold pieces: five, ten, fifteen, twenty, twenty-five, and assorted smaller stacks of silver, and fingered the stout linen of the handkerchief, with its over-elaborate embroidery: AM. 'She piled up more than I thought,' he added softly, in that deep, velvety voice. 'Poor silly bitch.'

January said nothing to that. *The memory of your limbs entwined with mine makes my heart pound . . .*

It went without saying that he'd made no such sweet-talk to Selina. When Pollack coughed again – the wet, heavy hacking of a man struggling to breathe – January thought, *You're dying, Mister*, and was glad.

Beyond Pollack's shoulder, January could see lamps and lanterns moving around in the hallway. Heard the voices of men, the crunch and rip of upholstery being torn or stair-risers taken up. As he and his captors had crossed from the corrals to the house, he'd seen men going through the barns and sheds, to see if there was anything they'd missed. They were even digging up Hookwire's grave, to make sure that all that was down there was, in fact, a man's body.

Good luck with that . . .

'And what's this?' Pollack coughed again, and pulled out the bundle of papers from the saddlebag.

'I don't rightly know, sir. My master took those from Mr Francis's study. He told me to hold onto them; said they'd help prove that Mr Francis forged Mr Taggart's will. Mr Francis claimed he'd found the will in a book or someplace in Mr Taggart's rooms, that gives everything to Mr Francis.'

'Huh.' Pollack poured himself another half-glass. 'Vin Taggart knocked his brother down, the one time that crippled little git asked him about a will – and in company, too. By what Alicia told me that hag-witch mother of theirs, and the older brother, Jack, nagged and pestered old George Taggart about his Virginia property til he swore he wouldn't have anything to do with any of 'em. In the end Jack got the old man drunk and had him sign a will that none of 'em ever told him about. Got two of his gambling pals to witness it, knowin' neither of 'em would get a dime of what Jack owed unless they did.'

He shrugged, and grimaced as he drank. Beside the door behind him, January was aware of Mudsill making a movement, as if he would have spoken. Evidently he thought better of it – or perhaps knew that there was no point. At length Pollack said, 'Everybody in the county knew it. The kid doesn't have a leg to stand on.'

Calculation flickered in the velvet-brown eyes. Tender, Malojo had called them. They were like chips of onyx now, wondering, perhaps, how best to seduce Valentina, or Madrecita Taggart, if she ended up in possession.

'That's what my master told M'am Valentina, sir,' agreed January respectfully – so that it wouldn't sound like he had any opinion of his own on the subject. 'I think that's why Mr Francis accused my master of the deed, when he found poor Miss Marryat's body.'

Pollack looked aside, his mouth tightening for a moment. Then he waved a dismissive hand. 'You got nuthin' to worry about, boy.' He tried to clear his throat, fighting for breath.

'No, sir. Thank you, sir.'

'So where *was* you and your master yesterday mornin'?' The dark eyes, though narrowed shrewdly, squinted, struggling to focus. 'He say anythin' about huntin' for somethin'?'

'Yes, sir, he did. We were down the arroyo where Miss Valentina was shot at, hunting for anything – any sign at all – that could prove that it happened as she said. Michie Sefton searched the old jacal down there, and it must have been four miles upstream, where he said there was another ruin of some kind. He didn't say why, sir.'

'Didn't he?' Pollack's frown deepened, and he turned his head as his brother entered again. 'You know anything about other ruins on Sauceito Creek? 'Bout four miles up from the jacal?'

Rance looked puzzled, but Shaughnessy said, 'There's

supposed to be what's left of a Spanish garrison fort someplace up that way, sir. I never heard exactly where it is . . .'

'Think you could find the place again, boy?'

January shook his head. It was one thing to divert their search from Witch Cave Canyon, quite another to accompany them as a prisoner. 'The way the creek rose with the rain, sir, I couldn't be sure of anything.'

Pollack grunted. 'Rance, take a couple of men and have a look.'

'Wasn't Sefton the feller, tried so hard to get that yeller wench away from you?' The younger brother stared hard at January. Pollack's velvety eyes were, in Rance's face, like hard little dark beads, sunk in pouches of fat.

'He's the man who saved my life.'

'You searched him?'

Pollack moved his hand to indicate the empty saddlebags, but Rance strode over to January and shoved hands into his pockets.

'Got a damn fancy watch for a nigger.' He tossed the silver watch on the table. 'And a damn fancy spyglass and compass.'

'They're my master's,' January explained. 'They were left in his room.'

Rance unfolded a half-sheet of crumpled paper that for a moment January didn't recognize.

Then he realized it was the list he'd found in Taggart's strongbox. And had pocketed, as he'd distributed coin throughout the house.

Shit. Damn. Shit.

Rance asked, 'You know what these names are, boy?'

January shook his head and felt as if both men could hear the pounding of his heart.

'Where'd you get this?'

'It was in Miss Marryat's little music-box, where she had the money.'

Pollack's face had changed. He regarded January for a long time in the lamplight, then said, 'Shoot him.'

Rance's small eyes widened. 'Shit, Gideon, Neumann'll give us a thousand dollars for a big buck like him.'

'Rance,' sighed Pollack, 'I love you an' you are the dearest brother a man could ask for, but if brains was gunpowder, you couldn't blow your nose. The last thing we need is a nigger wanderin' around knowin' more than he's sayin'. Shoot him. Shaughnessy, Mudsill, bury him in the same hole with that poor bastard Creed told us about, that got sliced up by the savages.'

As Rance took January by the arm and thrust him at gunpoint toward the door, Pollack rose, and said quietly to January, as if continuing a conversation that had already gone on for an hour, 'I didn't tell her to kill him, you know.'

January turned and looked back at him. Just as softly, he replied, 'It doesn't matter to me, sir. And it won't to you, in about two days.'

Rance looked absolutely baffled by this, but January felt Mudsill's hand flinch, where it closed around his arm. Pollack's mouth hardened again as he turned his face aside, like a man trying to duck a blow.

He said, 'Believe me when I say I was as knocked down as anybody, when I heard. Yeah, I told her Vin was a traitor – which he was. An' when she said he'd meddled with her back home, an' had brought her here to Texas so's he could have his way with her again – I agreed with her, yeah, I'd heard him say so. Although I knew for a fact, Vin was horrified at havin' her under his roof, whatever he'd done in the past . . . Well, I needed someone in the household. Someone close to him, who'd be able to find out what he was up to. Someone who wouldn't feel one shred of loyalty to him.'

He coughed again, this time almost doubled up by the violence of it. January glanced sideways and saw in Rance's face both pity and absolute terror. Terror at the thought of being left alone. Leaving January in the grip of the two cowhands, he stepped back to the table and poured another glass of whiskey, which Pollack drank.

'That's better,' Pollack whispered. 'I hope you believe me, boy. I had to do it. Had to turn her. Just payin' that hound-dog Creed wasn't enough. An' by damn,' he added, 'I was glad I did, when Rance told me . . .' His eyes narrowed a little, as if trying to recall how much January knew or might have guessed.

'Well, I never meant her to kill him. She said he deserved to die an' I said yes, he sure did, but she was always goin' on like that. She'd say that about her sister, too, an' two days later I'd see the two of 'em gigglin' like schoolgirls over some gossip or other. It didn't mean nuthin'. When I told her to clear him an' that Mex wife out of the house for a couple days, I meant set the kitchen on fire, or run cattle through the place – she was a smart rider, an' knew how to shoot. She coulda done it an' not been caught. She was clever, if you got to her in the mornin' 'fore she started in on the dope. Damn if I thought she'd do what she did.'

'But when she did it,' replied January, 'you had to be rid of her, didn't you?'

Rance's face convulsed with fury at this *lèse majesté* and he raised his gun-hand to strike, but his brother gestured him still.

'She was crazy,' said Pollack quietly. 'She wasn't stupid, not in the least. But crazy. An' she got crazier, after she did it.'

'He had raped her,' returned January. 'Whether he'd been pushed into it by his brother, whether he regretted it afterwards, did you think she wouldn't feel anything?'

Pollack gestured again, impatient at the argument. 'Ah, he hadn't hurt her. Women don't really care that much about bein' raped.'

January was silent for a moment. Then, quietly, he asked, 'Or were you just afraid she'd start asking about your divorce?'

Rance hit him, that time, a blow that made his head ring. He staggered, and as Mudsill and Shaughnessy pulled him upright again and he flinched away from a second blow, he heard Pollack say, 'Rance . . .'

His skull pounding, January met Pollack's eyes again.

In them he saw that the man knew he was dying.

Only to see what he'd say, January asked, 'What *are* you looking for, sir?'

Pollack whispered, 'The future of Texas.' And sank back, as if he, not January, had been struck, into his chair, and buried his head in his hands.

'Fucking goddam nigger –' Rance's voice was shaking as he thrust January out the back door into the darkness – 'I'm

gonna fucking kill you for that. I'm gonna shoot you to pieces,
one piece at a time . . . It's your goddam doin' he's failin'!
Your goddam meddlin' with Doc Meredith's takin' the bullet
out.' His grip was like an iron shackle but January could hear
that he wept. 'He'd been fine, if you hadn't throwed Doc
Parralee out, if you hadn't messed with him. Creed!' he yelled.
'Creed!'

The sandy-haired man came running from one of the barns.
'Get the ox-whip. An' a chain.'

In the torchlight, Creed saw the fear in January's face, the
murder in Rance's, and smiled. Like a child, at the prospect
of sweets.

Three more men came running up from the direction of the
orchard and Rance yelled to them, 'Get a rope, an' let's get
this damn nigger –' before he realized – and indeed, before
January realized – that the three men were Jalisco, and the
vaqueros Borrachio, and Yanez.

January wrenched and twisted aside from the pistol that
Rance had pressed to his back, dropping to his knees as the
pistol fired, the ball skinning across his back like the stroke
of a red-hot poker. The next instant one of the vaqueros fired,
and Shaughnessy buckled and fell. Rance and Mudsill fled for
the shelter of the water-trough beside the corral. In the darkness beyond the torchlight January saw riders, gunshots
cracking . . .

'Get your men out of here!' he yelled, as Jalisco caught
hold of him, dragged him back toward the darkness. 'Pollack's
dying – and I know what he wants. I know what's going on.'

'Shit,' gasped the vaquero, 'I'm glad somebody does.' He
raised his voice. '*Vamanos, bravos*! Let's get out of here!'

TWENTY-FOUR

The raid on Hacienda Perdidio had actually been organ-
ized by Jalisco to obtain horses, salt, beans, and flour
from the rancho's stores. It was only chance, Jalisco

said – later, around a campfire in the hills beyond Witch Cave Canyon – that Twenty-One had spotted January being brought in to the hacienda. 'I doubt Pollack told his own men what they were looking for,' January said, sipping coffee from a borrowed tin cup and gnawing from the bone the final fragments of beef. 'Other than that there were three wagons involved – and three wagonloads of boxes. All ten of the men Pollack hired – or instructed Silver Joe Fleam to hire – were from out of the area, Missourians, deserters from ships in port, or Comancheros. Men who had no opinion about and no stake in what Texas was or might be. I think it's what took him so long to put the theft together.'

'So long?' Jalisco raised his shaggy brows.

'I think Pollack has been working on this,' said January, 'since October. And it's a good thing,' he added, looking around him at the little camp, men and horses in the flickering light of the camp-fire against the rock and woodland of one of the innumerable gullies in the hills, 'that you got as many horses as you did.'

'Half of them we found,' explained the vaquero. 'Horses and mules – branded with the Pollack brand, loose on the hills.'

January nodded. He was just beginning to stop shaking from the exertions and shocks at the hacienda. 'I thought you would.'

Seventeen of Vin Taggart's cowhands – plus Noah, and Enoch's wife Juana – had retreated to the hills when Sheriff Quigley had turned up with his warrant yesterday afternoon. There they had been joined by the bodyguard Ortega, stringy and silent as ever. January worried that their numbers might not be sufficient, should Pollack attempt to stop the next day's cavalcade back to Austin. But Ajo and Missouri, who were watching the hacienda from a distance, reported in the morning that Pollack's men were staying close to the house, with the exception of Eli Creed, who had slipped away before daybreak with three horses and what looked like provision for a journey, headed south.

'I'm not surprised,' said January, as he helped saddle up – stiffly, his grazed back aching from the rough-and-ready treatment his wound had been given. 'Pollack's dying. He may be beyond giving instructions by this time, and from what I hear, Rance couldn't organize an expedition to the out-house. And though the men may know this country, they don't know what they're looking for. Let's get ourselves away before one of them figures it out.'

On the ride to Witch Cave Canyon, January fell in beside Ortega, and confirmed what he had suspected: that the bodyguard had been summarily dismissed on the fifteenth of April, less than twenty-four hours after Silver Joe Fleam and his men, led by Rance Pollack – standing proxy for his incapacitated brother Gideon – broke into the new Record Office in Austin, loaded up the republic's archives, and drove off with them into the night.

'He said nothing to me of Madame Valentina,' reported the bodyguard in his slow, deep rasp. 'He had not the air of a jealous man. I asked him, what had I done, and he said that his aunt would have no Catholics in the household. He begged my pardon, señor, and gave me ten dollars above my pay.'

He relapsed into silence, lean body moving only with the motion of his horse, dark eyes scanning the prairie which they crossed. After a time January said, 'I notice you didn't leave the area.'

The snowy brows deepened above Ortega's nose. 'It stunk,' he said. 'Señor Taggart wasn't the man to let that wittery hen woman make him do things, Catholic or not. He didn't get rid of Juana, or Jalisco.' He shook his head.

'I knew the Madrecita, and the aunt, hated Madame for her faith. I knew the brother had his own schemes about the lost mine, and no more brain than my horse. I knew something was wrong.'

He continued slowly, bringing out the words as if language – any language – were some half-forgotten skill, like a childhood game barely remembered. Jalisco had said of him once that he would go for weeks without speaking to anyone but his horse. 'Father Monastario told me, when he sent me to work for her – when she wedded this Taggart, and would come into town to be confessed – to watch over her, because her heart is pure. I didn't think it was so,' he admitted. 'She is a woman, and you cannot trust them. Not the pretty ones, not the ugly ones, not the ones who are stupid and especially not the ones who are smart. But he spoke true. I would not see her harmed.'

He fell back then, his rifle propped ready on his thigh, and returned to watching the canyon rims as they entered the wooded shadows of Witch Cave Canyon, the men spreading out in a loose circle of scouts to warn of attack. The creek had gone down. The little herd of horses and mules made no trouble as the vaqueros drove them up the old, flooded road to the entrance of the disused tunnel. While the men dragged the wagons into the open, and harnessed the teams, January climbed and scrambled up to the high cave where he'd spent the night before last, and fished out the elements which would, he hoped, prove – or at least corroborate – his story.

Gervase Hookwire's satchel of inks, pens, and parchment.

Vin Taggart's bloodstained shirt and trousers.

Gideon Pollack's letters to Alicia Marryat.

Would any of them prove anything? He didn't know. And his own testimony would not be admitted in a Texas court. Nor would that of Noah, or Enoch, or any slave in the household. Quite possibly neither Jalisco or Ortega as well.

But we can only, he thought as he roped canvas over the boxes of government records, deeds, property specifications, *do what we can do.*

The originals of the San Saba and Valenzuela deeds he kept in his satchel.

They reached Austin shortly after dark, and drew up before the single-story clapboard house that sheltered the sheriff's office and the jail. Quigley was on the porch to meet them.

'Well, well.' He folded his shirtsleeved arms. 'And what do we have here?'

'The National Archives,' said January, 'of the Republic of Texas. Stolen from up the street –' he nodded along Congress Avenue – 'a week ago Tuesday night, by a fellow named Silver Joe Fleam, assisted – I'm pretty sure, but can't prove it – by Rance Pollack. They were supposedly headed for Houston, but Fleam shook Rance off somehow – it couldn't have been hard – and cached the wagons in the old Bruja mine on Vin Taggart's property, on promise of payment of a thousand dollars in gold from Taggart, something else I can't prove. Not,' he added, carefully keeping his voice neutral, 'that my testimony would be acceptable in court. I believe that theft was the reason that Taggart was killed.'

'So Pollack could steal them back?' The sheriff considered the wagons thoughtfully by the light of the lantern on the porch.

January nodded. 'So Pollack could search the house, which is where I think he thought they were. At least, that's where his men were searching the moment everyone was cleared out of the place Thursday night.'

'Sounds like there's a lot of speculation and surmise in the story you're about to tell me.' Quigley stepped down from the porch, put a foot on the spoke of the near back wheel of the wagon that January drove and hoisted himself up to look under the canvas. 'But John Watrous – that's the attorney general – and the land office recorders, will be happy to see this, whatever the story really is. And if your men will be so good as to stand guard for another half-hour, I'll send to him to have these returned to the General Records Office. And I'll send a man over to the Eberly House,' he added, as January climbed stiffly down from the wagon-seat, 'to fetch your master.'

'Eberly House?'

'That's where he went for dinner,' said the sheriff, climbing to peek under the covers of the other wagons. 'After the arraignment this morning, where that friend of his testified to bein' with him all Thursday mornin' when Miss Marryat was strangled.' He raised an eyebrow at January, pale eyes observing him sharply.

In a voice of pleased surprise, January exclaimed, 'M'am Passmore? Michie Taggart's – uh – lady-friend?'

It was a bow drawn at a venture, and he fought not to sigh with relief when Quigley's shoulders relaxed just slightly. 'That's the one.'

January wondered how long it had taken the lady to walk back to Austin after he'd stolen her stolen horse. Or had she just helped herself to another from the unguarded corrals? 'I wasn't sure if she'd speak up for him, sir – or even if she was

still in town.' He reminded himself that as far as anyone on
Rancho Perdition knew, the woman who'd been at the hacienda
Thursday morning was a Turkish lady who spoke nothing but
pig-Latin. Had part of that twenty-four-hour delay been to
rinse the flour out of her hair?

'She's in town.' The sheriff returned to the porch, shaking
his head. 'Gonna be a hell of a job inventoryin', that's all I
got to say. And M'am Valentina will be at the Capital City
Hotel, havin' supper with Doc Meredith, since she couldn't
very well join your Mr Sefton's party. Her mother-in-law's at
the Capital City as well, an' that cold little weasel Francis. I
will say,' Quigley went on, leading the way into the shabby
and smoke-smelling office, 'the both of 'em was damn shook
up by Miss Marryat's death. The boy looked sick as a dog,
even before he finally admitted he hadn't seen M'am Valentina
anywhere's near the hacienda last Monday mornin'. You want
some coffee?'

'I would, yes, thank you, sir.' January sat in the ladderback
kitchen chair the lawman gestured him to. 'And I realize it's
a terrible imposition, sir, and probably tampering with evidence,
but – Jalisco and the men have worked since sun-up, retrieving
those wagons and guarding them into town. Every penny I
possessed – which includes the money that was in Michie
Sefton's saddlebags – was taken from me last night by the
Pollacks.'

He opened the saddlebag he carried, and held it so that
Quigley could look inside. 'These four gold pieces were in
here when I found the bag,' he said. 'They're part of the story
of the archives and what became of them – and, I think, of
what happened to Michie Taggart. May I have your permission
to give one of them to Jalisco so the men can at least get some
supper?'

'I can't allow that.' Quigley opened a drawer of his desk,
looked inside, frowned, and dug into his trouser pocket. From
it he took four US silver dollars, and from the desk drawer,
five more. In his entire sojourn in Texas January had never
seen the slightest evidence that the republic coined money,
nor that any Texan accepted the republic's printed red scrip
unless he or she absolutely had to. 'I'll take your master's

IOU for that,' the sheriff said. 'And I take it you're going to tell me who really shot Vin Taggart?'

'I am, sir.' And he handed him the packet of Pollack's love letters.

'I think the whole thing started,' he said, as he sat down again in the sheriff's office with the lamplight falling in a dim golden pool around the desk, 'last October, when President Lamar moved the capital from Houston to Austin. I gather there was an uproar over it—'

''Bout the degree of uproar as when Joshua showed up outside the walls of Jericho with his marchin' band,' agreed Quigley comfortably. 'But with newspapers thrown in.'

'And I gather Gideon Pollack decided he was going to do something about it.'

'Well, at one point he was writin' letters to the *Texas Register* callin' on all right-thinkin' men to burn Austin to the ground.' The sheriff lit a cigar, and offered one to January. This was illegal in New Orleans, and January wondered if that went for Texas as well, but accepted. 'Week after that he wrote there was a Mexican army marchin' north to invade the new capital – which was pretty much all hogwash. The Rangers rode out an' couldn't find so much as a hoof-track, anyways. So I ain't surprised he thought of liftin' the archives – lock, stock, an' barrel – an' takin' 'em back to Houston – if that's what he intended to do with 'em.

'I will say for Sam Houston –' the sheriff poured out a tin cup of coffee and pushed it across the desk to January – 'that he'd probably have ordered 'em back. Or at least would have promised to send 'em back, though he might not have got around to it in any tearin' hurry. So where'd Taggart come into it? It was long about October,' he added thoughtfully, 'that Taggart switched over from callin' Pollack a skunk an' a traitor, to shakin' hands with him after church.'

'It was,' agreed January.

'I always wondered what Taggart was up to. He was smart. He musta got wind of Pollack's plan somehow. Between readin' law an speculatin' in town he always had his ear to the ground for rumors, an' odd bits of news. An' he hated Pollack. Many times he said to me, that those that wanted to hook Texas onto the United States were cowards and fools, screwin' up the finest chance they'd ever have to found a republic the right way, based on sound economics rather than a bunch of Northern preachers singin' hymns through their noses. Then all of a sudden he's lettin' Pollack run his sheep on Perdition land, an' invitin' him to dinner.' The sheriff turned the packet of letters over in his hands, then untied the ribbons that bound them. 'Like my mama always said, somethin' about that didn't listen right to her.'

'That's what my mama says, too.'

Quigley glanced over the first of the letters, then the last, face expressionless as a poker-player's behind a drift of smoke. 'Where'd you find these, Ben?'

'Hidden with Miss Marryat's cache of money, under the steps of the backstairs.'

The sheriff made a growling noise in his throat. 'Can't say I'm surprised. Taggart told me . . . Well, one night when he was drunk he said he'd done Miss Marryat a wrong, back in the days when they were both in their teens. Said his older brother had pushed him into doin' what he knew was wrong, and he'd always felt responsible for his aunt turnin' a little crazy. This was years ago, before he ever thought she'd be livin' under the same roof again. So it must have been easy, for Pollack to turn her against him, 'specially if she thought—'

Here he glanced at one of the notes, with a wry twist to his mouth.

''Specially if she thought he was going to divorce his wife and marry her. It's all she ever wanted,' he added. 'To get away.'

Like Selina, thought January. *Like Valentina*.

'I think,' he said after a silence, 'that round about last October, Taggart did indeed hear somehow that Pollack planned to lift the archives, and had hired a man named Silver Joe Fleam to put together ten men from outside of the area – men who wouldn't blab to anybody in Austin – to do the job. Now, it just so happened that Taggart had been wanting to have a few days in private with the archives himself.'

He saw in the sudden widening of Quigley's eyes that the reason for this wasn't a new thought to him, either.

'He knew Texas land is going to increase in value,' continued January, 'the minute the republic gets on its feet – or gets into the Union. Since the banks crashed in 'thirty-seven, you can't buy land in Alabama and Mississippi the way you used to. But England's still screaming for cotton. And you *can* still get land on credit in Texas. Lamar's whole program of exterminating every Indian tribe he can get in his sights is about making investors and buyers in the United States feel safe enough to settle here.'

'An' Taggart knew –' Quigley jabbed a finger at him excitedly – 'that when land prices went up, there'd be speculators lookin' into the San Saba land grant that he bought his land from. Maybe lookin' into his wife's land as well. That San Saba grant's already been called in question by a feller in Houston. Pollack himself got two *labor* an' about three leagues by callin' in lawyers on a man who *thought* he was buyin' all rights to the San Marcos grant over on Sunday Creek near San Antonio. *Damn!*' he cried, enlightened, as the truth broke over him like surf on the shore.

'Damn indeed, sir,' January agreed. 'That was no accident, back in the lobby of the Capital City Hotel after the duel. Taggart must have been waiting for days, for the right moment to lose his temper and put his men in a cordon around his land.'

'I thought it wasn't like him,' remarked the sheriff. 'Or at least, I'd like to think I'd have thought so, if I didn't have about ten of Pollack's men jumpin' down my throat. Even when he was drunk, Vin always knew what he was doin'.'

'Pollack and his brother met with Silver Joe Saturday night – the eleventh – and paid him half the money for the job. But long before that, Taggart promised Silver Joe a thousand dollars in gold if they'd divert the archives, when they got hold of them, to the old Bruja Mine on Perdition land. While he was collecting the gold – and it took him several months to do it – he sent for a professional forger from New Orleans, a man named Gervase Hookwire. I know this because Hookwire was on the *Rosabel* that brought Mr Sefton and myself to Houston from Galveston on the eighth. Mr Sefton knew him slightly. And Mr Sefton identified him Wednesday morning, when we found his body in a cave up Witch Cave Canyon, staked out naked and cut up pretty bad. He'd been dead about four days. I helped bury him.'

'Wednesday?' Quigley's mouth hardened for a moment. January could see him counting back days. 'You sure about that?'

'Fairly sure. The body'd gone limp again – completely – and the maggots in the wounds were not only big and fat, but some of them had had time to turn into pupae. My sister's protector back in New Orleans,' he added, a little apologetically, interpreting Quigley's frown, 'collects insects – he told me all about this.' He knew this would sit better with a white Texas sheriff than, *I went to medical school in Paris and I'm not really a slave at all . . .*

'Then he was killed – what? – Sunday or Monday. And if Taggart had put guards all around his land on the twelfth . . .'

'The archives were stolen – twice – on the night of the fourteenth. Hookwire's throat was cut before his body was cut up. The other wounds had hardly bled at all, and the stakes that held his wrists and ankles hadn't been so much as tugged on. They'd never have held a man being tortured.'

The sheriff drew breath to speak, then sat back again, the glow of his cigar like a demon eye in the semi-dark.

'Michie Sefton and I went back Thursday morning,' continued January, 'and had a look at the other caves along the canyon. We found this.' He opened Hookwire's saddlebag again, and brought out its contents: parchments, inks, pigments, all varieties of pens. Four ten-dollar gold pieces.

Quigley studied the kit, and remarked, 'I will be dipped in shit.'

'I hope not, sir.' From his other saddlebag, January took Taggart's bloodstained shirt and trousers, and the forged deeds and conveyancing papers pertaining to the original Perdition lands, before Taggart had tripled his holdings by marrying the niece of Don Gael Valenzuela.

'As for who killed Hookwire,' he went on quietly, 'I found these stuffed in the back of the top shelf of the armoire in Taggart's room.'

The sheriff turned them over in his hands: first the land office papers, confirming beyond all shadow of doubt Taggart's ownership of the Perdition lands. Then the shirt and trousers,

matching up with the eye of long practice what it meant, that
some of the bloodstains marked the sleeves, and others, the
back of the shirt, and the back of the trousers, where a carried
body would leak from a cut throat.

With no doubt whatsoever in his voice, he said, 'Taggart
was gonna swap 'em in.'

'I think so, yes, sir.'

'An' he wanted to shut this Hookwire's mouth for him, an'
blame the Comanche, if anybody found the body.'

January nodded. 'That's how it looked to me, sir.' The
forgeries pertaining to the Valenzuela lands, the lands Valentina
had brought to her husband, he had left where Taggart had
put them in the archive wagons. The originals were now stowed
behind some rocks in the Bruja mine. At a guess, absent a
will – and he knew Francis Taggart's opportunistic efforts in
that direction would not stand up in court – Taggart's original
purchase from the San Saba grant would almost certainly be
awarded to his family, while Valentina would keep the
Valenzuela lands that had originally been her uncle's. He knew
Quigley would never accept the story of a planned forgery
unless *some* forged documents were presented, and while
the wagons were being loaded and hitched, had replaced the
original Perdition purchase forgeries with their originals.

That would, he hoped, discharge his debt to an extraordinary
young lady, and make her sale of those lands – if she chose
to sell – that much easier.

And with any luck, he would never have to see her again.

TWENTY-FIVE

H is mind had barely framed this thought when feet
thumped on the boards of the porch outside. He heard
Valentina say, 'But surely at this hour—'

'I behold light within, domina. *That orbed continent the
fire/ That severs day from night . . .*'

Quigley rose, and went to open the door.

'I'd heard a rumor,' Hannibal began, and then, looking past him, 'Benjamin! *Amicus meus*! Or, as Homer would say –' he switched to classical Greek: you never could tell who might have gone to a boys' academy and remembered some of the Latin he'd been taught – 'is everything all right?'

January's command of that language wasn't extensive ('More a suggestion than a command,' his wife Rose would say), but he replied, in Greek, as he got to his feet, 'All seems to be well, unless this warrior is lying,' and added in deprecating English, 'as your old grandpa used to say, sir.'

'My old grandpa,' returned Hannibal in Greek, 'would have thrashed the lot of us with a riding-whip for interrupting his drinking,' and turned back to Quigley with a punctilious handshake and a little bow. 'I trust all is well here, sir? I encountered Jalisco and his men outside Eberly's, and they said something about the Texas National Archives?'

Valentina, startled, said, '*What*?'

'It seems, sir – m'am,' said January, bowing, 'that that's what this has all been about from the start. Which I should have realized,' he added, 'when I heard that your husband dismissed your bodyguard – on a fairly flimsy excuse – on the afternoon after Mr Pollack's hired men raided the Records Office, and then turned three wagonloads of archives over to Mr Taggart. Your husband wanted to keep you from riding out,' he added, seeing her baffled expression. 'To keep you from seeing some clue, some sign, that might lead you to where they were hidden. A tribute to your intelligence, in fact. And to his respect for you.'

She said softly, 'Oh.'

'I think when he came in on Sunday,' went on January, as he fetched the office's third chair for the young widow, 'he had just – as I was only this moment telling Sheriff Quigley – murdered Mr Hookwire. Mr Hookwire was the forger he'd hired to make substitute documents to put into the land office records, so there wouldn't be any question about the portion of Rancho Perdition that he'd acquired from the successors to the old San Saba land grant.'

'He did worry about that.' Valentina took the chair, and Hannibal would have perched himself on the corner of the desk had not January motioned him, with his eyes, to take

the old ladderback in which he'd been sitting. 'He spoke to
me of it, just after we wed. My uncle Gael . . .'

January caught her eye, shook his head slightly, praying
Quigley wouldn't see this. Fortunately, the sheriff was fetching
a cup of coffee from the stove.

He didn't underestimate her. She finished quickly, '. . . said
that all over Texas there are quarrels and questions about
land grants.'

His eyes on hers, January said, willing her to accept this
and be quiet, 'My understanding is that there is *no question*
about the Valenzuela lands that your uncle gave you –' she
looked extremely surprised at this but – *thank goodness!* – kept
her mouth shut – 'but yes, you're right. But your husband
wanted to make sure of *his own* lands. And for that, he needed
access to the archives – and he needed to close his tame
forger's mouth and keep it closed. When he came in on that
Sunday night – Easter Sunday – I'm pretty sure he'd just killed
Hookwire. Killed him, carried his body to another cave,
staked it out as if the Comanche had killed and mutilated him.
The last thing he needed was for his wife to greet him with
accusations of infidelity.'

'Oh.' Valentina turned her face aside. 'I was . . . I was
angry . . .'

'Of course you were,' said January. 'Don't you see, m'am?
You were meant to be.' He turned to Quigley. 'Did Mr Francis
Taggart say where he heard about his brother's mistress? If
he never went into town himself . . .?'

'He said he'd heard it just that day from Miss Marryat. That
she'd heard it at church.' He paused, putting together the pieces
– the timing – in his mind. 'So she wanted them to fight.'

'I think so, yes, sir.'

'Francis was shook up bad over her death,' the sheriff went
on after a moment. 'Shook up bad over the whole thing, for
all he tried to turn it to his own advantage, accusin' Mr Sefton
of the deed. He's a cold-blooded little polecat, but he did love
his aunt. He carried on – the way most folks will – about
whether somethin' he'd said or done would have saved her,
or could have caused what happened. He said his aunt went
on about how M'am Valentina – begging your pardon, m'am

– was a hypocrite, when Mr Taggart – who was a hypocrite too, she said, an' a traitor an' a monster – was carryin' on with this woman in town. Knowin' the three of them, she guessed he'd go straight to you with that story, m'am.'

'You've said yourself, Mrs Taggart,' said January slowly, 'that it wasn't the first quarrel you'd had . . .'

'No.' Color flushed up into her cheeks. 'We fought – oh, horribly! – when he told me he'd sent Ortega away. *And* for such a . . . such a *stupid* accusation . . .'

'So Miss Marryat knew she could count on there being another quarrel. And it being Sunday – and Ortega being gone – she could count on *you* being gone, and without any good account of your whereabouts, the following morning.'

'An' there's no tellin',' said the sheriff quietly, and riffled his thumb again over Gideon Pollack's letters, 'what Pollack said, or implied, to poor Miss Marryat when they met. Or what went on in her head, from what he said.'

'Another thing I can't prove in court.' January nodded towards the letters. 'After Pollack ordered his brother to kill me last night, he said to me, *Damn if I thought she'd do what she did.* But I can think of no other reason that he'd have one of his men kill her.'

Quigley was silent for a time. Then: 'He say which man?'

January shook his head. 'By that last note in there, I'd guess it was Creed.'

'If she was keepin' these letters for some other purpose,' murmured the sheriff after a time, 'some more *legal* purpose, shall we say, it crosses my mind that the result would have been the same.'

January thought about it. About the phrases of the letters, the repeated admonitions to burn them.

About Pollack's flash of rage when he'd spoken of that possibility. 'If that was what was in her mind,' he said slowly, 'I'm guessing Pollack's defense would have been to tell her, publish and be damned. Disown her and claim that it was entirely her idea – which is probably what he's going to do,' he added after a moment, 'when those letters show up in court. And I'm thinking that she'd have shot him, rather than let him go.'

'Which would make two of 'em,' added Quigley, 'countin'

his wife. Or Mrs Pollack would have shot *her*. You ever met Mrs Pollack? Most beautiful woman in Travis County – like what an angel would look like who was goin' to boardin' school. But she'd never have let him go. The pair of 'em make the Macbeths look like Mary an' Joseph in the Bible. An' I tell you, I do *not* look forward to ridin' down to Los Lobos tomorrow an' tryin' to charge Gideon with conspiracy to do murder. I'll be lucky if *she* doesn't have the place guarded like Taggart did Perdition. Or shoot *me*.'

And he stared for a time, morosely, into his coffee, turning the letters over in his hands. Then, turning a wry glance back to January, he added, 'I appreciate you findin' all this – not to speak of returnin' the archives. But I will say, Ben, you sure have handed me a pip.'

'Alicia could ride,' said Valentina slowly. She had set down her cup, sat looking down at her hands, turning on her finger the wide gold circle of her wedding-ring. 'And she could shoot. And I think Enero was right, when he said he didn't think whoever attacked me at the jacal meant to kill me. She may even have known, that an accusation against me would not hold up, but would serve to have me taken away from the house for a few days.'

'It would be easy enough,' said January, 'for her to ride out to Sauceito Creek early, and wait for you, Madame Taggart. To frighten you badly enough to keep you in hiding for an hour or two in the ruined jacal, to take your horse, and be back in the orchard in time to keep the rendezvous she'd arranged with your husband. Again –' he spread his hands – 'I have no proof. But Pollack speaks of the absolute necessity of getting the house and the property cleared out, unguarded and unobserved, as soon as possible.'

'You know,' pointed out Hannibal thoughtfully, 'Taggart well may have had some hand in putting Pollack in touch with Mr Fleam in the first place. His – um – friend Mrs Passmore certainly knew the man. And Pollack put two and two together pretty quickly, when Rance came back and told him that Fleam and the three wagonloads of records had disappeared. Personally,' he added, 'I'm surprised Fleam and his men didn't kill Rance.'

'I'm surprised *Pollack* didn't kill Rance.' Quigley glanced up from the love letters with a wry face. 'Wouldn't take a college professor to get Rance to turn his back or ride off in another direction – the man's an idiot. I'll bet you ten US dollars to a Texas redback, Pollack meant to head up the raid himself, 'fore he was shot in that damn fool duel with Stanway. He musta been spittin' blood when he learned Rance had gone an' lost the archives within a few hours of stealin' 'em.'

'And Pollack may already have heard of Taggart collecting up gold,' said January. 'He knows he has to act fast. He writes to Miss Marryat of how her nephew's a traitor to the United States – arranges a meeting – whispers to her that he, Pollack, will be ruined if Miss Marryat can't somehow get the hacienda Perdition cleared out . . .' He extended a finger, touched the corner of the thickets of the love-notes. '*For my life, and for our future*, he says . . .'

'An' doesn't much care,' murmured Quigley, 'what means she'll use. He wouldn't.'

'But if she killed us both,' concluded Valentina softly, 'someone would ask, who would benefit by our deaths? And that would be Francis. And that, she could not permit.'

There was silence for a little time in that cramped, dim-lit office. Through the thin board walls came the sounds of horses jangling past in the street, of a piano played in some building nearby, faint and muffled. Of someone shouting about how all Injuns should be shot, and all Mexicans too . . .

The sheriff said softly, 'Nor did she feel she had a grievance against you, m'am. You may be a Catholic, but I doubt she ever thought that *you* deserved death.' As the lawman opened his notebook once again, and began listing all the things he'd need to check, arrange, and do with the evidence January had brought him, January recalled his dream in Witch Cave Cavern. The young woman on the bed, the big youth bending over her, sandy hair falling into his eyes. The three-quarters-grown boy standing in the doorway . . . *Go ahead Vin. What's the matter? Can't get it up?*

Was that, he wondered suddenly, why Vin Taggart had fled from Elysium in the first place? Shamed and horrified at a wrong which could not be put right?

Or had he, like Pollack, believed in his heart that a woman didn't really mind being raped? Had that just been one more element that convinced him that he must flee that poisoned mess of drunken violence that was his family? Get away from it, as far as he could . . .

I thought he was gonna choke, when they came drivin' up from town with all their trunks an' plunder, Noah had said, as he dug Gervase Hookwire's grave. *It'd be funny, if they hadn't moved in.*

And, *You'd never see a place less like Heaven if you walked til your toenails bled.*

'Looks like he met with her at least twice after the archives was stolen,' remarked Quigley, pausing in his note-making to check the letters again. 'So we can at least get him on conspiracy. He's lucky it didn't kill him right then. But she must have been in a state to do anything, after that.'

'And it certainly looked to me,' added Hannibal thoughtfully, 'that she thought her accusation would have the effect of driving you away, Valla, rather than getting you actually hanged.'

Valentina made no reply for some minutes, but rather sat looking at her folded hands. Then she said, 'I saw my mother-in-law at the hotel tonight, señor. Having dinner, alone. Alone, and so . . . so still. And I pitied her. Even for all that she had said, had done. I went and spoke to her – thanked her for what she said at the arraignment this afternoon. That she had not seen me, that Aunt Alicia claimed that she had, but neither Madre Taggart nor Francis did. And she–she wept, señor. She asked my forgiveness.'

She looked aside again, as if she saw once more that tall, stern-faced figure in black, humbled suddenly by the death not only of the son she had scorned, but of the little girl she had raised.

'This is why I made Señor Sefton bring me here tonight, señor. She said that she suspected in her heart that Aunt Alicia had killed my husband. Not at first, you understand, but the more she thought about it. She could have, she said. She had not seen her sister all the morning, until the alarm went up when the body was found. This was not unusual. But the more she observed her afterwards, the more she thought. Like Hannibal –' her eye flickered to the fiddler, and a half-smile touched her lips – 'it occurred to her that a shawl was a very *silly* thing to leave at the place of the murder. And maybe Señor Enero is right, and Aunt Alicia had no intention for me to actually do more than spend a few nights in jail.

'Alicia . . .' Usually straightforward, she struggled suddenly, how to say *rape* without actually saying it, the way, January had observed, so many well-bred women were taught to do. 'There had been . . . wrong-doing. Back in Virginia, when Alicia was sixteen, and my husband's brother Jack much the same age. But a man, she said, and . . . and a drunkard already, and . . . base.'

Very softly, Quigley said, 'That is what I heard from your husband, m'am.'

She raised her eyes to the sheriff's. 'My mother-in-law swore that my husband would never have done more than keep silent about what he saw his brother do – the brother whom he worshipped, at that time, anyway. But she said – my mother-in-law – that Alicia sometimes said there were both of them, and sometimes only Jack. That she only spoke of it when she'd taken too much laudanum, and then her story would change. Myself, I do not know. I don't want to think of him doing such a thing – or even helping, or keeping quiet . . .'

Again she turned her face aside, from the memory of the man whose bed she had shared rather than risk the helplessness of poverty. The man she had barely known.

'But in truth, señor, I don't know. He was a boy then, a different person, and almost certainly drunk. Yet it explains things about Aunt Alicia, and the way she would look sometimes at my husband, and sometimes leave the room.'

She brushed quickly at her eyes with her black-gloved fingers. It was the first time January had seen her weep, since her husband's death. She managed to say, 'It is not a very good story,' and Hannibal rose, and stood behind her chair, to put his hands on her trembling shoulders.

Quigley went to a shelf and took down another cup, which he filled with coffee. This he handed to her, and fetched a clean handkerchief from his desk drawer. 'My daddy was a preacher, m'am,' he said gruffly as he handed it to her. 'And I been a sheriff, one place an' another, for fourteen years. It ain't nuthin' I ain't heard before. But I am sorry you had to speak of this.'

Valentina shook her head. 'You had to know,' she said simply. 'I feel terrible – *horrible!* – for poor Madame Taggart, keeping this silent, all these years. Loving Alicia as I know she did – yes, in spite of the way she acted when she was drunk. Knowing what she thought had happened and not knowing if it was the truth, that her son – or maybe two of her sons – would do such a thing. But it was true that her husband, and Jack, and my husband when he was a youth, fought and fought, and came to hate one another – and to hate Francis, who did nothing but hide behind his mother and Alicia – and that the house was a lake of poison, a house of Hell in which one could believe anything.'

She wiped her eyes again. 'My father is insane, Señor Quigley,' she added in a calmer voice, and glanced ruefully over her shoulder at Hannibal. 'He talks to statues and sees visions of ancient gods. But it was not like that.'

'Someday,' said Hannibal to Quigley, in an effort to lighten the darkness, 'I'll tell you stories about her father.'

But not, January guessed, about the skeletons he'd found, one of which had worn the sapphires that had belonged to Valentina's long-vanished mother.

Quigley was silent again, tapping the little bundle of love letters against the side of his hand.

'You say you looked through the house, Ben. You find the thousand dollars you say Mr Taggart put together to pay off Silver Joe an' his boys?'

'No, sir,' lied January.

His glance crossed Hannibal's, and the fiddler said – again in Ancient Greek – 'I daresay I saw some of it tonight, when Cornelia paid for my dinner.'

January went on, 'I came across nearly two hundred dollars with those love letters, sir. Some of the household servants had told me, that Miss Marryat would–would pick up any spare money she could find.' It wouldn't do, he knew, for a black man to out-and-out accuse a white woman of theft, even one acknowledged to be mentally unstable and almost certainly a murderess. 'I understand that before she met Pollack she was saving up to get out of there. Away from her older sister – and away from her nephew. I think that's what it must have been. Pollack took it from me, when they caught me last night.'

'Damn it,' murmured Quigley. 'I can see I'm in for a treat tomorrow.'

'I'm not sure he'll be able to speak to you, sir,' said January. 'He was feverish last night, and looked to be getting worse. I did find the list of Silver Joe's boys, with the date of the theft on it, and "one thousand – gold" written at the bottom. They took that from me, too.'

The farther Mrs Passmore can be kept from all this, the better. There was no telling what accusations she might bring – or what trouble she would cause – if she was questioned.

He added, 'You can probably corroborate some of this by questioning the Taggart servants. The houseman Noah, and Melly, Madame Taggart's maid. The stableman Malojo too. He may very well have seen what time M'am Valentina, and Miss Marryat, rode out Monday morning. But how much of that would be admitted in court I don't know.'

'Well, not yours or Noah's or Melly's, that's for sure. An' if it comes in front of Judge Long, he's like to throw the whole case out, rather'n convict Pollack. But I'll have a word with 'em. I think that was Noah I saw, drivin' one of those wagons into town.'

'It was, sir.'

Quigley growled a little in his throat. 'Of course, with Mr Taggart's death –' he glanced apologetically at the young widow – 'that means nothing much can be proved against the Pollacks anyway. And it's even money Creed's across the river and gone. An' two to one Cilly Pollack'll have her men take a shot at me for disturbin' him. Still—'

The clink of wagon-chains sounded in the street, and the clatter of many hooves. Torchlight splashed through the windows. The sheriff got to his feet and went to the door, opened it and looked out. 'You're in town late, Rance,' he called out, and January – who, with Hannibal, had risen to follow Quigley to the door – stepped back again into the room and moved to the side of the window, where he could look out and not be seen.

Rance Pollack sat his horse beside the wagon-team, the light of the torches held by a circle of cowhands glinting on the tears that tracked his heavy, unshaven face. He said nothing, but Mudsill, on the box of the wagon, drew rein and called out, 'It's Mr Pollack, sir. He's dead.'

'An' I'm gonna kill Doc Meredith.' Rance seemed to choke on the words. 'If that fucken bastard had let my brother alone . . .'

Mudsill said, his voice strangely gentle, 'It weren't Doc's fault, Mr Rance. Shit happens. You know it does.'

'Don't you fucken tell me whose fault it was, nigger!' yelled Rance, rising in his stirrups. Snot dripped from his swollen nose, glinting in the torchlight. Ridiculous, but for the man's devastating grief. 'The one I *am* fucken gonna kill is that feller Sefton's goddam nigger! It was his fault!' He dragged his rifle from the saddle holster, brandished it at the black, star-stitched sky. 'He was the one kicked out Doc Parralee. If it weren't for him, my brother woulda got over his wound in two days! Gideon was at San Jacinto, shot thirty-five Mexicans in the swamp, took a bullet in his hip an' not a penny the worse for it! An' he was shot by Comanche in '38! An' he took a bullet in his shoulder, killin' Butler Simm back in Mississippi, an' he was up an' walkin' around inside a day—'

'You better take him on to the hotel, Mudsill,' said Quigley quietly, stepping out onto the lantern-lit porch. 'Finn . . .?' He picked out another of the riders beside the wagon. 'Soon as you get Mr Pollack delivered to Firkin's, come on back here an' tell me the circumstances. I'm guessin' his wound went bad on him?'

'Yes, sir,' said the man Finn, the young Irishman, January recalled, whom he'd met en route to Austin. *Was it really only three weeks ago*?

The man nudged his horse closer to the porch, and spoke beneath Rance's furious ranting as two of the other riders gentled the rifle away from the huge man and got the cortège again on its way. 'Damned if I've ever seen a man hang on the way he did, sir, but he took to his bed last night, an' it

seemed he just burned up like touch-paper. He died this mornin'
'fore we could send for a doctor or a preacher or nuthin'.'

Valentina rose from her chair by the desk, brushed past
January to step into the doorway. 'Is there anything that I can
do for his wife?' she asked quietly, of the half-seen rider in
the darkness. 'Any help that I can be?'

Finn touched his hat. ''Tis most kind of you, Mrs Taggart,
most kind indeed, and I'll be askin' her if she needs anythin'.
Sheriff,' he added, with a glance after the wagons and the
torches, creaking away down Congress Avenue, 'you might
want to go find Doc Meredith, tell him maybe to make himself
a little scarce for a couple days, til Rance calms down some.
He don't mean what he says, but if he gets to drinkin' he may
do what he'll later regret.'

'I'll do that,' promised Quigley.

'You might also want to look up that feller Sefton, give him
the same word, if he's still in town.'

'I will.'

The young man touched the sides of his straggly-tailed
gray, and moved off up the street, appearing and disappearing
in the thrown glow of the lamps in front of the barrooms.

'You heard that?' Quigley came back into the dim-lit office,
and shut the door. 'I heard of people having to flee the United
States and run to Texas . . . but where do you run if you have
to flee Texas?'

'Hell?' suggested Hannibal. 'That seems to be the only
place left.'

'Been there,' sighed January. 'At the moment, the only place
I want to go is home.'

TWENTY-SIX

With the assistance of the obliging Marcus Mudsill,
Hannibal and January kept a wary eye on Rance
Pollack's movements through the following day,
which was Sunday. Mrs Eberly, proprietress of the tavern

where they again stayed, directed January to the apothecary
shop of one Señor Pardo, in whose back room Father
Monastario held Mass for the Catholics of the largely Protestant
vicinity. The priest proved to be elderly, hugely fat, and with
a twinkle in his dark eyes. When Mass was over, January saw
Sheriff Quigley approach him outside, and knew the lawman
was tidying up his case.

His own part was done.

Mrs Passmore visited with Hannibal in the afternoon, and
reported that the sheriff had also questioned Noah, Melly, the
elder Mrs Taggart, and Malojo. 'Doubtless trying to find
someone whose evidence the court will accept,' the lady sighed.
She had retreated – with Hannibal – to the tavern's rear porch
'for a breath of fresh air', meaning a surreptitious cigar and
a sip of cognac from her silver flask. 'With Gideon Pollack
dead and Eli Creed on his way to parts unknown, there really
doesn't seem to be anybody left to try for murder, though I
suppose Quigley could prosecute Rance Pollack for conspiracy
to steal government property.'

She had resumed her quiet, well-cut gown and her hair had
returned to its customary sable richness. With her lace mitts,
and the subdued cameo at her throat, she looked so respectable
that no one, January reflected, would think twice about leaving
her in the same room with his money.

But when Hannibal inquired after this of the sheriff himself,
who dropped by the tavern that evening to give his formal
leave to their departure, Quigley shook his head. 'Like as not
the case would be tried before Judge Long,' he said. 'And he'd
throw it out 'cause he'd love to see the archives – and the
government – back in Houston. So we might just as well save
ourselves the trouble. And it might be,' he added, pushing his
hat forward to scratch his thin gray hair, 'that losin' his brother
is punishment enough, for Rance.'

The mail-coach for Houston left early Monday morning.
Valentina Taggart had given Hannibal seventy-five dollars to
pay passage back to New Orleans, and had sent Ortega into
town with the remaining four horses that they'd purchased
in Houston. 'Which I suppose we'd better ride,' remarked
the fiddler, with a certain degree of regret. In the course of

conversation that afternoon Mrs Passmore had let fall the information that she was taking the stage, and had said how much she looked forward to playing cards with Hannibal, to while away the jolting hours in the coach.

Hannibal looked thin and spent, and had developed a persistent cough, but remarked that night, as January spread his pallet – like a good servant – on the floor of their mutual room, 'There are fates worse than death, *amicus meus*, and playing cards with Cornelia Passmore is a sure path to one of them.'

Certainly when she came down to the coach in the gray of pre-dawn and saw January tying saddlebags onto their independent equipage, she looked vexed as well as disappointed. 'Are you certain you're well enough to ride?' she asked, laying an anxious hand on Hannibal's thin shoulder. And, when he assured her that his doctor had recommended the journey be done thus, for his health, she smiled brightly and said, 'But you will, I hope, join me for dinner at the posting-inns?'

At this point, to January's surprise – and infinite relief – Valentina Taggart rode into the square, having left Perdition by the late-setting moonlight with an escort of Ortega, Jalisco, and Lope. 'I'm so glad to have caught you,' she smiled, through the cloudy black gauze of her widow's veil. 'I came to beg of you, to accept Jalisco and Lope as an escort. The danger of the Comanche, you know.'

And she turned her radiant warm friendliness upon the deeply annoyed Mrs Passmore. 'One cannot be too careful.'

'You shouldn't,' murmured the older lady sweetly. 'My dear, the roads are perfectly safe.'

January wondered if she'd already made a deal with the owners of one of the posting-inns where they were scheduled to spend the night, to incapacitate Hannibal and kidnap January for later sale.

'It is such a dangerous country, madame,' cooed Valentina. 'Far better to be safe than sorry.'

Mrs Passmore returned the smile, with a forced gratitude which confirmed January's suspicion. 'Dear Mrs Taggart, you *shouldn't* have . . .'

With deepest sincerity, Valentina replied, 'It is my pleasure, madame.'

As he turned towards his own mount, January halted beside Valentina, and drew from his jacket pocket a thick packet of parchment. 'For you, madame,' he said in a low voice. 'A gift from your husband. The original deeds pertaining to the Valenzuela lands.'

She glanced quickly up into his face.

'He obviously thought there was enough question about their provenance – through the King of Spain to the Franciscan Order, through the San Saba Mission to your great-grandfather – for them to be questioned in a Texan court. Or an American one, if things fall out that way. Documents clarifying the transmission of these lands – I presume in such a way as to make your title stronger – were substituted into the National Archives while they were hidden in the Bruja mine. These are the originals, in case you ever need them. Hannibal assures me that the forgeries are first-rate, professional work. If nothing else, even if you decide not to remain in Texas, they should greatly help the sale of the land to some American.'

Valentina smiled, and tucked the deeds into the deep pocket of her skirt. 'Thank you,' she whispered. 'That is very good of you, Señor Enero. You know I would kiss you, if it wouldn't get you hanged.'

'And I would kiss your hand,' he returned, 'in another place and another time.'

Her smile was warm behind her veil. 'Please give my best wishes to your lady Rose. And – with all that has happened, I have never asked! – have you children? *Two*! Wish her all my blessings. And write to me,' she added, 'to let me know how it goes with Selina – if she is well, if . . . if all things are well with her. And if they are not, tell me how I may help.'

'I'll do that, madame.' He bowed again. 'We all of us owe you our lives. We will not forget.'

'Much as you'd want to?' Her smile gleamed, bright and briefly mischievous as of old. 'And I owe you –' she touched the pocket of her dress – 'my life as well. Not just keeping me from being hanged, but my real life – my future life – my freedom.' She pressed his hand. 'Go with God, my friend.'

January swung into the saddle, and checked the long leather *riata* that connected the two re-mounts to his cantle, as the coach clattered away down Congress Avenue. The lights that had burned in a few of the more distant houses of the half-built little town were being blown out, as broad yellow sunlight splashed across the shabby wooden houses and cabins, the imposing, false-fronted, whitewashed edifices of the new capital. Hannibal bent from the saddle to kiss Valentina's hand and address her with praises cribbed from Pindar and Horace.

When they rode out – trailed by their vaquero guards – January looked back, to see the small black figure of the widow, lifting her hand in farewell to him in the bright bold light of the new day.

In other circumstances January would have been amused to watch Hannibal, over the next four days, fencing with Mrs Passmore at the execrable roadside taverns where they – and the mail-coach – stopped for meals, or to change horses, or to spend the nights. Hannibal flirted outrageously with the lady, who made several determined efforts to get him alone with her, or into a game of cards. January observed that he was careful not to be alone with her, nor to eat or drink anything that wasn't part of the common fare.

This made for an extremely wearing journey. January slept little, conscious always that he was worth twelve hundred dollars to this woman and that if anything should happen to his 'master', Mrs Passmore almost certainly had forged sale-papers somewhere in her luggage proving that he was her property, to do with as she wished.

Exactly like Selina.

Or like Valentina, he reflected, at the mercy of Texas courts and Texas law.

It wasn't until the French steam-packet *Suzette* churned away from the Galveston docks on Walpurgis morning – the thirtieth of April, a Wednesday – with Mrs Passmore waving her handkerchief (and doubtless cursing under her breath) at quayside, that January felt himself begin to relax. He felt that he wanted to sleep for a week.

As the slow, oily swells of the Gulf widened between the ship and the wharf, Hannibal glanced sidelong at him, and asked quietly, '*Will* Selina's father take her back, do you think?'

'I don't know.' January leaned his elbows on the railing, watched the brown cohorts of pelicans glide low over the water. South of the town, the dark wall of mangrove and cypress concealed where the wood-store had been, where Seth Javel's body had burned up less than a month ago. 'I think so. My impression is that he loves her very much. But people don't always forgive, if they feel they've been betrayed, or their pride has been hurt. Or if their families tell them they've been fools,' he added with a sigh. 'People are stupid and cruel. Others, simply weak.'

'And people used to ask me,' sighed Hannibal, 'why I drank.' He coughed, his hand pressed hard to his side. He looked like ten miles of bad road.

Or a couple of hundred. From Houston to Austin and back.

After a long time, January said, 'Thank you.'

'For keeping the beautiful Cornelia occupied with flirtation? I feel like I've spent four days chained to an affectionate leopard. *Alas, the love of women, it is known/ to be a lovely and a fearful thing* . . . She's the real gorgon,' he added. 'Not that frightful Madrecita Taggart, or poor Aunt Alicia.'

'Thank you for coming to Texas,' said January. 'You didn't have to do that.'

'If it comes to it, neither did you.'

'I did. Who else would have?'

Hannibal made no answer.

'Selina Bellinger is sixteen,' January went on. 'Valentina was that age, when she ran away with John Dillard and came to Texas. She wasn't betrayed, except by fate; the wound she took at least wasn't a poisoned one. But sixteen is too young to lose your life – the whole of your life – for misjudging a man.'

'It's what Rose said,' agreed the fiddler, 'when she asked me to come with you. And I don't doubt that Rose could look after herself – and the children – had you not come back. Better anyway than poor Selina, who is, I fear, going to have a very hard time of it, whatever her father decides. You still didn't have to do it. I suppose soldiers' wives feel the same thing, when their men go off to war.'

'It is war.' January understood, then, the tiredness he felt.

He'd seen it, after the Battle of New Orleans, as a youth: that burned-out cold in the heart. That compound of exhaustion, disgust, and futility – *Tell me again why I did this*? His only real emotion a mild surprise that he'd survived.

He'd feel better, he knew, after he'd slept.

After he'd returned home, and gone to confession and Mass, and woke again in Rose's arms.

Galveston had shrunk behind them to a pale line of mud, a dark line of trees and houses, no higher than a sand-bar, across the water. White sails made chips of brightness against it, slave-ships, smuggling in men and women from the Caribbean, from Africa, from Brazil, to be sneaked across the Sabine into Louisiana, for sale to cotton-planters all up and down the Mississippi. Andreas Neumann was still offering his customers free samples of the women in that dim hot dust-stinking 'exchange'. Pharaoh at the Capital City Hotel still dreamed of the wife and children he'd been taken from, back in South Carolina, whom he would never see again. Rance Pollack still owned men and women and could sell them or rape them or beat them to death without a question being asked.

A slaveholder's republic. Would it always be so? He sensed the strength and the wealth of the land, and wondered what would become of them – white, black, Comanche and Tejano – in the years to come.

'It is war,' he said again. 'The battles are smaller, and different, but it is war. And thank you,' he added more lightly, 'for not giving in to the temptation to try to relieve Mrs Passmore of some of Mr Taggart's gold over a hand of cards.'

'You've got to be joking.' Hannibal coughed again, and put a hand back, to where the silk ribbon that tied his queue was coming unbound. January recognized the violet velvet band as one he'd seen in Mrs Passmore's hair. 'The woman cheats like a moneylender! It would be nice to retrieve that seven hundred and fifty dollars that you'll owe to your mother and the Viellard family and whoever else you borrowed from, but not if it meant chasing all over Texas looking for whoever Mrs Passmore managed to sell you to while I was unconscious from whatever she'd manage to slip into my drink. I completely agree with you, *amicus meus*. I only want to go home.'

They turned from the rail; against the dark of the *Suzette*'s superstructure the open door of the tiny dining salon glowed faintly now in the gathering dusk. Most of the cargo was cotton. The whole ship seemed permeated with its faint, fusty smell, its dry haze of dust. *Two days*, January thought. Two days of eating at the tiny table in a corner of the salon reserved for servants – and the slaves of the Americans *en route* – and sleeping on a hammock in Hannibal's closet-sized 'stateroom'.

He thought of the dream he'd had – he didn't even recall when – of Rose sitting with Selina in the parlor of the house on Rue Esplanade. The house that was her boarding-school, her life. *How could I have left her alone? How could I have risked my life – her life, her livelihood, the wellbeing of our sons?*

It is a hard country, Valentina had said, *for a woman alone.*

And that, he knew, was true of anywhere.

But in his dream, he'd seen the French doors open from the gallery on the street, and Roux Bellinger standing in the doorway. Standing for one instant, before he stumbled, weeping, to clasp his daughter in his arms.

It is a war, thought January. *And that is victory.*

And I couldn't not go to fight.

'Hannibal?'

'*Amicus meus?*'

'If this situation ever arises again, when I'm going to set out for Texas to help someone . . .'

Hannibal raised his brows.

'Hit me. Hard.'

The fiddler bowed. 'It shall be as you say.'

THE ARCHIVES WAR

The National Archives of the Republic of Texas were, in fact, hijacked in 1842 (two years after the date of this fictional story).

In the face of a Mexican invasion which took San Antonio, Texas President Sam Houston – who had been re-elected after the defeat of President Mirabeau Lamar – announced that Austin was no longer the capital of Texas, and ordered that the archives be re-located to Washington-on-the-Brazos. The citizens of Austin formed a Vigilance Committee to prevent this, and promised armed resistance to any attempt to do so. Houston sent a band of Texas Rangers, who successfully loaded up three wagonloads of state papers before boardinghouse-keeper Angelina Eberly, proprietress of Eberly's Tavern, fired a cannon at them. The Rangers made good their escape, with the wagons, but the vigilantes seized another cannon from the arsenal and pursued them, catching up with them at Brushy Creek. Only a few shots were fired, and the archives were re-captured at gunpoint and hauled back to Austin, where they remained.

Austin again became capital of Texas two years later.

The history of the American West contains several other instances of similar activities in the so-called County Seat Wars, of violence between towns (including archive-stealing) in competition for rulership over the new counties of the West.

A statue of Mrs Eberly firing her cannon still stands in downtown Austin.